Praise for *Infinite S*

'A brilliant, heartbreaking portrait of a (
   —Susan Wyndham, *Australian Book Re*

'*Infinite Splendours* deserves a place in that slender collection of brilliant Australian novels about art.'
   —Geordie Williamson, *The Australian*

'One of the best novels of 2020.'
   —Stephen Romei, *The Australian*

'Laguna explores in intricate detail the ways in which an act can have ramifications far and wide . . . it is her unfailing commitment to truth of children's innocence that makes her novels so wholly devastating.'
   —Louise Swinn, *The Sydney Morning Herald*

'True to form for Laguna, *Infinite Splendours* has its moments of sheer delight among the deeply disturbing and uncomfortable. I really loved this book.'
   —Booktopia

'*Infinite Splendours* is filled with vivid descriptions of colour, movement, and grace. It also brims with unfathomable grief . . . Do read this novel knowing that it is painful, but also read it because Laguna's writing is kind and truly a type of poetry in action.'
   —*Readings*

'Written with compassion and tenderness, and Laguna's aptitude for inhabiting the inner spaces of a vulnerable preadolescent, *Infinite Splendours* is suffused with outward radiance, which makes its excursions into darkness all the more horrifying to read.'
   —*The Guardian*

'Beautifully devastating . . . Masterful, insightful and compassionate.'
   —*Courier Mail*

Praise for *The Choke*

'The perfect title for a book that seizes you by the throat from its opening pages and never lets go. As brave and memorable a heroine as any in Australian literature. Raw, real, heartbreaking.'

—*AFR Magazine*, Books of the Year

'. . . unsettling, confronting and profound. *The Choke* does not take a step backwards. I think it is her best novel yet it is deeply disturbing, all the more so because the genesis of its darkness is ordinary people and everyday life . . . Laguna's empathetic inhabitation of the minds of young children . . . is one of the great strengths of her work.'

—Stephen Romei, *The Australian*

'Sofie Laguna's third book for adults gave me that sweet reading moment we all pine for . . . You cannot put the book down because you are immersed, completely and utterly, until the story finishes. Laguna was awarded the 2015 Miles Franklin Award for *The Eye of the Sheep*. It is possible that this novel will give her even more, deserved, acclaim . . . Readers who enjoyed Tim Winton's *Cloudstreet* or Georgia Blain's *Between a Wolf and a Dog* will be delighted with this novel.'

—Chris Gordon, *Readings*

'At the moment when other authors might give in, go soft, let their world shift and open up for their characters, Laguna holds on tight, pushing her characters through the small and unforgiving spaces she has created for them, like waters rushing through the narrow banks of the Murray, squeezing through until they feel as though they might choke. But always, in the very darkness of her tales there is light, there is breath, and above all, there is voice.'

—Rebecca Slater, *The Lifted Brow*

'Don't for a moment imagine that, after taking out the Miles Franklin Award for *The Eye of the Sheep*, the best of Sofie Laguna's work is behind her. *The Choke* is every bit as masterful and devastating, as well as being utterly addictive.'

—*Herald Sun*

'Calling all Sofie Laguna fans: you are in for a treat. *The Choke* will not disappoint . . . Celebrates the power of the human spirit, offering hope.'
    —*Sunday Times*

'Laguna builds suspense deftly and without mercy. From the moment *The Choke* begins, a slingshot's elastic is precisely, steadfastly being pulled back . . . And the stone Laguna lets fly ricochets inside you for days afterwards.'
    —*The Age/Sydney Morning Herald*

'This is a heart-breaking read of uncompromising compassion and intimacy. I don't think I've ever read a child's perspective so fully realised in contemporary Australian fiction. A powerful achievement.'
    —*Booktopia*, Books of the Year

'Sofie Laguna is a writer who can wrench beauty even from the horror of a child caught up in the toxic world of bastardised masculinity. Fearsome, vivid and raw, *The Choke* is emotionally intense, deeply engaging and quietly haunting. FIVE STARS.'
    —Simon McDonald, *Books + Publishing*

'My eyes were full of tears when I finished *The Choke*. There is great emotional depth to Sofie Laguna's writing, and her characters are alive in their vulnerability and beauty . . . Laguna is one of the most gifted writers in Australia right now. Don't miss this.'
    —*Good Reading*

'It is rare to come across a novel where the author's powers of empathy are so brilliantly addressed as they are by Laguna in *The Choke* . . . Reading it, I felt as if I were being drawn deeper and deeper into a nightmare with no way out. Laguna is in my view one of the most interesting writers to have emerged in the past few years.'
    —Alex Miller, *The Age/Sydney Morning Herald*

'Full of richly drawn characters, with a dialogue that crackles and a narrative that draws you right in.'
    —*The Big Issue*

Praise for *The Eye of the Sheep*

'Full of achingly true insights into family violence and the way trauma passes from one generation to the next. Laguna dissolves the barriers between author and reader, getting the voice of odd, funny, love-hungry Jimmy so right that I still don't quite believe he isn't out there somewhere, spinning and spinning in ever-faster circles.'

—Emily Maguire, author of *An Isolated Incident*

'The power of this finely crafted novel lies in its raw, high-energy, coruscating language which is the world of young Jimmy Flick, who sees everything . . . *The Eye of the Sheep* is an extraordinary novel about love and anger, and how sometimes there is little between them.'

—Miles Franklin Literary Award 2015, judges' report

'Sofie Laguna faultlessly maintains the storytelling voice of Jimmy, who is oblivious in some ways and hauntingly knowing and observant in others. There are many places in which such a story could tip over into sentimentality or melodrama, but Laguna's authorial control and intelligence keep the story on track and the reader engaged and empathetic, and she manages both the humour and the darkness of this story with great sensitivity and control.'

—Stella Prize 2015, judges' report

'The greatest achievement here is making this family's world not just compelling but utterly entertaining. Laguna does this by showing the way her characters are the sum of all the parts that make them . . . It is quite a feat to write characters with such nuance. In harnessing her storytelling facility to expose the flaws in the system with what is becoming trademark empathy, Laguna is an author proving the novel is a crucial document of the times.'

—*The Australian*

'This book should be impossibly bleak, but Laguna has managed to imbue it with luminosity. This is a story about how to find your place in the world and how to accept what you have been given. *The Eye of the Sheep* will break your heart—a small price to pay to hear Jimmy's story.'

—*Readings*

'A beautifully written novel, refreshingly raw, through the eyes of a child. I couldn't put it down.'

—*Launceston Examiner*

Praise for *One Foot Wrong*

'An extraordinary achievement . . . original and compelling . . . compels us to see our familiar world as new and intriguing—no small feat.'

—Jo Case, *Big Issue*

'. . . a book that intrigues and affects every essence of your humanity . . . a dark and terrible tale told in lyrical, poetic language and stark imagery.'

—*Australian Bookseller and Publisher*

'. . . intense, disturbing and hallucinatory.'

—Kerryn Goldsworthy, *Sydney Morning Herald*

'The language is pitch-perfect—it is the light in this dark tale . . . a haunting story of horror, but also of friendship and love . . . Despite the darkness of the subject matter, it is surprisingly uplifting, cathartic and affecting.'

—Louise Swinn, *The Age*

'. . . harrowing, beautifully written, insightful and absorbing . . . unique, forceful and absolutely hypnotic . . . Fresh, honest writing . . . makes this dark journey well worth taking.'

—Emily Maguire, *Canberra Times*

'An authentic voice, an evocation of childhood and memory that, for all its terrors, evokes the sublime, tragic moment when innocence submits to experience. Laguna creates a world and a character and a language that we become immersed within. That she does it with a subject matter of such destructive cruelty, that she does it with such rigour and power, is a testament to her craft, skill and maturity. This is the opposite of what the tabloids do: this is humane, passionate, true.'

—Christos Tsiolkas

Sofie Laguna's first novel for adults, *One Foot Wrong*, was published throughout Europe, the US and the UK, was longlisted for the Miles Franklin Literary Award and shortlisted for the Prime Minister's Literary Award. Her second novel for adults, *The Eye of the Sheep*, won the 2015 Miles Franklin Literary Award and was shortlisted for the Stella Prize and longlisted for the International Dublin IMPAC Award. Sofie Laguna's third novel, *The Choke,* won the 2018 Indie Book Award for Fiction, and was shortlisted for the Victorian Premier's Literary Award, the Voss Literary Prize, the Australian Literary Society Gold Medal and the Australian Book Industry Award, and longlisted for the Stella Prize, the Kibble Award and the International Dublin IMPAC Award. *Infinite Splendours* won the Margaret and Colin Roderick Literary Award in 2021, and was longlisted for the Miles Franklin Literary Award 2021, the Literary Fiction Book of the Year, ABIA Awards 2021, and the Best Fiction, Indie Book Awards 2021. Sofie's many books for young people have been published in the US, the UK and in translation throughout Europe and Asia. She has been shortlisted for the Queensland Premier's Award, and her books have been named Honour Books and Notable Books by the Children's Book Council of Australia.

Sofie Laguna

Infinite Splendours

ALLEN&UNWIN
SYDNEY·MELBOURNE·AUCKLAND·LONDON

This edition published in 2022
First published in 2020

 This project has been assisted by the Australian Government through the Australia Council, its arts funding and advisory board.

This project is supported by the Victorian Government through Creative Victoria.

Allen & Unwin
83 Alexander Street
Crows Nest NSW 2065
Australia
Phone: (61 2) 8425 0100
Email: info@allenandunwin.com
Web: www.allenandunwin.com

 A catalogue record for this book is available from the National Library of Australia

ISBN 978 1 76106 703 7

Set in Adobe Jenson Pro by Bookhouse, Sydney
Printed in Australia by McPherson's Printing Group

10 9 8 7 6 5 4 3 2 1

In memory of my teacher
Dorothy Kellett

The lamps are burning,
and the starry sky is over it all.

VINCENT VAN GOGH,
The Letters of Vincent van Gogh

PART ONE

Hughlon, Southern Grampians, Victoria

1953

1.

'THREE! FOUR! FIVE!' PAUL COUNTED from the porch.

I stood in the middle of the yard; I'd hidden in the apple tree, Gert's shelter, by the trough, and the outhouse. I needed somewhere new.

'Seven! Eight! Nine!'

I looked to the bunker door lying against a slope in the grass, opposite the outhouse. *Fire will come again, Louise. It was fifty years ago but I'll never forget it. You make sure that bunker is dug out and ready.* I ran down to the door and hooked my fingers through the iron handle. *If there's a fire, Mrs Barry, we'll get out in the orchard trucks. I want the bunker door kept closed, and the boys to stay away.* I pulled as hard as I could.

The door was wedged in its frame.

'Fourteen! Fifteen!' Paul counted.

I pulled again, but still the door didn't open. I'd miss my turn if Paul found me before twenty.

'Sixteen! Seventeen!'

I pulled one more time, falling back into the grass as the door opened. I got to my feet. The bunker was filled with dirt almost to the top. Almost. I lay against the shallow space, tilted at an angle by the slope in the grass, then I brought the door down over me, spreading myself flat beneath it.

Paul called out, 'Nineteen! Twenty! Coming ready or not!'

Then everything went quiet. I could hardly move underneath the door—even my feet were flattened, pushed out to the side like Flat Man in *The Loons*. I blinked in the darkness. My skin itched under my clothes. It would take Paul forever to find me. Or maybe he wouldn't find me at all. Maybe I'd be here for hours. Lucky Mother wasn't home. I'd be in trouble if she knew. On Saturdays Mother did the numbers at the dairy the same way she did Monday to Friday. If it weren't for Mrs Barry to keep an eye on us, Mother didn't know how she'd keep the wolf from the door.

I couldn't hear Paul out there. How much time was passing? I took a deep breath, and as I breathed out, felt myself sinking into the spaces between the grains of dirt. The two temperatures, cooler underneath and warmer above, met in the middle. Everything grew still. Was this what it was like for the animals that lived underground?

Once Paul and I found an old rabbit warren at the foot of a tree outside the turnstile. 'Do you think there're still rabbits living here?' Paul asked.

I shook my head. 'No fresh droppings. And the earth is too dry. Look.' I dug into the warren, the ground crumbling around my stick.

Paul started digging too. There were burrows going off the sides, like homes in an underground town. We called rabbit town Pawville.

'Let's give it more roads,' said Paul.

'One leads to Pawville School,' I said, scraping dirt from the warren.

'And one to Pawville Cemetery,' said Paul.

'And one to Pawville Church.'

'Let's bomb the school,' said Paul. We picked up rocks and bombed Pawville School until the walls caved in. 'Take that, you Krauts, take that!'

'Got you Fritz!' I threw in handfuls of dirt.

There was one rabbit hole left, deeper than the rest, and when we dug off the lid, we saw it was lined with white and grey fur.

We sat back on our haunches and looked at the small circular burrow. 'It must've been a nest,' I said.

'How do you know?'

'The fur . . .' I touched the soft lining. 'The mother pulled it out of herself. From her stomach . . . or her chest.'

'Oh . . .'

I said, 'Don't worry, the babies that once lived here have grown up by now.'

Even though we knew the warren was empty we rebuilt the walls of the mother's burrow, making a new roof by laying sticks side by side over the top which we covered with dirt.

Now, lying in the bunker, I thought of the burrow and wondered if this was how the baby rabbit felt in its nest. It was very quiet; the only sound was my own breath. I kept listening as the breath went in and out. Who was making me breathe, I wondered? Soon, I couldn't feel my body anymore and could imagine what it would be like if I didn't have a body. I was inside my thoughts and outside my thoughts, as if I had two selves.

'Lawrence! Lawrence!' I heard Paul shout. I felt myself being called from far away. 'Where are you?'

All of a sudden, I could feel how cramped I was. How long had I been here?

'Lawrence! Lawrence!'

I pushed against the door. 'Paul! I tried to call. 'Paul!' My voice sounded small and croaky.

'Lawrence! Lawrence!'

'Pull at the door!' I tried to call to him again.

'It's stuck, Laurie!'

'Harder! Pull harder!' Paul was out there on his own. What if we couldn't open the door and I ran out of air? I pushed against it as hard as I could but it was difficult with so little room to move my arms.

'Lawrence! It won't open!'

'Pull!'

'I'm trying!'

'Harder!'

Paul pulled and I pushed.

Suddenly the door opened and there was Paul, standing beside the slope.

'You cheated!' Paul's face was red and damp.

'I did not!' I sat up, the sun bright in my eyes, and coughed. I felt like a body that a coffin had opened on.

'I was looking for hours. We aren't allowed to go in there.'

'I was only just under the door. And it wasn't hours.' I shook my head and dirt fell from my hair.

'It was.'

'It wasn't hours. Don't tell Mother.' I got up and out of the bunker.

Paul and I stood looking at the space where I had lain.

'What if you couldn't open the door?' he said.

'But I could.'

'You might have suffocated.'

'I got out, okay?' My legs were shaking and my throat was dry. 'I need water.'

'You won't go in there again, will you, Laurie?' Paul said as we walked back to the house.

'No, I won't. And don't you.'

For the rest of the day I didn't think of the bunker at all. It was like every other Saturday; while Paul and I played in the yard or helped Mrs Barry or fought or scored or raced the bikes, we were waiting to hear the sound of the Austin in the drive. For it to be Mother come home. But in bed that night, when Paul was asleep on the other side of the wall and Mother was doing the last tidy, I closed my eyes and felt the earth around me. There was no time; all the activity was above me. I was no longer an object in the world and did not live or die. In that second behind the breath, I didn't belong anywhere or to anyone.

2.

IT WAS NEARLY THE END of fourth class at Hughlon Consolidated and Mr Wade was handing out the reports. He gave out mine last, when I was the only one left in the room. 'Lawrence,' Mr Wade said, placing the thick envelope onto my desk. 'You are a good boy.' He tapped the report. 'My word, you are. Your mother will be proud.'

'Thank you, Mr Wade.' I placed the envelope against the ledger in my satchel and left the classroom.

Paul was waiting for me at the bike rack. 'Wade keep you?'

'Reports,' I answered pulling out my bike.

'Don't remind me.' Reports for the second class had come home the week before. Paul's said he was only good at sports.

We climbed on the bikes and pedalled onto the road that led out of Hughlon. You could see the Grampian mountains from the school. Everywhere we went they were there. The land flat and green, broken by fence lines, dirt roads and tree belts, and then the mountains, rising sudden and steep and rocky.

I stood on my pedals and when I felt Paul coming closer, pushed harder. He was eight, almost two years younger than me. I stayed in front for a while, my legs burning, and then I dropped back, and let Paul take over.

Soon the school bus came by. We kept pedalling, wobbling in the stones beside the road, squinting in the dust that rose up under the wheels. Now there were no more buses or cars. The other children who rode bikes peeled off to James Street and High Street, and then it was just Paul and me. Wallis was ahead of us. He never moved. You thought he did, but it was the clouds moving past him. Then, when we were closer, he was all we could see. We knew the others were there behind him, Piccaninny, Abrupt and Signal Peak and, further back, William and Young and the Pinnacle, but Wallis was in front, like the bow of a giant ship.

We passed Mrs Barry's first. Our two houses—Beverly Park, and Mrs Barry's—were the closest houses to Wallis on the eastern side. Mother and Father came out before the second war ended and bought the property, a house on forty acres of land. The wooden sign on our gate said *Beverly Park* when we first arrived, but the *Park* soon faded, until it said only *Beverly*.

We went through the gate, parked our bikes at the front and went down to the kitchen. Mother was at the bench chopping onions for the dinner; she did everything early. There were cheese sandwiches and glasses of cold milk on the table.

'Hello, Mother.' Paul drank all his milk at once, leaving a line of Gert's cream along his top lip. He took two of the sandwiches and headed out the back.

'Paul! That door!' Mother called when the screen door slammed behind him.

The bird clock chimed four. I saw the wooden birds bending to sip from the dish as I pulled the report from my satchel. 'Mother . . .'

She put down her knife, tucked her hair into her scarf and took the report. Mother wore scarves tied at the back of her neck to keep her hair from escaping.

'Drink your milk.'

I picked up the glass and took a sip of the milk. Mother wiped sweat from her forehead with her apron, sat down at the kitchen table and opened the envelope. She read the first page of the report, then she put it face down on the table and read the next. She looked up at me where I stood, dabbing at her eyes with the corner of her apron, then back at the page in her hand. I liked Mr Wade. I liked mathematics, and geography because of the places—Iceland and Borneo with the pythons, and the Sahara Desert. It was Mr Wade's class where I saw the castles in the book called *Ancient Buildings of the European Continent*.

After she was finished reading, Mother put down the page and pulled me to her so tight I felt her bones against my cheek. Then she set me back, her eyes shining. 'My Lawrence . . .' she said. I was pleased—not for myself, but for my mother, who was out here on her own without a husband. 'Off you go and play now.'

'Yes, Mother.' I took a sandwich from the plate and walked out to the back yard.

Paul was almost at the top of the apple tree. He tossed down a half-grown apple and caught me on the head. 'Teacher's pet,' he said.

'Ah, you got me, you bastard!' I called to him, pulling myself up.

We were at the table eating dinner that night when Mother put her hand over mine. 'You are like my brother, Lawrence,' she said. I knew it was because of the report. She had told us before how clever our uncle was. How good at school. 'So very like him.'

If it hadn't been for my brother, Eileen, I would never have endured . . . she told Mrs Barry.

Mrs Barry said, *The horrors are in the past now, Louise.*

I wondered what shape the horrors took. Were they like the ghouls in the Lombardy Mansion? Were they like a poison mist, were they skeletons? Ghosts?

Paul dipped bread into his soup. 'Where is he now?'

'Your uncle had dreams for himself. But one day he'll come. He knows where we are.' Mother had said that for a long time and we'd never once met him.

'You don't think he's forgotten?' said Paul.

'Finish your dinner, Paul, or there'll be no custard,' said Mother, frowning at him.

'Yes, Mother.'

After dinner we climbed to the top of the fence that was between our place and Mrs Barry's, and from there onto the roof of the shed. The two houses, Beverly Park and Mrs Barry's, huddled together, as if they were afraid of Wallis, standing tall and jagged behind them, clouds catching on his head.

The iron roof of the shed was hot under the skin of our legs. Paul said, 'I hope he never does come.'

'Why don't you want him to come?'

Paul shrugged.

'He looked after Mother, you know. When they were young. Otherwise she wouldn't have endured.'

'Endured what?'

'What happened to her.'

'What did happen to her?'

'I don't know. But he looked after her, whatever it was.' I flicked the side of Paul's ear. 'The way I look after you.'

Paul punched my arm and I punched him back.

'If she ever does tell you, you have to tell me.' He kicked the side of my foot.

'Tell you what?'

'What happened to her.'

'I don't know what happened to her.'

'I know, but if you ever find out . . .'

'Alright, if I ever find out.'

We were quiet for a while. The sun was beginning to set; melting stripes of gold and pink over the mountain. 'Do you know that if the sun came any closer the earth would catch fire?' I said.

'Will it come closer?' Paul asked.

'Nobody knows.'

We lay on our backs, the iron warm beneath us, watching the changing sky.

3.

ON THE LAST DAY OF school, Mother was at the gate to greet us. It was because of my birthday; Mother was never at the gate the other days. She had Gert to milk, the dinner to prepare, and the numbers to finish. But today she was there at the gate, a hand over her eyes to shield them from the sun, hair trying to escape from underneath her scarf. She said, 'Boys.'

We followed her through to the kitchen. On the table was a large box wrapped in brown paper.

I turned to her. 'Mother?'

'Happy birthday, Lawrence,' said Mother.

The other years it had been a top, or blocks. One year it was playing cards.

I tore back the paper and opened the box. Inside was a large wooden boat. When I lifted it out I saw that the boat had two sails, and a wide hull. Rope rigging led to a crow's nest at the top of the mast. A rope ladder hung over the side, between two sets of oars. *The Lady Bold* was written in gold letters along the boat's curved body. 'Mother . . .' I looked up at her.

Mother took a wooden box from the cardboard. 'You mustn't forget this.'

I put the boat on the table and opened the lid of the wooden box. It was full of pirates and redcoat soldiers the right size to man the ship. Paul picked up one of the pirates. The pirate was painted and held a sword. 'Crew . . .' He looked up at Mother, eyes wide.

It had always been something small. One year it had been a Dick and Jane reader. 'Mother . . .' I said. I wished I could put my arms around her. Paul and I always wanted to know if she loved us and needed us. Even if Mother was close, washing our hair in the bath or doing our buttons or sticking plasters to our knees, she kept a part back, and that was the part we wanted. It was as if she were at the other end of a bridge.

'You still have light,' she said. 'You can go all the way to the stream, if you like.'

'Mother . . .'

'Go on, off you go.'

I took the boat from the table—it had only ever been a top or the blocks or a ball.

'Come on, Laurie,' said Paul. 'Let's put her in the stream.'

'Off you go,' said Mother.

'Mother, thank you . . .' I wanted to cross the bridge, stepped closer.

'On your way, boys, before you lose the light.' Mother moved away, picking up the broom.

'Yes, Mother.'

Paul and I left the kitchen.

*

We went out the back, past Gert's shelter, and through the turnstile. Wallis loomed ahead of us as we walked across the field. Paul and I talked a lot about the day we would climb him. So far Mother only let us go as far as the stream. Other children at school had climbed him and said you could do it, that there was a path. If you didn't get lost, you could be up and back in a day. Paul and I asked Mother, but she said no and told us about a girl and a boy who'd fallen when the father wasn't looking. 'Leave it alone. It's not safe up there.'

Paul and I followed the track through the field towards the mountain. The field was going to have orange trees planted in rows. Father was going to leave the air force and never lay eyes on another plane; he was going to spend his time taking care of the trees until they grew bright and heavy with fruit. Mother was going to juice oranges so that every morning there'd be pitchers of cold juice to drink with breakfast. The last time Father came to visit us in Hughlon he said to Mother, *Not much longer*, and left Paul to grow in Mother's stomach. Then off he went, back to fight the Germans. He was flying over the Atlantic Ocean in his B24 Liberator when a German gunner flew over the top of him and fired.

The air force sent the Atlantic Star home to Mother. I was two years old and Paul wasn't yet born. Mother put the medal in the spare room, on the shelf beside a photograph of Father in his pilot's uniform. Father looked like Paul; he had the same eyes and face and body and hair. The Atlantic Star and the photograph had a whole room to themselves. Mother kept the room and the shelf dusted and the bed made, as if she thought one day the Atlantic Star and the photograph might climb down from the shelf looking for a place to sleep.

'Must seem like a cruel joke,' Mrs Barry said to Mother over the fence. 'To come so close.'

'No use crying, though, is it?'

'No use at all,' said Mrs Barry, passing a bunch of carrots over to Mother.

Mother never sold. She told Mrs Barry she ought to. The orchard next door had offered to buy the land more than once. But Mother refused. 'This place was our dream.'

The stream that came from the top of the mountain dripped over the rocks, dampening the moss, making puddles under the ferns. We played with *The Lady Bold* in the water, pitching pirate against redcoat on rafts of bark, until the light faded and the mosquitoes began to bite.

After dinner Mother lit the birthday candles on a chocolate cake. *Happy birthday to you, happy birthday to you*, Mother and Paul sang, their faces glowing. Ten white candles quivered on the cake. *Happy birthday, dear Lawrence, happy birthday to you!* I saw a row of ten lights reflected in the window behind Mother, going back further and further, never-ending.

I was drying the dishes when Paul put his hand on my arm. 'Come with me?'

'Go on, Paul, off you go on your own,' said Mother.

'It's alright, Mother, I don't mind,' I told her, running the cloth over the last plate. Paul didn't like to go to the outhouse by himself at night.

'Well, be quick about it, both of you,' said Mother. 'There's still your readers to do.'

'Yes, Mother.'

The sky was darkest purple and grey as Paul and I went down to the bottom of the yard, the track worn deep from all the years Mother or I or Paul had walked it. When Paul pulled open the outhouse door, I smelled sawdust. Mother made us throw a handful down the drop once we were done. Paul closed the door and I sat on the grass outside. I leaned back on my elbows and looked up at the outline of Wallis, like a great black sail.

Soon I heard Paul straining over the outhouse bench.

'Hoo hoo . . .' I called. 'Hoo hoo . . .'

'Don't, Laurie!' The smell of his shit wafted from the top of the door.

'Hoo hoo . . . It's the ghost of the Lombardy Mansion . . . Hoo hoo!'

'Laurie!'

'Coming for the Lady Lavinia . . . hoo hoo . . .'

'Laurie, don't!'

'Alright, alright, take it easy. That smell would scare off any ghost.'

That night in bed Paul whispered through the crack between the boards that separated our rooms. 'The boat was a good present, Laurie.' We covered the crack with posters so Mother wouldn't see. It was the British Naval Line on my side and the Red Funnel Steamer on his.

I lifted my poster and answered him. 'The best yet.'

'By far.'

'By far, me hearties.'

'By far, me farties.' Paul let one off under his blankets.

'Death bomb,' I said.

'That's how I'd kill the enemy.'

'You'd win the bloody war.'

'Want to go to the Marbles again?' he said. The Marbles was the empty hut behind Hughlon Cemetery. Thomas Marbles was the caretaker before he died there. The hut had money buried underneath it. 'We could bring the shovel.'

'Yes,' I whispered. 'Then the stream?' Two knocks meant *tomorrow*.

Knock knock. *Tomorrow!*

I waited for him to fall asleep first. I was the eldest by two years, Father was dead in the war and Mother was only a girl. Not until I heard his slow sleeping breaths could I leave the world behind to drift through the pictures of the day. That night Paul and I manned the deck of *The Lady Bold*, two pirates against the redcoats, as the boat sailed upwards, past the stream, then higher, all the way to the top of the mountain.

4.

THE FIRST FRIDAY MORNING BACK at school, Mrs St Clair, our new teacher, gave everybody an old oversized shirt. 'Put them over your uniforms, please.'

While we put on the shirts Mr Croft dragged in the easels. Mrs St Clair placed them around the room, moving them a little one way, and then another. 'Quiet, class. Please go and stand behind an easel.'

As we chose an easel, Mrs St Clair poured different coloured paint into steel trays shaped like the bottom half of an egg carton. Then she went around the room sliding down the tops of all the windows. When she passed I smelled her lavender perfume, warmed by the heat of February.

'Make sure you can all see a window without obstruction. Let me know if you cannot see a window. Quietly, please, class, no talking. No need for noise of any kind.' Mrs St Clair gave us each one of the trays of coloured paints, and a paintbrush. The paints shone in their little round compartments in the tray—blue, white, green, brown. She said, 'Look through the windows.'

I turned to a window and saw treetops on the far side of the playground, the brick sports shed and, above these, the blue sky.

'Class, you may begin,' said Mrs St Clair. I dipped my brush into the blue paint, then into the white, and put my brush to the paper. A layer of white cloud spread over the sky, like a veil. The cloud collected more thickly to one side, as if the veil had been drawn across. I looked at the sky and painted, and then looked at my paper then back to the sky, until I was not sure of the difference.

After a while I noticed that everyone was standing back from their easels. What had happened?

'Please remove your smocks, class,' said Mrs St Clair.

The lunch bell rang. I felt as if I were returning from far away, the way I did when I was in the bunker.

Mrs St Clair looked at my painting. 'Ah, Lawrence,' she said softly.

I did not recognise the painting on the easel in front of me. Who did that? I wondered. It was one sky on the way to the next.

'You enjoyed yourself, I see,' said Mrs St Clair.

I didn't know if I had enjoyed myself. Had I?

Outside in the playground, when I looked up, I saw the sky differently: I saw that it was living, that although it was silent, it seemed to speak.

On my bike on the way home, looking ahead to the mountain, I imagined him in paint. The dark green strokes of the trees at his base, where his strength began, the grey and brown of his body covered in stringybarks, the blue of the sky behind him.

When we were almost home, I saw Mrs Barry at the front of her house pruning her roses. All around was the silver-green of the grass in the fields, and the silver-white coats of the grazing sheep and the silver-grey of the road ahead, and then there were Mrs Barry's roses—blazing pink and crimson and orange.

Mrs Barry waved her cutters. 'Boys!'

We slowed down.

'I have something for you. Wait there.'

Paul looked at me and rolled his eyes.

Sometimes, after school Mrs Barry gave us meatloaf. The beef was pressed down so hard, it turned the carrots and the onion and parsley into tiny flat flecks; the rest was grey. The meatloaf crumbled from the fork on its way to the mouth, and then stuck in the throat. 'Oh, Mother,' Paul would say, grimacing. 'It's awful.'

'You eat up and be grateful. It's important for Mrs Barry. She doesn't have a family to cook for.'

'The meatloaf killed them.'

Soon Mrs Barry came back out with a basket full of potatoes and a plate of the meatloaf. She snapped three pink roses from one of the bushes, laid them over the top of the potatoes and gave the basket to Paul. 'You put them in a jar of water for your mother.'

'The spuds or the flowers, Mrs Barry?'

'You're a cheeky devil, Paul. Keep it up and give your mother a laugh.' She pinched Paul's cheek.

That afternoon, when Paul and I played in the stream with *The Lady Bold*, I saw the water dripping over the moss, the wet leaves that drifted in the puddles, the circles of lichen, all in paint. As Paul and I built a fortress of stones, with turrets made of twigs, I imagined the view of the sea from the highest tower in brushstrokes. I imagined how the colour would deepen from green to grey-green into deeper grey, almost black. I pictured the last rays of the sun over the sea. The line of gold at the crest of every ripple.

Later, when we came into the house, I saw Mrs Barry's three roses in the glass jar Mother had chosen, sitting on the table, and imagined the flowers in paint. How bright the pink of the petals. I didn't say anything about it to Paul. It was something only for me; everywhere and everything had two lives.

From then on, all hours of every day led to Friday morning, when Mr Croft would bring in the easels and Mrs St Clair would take out the smocks. When there was no time. When there was nobody else in the room. When I felt myself entering the painting, through the brush, my hands like puppets acting for some other part. Mrs St Clair might place fruit on her table or ask us to look through a particular window, or to work from our own imaginations. Once she sat on her chair at the front and asked the class to paint her seated figure.

All hours of the week led to painting, but I liked the other hours of school too. I was the first to raise my hand. *What is one third of thirty-six? At what temperature does water boil? How do you spell 'thunderstorm'?* I liked to speak the names of places. *Florence—home to many masterpieces. Paris—crisscrossed by the River Seine. Prague—the city of a hundred spires.* I was curious about the earth; glaciers that moved at a snail's pace, jungle so thick it blocked the sun. The globe sat tilted on its axis on Mrs St Clair's desk. She showed us Africa with her pointer, where the Masai bled cows and wandered the savanna. The Arctic Circle, where the Inuit used spears to hunt for caribou. India, where the religion was Hinduism, made of three principal gods. She said we must write a poem for every colour. My poem for white began, *White is a sheet of paper, words yet to be written.* She read us a book called *Robinson Crusoe* by Daniel Defoe. *By this time it blew a terrible storm indeed, and now I began to see Terror and Amazement in the Faces even of the Seamen themselves* . . . All of fifth class cross-legged on the floor, looking up at Mrs St Clair where she sat in her matching suit, her face damp and shining, glasses slipping, book open in her hands, our cares with Crusoe and the storm, the boat rocking on the waves, Crusoe begging the Lord, *Be merciful!* Tears came down Mrs St Clair's face when she read. She allowed them to fall, mixing with her sweat, as another wave of heat came over her. Not a single one of us spoke or laughed; we too battled the storm, lost our men.

One day Mrs St Clair brought a bunch of yellow flowers into class. She placed them in a green vase on her table at the front. 'This morning your subject will be parrot peas,' she said. 'From my garden.' Mrs St Clair put yellow and orange and red and white and green paint into our trays. The parrot peas were bunched together in clusters; no flower, petal or leaf was alike. The vase that held the flowers was its own subject—the widening stripes in green and darker green, the small crack beneath the rounded handle. I dipped my brush into the yellow paint. Soon I could not hear the rustle of paper, or the scraping of chairs, or Mrs St Clair moving from easel to easel.

'Oh, Lawrence,' I heard Mrs St Clair say. 'This one I think you should take home for your mother.'

Later Mrs St Clair put the painting between two pieces of cardboard and helped me slide it into my satchel.

On the way home Paul pedalled along behind me singing, *'Reach for the sky, reach for the sky, hands up high, hands up high . . .'*

That afternoon Crusoe had seen footprints on the island. As I looked at Wallis, I imagined he was surrounded by sea. There were no fields or houses, no Grampians, no roads. I stood straight on my pedals. 'Crusoe!' I shouted. 'Crusoe!'

When we came home, Mother wasn't in the kitchen and there were no sandwiches, glasses of milk or apple quarters set on the table. The back door was open. We went through to the porch and saw Mother sitting on the canopy swing, still wearing the dress she wore to the dairy. The first thing Mother did when she came home from work was change into her pinafore and tie on her apron.

'Mother?' I said.

She turned to us, holding a letter in her hands.

'Who's that from?' Paul asked.

'It's a letter . . .' Mother seemed in a daze.

'But who from?'

'From your uncle. Reggie. Reginald.' She looked down at the letter.

'What about him?' Paul asked.

'He's coming.'

'Here?'

'Yes.'

'When?' I asked.

'In two weeks. Reggie . . .' She held tight to the letter. 'It's been so long . . .'

'How long?' Paul asked.

Mother didn't answer. She folded the letter, pressing it into her pocket, and counted under her breath. 'That's the third Sunday from now,' she said, standing suddenly. 'Boys, you need to throw Gert's manure over the fence to Mrs Barry. Come on. Out of your uniforms. Only two weeks to have the place ready.'

Paul and I changed our clothes and went down to Gert's shelter, where we shovelled the cow's messy pats over the fence. It was only ever Paul and me, Mother and the medal. Where would he go, the uncle?

'Damn him,' said Paul.

'Paul,' I said. 'He's our uncle.'

'I don't care.'

'What do you mean, you don't care? You have to care.'

Paul drove his spade into the shit. 'I don't have to do anything.'

That evening, after his bath, Paul stopped at the door of the spare. 'Imagine Father,' he said. 'In his Liberator. *Rut-a-tut-tut-tut.*' Paul pretended to hold a steering wheel, pulling it back as he fired. He went into the room and took the medal from the shelf.

'It's not a toy,' I said.

'How many would he have taken out?' Paul turned the Atlantic Star in his hands.

'Twelve. Maybe more.'

'In one hit like that?'

'In one hit. Then he would have gone back for fuel,' I said.

'Yes. And then he would have fired again.'

'It's from the King himself,' I said, taking the medal from Paul.

'How do you know?' he asked.

'Look at the crown.' I showed him the engraved crown at the top of the star. 'That means it's from the King.'

'The King.' Paul took the medal and put it back on the shelf. 'The King probably knew Father.'

'He would definitely have known *about* him,' I said.

'Same thing,' said Paul.

We stood and looked at the picture of the man so like Paul, and the medal beside it. It was as if Father himself was a medal. With a star for a head, and a body made from bright green and blue ribbon. Once I heard Mother say to Mrs Barry, 'I would have liked the boys to grow up with a father.' Mrs Barry answered that half the country was growing up without a father. What would it be like if Father the medal walked through the door, opened his ribbon arms, and said, *I'm home*?

'Mother,' I said after dinner. 'Mrs St Clair wanted me to give you this.' I spread my painting of the parrot peas on the table before Mother, where she sat working on her numbers.

'Oh . . . Lawrence. Is this what you spend your time doing at school?'

'Fridays, Mother. Mrs St Clair wanted me to give it to you.'

Mother put down her pencil and looked at the painting. 'It's very lovely, Laurie. Parrot peas. They are almost real.'

'Thank you, Mother.'

She gave me back the painting. 'Only Fridays. Well, good. Good.' She kept ticking down the rows. Without looking up she said, 'When your uncle comes you can show him your report.'

'Yes, Mother.' I took the painting into my room and propped it against the wall between two Dick and Janes. I could hardly believe he was coming. That he was real.

5.

THE NEXT DAY WAS SATURDAY; before she left for work Mother said, 'You can try the milking this time, Lawrence. My hands are terrible.' Mother's hands became arthritic when the weather turned cold. They would ache and stiffen and she couldn't write properly or sew or do her hoops. Now it was autumn, and soon it would be winter.

I followed Mother down to Gert.

'Come on, Gert, into the stall,' Mother said, waving her arms.

Gert was already on her way, her udder full.

'She'll kick me, Mother,' I said.

The cow stood close to the fence under the shelter.

'Not if she's tied.' Mother knotted a rope to the rail and looped it round Gert's back leg. 'Make sure you dig the seat in an inch or two,' she said, pushing the milking stool into the dirt. She placed the steel pail underneath Gert.

'Are you sure, Mother?'

'Of course I'm sure. I want my hands better before Reggie comes. And you can impress him with how much you're able to do about the place.'

I sat on the stool at Gert's belly.

'Go on, both hands,' said Mother, squatting beside me.

Gert's udder was like a big pink upside-down glove close to bursting. I put my hands on the two front teats and Gert stepped sideways.

'Mother?'

'Take no notice. Come on, Gert. I need a rest. My hands are awful. Let your milk down for Laurie.' Mother moved to Gert's shoulder and gave her a pat. 'Give them a squeeze, son. Go on, nice and firm.'

I squeezed the teats as Gert strained at the rope.

'Harder, Laurie.'

I squeezed harder.

'From the top down.'

Gert tried kicking and the rope pulled tight.

'But, Mother . . .'

'Again, Laurie. Come on, Gert, my old hands can't take it. And I don't need the veins.' Veins ran from Mother's wrists to the crooks of her arms, like rivers under her skin. 'Try again, Laurie. Fingers right around the teats with a squeeze and a pull.'

'But, Mother, I don't think she . . .'

'Come on, Laurie, a nice strong pull.'

I kept trying, pulling and pulling, until Gert gave one big kick with the leg that was free, knocking the pail into the mud.

'Damn you, Gert!' said Mother. 'Alright, alright, you win. I'll do it.' She sighed. 'Go on, Laurie, help your brother fill the trough.'

I got off the stool and Mother took my place. I leaned against the fence and listened as the milk came down into the pail, one teat and then the next, *squirt squirt, squirt squirt*.

'Where did you learn it, Mother, to milk a cow?'

'Oh, Laurie.'

'Where, Mother? Did you have a cow when you were a child?'

'No. No, we didn't have a cow.' Her voice was muffled in Gert's side.

'And you and Father never had a cow?'

'No. Gert came after. You know that.'

'When then?'

'I learned it at the Hartfields',' she said.

'The Hartfields'?'

'Yes. Didn't I tell you? When we . . . when I was there with your uncle. Off you go and help your brother.'

'You never told me, Mother. Who were they?'

'Who?'

'The Hartfields.'

'Oh, Laurie . . .'

'Who were they?'

The milk came down, between my questions, *squirt squirt, squirt squirt.*

'Will you let me do this, please, Lawrence? Go and help your brother.'

'But, Mother . . .'

'Lawrence!'

'Alright, alright.'

I left Mother there in the shelter, her scarf as bright as a tomato against Gert's black belly. She had never told us about the Hartfields.

When Mother came home from work that afternoon, she was carrying a large tin of white paint. 'Boys, help me clear the spare.'

'What for?' I asked.

'What do you think? For your uncle. Come on, pull out the chair and the trunk.'

'Are you painting the room?' Paul asked.

'What does it look like? Yes, I am. And if there is enough left over, I will do the lounge and kitchen.'

'Why are you painting it white when it's already white?' Paul asked.

'Because it needs a fresh coat. I have been meaning to do it forever.' She swiped dust from the walls with a cloth. 'And now your uncle has given me a reason.'

Paul sighed.

'Have you a problem with that, Paul?'

'No, Mother,' he said.

'So, help Lawrence, please.'

'Yes, Mother.'

We cleared the shelves and put the chair and trunk in the corridor. Mother took the medal and Father's picture from the shelf.

Paul asked, 'Where are you going to put them?'

'They will be quite safe,' said Mother, going into her room. 'I will keep them in my dresser.'

Paul frowned. The medal and the picture were always in the same place on the shelf, and when Mother dusted, she picked them up and cleaned underneath and then put them back in exactly the same place.

Mother came out wearing her pinafore. 'The room will belong to your uncle while he is here. He can make it his own.' She threw a drop sheet over the bed. 'You boys go and get yourself some fruit, and there are tea biscuits in the tin above the fridge. Take them and go outside, and Lawrence, wipe those webs from the outside windows.' She cracked open the lid of the paint can with a butter knife. 'Go on, boys, out you go.'

We did what we were told, and left the house, keeping quiet, not laughing and looking for ways to muck about and have fun. It had only ever been the three of us, Mother, Paul and me, and the medal on the shelf.

For the next two weeks Mother worked on the house every minute she had. She stood on the milking stool, hair escaping from her scarf, her narrow arms moving up and down across the walls with the paintbrush. As soon as a daddy-long-legs made a web, Mother was at it with the broom. 'Away with you, blasted things,' she said, attacking the sticky web with the bristles. After she painted the room where Uncle was going, she did the kitchen and the lounge. When the painting was done, we worked outside, trimming the blackberries and pulling up the weeds that grew around the fence posts. I had to do the grass with the push mower while Mother pruned the branches of the apple tree and the camellias. One day we came home from school and found her at the top of the ladder dragging damp leaves from the gutters with her bare hands, slapping them down where Paul and I stood at the bottom.

'What are you doing that for, Mother?' I called to her. Mother only cleared the gutters in summer, in case of fire.

'They look awful with everything stuck over the side,' she called back. She didn't stop. She didn't do her hoops. At night she wiped down the insides of all the shelves and scrubbed the black bits off all the pots and pans. Paul and I had to gather enough kindling from the field to last a month. It sat in a big pile at the back door beside the wood that Mrs Barry's man delivered, chopped and ready. 'An arm and a leg,' Mother said. 'But I can't have Reggie freezing.'

*

We were in the back yard setting up obstacles for the bikes when Mrs Barry called to us through the gap in the fence. 'Boys!'

'What is it, Mrs Barry?'

'I need a man to look after the vegetables,' she said. 'And I want help getting him to his feet.'

We followed Mrs Barry into her yard. Mrs Barry kept a big vegetable garden and gave us anything she didn't need. In return, Mother gave her fresh milk that Mrs Barry delivered to the patients without hope at the back of Stawell Hospital.

She picked a long iron stake up from the ground. 'You boys take this—' she passed us the stake '—so I can make his arms.'

Paul and I held the stake while Mrs Barry tied an old broomstick across the middle. 'Here, take my bucket and bring back some of your sawdust. And as much of Gert's straw as you can carry.' When we returned with the sawdust and straw Mrs Barry was tying a man's shirt and trousers with twine onto the broom. 'Lucky I didn't toss out all the old bastard's clothes. Here, stuff him.'

We filled the shirt with straw, so the chest stuck out wide, then we filled the trousers, tying ankles with more twine.

Next Mrs Barry brought out a cloth bag and filled it with the sawdust. She took a black marker from her pocket.

'The man needs a face. Those crows won't clear off without a face. Here, Lawrence, you can do the honours.'

I drew big black eyes and eyebrows on his cloth face. Then his mouth, not smiling, not sad. And a long nose.

'That's it, nice and angry. *Get away, birds, get away!*' Mrs Barry shook the straw man.

'Piss off, birds!' said Paul.

'Paul!'

'Can I put something on him?' Paul asked.

'Give him the marker, Lawrence. Have a go, Paul.'

Paul did a line down the straw man's cheek, then crossed it with stitches. 'He's been in a battle,' he said.

'Now he can do battle with the birds.' Mrs Barry pushed one of her old gardening hats down onto the straw man's head. 'That should keep the sun out of his eyes.'

I helped her tie the bag head to the top of the stake. 'Alright, boys, let's stand him up.'

Paul and I took hold of the stake.

'Ready?'

'Ready!'

'One . . . two . . . three and . . . up!'

And up he went. The straw man stood over the vegetable garden, his legs and arms thin and lumpy and long, his black eyes fierce.

'There,' said Mrs Barry. 'At last—a man in my life.' She brushed straw from her apron. 'Wait there, boys. I have something for you to eat.'

Paul, frowning at me, mouthed *No*. I shook my head at him.

Soon Mrs Barry came back out of her house with three bowls of blackberries she had bottled, and a pot of yoghurt.

'Not long now until Uncle,' I said, taking a bowl from Mrs Barry.

'He sent a letter,' added Paul. 'Can I have sugar on these, Mrs Barry?'

'No, you can't, Paul, sugar will rot your teeth.' She passed us spoons. 'I know all about the letter,' she said. 'Took him long enough.'

'Yes,' said Paul. 'What took him so long?'

'He's our uncle,' I said. 'If it weren't for him . . .'

'If it weren't for him—what?' Mrs Barry dolloped yoghurt onto the berries. 'Your mother has done a sterling job on her own out here. Look at the two of you. And she has kept her position at the dairy at the same time—never had a day off. If it weren't for him . . . If it weren't for *her*, you mean, Laurie.'

I shrugged. Suddenly I didn't know. I looked up at the straw man, his face stern, without answers.

Mrs Barry sighed. 'Well, I am happy for her, I suppose. Her long-lost brother at last.'

'Yes,' I said. 'At last.' I swallowed a spoonful of yoghurt, so bitter it stung my mouth.

6.

WHEN ALL THE OTHER CHILDREN had left the room for morning break, Mrs St Clair called me to her desk. My painting of a nest was spread before her, its twigs and bark and string carefully woven. She said, 'You like painting very much, don't you, Lawrence?'

'Yes, Mrs St Clair.'

'Do you get the chance to do very much of it outside of our class time?'

'Not really, no,' I answered. We didn't have the paints at home, and there was homework and chores to do.

'No, I didn't think so. It can be difficult with everything else. I have something for you that might make it a little easier.' She took a black book and a flat rectangular tin from her bag. 'This is an artist's sketchbook,' she said, opening the black book. 'See the quality of the paper, Lawrence. It's thicker than the butcher's paper we use in class. It's textured, see.'

I touched the thick paper and imagined the way it might hold paint. 'Yes.'

'And the pencils.' She pulled open the tin. 'They run from ordinary HBs to 7 and 8Bs.' She ran her fingers over the row of pencils. 'You'll get better results with these.' Mrs St Clair closed the tin and pressed it into my hands.

'For me?'

'Yes, Lawrence. You can use the sketchbook whenever you like without a fuss. No paints or water or mess. You can just take it with you wherever you go. It will fit nicely into your satchel.'

'Thank you, Mrs St Clair.'

'Lawrence,' she said, 'you have a gift. I want to encourage you to keep using it. I believe it to be important. Do you understand?' Mrs St Clair looked into my eyes.

'Yes, Mrs St Clair.'

'And you will continue to draw. And to paint?'

'Yes.'

'Good.' She stood, gathering up papers from her desk. 'That's good. Now go and join the others outside.'

'Thank you, Mrs St Clair.' I put the sketchbook and the pencils into my satchel and left the room.

While I was eating my sandwich, and bowling marbles, and then returning to class for mathematics, I thought of the pencils and the feel of the thick and textured paper under my fingertips. When I looked through the window at the mountains, joined in a chain behind the school, I wondered how the pencils would make them appear on the new paper.

In the last hour of the day Mrs St Clair read from *Robinson Crusoe*: '*I began to conclude in my mind that it was possible for me to be more happy in this forsaken, solitary condition than it was probable I should ever have been in any other particular state in the world.*' The class sat on the floor looking up at Mrs St Clair; we didn't notice the cold that crept in under the door and didn't care that the bell was about to ring and forgot we were in school.

We were on the island with Crusoe as he learned there was not a better place to be.

I thought of Crusoe as Paul and I rode home that afternoon. When Crusoe was on the island, he didn't have company, only his own thoughts. *I learned to look more upon the bright side of my condition, and less upon the dark side*. He taught himself to change his thoughts. Even after he was shipwrecked and lost his friends and his boat and didn't know if he would ever go home. As I pedalled along on the bike, everything that I saw—the fences, the sheep, the road—and everything and everyone that I would soon see—Beverly, the yard, the house—I could learn to 'look upon them' as bright or dark. 'Bright or dark!' I shouted to the trees and the mountains and the clouds. 'Bright or dark!'

After the school bus had passed, Paul and I raced each other. Paul won, then I won, then we rode for a while side by side, him reaching out to push me, me to push him. All the time we pedalled Wallis was in our sights, as if it wasn't only Mother waiting for us.

When I got home, Paul saw me unpacking my satchel. 'What have you got?' he asked, his mouth full of biscuit.

'A sketchbook. And pencils.'

'Where did you get them?'

'Mrs St Clair.'

'What for?'

'What do you think?' I snapped open the lid of the tin. 'For drawing.'

'Oh,' said Paul, taking another biscuit from the plate. 'Penny Wilson said you were the best at painting that Mrs St Clair has ever seen.'

'Did she?'

'Yes.' Paul took his marbles out to the yard.

I went through to the back porch, and sat on the edge with my legs over the side. I chose one of the pencils from the middle of the tin and opened the sketchbook, running my fingers over the paper. I looked at the peak of Wallis cutting into the autumn sky. The air held the warmth of the day, but the cold was not far behind. My hand moved the pencil across the paper, making a small scratching sound, back and forth. My eyes were on the mountain—his body of rock, broken with indentations in a vertical pattern, one after the other, each filled with shadow—while my hand was on the paper. Paul played marbles against himself as I drew, shooting cat's eyes across the path.

'Paul! Laurie! I've got a job for you!' Mother called from the kitchen.

'Yes, Mother!' I called back.

'What is it, Mother?' Paul shouted.

'I want you boys to clean the outhouse. Come and fetch the hot water!'

'Perfect,' Paul grumbled, gathering his marbles.

I stopped and looked at the drawing I had made. It was the inside of Wallis come to the outside. His hidden self. And above him the sky, a witness to the mountain and the world below. I touched the clouds at the top of the paper. A witness that chose to allow this much smaller world below. Who did this? I wondered. Was it me? I put the sketchbook into my satchel and followed Paul inside.

Mother sent us down to the outhouse with a bucket of hot soapy water and the scrubbing brush. 'First I need to go,' I told Paul.

'Great!' said Paul.

I pulled open the wooden door of the outhouse, carved at the top with three leaves.

'You'll never get me, you Jerry numbskull!'

I heard Paul bombing rocks outside as I looked up to the ribbon of sky between the roof and the carved door. Lorikeets and rosellas squawked in the trees. I could hear the scratch of the doves on the tin of the outhouse roof. I lowered my eyes, following the grooves in the planks, until I reached the framed picture of the sunflower that Mother had nailed to the back of the door.

'Damned Krauts! Take what's coming!'

I heard Paul bomb more of the Germans.

I shifted my weight on the bench. Home was about to change. Books and stories and the things I learned in school were the things that changed. Mr Wade had taught us about a desert with flowers that grew without water, about Antarctica where penguins leaped from cliffs of snow. About the River Thames where boats carried fruit to market. Mrs St Clair taught us about Crusoe's struggle, she taught us mathematics and painting. The things I learned at school entered me as if I were a sponge, but home stayed the same. One allowed for the other. Now home was changing too. What would happen?

After I was done, I threw down a handful of sawdust, crumpled three of the newspaper strips that Mother made Paul and I tear up at the kitchen table, and gave myself a wipe.

'You just took out a fleet of Messerschmitts,' Paul said, waving his hand in front of his face when I opened the door.

I sighed. 'Come on, we better hurry—Mother wants us back inside to do the damn silver.'

We scrubbed down the bench with eucalyptus oil, swept the floor and dusted the spider webs from the corners.

'Clean enough for the Queen to take her tea off the bench,' I said.

'Then drop a scone into the hole.' Paul grinned.

7.

IT WAS ONLY A FEW days now before Uncle. Mother was inside finishing her numbers, and Paul and I were in the back yard practising for his match against Glenthompson.

Paul placed a stick at the top of the yard. 'You have to bowl from here, Laurie. You get ten paces. So, go back a bit. Ten paces.'

'I know how to bowl.'

'From this line, as hard as you can.' Paul touched the stick with his bat. Mr Tonks had let him take home the Dynamo.

'I know.'

'You aim for the stumps.'

'Paul . . .'

'Okay. You ready?'

'No, I need a cup of tea first.'

He turned to face me from the bottom of the yard. 'As hard as you can!' he yelled, tapping the Dynamo on the grass.

I went back from the stick ten paces, then I took a run-up, and bowled. Paul raised the Dynamo and whacked the ball. Paul and I both turned and watched as it sailed through the window of Mother's bedroom, smashing the glass.

Paul gasped. We didn't move. Seconds passed. Mother came outside onto the back step, holding up the ball. 'What the hell?'

'We . . . we . . . it was an accident,' I said.

'An accident? An accident?'

'S-sorry, Mother,' I said.

'You just broke my window! And the mirror on my dresser!'

'We're really sorry, Mother.'

'Sorry. *Sorry*. I can't afford to fix the bloody window this week! Reggie will think we live like animals. And I could never replace that mirror. It was one of the only things nice left from my marriage. How could you boys?'

Paul dropped the Dynamo. 'We didn't mean to, Mother.'

'I cannot tolerate it. You boys!'

Mrs Barry put her head over the fence. 'Everything alright, Lou?'

'No, it is not.' Mother went back inside, slamming the screen door behind her.

'What happened?' Mrs Barry asked.

'We broke the window,' I said.

'And the mirror in her room.'

'The one from her wedding?'

I nodded.

'Oh dear.' Mrs Barry's head went down and a minute later she came into our yard through the gap in the fence. 'Why don't you two go and pull some of the snails off my cabbages, and I'll go in and talk to your mother, alright?'

We went into Mrs Barry's and sat under the straw man. He pointed at us, his mouth grim.

'Bloody hell,' I said.

'Jesus,' said Paul.

Ever since Uncle had sent the letter Mother had stayed on her side of the bridge. She was less patient when we didn't finish a task the way she wanted it. She didn't stop so often and say, *We do alright out here on our own, don't we, boys?*

'For God's sake,' I said to Paul, and kicked at the dirt. Suddenly I didn't want Uncle to come either. I wanted things to be the way they were before he sent the letter.

Mrs Barry came back out to us. 'It will be alright, lads. I know someone in Hamilton for the window. I'm sure he can have it ready before your uncle arrives. I don't know about the mirror. Might have to remain as one of life's minor disasters, I'm afraid. Oh, boys, don't look so worried. I'll bring you a plate of bran biscuits and you can just forget about it for now, alright?'

I had never seen Paul look so glum.

That night when we came inside, Mother hadn't lit the wood stove. She only turned on the corner lamp, leaving the rest of the house in shadow. At dinner, she was quiet. I noticed the dark half-moons under her eyes, how pale she was, the untidy hairs coming out from underneath her scarf. Paul and I moved around her nervously, watchful.

As she was filling up the sink, I said, 'Mother, do you want me to do the dishes tonight?'

She didn't answer, her hands in the soapy water, her face turned towards the window.

'Mother?' I said. 'I can wash and Paul can dry, then you can sit and do your hoop.'

Mother was only able to do her hoop when every number had been added and the dishes done, and the cow milked and everything off the floor.

'Mother? Why don't you sit and do your hoop?' I said again.

She just stood there, hands submerged, turned to the window and the night outside.

'If it weren't for your uncle . . . my brother . . .' she said. 'We endured . . .' She sniffed and shook her head. 'If it weren't for him . . .'

It was as though Paul and I weren't in the room.

'And then he was so sick, poor thing, and there was nothing I could do for him . . .'

I shivered. It was as if we had let in the horrors when we had broken the window, and now they drifted around Beverly like ghosts.

She placed the last plate on the rack. 'You boys don't know anything . . .' She wiped a wet hand under her nose. 'You've been spared . . .'

After she had finished the dishes, she sat down in her rocker. She did not get it rocking and did not pick up her hoop or her ledger. Mother was always moving, her legs as hard and narrow as our own were from the pedalling. She was busy and no nonsense, sure of herself and her movements. But this night she sat still, looking into the cold wood stove. Her face was blank, empty of stories and feelings and thoughts, all lines dropped away, all expression.

Later, when she was taking her bath, I went into her bedroom and switched on the light. The dresser from her wedding had a marble top and green leaf tiles. Above it sat the mirror, cracked in one corner, reflecting my face in pieces.

Paul and I took our bath quietly that night, no shooting each other with the water pistol, no bombing with the flannel or daring Paul to eat the soap. Just quietly washing without forgetting

43

behind our ears or under our arms, and quietly climbing out and staying on the mat so as not to spread the drips.

We were both in bed when I heard the rustle of Paul's Steamer. 'Laurie?'

'What?'

'We really did it this time.'

'*We* did? You mean, *you* did.'

'It was my first time with the Dynamo.'

'The bloody Dynamo.'

'Do you think she'll be angry for long?'

'I don't know. Could be.'

'What if she doesn't let me play at Glenthompson?'

'She might not.'

'Christ,' whispered Paul.

'Just be polite and don't make noise or swear and we'll chop the rest of the logs and get rid of all the webs outside and do every stick of homework you get from Mrs Smythe and say to Mother, "Is there anything I can do for you, Mother?"'

'Alright, alright.'

'And leave the bloody Dynamo at school.'

'Alright!'

I put down my poster and thought of Mother's words as she stood at the sink that evening. 'If it weren't for your uncle . . .' Last week Mrs St Clair had read from *Robinson Crusoe*. Crusoe *looked back upon his past life with such horror*, and I thought that was the same way Mother looked back on her past life and I wondered what had happened to her. What was the horror? I thought of her face as she sat by the unlit wood stove. She wasn't our mother, or not our mother at the age she was then, which was thirty-six; she was younger. She was a child with her years stripped away, the horrors still to come.

I pulled the blankets tighter around me. He would be here soon. Uncle. Then Mother would have someone else who remembered the horrors. She wouldn't be all alone. I looked through the window above my bed. Wallis was a line of darkness against the night sky. The others were behind him—Piccaninny, Abrupt and Pinnacle and Signal Peak, all of the Grampians, their bodies like a giant family, with Wallis at the front.

I wondered if the reason I could see Wallis at night was because I had looked at him so often in the day and knew his shape so well that it was impossible to look at the sky and not see him. As if without him there was no sky, no Beverly Park, no Hughlon. I rolled to my side and thought of all the things that happened at the base of Wallis—the potatoes growing in their gardens, the children going to school, the Austins on the road, the uncles on their way, and the horrors being endured, and him, Wallis, unmoving, seeing it all from above.

In the morning, Paul and I got up, dressed ourselves and went into the kitchen. Mother came through the back door carrying the steel milking pail full of milk.

She placed the pail onto the kitchen bench, milk lapping at the sides. 'Get a move on now, boys, I don't want you starting the week late. Porridge is ready in the pot.' Her busy and no-nonsense self was back.

Paul and I had breakfast and got ready for school.

The day before Uncle was due to arrive, Paul and I looked around our new lounge; the walls were bright white, the windows clear and the ledges free of dust. The bird clock had been moved to the centre of the mantelpiece above the wood stove, and a small round high table set with two lace doilies and an ashtray had been placed between the two lounge chairs. On the sideboard next to the wood stove was a silver tray that held Mother's good crystal glasses and a bottle of whisky labelled *Teacher's*.

'Looks like the Queen is moving in,' I said.

'Hell,' Paul said.

'Have you seen the spare?' I asked.

We opened the door of the spare room, which lately Mother had kept closed.

'Looks different, doesn't it?' I said.

Paul nodded. The walls were white and clean, and Mother had sewn a curtain with a border of roses. The bed had been made with new linen that was white and smooth. There were two new pillows that Mother had bought from Home and Hearth in Stawell. Paul and I and Mother only had one pillow each, flat from our heads lying on them night after night; Uncle's two pillows looked plump and soft.

Paul got on the bed, lay back against the pillows and pretended to read a newspaper. 'Oh me, oh my, how lovely these pillows are, can I please stay forever? Pass me a glass of whisky, boys.'

'Get off, Paul. What if Mother sees?'

'I wish he wasn't coming,' said Paul, climbing down from the bed.

'Well, he is coming.' I didn't feel the same as Paul. I was curious. Uncle had only ever been a dream from Mother's past, not a real man on his way to Hughlon. I wondered what sort of things he might do, and if he would like me.

I pulled Paul from the room and shut the door.

8.

MOTHER WAS GOING TO PICK up Uncle from the station in the Austin.

'Where has he been all this time?' Paul asked.

'I am sure he'll tell us, Paul,' said Mother, smoothing the skirt of her good dress. 'You can be sure that he's travelled far.'

'But didn't he let you know in the letter?'

'Of course he didn't let me know in the letter. He wasn't going to send me a book, was he? It was a letter telling me when he was arriving, that's all.'

Paul frowned.

'He's family, Paul. You'll see,' said Mother, pulling on her gloves.

The house had never been as tidy; the floor was so clean that Mother made us take off our shoes before we came inside.

'I want you boys to stay home for the day. Mrs Barry is next door. She can watch over you. You can ride in the field but keep a lookout for snakes,' she warned.

'There are no snakes now, Mother. It's too cold,' I said.

'Still, be careful,' she said, buttoning her coat.

'Yes, Mother.'

'Paul?'

'Yes, Mother.'

'And you are to let Gert in at three. She'll have to wait until tomorrow for milking. She's lessening off—she'll be alright.' Mother checked her face in the mirror. She was quick and rushing, bright with lipstick and hair tidily put away under her scarf. 'Your uncle has come a long way, and there are things I need to talk to him about.'

'You look nice, Mother,' said Paul.

She touched his cheek.

'And there are things he'll want to tell me, no doubt.' She picked up the keys to the Austin. 'His train comes into Melbourne at twelve, so we should be home by five.'

'Yes, Mother,' I said.

We stood in the drive and waved as she reversed the car, mud splashing up around the wheels. We waited there until the Austin disappeared. It was the first Sunday Mother wouldn't be home with us. The first Sunday Paul and I would be alone the whole day. Mrs Barry was next door, but she trusted us to take care and do what Mother said.

I turned to Paul. 'Want to go up the mountain?'

'Wallis?' Paul eyes widened.

'Yes. Do you want to?'

He nodded slowly.

'All the way?' I asked.

'All the way,' he answered.

'We need to be back by five.'

'*Before* five.'

'Yes!'

*

Our feet left faint prints on the mopped floor as we put apples and bread and cheese into the string bag.

'Should we ask Mrs Barry for some of her meatloaf?' Paul said, grinning.

'Please, no.'

'Or would you prefer Uncle's ham?' Paul opened the fridge and took out the ham leg wrapped in muslin.

'You better leave that. Mother bought it specially.'

'Can't we cut a piece from the top?' The ham sat pink and glistening on the plate; we only ever had ham off the bone at Christmas. 'He won't need a whole leg to himself.'

My mouth watered. 'I don't suppose she'll notice.'

I took Mother's carver from the block and cut off two thick slices of the ham, wrapping them in newspaper. 'Perfect,' I said. 'Read the paper while you eat your ham.'

'Then use it to wipe your arse.' Paul pushed the ham into the string bag.

We took the bikes to the back of the yard and dragged them under the rails beside the turnstile. It was very quiet; no trucks driving by, no tractors cutting hay, no cockatoos screeching over the banksia pods. We wheeled the bikes through the bumpy grass, neither of us speaking. With Mother far away—the pressure of her, the things she did and wanted for us, the waiting for her touch—there was enough space to hear the silence. A silence so thick it made sound. The clouds passing made sound; the grass growing made sound; the trees and flowers, the rocks, the leaves, the trail of dirt beneath our feet, all made sound. I looked up ahead at Wallis, jutting into the blue sky. The silence seemed to come from the mountain itself, beginning inside him, radiating outwards.

When we came to the trail we started pedalling, standing up when it became rocky. Paul bumped along the track in front of me, bombing fleets of Messerschmitts. 'Take that, you Krauts, take that!' Soon he went quiet, and I could see that he was working as hard as he could to keep his bike moving forwards over the path. It was getting more and more difficult.

'We'll walk from here,' I said. We dragged the bikes away from the narrowing path and hid them behind rocks, covering the rocks with branches. The trail, as it entered the trees, sloped upwards.

'Paul, look!' I whispered.

An emu was pecking its way through the bush.

'Heil Hitler!' Paul raised his arm.

'Shhh . . .'

Another emu appeared. If I were on my own, I would sit and draw the emus with their long feathery backs, their bare blue necks and hairy heads, and then I would draw the flowers that grew along the trail like miniature bells. I might draw the pink needle flowers too, and the ferns curling into their own centres, and the circles of lichen on the rocks, each like a small green sun. I wondered if I could ever come again by myself.

'Where has the track gone?' Paul asked.

'This way,' I said, seeing it narrow and winding between clumps of balga.

I heard Paul breathing harder as the path steepened. The gum trees grew more thickly around us, the bark peeling from their bodies in long papery strips. The air felt damper, the ground moist. I noticed puffs of wattle caught in Paul's hair and in the wool of his jumper as he took shots at imaginary soldiers in the trees. I watched his boots and his legs in his trousers as he walked ahead of me. Mother had patched and re-patched the seat so many times they looked like the trousers of a clown.

'You okay, Paul?'

'Aye aye, captain,' he said over his shoulder.

It was my job to take care of Paul. If we were the only brothers left in the world and the mountain was our home, and we didn't have a mother or Mrs Barry next door, it would be up to me.

The trail steepened further, becoming narrower as it wound its way through the rocks, fallen branches and scrub.

'I'll go in front,' I said to Paul, stepping past him. I could hardly believe we were here; I had looked at Wallis from afar, every single day, in all his changing lights and skies and weathers, for so many years, and now I was climbing the trail to the summit.

The walk become much harder, and the path more difficult to follow. Neither of us spoke, both breathing heavily. How long had we been climbing? I kept thinking the trail had ended, and then I would see it again, faint and sandy between clusters of rocks.

At last the trail flattened out. We had reached a wide plateau of smooth stones. When we looked out over the edge we saw the valley, thick with trees, sweeping away beneath us to Abrupt on the other side.

'How far have we come, do you think?' said Paul, out of breath.

'About halfway, I think,' I answered, though I wasn't really sure.

Paul stepped closer to the edge of the plateau, sending small stones over the side.

We watched as the stones knocked against branches and rocks all the way to the bottom.

'Could've been us,' said Paul.

'Do you think he tried to save them?' I asked.

'Who?'

'The brother and the sister. The ones Mother told us about. Do you think the father tried to save them when they fell?'

'He must have.' Paul picked up a stone and threw it over the side. 'If our men could have seen the Germans from here, things would have been different. Father could have shot them down with a rifle before they saw him.'

'What about a grenade?'

'Yes. He could have taken them out that way. The Germans wouldn't have known what hit them,' said Paul.

'The King would have sent us two of those Atlantic Stars,' I said.

'One each.'

'Three. One for Mother to keep in her room.'

Paul squatted beside a small pile of bones on the rocks. 'What do you think it was?'

I picked up one of the small curved bones. 'Kangaroo,' I answered, seeing the bones as they might appear on a page of my sketchbook.

We sat on the flat rocks and I took two apples from the string bag.

'I don't want him to come,' said Paul, biting into his apple.

'I know you don't.'

'There isn't room.'

'Yes, there is.'

'The spare is for Father's things.'

'A medal doesn't need a whole room,' I said.

Paul poked at the ground with a stick. He flicked dirt from inside an ant hole.

'Mother says he is clever,' I said.

'*You're* clever.'

'He could show us things.'

'Like what?'

'I don't know. How to make things. How to do things.'

'We don't need him,' said Paul, squashing ants under his shoe.

I got to my feet. 'He's coming anyway.'

'Bloody hell,' said Paul. He stood and walked towards the trees. 'I need to pee.'

'Me too.' I stood beside him.

'Ha ha!' Paul sprayed the ground in an arc.

'You got my shoes!'

'Ha! Take that and that!' Our streams of piss crisscrossed in the dirt. It felt good to be away from all the ordinary rules and Mother fussing around us and making us do the right thing.

'Keep going?' Paul asked, buttoning his trousers.

I picked up the string bag. 'Aye aye, captain.'

We kept going along the trail. When we came to some higher rocks, I gave Paul a knees-up.

'Much further do you think, Laurie?'

'Not much.'

We climbed from rock to rock, higher and higher. I was hot, sweat dripping under my clothes. Paul was climbing more and more slowly. My legs were on fire. It began to feel as though we would never reach the summit, as though there was no summit. The mountain kept going and going and it had been a mistake to think that it would ever end. Wallis went all the way to the sky, and nobody had ever even tried to climb him. We were both panting. And then we reached a higher set of rocks and I could see we were almost there.

Our chests heaved as I took Paul's hand and pulled him up and over the last rock.

I was still holding his hand as we looked out at the view spread before us—at the orchards and farms, the fields separated by lines of fence and roads; at the town of Hughlon on one side and Hamilton on the other; at the whole flat human world, and then the up-and-down lines of the mountains behind Wallis, like waves turned to rock. Way down below, small and far away, was the red roof of Beverly, and the grey slate of Mrs Barry's beside it, with the dark trees standing guard. I sensed the enormity of the space around us, at the same time as feeling the warmth of Paul's hand in mine. The faraway world and the close.

A wind blew around our heads. Paul put out his arms, tipping from side to side as if he was on the deck of *The Lady Bold* as she was tossed about on the ocean. 'Batten down the hatches!' he shouted.

I pulled my sword from its sheath. 'Take that, you blaggard!'

'Get off me!' He fought back, tearing my pirate shirt, leaving stripes of blood across my arms.

I stuck him in the chest, pinning him to the ground. 'I've got you this time! Cry mercy!'

'Never!'

'Cry mercy!'

'I'll die before I surrender!'

'Cry mercy!'

'Never!'

'Then die!'

'Vengeance!' Paul wriggled out from under me, and ran. 'Vengeance!'

We chased each other from one side to the other, our cries carried away by the wind.

Paul and I sat on the rocks in the middle of the summit, and I took the parcel of ham from the string bag. I gave one of the pieces to Paul and took the other for myself.

'The sun revolves around the earth or the earth around the sun. Which do you think it is, Paul?' I asked him.

'Don't know,' said Paul, stuffing ham into his mouth.

'Earth around the sun,' I said. The meat tasted sweet and salty.

'Good ham,' said Paul, his mouth full.

I imagined the earth turning around us as we sat cross-legged on the stones with Paul and me at its centre, eating ham.

We stood for one more moment at the edge, looking out at the world below. I understood that Paul and I were on the surface of the earth, and that the earth was finite, but I could see that there was something else, greater, that was infinite—the earth's invisible self. Wallis whispered, *See this.*

We didn't walk down the mountain; we ran, jumping from rock to rock, as though Wallis himself was tipping us. All the way down, not a step out of place. Not caring how hot we were, how out of breath, how tired, as if the top of Wallis had given us the strength to reach the bottom. We found our bikes where we had left them and rode the last part of the track to the field, our legs burning and aching, then pushed the bikes through the grass, to the turnstile. The cow was waiting at the gate. 'Get in there, Gert!' we called, waving our arms. 'Get in there!'

Gert bellowed and went through as I pulled a biscuit of hay from the bale and spread it in the rack.

'Look!' Paul said.

There, coming along the road, was Mother's Austin.

'Jesus,' said Paul.

My heart pounded; we had made it just in time. Mother was home, with Uncle.

9.

PAUL STOOD BESIDE ME ON the porch as Mother and Uncle Reggie got out of the car. He was wearing a dark brown suit, with a waistcoat and tie, and a dark trilby hat on his head. A white stripe ran round the sides of his shoes.

Mother walked to the back of the car.

'Let me,' Uncle said, taking his suitcase from the trunk. He looked much older than her, even though the difference was only two years. Mother was like a girl, and he was a man.

As they came up the path towards us, I noticed that Uncle limped.

'Boys, this is your Uncle Reggie,' said Mother. There was a smile on Mother's face, coming and going as she looked to Paul and me.

Uncle put down his suitcase. 'You must be Lawrence,' he said, taking my hand in his. Uncle smelled of a perfume I didn't know, one belonging to a man. His hand felt warm and firm and his eyes glittered. 'You must be Paul,' he said, taking Paul's hand. Paul didn't smile and his hand stayed slack.

'Come inside, Reggie. Surely you're exhausted. Come and have a drink,' said Mother.

'Yes, yes, of course, although I am quite struck by the beauty of this place.' Uncle looked all about him. 'I hardly want to go inside.'

'Beauty?' said Mother. 'I don't know about that. Out here in the middle of nowhere.' She shook her head at the fields and mountains all around. Even though she was saying the place we lived was not beautiful, she looked and sounded proud. Her cheeks were flushed, her eyes shining.

'Yes—beauty and space. The city is so crowded; everything moving so fast,' said Uncle, breathing in through his nostrils. 'And the mountain is quite staggering. Like a great lion on his paws. Is Wallis the tallest in the range?'

'No, there are taller. William is the tallest. And Abrupt is taller too, though it doesn't appear so from here. But still, Wallis does a good job of putting the place in shadow.' She picked up Uncle's suitcase. I saw that it was dented and worn. Like it belonged to a different man.

Mother ushered Uncle through the door, and we followed. The smell of the new paint on the walls mingled with the smell coming from Uncle. Mint and pine and lemons. Where was it made in his body?

Mother took off her coat and hung it on the rail in the corridor. 'Give me your coat, Reggie,' she said. 'Your hat.'

'Thank you,' said Uncle. He took off his coat and hat and passed them to Mother. His shirt and his trousers were so long and loose you couldn't see where his body began inside them. His dark hair was slicked back and oiled. That was where the smell was made—in his hair. I took a deep breath as we followed Mother into the house.

'There is the lounge,' she said. 'This is the kitchen, and this is your room.'

The four of us gathered in the doorway of the spare and stood looking at the puffed pillows, the rose curtains, the clean and dusted shelves.

Mother said, 'I hope it will do, Reggie.'

'It's wonderful, sister,' said Uncle. Mother had always been Mother. Mrs Barry called her Lou, or Louise. And now she was *sister*. Everything was changing. A man was in our house, a grown man, a man who was not a medal, a man who knew our mother from years before. And this man would be sleeping in the spare room, here.

'Well, you can get some rest at least. It will be a lot quieter than you are used to, I'm sure,' said Mother.

We were still standing at the entrance to the spare—the four of us—as if we were trapped there.

Then Uncle said, 'Perfect,' and stepped into the room. 'Just what I need.' He put his case down on the floor.

Mother said, 'It's so good to see you. I've missed you.'

'And I have missed you, sister.'

'Oh, Reggie, sometimes I wasn't sure if . . .' She sniffed and her eyes reddened.

Uncle reached out and took her in his arms. Paul and I stood where we were, not belonging to their moment, not expecting it, but held spellbound. We had never seen Mother in the arms of a man, never seen her look so small.

Uncle set her back, and Mother put her handkerchief to her eyes. 'Come on, come on, I don't want you dying of thirst. Come on, boys. Oh dear, Reggie, you'll die of thirst,' she said, trying to find her no-nonsense self again.

We followed her into the lounge.

'You take a seat, Reggie, and I'll fetch you a drink.'

'A glass of water first, Lou?' he said.

'That I can do.' Mother smiled.

Uncle walked to the side window. He looked out of it, then Mother came in with a glass of water. Paul and I waited, not knowing where to sit or what to do.

Uncle took the water. 'Thank you, Louise,' he said. 'What a day it has been.'

Paul and I watched as he drank.

Mother went to the bottle of Teacher's, opened the lid and poured whisky into the two crystal glasses. She passed one to Uncle.

'Ah, wonderful,' he said. 'To you, Louise.'

'To me?' she said. 'I hardly think so.'

'Why not?' said Uncle. 'You have earned it.'

They looked at each other as their glasses touched. We had never seen Mother drink whisky. Whisky killed Mrs Barry's father. *The fires took everything, then he spent the rest of his bloody life trying to douse the flames*, Mrs Barry told Mother.

Mother said, 'Sit down, Reggie.' She held out her hand to one of the chairs. Then she put down her glass, went to the wood stove and crouched before it, opening the iron door.

'You should let me do that,' said Uncle, half standing from his chair.

'No, no, it's all set, no trouble at all.' Mother struck a match from the box she kept in the wood basket and the flames jumped inside the stove. 'It will be warm in no time.' She looked up at him, her face open, smiling. 'Do you remember how cold it used to get?'

Uncle swirled his drink in his glass. 'That's a cold you don't forget.'

'You haven't forgotten?'

'Not for one day.'

Paul and I stood at the side, not yet knowing where to sit.

Uncle took a sip of his Teacher's and turned to Paul and me. 'Boys,' he said.

Mother said, 'They were meant to be dressed and tidy.'

'Boys don't need to be dressed and tidy,' said Uncle. 'They have been out having fun, I hope. Making the most of it. Right, boys?'

Paul and I still could not seem to move or speak.

'Paul, Lawrence,' said Mother. 'Answer your uncle. Sorry, Reggie, I think they are just a little too excited.'

'Well, I am excited too, Louise,' said Uncle, 'to meet my nephews. Charlie would have been proud.'

Charlie. That was Father. I looked at Mother's face. Tears came to her eyes. 'Yes, yes . . . he would have been.'

'Young Paul is the spitting image.'

'Yes . . . I am reminded every day.' Mother sat in the chair beside Uncle. 'Sit down, boys,' she said.

We sat on the couch, looking at Uncle.

'What classes are you in at school?' He turned to me when he asked his question.

'I am in the fifth class,' I said. My voice sounded light and soft like a girl's.

'Ah, the fifth class,' he said. 'You must be . . . How old are you?'

'Ten,' I said.

'Ah, ten! I think I was ten when I first realised all that I didn't know and all there was to learn.' He took another sip from his glass.

'He is just like you at school, Reggie. Just as clever. I will show you his last report.'

I sat as tall as I could in my chair. This was better than a medal on the shelf. This was a real man who was in our family. I noticed that Paul was leaning back, his arms folded across his chest.

'Do you like school?' Uncle asked me.

'Yes, sir.'

'He does like school,' Mother answered. 'And he likes all of his subjects.'

'Is that true?' Uncle asked me.

'Yes, sir.'

'But surely there must be something you like most of all. A favourite subject. What is it? History? Mathematics? The sciences?'

'Yes . . .'

'Well, what is it?'

I wanted to tell him the truth. Even with Mother there. 'I like to paint.'

Uncle's eyes widened. 'To paint? How wonderful.'

'Let me show you his report,' said Mother, standing from her chair.

'I would like to see a painting,' said Uncle, his eyes on me.

'I try to remind Lawrence that he must remember all his studies.'

'But I do, Mother.'

'I know you do, Lawrence, I know.' She smiled. 'It was all there in the report.'

'Do you have a painting you might show me?' Uncle asked.

I looked at Mother. She knew I did have a painting I could show Uncle. The parrot peas.

'Oh, Reggie, that can wait. You must be tired.'

'Never too tired to look at a work of art.'

Mother said, 'Oh, go on then, Laurie, and bring your picture.'

I got up from the couch and went to my room. I heard Mother say, 'I don't know you should be encouraging him, but it's true, he is good at all his studies. He is so like you, Reggie.'

As I came back into the lounge, Uncle said to Paul, 'Do you have similar interests to your brother, Paul?'

'He likes sport,' said Mother. 'And he is very good. But he has to learn that he must value his studies.'

'Sport is as important as anything else,' said Uncle.

Paul kept his head down.

'Yes, but sport won't pay bills, will it? Or help him find a good job.'

'I am not sure you can claim that sport won't contribute to his success, Louise . . .'

Mother pretended she hadn't heard him. 'Go on,' she said to me. 'Show your uncle, Lawrence.'

'Ah, let me see,' he said. He placed his drink on the round table on the lace doily, then he took the corners of my picture. He looked for a long time. 'My, my, Lawrence,' he said softly. 'It is a very good painting. Very good indeed. Did it take you long?'

I had never spoken at home about painting. I felt shy in front of Mother. 'I don't know,' I answered. 'I don't think so.'

'Not that the time it takes tells us anything,' he said, still looking at the painting. 'Nothing is of less relevance, really. Lawrence—' he turned to me '—I feel as if I could put my face to these and inhale their scent.'

'Well,' said Mother. 'Tomorrow perhaps he can show you his school work. Would you like another drink, Reg?'

'No, thank you, Louise. One is plenty.'

'I must prepare the dinner.' Mother held out her hand and Uncle gave her back my flowers.

Uncle picked up his glass and drained the last drop. 'Paul,' he said, 'why don't you show me what you can do with that cricket ball before it is time for us to eat?'

'Oh, Reggie,' said Mother. 'You haven't changed a bit. Surely it's too late. It's almost dark.' I could see she was pleased. She had never been able to share us. There had been no other family to tell about our reports or our sport or what she wanted for us. And now here she was sharing us with her brother. I couldn't take my eyes from him. Even though he wasn't much taller than Mother, he seemed much bigger, and made of something completely different.

'Just a very quick play, so we can see what Paul can do.'

'There isn't enough light.'

'Oh, go on, Paul. Your uncle has asked you,' said Mother.

Paul grumbled and stood.

'Out here?' said Uncle, going to the back door.

'Yes,' I said. 'Use the new ball, Paul.'

We opened the door, and Paul went ahead to fetch the ball and bat from the shed. Uncle was beside me as we stepped outside. The air was cold and clean, free of the smell of house paint and fire and the disinfectant Mother used to mop the floors. There was Wallis before us, with the mists of evening around his head, his body of trees dark and rough.

'Majestic,' said Uncle. 'Truly majestic.'

Majestic . . . truly . . . The words he used . . . He was like a book where I didn't know what would happen next.

'Have you painted it yet?' he asked me, as we stood together on the bottom of the porch.

'What?'

'The mountain. Mount Wallis.'

'I only paint at school. On Fridays. With Mrs St Clair.'

'Ah, your teacher?'

'Yes.'

'There is no need to wait for Fridays and Mrs St Clair.'

'I have homework to do.'

'Your mother wants what is best for you, but not everybody can understand the value of artistic expression.'

'Mrs St Clair likes painting.'

'Mrs St Clair has set you on your path. But it's only the beginning.'

'Oh.'

'And your Mount Wallis would make a splendid subject. He will sit without moving for hours. And he won't charge a penny.'

Uncle was sharing things with me; I was the person he thought most clever and the best at painting and could understand his joke about Wallis staying still. I did not understand the joke about not paying a penny, and yet I knew that it was intended for me.

'Have you ever climbed him?' he asked me.

I didn't know how to answer. I didn't want to lie. 'Mother doesn't want us to climb him . . .'

He looked down at me, a smile playing on his lips. 'That's not what I asked.'

Just then, Paul ran up to us from the bottom of the yard. 'Here,' he said, tossing the cricket ball to Uncle.

'So, you're a batsman?' said Uncle, catching the ball.

'Yes,' Paul answered.

'Well, get down there and defend your stumps.'

Paul ran down to the fence. Uncle moved back and rolled up the sleeves of his shirt. 'Ready?' he called to Paul.

'Ready!'

Uncle took a run and bowled hard into the fading light. I heard the hard *thwack* of Paul's bat as he returned the ball.

The four of us sat at the table as three white candles flickered in the centre. Mother had lit the dinner candles in the candelabra.

Uncle patted his lips with the serviette. 'Delicious, Louise. You always could prepare a fine meal.'

'It's hardly anything fancy.' Mother smiled. She had cooked lamb chops with Mrs Barry's potatoes and beans and baby beetroots.

'But you always made the best of whatever we had.'

'I was so young then.'

'We both were,' said Uncle.

'I am glad things are different now.'

It was quiet. Uncle reached for Mother's hand. They looked across at each other, their faces sorry. Sad.

Paul turned to Uncle. 'What have you been doing all this time?'

'Paul!' Mother frowned.

Uncle answered. 'The boy can ask me what he likes, Louise. It's a fair question. He wants to know why I haven't come sooner, why I haven't been an uncle to you boys before now—isn't that right, Paul?'

Mother glared at Paul, who was looking down at his chops.

I waited.

Mother waited too.

'The truth is, boys, that I needed to go far away before I could return. Your mother is home to me—the only real home I have, but she knows that I am cursed with an adventurous spirit, and that spirit took me far.'

'To where?' I asked him. I imagined him in the places Mr Wade had taught us: Borneo and the Sahara and the Nordic Isles. I saw him on a camel and in a boat and in a sled with wolves to pull him through the snow. I saw him wearing all the costumes that were the custom and I saw him in the great art museums Mrs St Clair had described for the class.

'Ah, so many different places in my travels abroad . . . I have never liked to stay in one place too long. I was always restless.'

Restless, travels, abroad. I watched his hands as they held his fork and shook the salt over his chops and raised his glass to his lips. When he rolled back the cuffs of his shirtsleeves I saw, peeking out from the bottom of his sleeve, a dark green hook. I had seen other men with tattoos on their arms—at the cricket match and at the fundraiser and at the Glenthompson Show. Some of the fathers had them drawn after the war. They put the date they lost a friend or a brother. I wondered where the hook on Uncle's arm led.

'But what did you do there?' Paul asked.

'Paul!' said Mother. 'Your uncle has come a long way and is tired.'

'That's fine, Louise. The boy is curious. And rightfully so.' He turned to Paul. 'I worked in England for a time. And in France. Spain. Spain was really something to see.' He glanced at me. 'The architecture was unlike anywhere else in the continent— La Sagrada Familia, of course, and the Casa Mila . . . I was involved with various businesses. I never liked to stay any one place too long. As soon as I knew the language—either the language of the country or merely the language of the company itself—then it was time to think of a new destination.'

Merely, company, destination . . .

'But, what did—' Paul said.

'Paul, your uncle will tell you more of his adventures, but that's enough for now.' Mother placed her hand over Paul's. 'Make sure to eat the vegetables. Mrs Barry's pride and joy.'

I looked up at the three faces: Paul and Mother and Uncle. I didn't know until then what we had been missing. The medal never spoke, never told us where it had been or shook salt on its lamb chops or said, *Boys, your mother has every reason to be proud.* We had been missing a man.

That night I lay in bed and lifted the corner of the British Naval Line. I could hear the rustle of paper from the other side of the boards as Paul lifted the Steamer.

'Paul?' I whispered into the crack.

'What?'

'What do you think?'

'About what?'

'About Uncle.'

'What about him?'

'Do you like him more now?'

'We hardly know him.'

'We will get to know him.'

'We don't need him.'

'Mother needs him.'

'She has us.'

'We aren't enough. He's a grown-up. And he's her brother.'

'I don't care.'

'But don't you like him?'

'I don't know.'

'You don't like him. I can tell.'

'How?'

'I can tell.'

There was quiet.

'He's good at cricket,' I said. I heard Paul sigh. 'It doesn't matter, Mother likes him. He is here for Mother. And he knows a lot, Paul. He probably knows more than anybody else we ever met.'

'Not more than Mr Wade.'

Mr Wade's passion was geography. He said geography was the relationship between different peoples and the natural world. But Uncle understood about a way of seeing. He knew about Wallis being a subject.

'Mr Wade only knows *some* things,' I said.

'All those years. What was Uncle doing? Why didn't he come before? We still don't know,' Paul said.

'He was being educated. He was . . . working in a business. In Spain.'

'But what was he doing?'

'He was travelling. He was—'

I heard the creak of Paul's bed as he rolled over.

'Goodnight, Lawrence.'

'Goodnight, Paul.' Who cared what Paul thought? Soon he would see how good it was to have Uncle here. He would like him as much as I did.

I looked through my window. Mother liked me to close the blinds to save the heat, but I never did. I could see the crescent moon in the night sky, while the rest was in shadow. If I put them together and did not separate the crescent from the whole, I saw a perfect silver sphere balancing on Wallis's peak. I turned onto my side and listened to the muffled sound of Uncle talking to Mother in the lounge as I drifted to sleep. Now it wasn't only Wallis keeping us safe.

*

The next morning when Paul and I came into the kitchen Mother was stirring porridge at the stove. 'Where is he?' I asked.

'Out for a walk in the field,' said Mother.

I went to the window and saw Uncle coming through the turnstile.

'Why does he walk that way?'

'What way?' Mother placed a jug of milk onto the table.

'He has a limp. Can't you see?'

'Yes, yes, I can see. Sit down please, boys.'

'Why does he have it?' Paul pulled out his chair.

'He was ill, when we were younger.' Mother spooned porridge into our bowls. 'Didn't I tell you?'

'No,' I said.

'Well, he was ill. The illness damaged his leg.'

'Can't it be fixed?'

'I thought it could. I mean, I thought it would fix itself.' Mother put the empty porridge pot into the sink. 'But, no, it seems it hasn't. Not altogether. Now, hurry up and eat your breakfast. I don't want you late for school.'

Uncle came through the back door wearing a long-sleeved undershirt and his suit pants. His face was red and damp. 'Boys.' He nodded at us.

'How was your walk?' Mother asked, smiling.

'The mountain is truly something to behold,' he said. 'A thousand moods in a single day, I imagine.' He looked at me. 'Quite mesmerising.'

I felt my face flush.

'I had better go and wash,' he said.

'You have the towels I left out on the bed?'

'I do, thank you, Lou.'

Soon we heard water splashing against the tiles. I could still smell Uncle's sweat and hair oil left behind in the kitchen.

'He'll use all the hot,' said Paul.

Mother raised her eyebrows at him. 'Since when did you ever want hot water, Paul?'

'Well, there won't be any,' he said, frowning.

Uncle turned off the taps.

The house shuddered.

10.

BEVERLY'S ROOMS WERE FULL OF Uncle even when he wasn't inside them. Even when he was in the spare—resting, reading or listening to the radio—it was as if he were throughout the house. The smell changed. Wood smoke and dinner and laundry soap mingled with the smell of the oil Uncle used to smooth his hair, the cigarettes he smoked in the evening, and the smell of his sweat when he returned from a walk. 'As if a man can walk away from what is inside him, hey, boys? What folly to think so.'

His voice warmed the house, his sentences like announcements. 'The skies here, Louise, so clear . . . The taste of fresh milk again . . . So much space, time to think, time to breathe; Louise, you are blessed . . .'

Other times he spoke low with Mother, the two of them on the back porch on the canopy swing, or standing at the kitchen window. *Where do you think? But how could they? And now? Have you heard anything? Anything at all?* If Paul or I came near at those times, Mother looked at Uncle and they stopped talking, and Uncle asked us how was school, what did we enjoy, and who were our friends? My answers were brief, my voice soft.

But I spoke more than Paul. He only spoke to Uncle if they did batting practice.

When Mother took Uncle down to meet Gert, I followed.

'Hello there,' he said, holding out his hand to the cow.

Gert dropped her head and went back to her salt lick.

'She doesn't like boys,' I told him.

'Ha!' said Uncle. 'Really? What's not to like about boys? How long have you had her, Louise?'

'A couple of years. She's the second we've raised.' Mother stroked Gert's back.

Uncle planted the stool by the cow's side.

'You haven't forgotten how?' said Mother. She smiled, her hand against Gert's rump. Her eyes shone. Strands of her hair that had gotten away from under her scarf curled around her ears. Her nose and cheeks were pink with the cold that came from the mountain.

Uncle said, 'Let's see if I haven't forgotten how.' When he rolled up his sleeves, I saw more of the drawing on his arm; a long hook with a green tail. I wondered if it was an anchor, or was it a snake? I couldn't imagine ever not being too shy to ask. Uncle put the pail under Gert's udder and sat down on the stool. As his shoulders worked back and forth, I heard the two streams of milk hitting the sides of the bucket.

'Ah, you haven't forgotten at all, Reg!' Mother wriggled her fingers. 'At last these poor hands of mine can have a rest.'

'Hands just like our father's, hey, Lou? The devil arthritis.'

'My only inheritance,' said Mother. She smiled. 'You're milking like an expert.'

'Once you learn you never forget.'

'Laurie, go and carry a load of wood in for the stove,' said Mother. 'And call your brother to help.' Paul was kicking his football against the shed wall.

As I walked away, I heard Mother say, 'Can you tell the boy has never had a father, Reggie? He doesn't leave your side.'

'Lou, I am happy to be there for him.'

'But it must drive you mad . . .'

'Not at all. Quite the opposite. I am delighted.'

Was it possible to grow taller in an instant?

A short while later, Uncle brought the steel pail into the kitchen full of fresh milk. It sloshed over the sides as he placed it on the table. 'You took more than me, dear brother,' Mother said.

'Your Gert was a lady.'

I was quiet around him; I wanted to hear the things he had to say, the warmth of his voice. I wanted to watch him. At school I thought of him and wanted the day to end so I could see him again. Mrs St Clair said, 'Lawrence, where is your attention this week?'

'My uncle has come to stay,' I told her. I told everyone in the class. Daniel Sheefer, Ian Lockey, Sam and James. I told all the other boys, some with fathers, some without. 'My uncle has come to stay.'

Every night, Uncle and Mother sat in the good chairs in the lounge and drank Teacher's from Mother's crystal glasses, while Paul and I did our homework at the kitchen table. I worked on my spelling words—*enough, parcel, collide*—while Paul did catch-up mathematics. I covered each word with the corner of my ledger to make sure I spelled it correctly without looking. Between words I would look up at Uncle, sitting and sipping and talking with Mother, a man to help keep the wolf from the door. When the bird clock chimed six—the two wooden birds bending to drink from the dish—Mother stood, smoothed her dress and said, 'Dinner is almost ready.'

Paul and I cleared away our books and Uncle came to the table, while Mother set out the four blue-and-white place mats that she kept for special occasions. The mats were decorated with bird patterns and a river lined with willow trees, and they'd come out of the side cupboard every night since Uncle arrived.

Mother was in the kitchen longer after school, *The Joy of Cooking* open on the shelf. She said, *Boys, out of my kitchen*. She was not outside so much anymore, milking Gert, or breaking sticks for kindling, or mucking out the shelter. Uncle did all that.

After she set out the mats, Mother served the dishes. Every night it was something different: chicken Maryland, beef stroganoff, bacon and egg pie, roast pork and apple.

Uncle said, 'You boys have it easy.'

'That much is true, isn't it, Reggie? It wasn't like that for us, was it?'

'It certainly was not.'

'Do you remember mutton soup?' Mother held her serving spoon mid-air. Her face glowed in the lamplight. She looked as young as the high school girls that came out of Stawell Secondary College.

'Mutton soup with turnip.'

'Turnip if we were lucky.'

'So lucky, hey?'

The two of them began to laugh. 'Bloody mutton soup, Reggie, do you ever eat the stuff? Mutton soup?'

'What do you think?'

'Never?' Mother snorted.

'Never.' Uncle grinned.

The heat from the wood stove filled every corner of the house. Since Uncle, Mother kept the flames behind the glass burning bright, not minding how much wood it burned. We went to bed slow and sleepy with full stomachs and heat. The coals were still burning when Mother opened the iron door in the morning.

When we came home from school, Uncle was there with Mother, waiting for us. He said, 'How was school, Lawrence?' as if he expected an answer. Mother didn't bother to ask how was school, because we never gave her an answer. We just grunted, happy the school day was behind us.

'It was good, Uncle.'

'And you, Paul? How was it today?'

'Alright,' said Paul, kicking off his school shoes at the door.

'School is not for everybody,' said Uncle.

Mother's face fell. 'But, Reggie, everyone must go.'

'Yes, Louise, everyone must go.' Uncle followed Paul into the kitchen. 'Paul, sometimes we have to be patient. Sometimes it's a matter of endurance.'

For once Paul seemed to be listening.

'He has to do well in school . . .' said Mother, placing our afternoon tea on the table.

'Of course, Louise. Paul will do fine at school. Don't fret.' He looked at Paul. 'You see how your mother worries, Paul?'

Paul reached for a sandwich and rolled his eyes.

'Take that outside, Paul,' said Mother. 'You and Laurie both. Take your afternoon tea onto the porch.'

*

I sat on the edge of the porch drawing the sheep in the field beyond the fence. The field appeared shiny with rain. The sky above was filled with wispy clouds, as if the fur the mother rabbit had taken from her chest was pulled thin and spread across the sky. The rest of the sky behind the clouds was divided in half, dark grey on one side and pale blue on the other. I knew, as I shaded the clouds with my pencil, that the sky would soon change. What would it be like to do nothing but watch the sky all day, I wondered, drawing every change?

'What is that you are doing?' Uncle asked, sitting beside me.

'Nothing.' I put down my pencil, suddenly shy.

'Nothing? Yet you looked so absorbed. Can I see?'

'It's nothing, really.'

'Let me be the judge. I would very much like to see.'

I passed him the sketchbook.

'Ah, Lawrence . . .' He touched the grass, then the sky. 'This depth, this perspective . . .'

Depth, perspective . . .

'And you are using your good paper too? And your proper drawing pencils.'

'Yes, the ones Mrs St Clair gave me.'

'Of course—Mrs St Clair.' He passed the book back to me.

'Uncle, what is perspective?'

'Perspective? Let's see . . . it's the way you show the dimensions of your subject. The way you make it real on the paper.' He touched one of the grazing sheep. 'Your animal here has dimension, and is the right size for your field, and your fence, so I believe it. At least, I do not question it; I enter the scene without effort and am immersed within it. You have communicated with me, do you understand? You have shared your vision. And because you have a natural feel for perspective, I am in no way distracted.'

'Oh.'

'It's a good thing, Lawrence.' Uncle smiled, placing a hand on my back. 'You can be proud of your sheep in their field.' Then he stood and was gone—I breathed the scent of him left behind.

Later Mother sent me through the gap in the fence to Mrs Barry's to bring home her extra cabbage. Mrs Barry was on her back porch drinking tea and smoking a cigarette. 'How are you, Laurie? How is Paul?' she asked me.

'We're good, Mrs Barry.'

'I'm glad.'

'Uncle is helping Mother. Do you want to come and meet him?'

Mrs Barry drew back on her cigarette. 'I did meet him, remember?'

Mother had introduced them when Uncle first came, but I wanted to show Uncle to her again. I wanted her to see the way he was helping around the yard, doing the weeding, checking for termites and tidying the woodpile.

'Would you like to meet him again?'

'I'm sure I will meet him again.' She passed me the basket of vegetables.

'You could come now.'

'In the middle of my tea?'

'He's in the yard. He's helping a lot.'

'What I want to know is, does he pay for anything?'

'I don't know, Mrs Barry. He does all the outside jobs for Mother, Mrs Barry. He fixed the gate. He's just in the yard.'

Mrs Barry stubbed her cigarette out under her boot. 'Well, Lawrence.' She got up from her chair. 'You are one man I can never refuse.' I waited while Mrs Barry drank the last of her tea. 'I can refuse the other fools no trouble.'

We went down past the straw man and through the gap in the fence. Uncle was at the bottom of our yard, bowling for Paul. He wore his suit; it didn't matter what he was doing, the white shirt was crisp and clean, and the crease stiff down the front of his trouser legs. 'Hands not too wide on the bat, Paul. Get them closer!' he called. 'Ready?'

'Ready!' Paul shouted, tapping his bat into the dirt, his face serious.

Mrs Barry and I watched as Uncle took a run-up and bowled. The ball went hurtling towards Paul who hit it hard. Mrs Barry, Uncle and I watched as it sailed out of Beverly and into the field.

'Out!' called Uncle. He crossed to Mrs Barry and me as Paul ran into the field to retrieve the ball. 'Nice to see you again, Eileen.'

'He can play cricket,' I said. 'He's good at bowling.'

'I can see that,' said Mrs Barry.

'And he helps Mother with the milking. Don't you, Uncle?'

'I try,' said Uncle, ruffling my hair. 'How long have you been living out here, Eileen?' Uncle wiped his brow with his handkerchief.

'Forever,' said Mrs Barry. 'My father built both of these houses.'

'They've certainly stood the test of time.'

'There have been changes made since then, of course, but he laid the foundations.'

'Charlie bought the place from you?'

'From my father, yes. But that's ancient history.'

Uncle crouched, tightening the lace on his shoe. He looked up at Mrs Barry. 'Who was it said history never truly passes? That history is with us every breath we take?'

'Whoever said it must be a fool,' said Mrs Barry. 'If history was with us every breath, I would bear a black eye dealt me by my father. History is history, thank God.'

'You are probably right,' said Uncle. 'May the ghosts of the past remain forever sleeping. I'm not sure who said that, but I like it. Eileen, if there is anything I can help you with . . . You have been a good friend to my sister, and the two of you are out here on your own . . .'

'We do alright on our own.'

'Yes, I can see that, but if there is anything, anything at all—it would be my pleasure.'

Paul came through the turnstile with the cricket ball. 'My turn!' he shouted.

'Yes, sir!' Uncle called back, saluting Paul. 'Please excuse me, Eileen. Duty calls.'

Mrs Barry nodded, frowning. 'Of course.'

I walked her back to the gap in the fence. 'Do you like him, Mrs Barry?'

Mrs Barry chucked me under the chin. 'I like you, Lawrence. I like you very much. Will that do?'

11.

IT WAS THE END OF the third week of Uncle, and Paul and I were riding home from school. Paul was quiet as he pedalled behind me; he didn't bomb or sing or come up with plans for tomorrow. As I rode, I was not thinking of Crusoe and what happened after the storm, nor was I thinking of the yellow-tipped cockatoo feathers that Mrs St Clair had brought in to paint that day. I was wondering what Uncle would be doing when we came home. What would he talk about? Would he want to help with my homework? Mrs St Clair had set us a project about the seven ancient wonders, beginning with the Great Pyramid of Giza. I wanted to show him the picture Mrs St Clair had given us—a great triangular limestone building with a King's Chamber, and a head.

My thoughts about Uncle weaved their way in and out of what I saw along the road—the mountains and fields and sky. Uncle described these things as *majestic, mesmerising, beautiful.* They were different to the words Mother used. To Mother the mountain was a danger and the field needed tending and the sky rained on her fresh laundry. Who chose the right words, Mother or Uncle?

*

When we opened the front door, Uncle called, 'Boys?'

'Yes, Uncle!'

'Ah, Lawrence,' Uncle said, coming out of the spare.

Paul walked past him and went straight through to the kitchen.

Uncle was wearing his suit with a waistcoat to match, his shoes with the stripe, his hair oiled and smooth. I wanted to breathe it and breathe it so I could know it and name it for myself. The smell of Uncle.

'Hello, Uncle.'

'I have something for you, Lawrence.'

'What is it?'

'Lawrence,' said Mother, from the kitchen, 'thank your uncle.'

'He doesn't know what it is yet. Come with me.'

I followed Uncle to his room where he took a long flat box wrapped in brown paper from his bed.

'For me?'

'Yes, for you. Don't look so surprised.'

I tore away the paper. Uncle's gift was a wooden box with the words *Artiste Propre* engraved on the lid.

I touched the letters, looking up at Uncle.

'Artist's own,' he said, smiling.

'Artists own,' I repeated, opening the box. *Artist's Own.* Was that me? An artist? I saw two long rows of coloured squares of paint, with three brushes lying in a section at the top. Two sponges with different-sized holes sat in a low dish in their own compartment beside the brushes.

'It's a pochade box,' Uncle said. 'You take out the panel here . . . see.' He slid out the wooden panel. 'And you can use it to lean upon, like an easel, and then you can tuck your paintings in when they are done, underneath, see here?' He slid out the wooden drawer, passed me the flat white dish that was inside and showed me where I could store the paintings. 'Watercolours,' Uncle said. 'Have you used those before with your teacher?'

'I'm not sure,' I said, running my fingers down the rows of colour. 'I don't think so . . .'

'Only the smallest amount on the dish,' said Uncle. 'Then add water.'

'Uncle . . . where did you get it?'

'I ordered it from the city, after I saw your painting of the parrot peas that first day.' He smiled. 'Do you know what *pochade* means, Lawrence?'

I shook my head.

'It comes from the French word for pocket. It means a little sketch that captures the atmosphere, the feel of a scene. Something rough, perhaps, that holds the soul of its subject.'

'Oh.'

'This box will help you do as many of them as you need. *Artiste Propre* is an appropriate name for it, don't you think?'

I shrugged, feeling shy. 'Uncle, how do you know . . . about painting? Did you ever paint?'

'Oh, it was never something I wanted to do particularly. I was always on the other side, wanting to see it. One can't exist without the other, if the truth be told. But no, it was never something I wanted to do. Although that doesn't mean I don't understand its importance to you.' He gave my shoulder a quick squeeze. 'You must go and try your new paints.'

'Now?'

'Yes. You must paint your mountain. Why not?'

'But Mother . . . There is homework . . .'

'I'll speak to Louise.'

I took the box with the rows of watercolour paint out to the back porch.

'Why don't you go a little further today?' Uncle said from the kitchen door.

'Further?'

'Yes. Closer to your beloved mountain. Take your box through the stile and sit in the field. That's why the box is useful; you can use the tray to lean upon. Just give yourself some time to learn the paints. They may feel unnatural at first, like anything new.' He filled a jar with water at the sink. 'Essential,' he said, screwing down the lid.

'Thank you, Uncle.'

'Go on,' he said, passing me the jar. 'Off you go.'

I wanted to put my arms around him. It wasn't something I had done with him before, or with any man, but he was so close, just standing there. I stepped towards him and felt his arms around me. 'Thank you. Thank you, Uncle,' I said, leaning against him. Feeling his warmth.

The pochade box was heavy and solid in my arms as I went down through the yard. Paul was there kicking a football between two sticks. 'What's that you've got?' he said.

'It's a paintbox.'

'What for?'

'To hold the paint and paper.'

Paul crossed his arms around the ball. 'Uncle gave it to you, didn't he?'

'Yes.'

Paul kicked the ball hard into the shed wall.

Mrs Barry put her head through the gap in the boards. 'Boys,' she said. 'Everything alright?'

'Yes,' said Paul, taking another kick. The teacher never showed him how. It was his body that knew. Or was it the ball that told his body?

'Paul!' Uncle called from the house.

'He'll have something for you too,' I said.

'There isn't anything I want.'

'Paul! Come inside!' Uncle called.

Paul frowned, shaking his head, and went up to the house.

It was the beginning of winter and the air was cold in my lungs as I went down through the yard. Once in the field I lifted my face to the sky; rays of gold light poured between the grey clouds. Wallis himself was draped in cloud, mist sinking low over his head. Sitting cross-legged on the damp grass, I ran my fingers across the label of the pochade box, *Artiste Propre*. I didn't need or want to paint, only to feel the weight of the pochade box in my lap and look at the clouds above the mountain.

Uncle, Mother, Paul and I were at the table for dinner. Uncle wore his blue suit and his hair glistened. A chicken pot pie sat in the centre of the table. Uncle said, 'Shall I serve?' I could not see where his body ended, and the suit began. Perhaps he had no body, only hands and a head, and shoes with a stripe.

'Thank you, Reggie,' said Mother.

'How was work today?' Uncle asked, serving the pie onto our plates.

'Oh, they probably need to employ another girl to help me, but on the other hand I like to be the one who knows what's what.'

'They are lucky to have you there.'

'I don't know about that,' she said, passing the salt to Uncle. 'I can be very cross if I am given the wrong sets of figures. I think I terrify them.'

'I can't imagine that.'

'Just ask Paul and Lawrence.'

'Boys ought to be terrified of their mothers from time to time,' said Uncle, smiling at Mother. 'Did Lawrence show you his paintbox?'

'No. No, he did not.' Mother raised her eyebrows.

'After dinner, Lawrence. You need to show your mother. And Paul, you must show her the knee pads.'

'Knee pads?'

'Yes,' said Uncle. 'To protect him when he plays cricket. That ball can be very hard, particularly when it's thrown properly. Something I am not much good at, I'm afraid.'

'You're better than I am, Uncle,' I said.

'Wouldn't be hard,' Paul muttered.

I felt strange. It had never mattered what else happened—who I had played with or spoken to—the day had begun and ended with my brother. But since Uncle gave me the paints, that had changed. I didn't feel paired with Paul anymore but with Uncle.

'Well, I hope the pads do a good job of looking after your knees. Every time I put you in the bath, I see another bruise.' Mother was quick to smile, her eyes bright. Each evening she wore her better dress, and would touch Uncle's hand when there was news she was pleased to share with him.

After dinner Mother placed a bread-and-butter pudding on the table. It had taken her all afternoon. The pudding sat in layers, with sultanas piping hot in the cream.

Uncle said, 'Louise, you know I am happy to take care of the boys in order for you to go out one night.'

'Oh, Reggie, I don't need to go out,' said Mother. 'I am so tired by the end of the day all I want is my bed.'

'You are far too young to take to your hoop and your bed. Of course you must go. It would do you good,' said Uncle, spooning the pudding into the bowls. 'I saw a poster for the Hamilton Dance in town—doesn't the dairy go to the dance?'

'Well, they do . . .'

'And so, you should too, Louise.'

'Surely I am past the age for dancing . . .'

'You are still a young woman,' said Uncle, lifting his spoon to his mouth. 'And beautiful.'

Mother caught her breath; her cheeks turned pink. I saw the veins that ran the length of her arms. Was it the veins that carried the beauty to the rest?

'You need to go out sometimes, Louise, just like everybody else. I'm happy to stay home with the lads.'

'I'll think about it, Reggie.' Mother took a small spoonful of pudding. 'Though goodness knows what I could wear. Perhaps Mrs Barry could help me sew something new . . .'

'Good, that's settled then,' said Uncle. He turned to me and winked.

Later, when we were in bed, I lifted the corner of the British Naval Line.

'Paul?'

'What?'

'Do you like Uncle yet?'

He didn't answer.

'Paul?'

'What?'

'Do you like him yet?'

'I don't know.'

'Do you like what he gave you? The pads for your knees?'

'I don't need pads.'

'But you like them, don't you? Won't Mr Tonks like them?'

'I don't know. I don't know how they feel to wear in a real match.'

'But when you do, they will protect your knees, won't they?'

'Yes, I suppose.'

I wanted him to say more, wanted it, suddenly, very much. I wanted him to tell a joke or drop a fart so we could laugh. I wanted him to come up with a plan for tomorrow. For it to be me and Paul who were paired, not me and Uncle. But Paul was quiet.

'Do you want to go to the Marbles soon?' I asked him.

'Sure.'

'When?'

'I don't know.'

There was quiet again.

'Don't you want Mother to go out?'

'What?'

'Don't you want Mother to go out?'

'No.'

'But it will do her good,' I said.

'I don't care.'

'Why not?'

'I don't know.'

'Paul, why not? Why don't you care that it will do her good?'

'I said, *I don't know*! Goodnight, Laurie.'

'Goodnight.' I sighed, punching my pillow into shape. It was me who said goodnight first. I was the oldest.

I don't know what time it was when I next woke. Everything in my room had turned to silver; shelves, books, wardrobe, bed and walls, door and ceiling—all silver. I heard the sound of crying. I rubbed my eyes and sat up in the bed. I saw the moon through the window hanging bright, white and round over Wallis. I got out of the bed and crossed to the doorway. Stepping into the shadows, I saw Mother turned to silver in her nightdress, standing in Uncle's arms at the entrance to her room. Her silver body shook with the sounds of her crying. Uncle held her, silver in his suit.

12.

THE NEXT EVENING, AFTER MY bath, I hung the towel over the rail and opened the bathroom cabinet. Mother's cold cream sat beside the extra soaps and cotton buds. A round tin stood on one of the shelves beside a black comb. I took the tin from the shelf and read the label. *Superior Men's Pomade*.

'Lawrence, hurry up in there, please,' Mother called from outside the door.

I unscrewed the lid of the tin and took a deep sniff of the waxy cream inside. It was the smell of Uncle—pine and mint and lemon.

'Lawrence! Hurry up, please! Your uncle might need the bathroom!'

I swiped at the cream in the tin with my finger, smoothing it over the side of my hair.

'Lawrence!'

My hair glistened in the mirror. 'Let the boy do as he pleases, Louise,' I whispered to my reflection.

*

'Oh, well done, Lawrence,' Mother said. She had come away from her cooking to look over my shoulder at the kitchen table. 'Come and see his work, Reggie.' I had written a list of facts about the Great Pyramid of Giza, beginning, *It is the oldest of the Seven Wonders, and the only one to remain intact.* Underneath the list of facts, I had drawn a map of Egypt.

'Hmm . . . so detailed,' said Uncle. 'Impressive, Lawrence.'

Paul was beside me putting together a model aeroplane with glue and balsa wood. He stopped what he was doing to listen.

Uncle placed his finger on the Red Sea. 'The way it forks right here into Saudi Arabia. Your map appears accurate, Lawrence.'

Mother nodded. 'I told you, Reggie. Just like you. Do you remember Mr Brindle?'

'I do.'

'Do you remember what he said about you? You got everything right.'

'I did for a while.'

Mother touched his arm. 'Oh, Reg, it was unfair.'

'Life isn't fair, Lou. We have all learned that by now.' Uncle returned to his chair. 'And Lawrence is very clever. The world will be his oyster.'

Paul looked at me, eyes narrowing.

Before bed, I went past Mother's room and saw Paul playing on the floor. The soldiers and pirates from *The Lady Bold* were arranged around the legs of Mother's dresser. Paul was holding Father's medal and flying it over the top of the men. 'Got you! There! There!' Paul dropped pretend bombs. 'You won't take me, all of you *down, down*, you dirty Franks!'

I wanted to be on the carpet beside him with my own soldiers to bomb. But at the same time, I wanted him to stop the game. To leave Mother's room.

'You better put that back,' I said, pointing at the medal.

'Why should I?' He knocked down more of the soldiers. '*Pch pch pch!*'

'You aren't allowed to take it from the drawer. Put it back.'

'Why should I?'

'Put it back.'

'I'll put it back when I'm ready.'

'Now.'

'When I'm ready.'

'Now, Paul. It isn't a toy.'

'When I'm ready!'

'Now!' I tried to pull the medal from his hand.

'Get away!' He pulled it back.

'Give it to me!'

'No!'

'Give it to me!'

I said, 'No!'

He punched me in the chest, and I punched him back in the face. He dropped the medal and hit me in the stomach. I hit him back again in the face, and then I couldn't tell where I was hitting him. We were fighting, hitting and punching and kicking at each other, not caring where our blows landed. I wanted to kill him and him, me.

'Boys! Boys!' Mother cried from the doorway.

Paul was on top of me, hitting me in my face, my stomach, everywhere. I fought back as hard as I could.

'Enough!' Uncle shouted, pulling us apart.

'Go to your rooms!' Mother shouted.

Uncle pushed me into my room, closing the door, and Mother took Paul. My face was on fire. I put my hand to my nose, and my fingers came away sticky with blood.

'They don't do this, Reggie, I don't understand it,' I heard Mother say, sounding upset.

'Boys will be boys, Louise.'

'But this was something more. If you hadn't been here . . .'

'Brothers rarely kill each other. We'll let them cool off then we'll go in and review the damage.' I could smell the smoke from his cigarette under the door.

I sat on the bed. My face stung and my head throbbed. I hated Paul. Mother was right; we didn't fight like that. And now we did. I missed Paul and started to cry. He didn't want me anymore.

Soon Mother came into the room with a damp cloth, some plasters and antiseptic. 'Sit up, please, Lawrence.'

I sat beside her on the bed. She lifted my chin and looked at my face, her forehead creased with worry. 'What happened, Lawrence?' she said, pressing the damp cloth to my nose, and chin.

I didn't know how to answer.

Mother sighed heavily. 'Other boys might do that in the school yard, but not you two here, at home.' She dabbed antiseptic onto my chin with a cotton ball and peeled back one of the plasters. She looked sad. 'You boys . . . you've always had each other.' She pressed the ends of the plaster across my chin. Her touch was soft, her hands warm. I wanted more. Wanted to lean against her. Wanted her to hold me. 'And now that Uncle is here, we have everything.' She shook her head, standing up from the bed.

'Really, Lawrence, I am disappointed. Disappointed in you both. You should be ashamed.'

'Yes, Mother. Sorry, Mother.'

After Mother turned off the lights, Paul and I didn't speak to each other through the crack and there were no plans for tomorrow.

13.

THE FOLLOWING SATURDAY NIGHT, PAUL and I were in the kitchen while Mother was getting ready to go out. Uncle was in the yard pruning the blackberries that grew by the stile.

Mother sang from her bedroom, *'And so, and so, when love is new, when love is new, when love, oh love . . .'* We could see her through her open door; checking herself in the mirror above her dresser, walking away from it and returning, as if something might have changed in the time she took to cross the room.

Paul ran his fingers down the crease of the paper plane he was folding at the table. 'Mother, how long will he be staying?' he asked.

'Paul . . .' I frowned at him as I turned a pencil in my sharpener.

Through her doorway I watched as Mother leaned close to the mirror and ran a lipstick over her mouth. 'Who?' She pressed her lips together.

'You know who, Mother. Uncle. How long will he be staying?'

'Why do you ask, Paul?' Mother said.

'Yes, Paul,' I said, lining up my pencils.

'I just wanted to know. Will he always be living here?' Paul sent his plane flying through the kitchen and into the lounge.

Mother saw. 'Don't do that inside, please.'

'But will he?'

'No doubt your uncle will soon find work, and then, of course, he will meet someone . . .' Mother held a pair of pearl earrings against her ears and stood again before the mirror. 'Then he will want a place of his own, somewhere nearby.'

'But until then . . . ?' said Paul.

'Of course, *until then*, Paul! He is family!' Mother came out of her room. 'Well, boys, how do I look?'

She turned a little so that her dark green dress swung around her legs. Her hair was shining and golden, free at last from its scarf, and her eyes were bright. The dress showed her narrow waist, the smooth white skin of her shoulders and her neck. She was glowing.

'You look beautiful, Mother,' I said. She smelled of soap, and the rose cream she smoothed onto her hands.

'You do, Mother,' said Paul.

'Thank you, boys,' Mother said.

Just then Uncle came through the back door, blackberry leaves caught in the buttonholes of his waistcoat. 'Louise . . .'

Mother flushed. 'Oh, get away with you.'

I hardy recognised her. The Mother who was there at the end of every school day, with sandwiches and tea biscuits, the mother who stuck the stool in the mud every morning to milk Gert, who shovelled shit over the fence for Mrs Barry—that Mother I knew. But this Mother, with pearl earrings, and a dark green dress that showed her smooth white skin, was one I was only seeing now. Now that Uncle was here. As if Uncle was a light.

We heard the sound of a car horn.

'That will be Elise,' said Mother, picking up her purse from the side table. 'Be good for your uncle, boys,' she said as she walked down the hall.

I wanted her to kiss me on my head or on my cheek, to cross the bridge. I knew Paul wanted the same thing. We wanted her to put her arms around us and hold us and say, *I love you*, but she was already on her way out.

An hour later, Uncle was preparing dinner at the kitchen bench, and Paul and I were doing homework. I was colouring in the second ancient wonder, the Colossus of Rhodes. Uncle opened the oven and took out a roast lamb, filling the kitchen with the smell of rosemary and cooking meat. 'Won't be long now,' he said, spooning the fat from the dish over the lamb. 'Lawrence—' he turned to me '—put another piece of wood into the stove.'

I looked to the stove. Mother asked us to stay clear. The door became hot and the handle didn't hold unless she gave it a twist.

'Go on, Lawrence,' said Uncle.

I took a piece of wood from the basket, turned the handle and pushed the wood into the flames. I gave the handle a twist, so the latch caught.

'That's the boy,' said Uncle. 'Can you turn up the sound on the radio while you are there?'

I opened the door of the spare. The bed was unmade; the sheets and blankets tangled, and I saw the dip in the pillow where Uncle had laid his head. The dented suitcase stood in the corner. There was his suit coat and another shirt lying across the chair. It was like looking into a secret.

'Go on, louder,' Uncle called from the kitchen. 'I don't want to miss the news broadcast.'

I turned up the volume on the radio. 'Is that loud enough, Uncle?' I asked, leaving the room.

'Shh!' Uncle held the potato peeler in mid-air.

'. . . *The trials in America have proved successful, where over sixty thousand children suffer from the disease,*' the newsreader announced. '*It is anticipated that Salk's vaccine will be available to all children across the world within twenty-four months . . . It is hoped that the disease will be completely eradicated within the next five years . . . Onto other news . . .*'

Uncle returned to peeling the potatoes. 'How different it is for you . . . your home here. Your mother . . . everything you have. It wasn't like that when we were young . . .' Uncle took beans from the fridge.

Paul looked up from his sums. 'What happened when you were young?'

'What do you mean?'

'When you were young. Mother said you were ill.'

I knew it wasn't polite for Paul to ask, but I didn't stop him.

'Hasn't she told you?'

'No.'

'My leg, you mean?'

'Yes. Was it from the war?'

'No. No, it wasn't from the war.'

'What was it from then?' Paul asked.

'When I was a boy, I suffered polio.' Uncle cut the ends of the beans and placed them in the colander. 'A great number of children contracted the illness. Only I wasn't at home then, with Mother and Father. I was with Louise, your mother.'

'Where?'

'At the Hartfields'.'

'Who were they?' Paul asked.

'She hasn't explained?'

'No,' Paul answered.

'She once said it was where she learned to milk a cow,' I said.

Paul turned to me, his eyebrows raised. 'She said that?'

'Yes, but nothing more,' I answered.

'She really never told you the story?' Uncle tipped the peeled potatoes into a pot of water boiling on the stove. 'Never told you how we came to be there?'

'No,' Paul and I said at the same time.

'No . . . well . . . I don't suppose she did.'

'Who were they?' Paul asked.

Uncle sat at the kitchen table. He took a sip from his drink, then put down his glass and leaned on his elbows. 'When our mother died, there was no one to take us. Father couldn't manage after he came back from France; he wasn't the same. It wasn't an uncommon story. The war left men without direction. They saw too much and no longer knew how to . . . how to live their lives, as if what they had seen made them wonder why they needed to try at all. What was the point? The point of the effort, I mean.'

He stood, went to the window, placed his hands on the ledge, and looked out. 'A wind blew in, I suppose you could say, and the direction it blew us was the Hartfields, old friends of Father's . . . they offered to take us, you see. We only had each other—your mother and I. We lived, for a while, apart from the couple. A house separate from the main house. I suspect it was once used as servants' quarters, though really it was too small for that. It was a separate building, at any rate. It was our home. Your mother's and mine. Our only home. But they could visit, of course.' He turned around to face us. 'The Hartfields. They *did* visit. Either your mother, or myself.' His face tightened. 'But we had each other. We slept head to toe in the same bed every night, Louise holding on to my feet.'

Paul and I listened, transfixed. Uncle was colouring in Mother's past the way my pencil coloured in the sun god's cloak.

'Then I became ill. We didn't know at first, thought it was just the ordinary flu, but then I lost the ability to move my legs. I could only lie on the bed in that small room looking up at the ceiling. There was no part of the ceiling I did not come to know. Every line and crack and patch of damp. How well I remember the damp; it appeared to me like a map in the ceiling of one corner in the room. But for a country I didn't know. Would never know.

'I lay there and said to my leg, "Lift, leg, lift from the bed," but my leg wouldn't move. I grew very frightened. I couldn't make sense of it, or at least, the ways I did make sense of it were . . . I thought . . . I thought for a time, you see, that there was something inside me that prevented me from moving. Didn't want me to move, though I didn't know the reason. I became certain it was something I had done. I was terrified. I was being punished by this thing inside me that knew better than I. And there was nothing your mother could do for me, of course. What could she do? She was as frightened as I was.

'The Hartfields didn't believe me to begin with. But that kind of thing can't be falsified. The illness was both a blessing and a curse. I was taken to the hospital, and Louise was left behind. I couldn't afford to think of her. I was the lucky one, if you can believe it. But it's still here with me, the disease—worse lately. Everything that happens remains hidden somewhere and eventually makes itself known. Nothing is exempt.'

Every mark of life was gone, his face bottomless, the way Mother's had been the day we broke the glass. He had no age. My pencil hovered over the second wonder.

'I couldn't return for her after I was in the hospital. I had to make my own way. Dear thing. She understood ... and I am here now. What difference does time make? And your mother has done a fine job with you boys.'

The years he had lived since then, his adventures and his education and the people he had met, returned to his face, like armour.

'Here we are all these years later, and Salk and his team have found a vaccine.' He picked up his glass of Teacher's from the kitchen table. 'The disease will be a thing of the past. Not in time for me, unfortunately, but for many others—in time for them.'

He drained his glass. Then he took the bottle of Teacher's from the bench and poured himself another.

'Dinner won't be long. Your Mrs Barry is a very useful neighbour, isn't she, boys?'

Paul stood, leaving his mathematics book, and went into his bedroom. Why did he have to leave just then? Now it was only Uncle and I in the kitchen. It didn't feel enough. I didn't know whether to join Paul in his bedroom or to stay here. Paul had made a teepee from a sheet and liked to sit under there making plans. At least he used to. I wanted to join him and close the door. I could feel the horrors that Mother and Uncle had endured floating about the kitchen, invisible and dangerous. Why hadn't Mother told us about the Hartfields? How long was she there after Uncle left? I didn't know how to think about it—Mother in bed beside Uncle, holding on to his feet, as if his feet might save her. But from what? The visits from the Hartfields. Cold moved through me, even though the fire burned.

Uncle came and stood behind me, one hand on the back of my chair. 'Do you know, Lawrence, that I have seen the ruins of your second wonder with my own eyes?' The room warmed with the sound of his voice.

'The Colossus of Rhodes?'

'Yes. It was over one hundred feet tall, wings spread ready to defeat its Roman enemy. Helios himself. Quite something. The ruins alone took my breath away. I could feel the lives of the centuries before me, in worship.' He took cutlery from the drawer. 'And who is to say that Helios is not watching us still? Rising over your mountain and seeing everything we do. Who is to say?'

I couldn't tell if he was waiting for an answer. I didn't have one for him. Could only listen. I saw pictures of Helios as he spoke, wings spread, centuries of lives in worship.

Uncle hummed as he moved around the kitchen, as comfortable preparing a meal as he was playing cricket. Did all men know as much as him? I didn't follow Paul into his bedroom but stayed at the table to write facts about the Colossus underneath the drawing.

'Boys, dinner.' Uncle took the Woodland china from the side drawers and placed them on the kitchen bench. Every piece had a pattern of wheat sheafs around the border.

Just then Paul came out of his room. 'We don't use those,' he said.

'Why not?' Uncle asked.

'They were from when Mother was married,' said Paul.

'And?' said Uncle. 'Is there a problem with that?'

'We might break one.'

'Everything breaks, Paul, eventually.' Uncle turned over one of the plates. '*Woodlands, Handmade in London*,' he read.

'Of course we shall use them. You boys worry more than you need. Let's just enjoy the evening, and trust she is doing the same.'

Paul and I were seated on either side of the table with Uncle at the head. Slices of lamb lay steaming on our plates, beside the beans and potatoes. Uncle had put fresh bread on our side plates. Mother only used bread for sandwiches or toast. He said, 'It isn't so bad when she goes out, now is it, boys?'

Paul kept his eyes on his dinner. The lamb was tender and the beans were bright green and crisper than when Mother did them. Each of the potatoes held a dab of melting butter.

'Eat, boys, please,' said Uncle.

It was quiet for a long time, with only the sound of the knives cutting the lamb on the plates and our glasses going onto the table when we had a drink. Then Paul put down his knife and fork and said to Uncle, 'Did you know our father?'

Uncle raised his eyebrows. 'Yes, Paul, I did.'

'You met him?'

'Yes.'

'How many times?'

'A number of times—when he was first taking out your mother.'

'How many?' Paul asked.

'Five, maybe . . . six. Before I left Australia. We were all younger then. A lot younger.'

'What was he like?' I asked him.

'Charlie?'

'Yes.'

'He was . . . he was quiet. He was concentrated. That didn't preclude a sense of humour; it was there, underneath it all. But he was a serious man. He took his responsibilities seriously, and it wasn't easy for him to forget them. That meant his family and his work. He was very good at what he did.'

'At flying, you mean?' Paul asked.

'Yes. He was dedicated and loyal. That's why your mother loved him. That's why he was successful. And he was the right man for her. To tell you the truth, I think he was the only man for her. The only man she could trust.'

Paul nodded slowly. It was the first time I had seen him look so long at Uncle and listen so attentively.

'He would have been proud of you both. And you would have been proud of him. He was a hero in the war, of course. Deservedly. I liked him very much and I am sorry he is gone, Paul. I am sorry for both of you he is not here.'

Uncle had spoken the words Paul and I had needed to hear our whole lives.

Paul placed his cutlery across his plate. 'You coming, Lawrence?' he said.

'There is still meat on your plate, Paul,' said Uncle.

Paul shrugged.

'I believe Lawrence hasn't finished,' said Uncle.

Paul looked at me. Who would I choose? I swallowed my lamb, and put a forkful of potato into my mouth.

'Enjoying that, aren't you, Lawrence?' said Uncle. We all knew who I had chosen.

Paul picked his plate up from the table. 'Can I be excused, Uncle?'

'We shall be sorry to eat without you, but I am never one to hold a man against his wishes. Off you go.'

Paul took his plate into the kitchen, scraping the remains into Mrs Barry's compost bucket. He went into his room and closed the door.

Now it was just Uncle and me again. It was hard to cut the fat away from the meat; I kept pulling at it with my knife and couldn't see where the fat ended on the lamb, and the meat began. I could tell Uncle was watching me. He could see me trying to use my knife and it made it even harder. It wasn't enough with only Uncle and me at the table; it felt as if there were nobody else in the world and Beverly was our house, and nobody lived here but Uncle and I, and these were our Woodland plates that we used every night. I wanted Paul to come back. I didn't know enough words to say to Uncle.

Uncle said, 'What do you think of the dinner?'

'It is very good, thank you.'

'It is, isn't it? Really, it's the simple pleasures that add up to the most, don't you think?' Uncle took a cigarette from his pack.

'I . . . I don't know.'

'Don't you?' Uncle sipped from his Teacher's. 'I think you do, though. And yet the things that bring pleasure are both simple and complex.'

'Oh.'

'Have you had enough?' Uncle lit his cigarette.

'Yes.'

'Then leave it. Come with me.' He stood and gestured for me to do the same. Our plates, still with some of the lamb and beans and potatoes, remained on the table. When we ate with Mother, we didn't leave our seats until our dinner was all gone. Then we had to clear the table. 'Come on, Lawrence.'

I followed Uncle to the lounge.

'Sit,' he said.

I sat down in one of the chairs while Uncle poured himself another glass of whisky and sat in the other.

'I have been deliberating about whether you are old enough.' He reached into his leather bag sitting by the chair and pulled out a large black book. 'And I have decided that you are.' The book appeared old with threads from its fabric cover coming loose. Across the front was the title in silver, pressed into the black: *Letters from the Masters*.

'When I saw it, I could hardly believe my eyes,' said Uncle, blowing out the smoke from his cigarette. 'Tucked into the back shelf of the second-hand store in Stawell. Really. How on earth did this treasure find its way there? Open it.'

I opened the book and saw that it was made up of both pictures and writing.

'The book is a collection of letters the greatest painters in the world have written, Lawrence. To each other, to their patrons and mentors, to their priests, their fathers . . . their wives.'

He stood from his chair and leaned down beside mine. 'Have a look at this one.' He turned the pages in the book until he came to a painting of a tower with Jesus on the cross. There was forest on both sides, and black branches coming from rocks. Uncle took the book from my hands and read, 'From Caspar David Friedrich to his pupils, 1811: *The artist's feeling is his law. Genuine feeling can never be contrary to nature.* Genuine feeling can never be contrary to nature. Friedrich was one of the masters of the German Romantic movement, Lawrence. He believed that all of nature was an expression of God. What do you think? Do you agree that there is a God who expresses himself through nature?'

I hardly understood what Uncle was saying. Yet I felt that understanding was there, just ahead of me.

He didn't wait for me to answer. When he spoke, his breath was warm with lamb and Teacher's and cigarette smoke. 'These paintings were done a long time ago, most of them more than a hundred years, and yet the ideas they hold are as fresh and important as if they had been painted today. Not all of the pictures in the collection were by the artists who wrote the letters, some of the works merely influenced those letters, or contributed to the development of a particular artist. Or the letters might be about another artist's work.' Uncle sounded excited. 'But what I find most interesting about the letters is that each artist's concerns feel so modern. Nothing has changed. Money, love, problems of confidence and faith, physical health—all the same.' He flicked through the pages. 'Here, look at this.'

He showed me a picture of people with no clothes, covering their private parts with their hands and dancing in a circle. There was a naked angel flying through treetops. A man wrapped in sheets had fallen to the ground, and one of the naked people was kissing the hem of the sheet. I was embarrassed and wanted to look away. I wasn't sure what Mother would think. What would she do if she were to walk through the door and see me looking at the people in the painting without clothes?

Uncle didn't seem to notice. 'Ingres never completed this painting,' he said. 'Tragic, really. *The Golden Age* indeed.'

He read from the book. '*Yet I love her, the wretch, and passionately, still; for when all's said and done, she loves me too . . .* Bedevilled by his own work, poor man.'

'Of course, you will need maturity to appreciate the meanings of the words . . .' He turned to the last pages. 'But you will get there, Lawrence, you will get there . . .' He closed the book and passed it to me. 'It is yours.'

'Mine?'

'Yes, Lawrence, why not?' He pressed the book into my hands.
'But, Uncle . . .'

I knew the book was important, perhaps the most important book I had ever seen, but I wasn't sure if I was ready. Could I show Mrs St Clair?

As if he could read my mind, Uncle said, 'Show whomever you want. That is what the book is there to give you. Permission.'

He stood, touched my back, then went into the kitchen, leaving me alone with the book. I folded my legs underneath me in the chair and turned back to the first page. It was a painting of a bouquet of flowers by Master Jan Brueghel the Elder. It was as if the artist had known something about flowers that nobody else knew. That there was no limit to their colour, their brightness, their richness. I turned from the flowers to paintings of churches and rivers, birds and trees, houses and children and cows and boats and flowers and Jesus on the cross. The book had far more pictures than letters; paintings by Master Gros, Master Gudin, Master Eeckhout, Master Rethel and more. I stayed in the chair so long my legs grew stiff. I stood from the chair, went to the window, the book open in my hands, and looked in the direction of the mountain.

Every master would have painted Wallis differently. Each artist would have chosen his own colours, his own brushstrokes. Each artist would decide for himself which parts of the mountain would come forwards, and which parts would recede. Where the light fell. Which time of day to show him. Master Turner might have given Wallis an arch of gold, Master Whistler might have painted him reflected in water, and in Master Gudin's painting there would be *The Lady Bold*, navigating his waters. Each painting would have told a different story. 'Because the painting comes from a person,' I whispered.

*

That night Uncle did not make us take a bath or brush our teeth. He cleaned the kitchen, listened to his radio, smoked cigarettes and let us do as we pleased. I wished Paul were out here in the lounge and not in his own room with the door closed. What was he doing in there? Uncle did not look at me as I walked past him into my room, much later, carrying the book, but I felt as if he was watching everything I did.

Lying in my bed, I wanted to open Paul's door and show him the book. But I did not. What if Uncle only bought a book for me and did not have anything for Paul? Perhaps tomorrow I could ask Uncle if he had a book to give Paul. I could tell him Paul might like a book on sport, that there might be one on another shelf in the second-hand store in Stawell.

I switched on my reading lamp and climbed into bed. The master on page 81 was called Master Corot. There was a painting of women dancing in a circle in a forest; their dresses fell from their bodies and showed their bosoms. The painting was called *Une Matinée. La Danse des Nymphes.* The trees were huge and, underneath, the circle of women danced, calling to their friends to join the circle. The words, difficult to see in the light of my lamp, read: *A letter from Corot to his friend Francais. You know, a landscape painter's day is delightful.*

'A landscape painter's day is delightful.' I said the words. *A landscape painter's day is delightful.* I put my finger over the painting and traced the trees around the dancing bodies, into the leaves and up to the sky. I turned onto my side so I could see the darkness of Wallis through the window. I imagined Master Corot's women dancing around him, holding hands, clothes falling from their bodies.

I put the book on the floor, slid it under the bed, and switched off the lamp. I could hear the faint crackle of Uncle's radio, could hear him moving around in the kitchen.

I wished suddenly that I could speak to Paul through the crack. I wanted to talk about our father, I wanted to whisper to Paul that Father was very good at what he did, wasn't he, that he was *dedicated*, *loyal*, *serious*. I wanted to hear Paul say he was a hero and whisper back, *No wonder they awarded him the star.* But I did not. Something was stopping me.

Soon I heard the water running into the bath. Why was he taking a bath when Uncle only ever took showers? I wished Mother was home. I wanted to hear the sounds of her doing the last tidy, to hear her locking the back door, the creak of her bed as she climbed under her blankets.

The next morning, when I went into the kitchen, Mother and Uncle were at the table drinking tea. Mother stood and kissed the top of my head. 'Good morning, Laurie.'

'What was it like?' I asked her.

Mother's colours sat against each other as if they had been chosen like paints on a tray: the green of her morning gown, the yellow of her hair, the pink of her slippers, the blue of her eyes.

'The dance?'

'Yes. Did you like it?'

Uncle said, 'I think she enjoyed herself very much, Lawrence.' He lifted his cup and I saw the hook peek from the sleeve of his shirt.

'I did enjoy myself, as a matter of fact, Reggie,' said Mother, pouring more tea into Uncle's cup.

'Good,' said Uncle. He spread a spoonful of jam onto his toast. 'You must go again. We boys survived the evening, did we not?'

'Did they behave for you?' Mother asked, smiling at Paul as he came into the kitchen.

'They did. Perfectly, as it happens. They were terribly worried about using your good dinner set, but I told them you would be pleased we were enjoying the evening.'

Mother glanced at the plates on the drying rack. 'Yes, good, of course—at last they are getting some use.'

A song came from the radio in the spare. *Oh, do, do, do you love me, pretty rainbows cannot tell me.* 'Oh, this was the song the band played last night!' said Mother. 'Right at the end of the evening, this very song!'

'This very song, hey?' Uncle put down his toast, stood and took Mother in his arms.

'Reggie, stop!' . . . *Oh, when love comes you will know, you will know, oh yes, you will know.* 'Oh, Reggie!'

He bent her right back over the chair, and she squealed.

14.

THE NEXT NIGHT, I WAS LYING in my bed looking at *Letters from the Masters*, when Mother opened the door. 'Laurie, dear, will you turn off your own lamp, when you have finished your reading?'

'Yes, Mother.'

'Good boy. Not for long, alright? I'll check for the light under the door.'

'Yes, Mother.'

I thought she might ask me where the book was from, but I brought home so many books from the school library, she mustn't have noticed that it was anything different. I was going to show her; I was going to say, *See the book that Uncle Reggie gave me, Mother*, but I didn't. I don't know why.

'Goodnight, Laurie.'

'Goodnight, Mother.'

She blew me a kiss from the door.

I turned back to the book, the painting on page 52 was by Master Constable and it was called *Dedham Lock and Mill*. It was a picture of a mill by a river, under a sky on its way to night.

In his letter to Reverend John Fisher, Master Constable wrote, *I associate my careless boyhood with all that lies on the banks of the Stour, those scenes made me a painter . . . I had often thought of pictures of them before I ever touched a pencil.* That was how it was for me too. I thought of the pictures before I touched the pencil. And I was in my careless boyhood, as Master Constable had once been in his.

My eyes rested on the painting. Sleep was coming. I did not close the book but kept my eyes open, on the painting, and soon I was there, where the painting began in the master. The desire contained in the first touch of the brush. Like the beginning of a road made of paint. I wanted to sleep, but refused it, travelling further into *Dedham Lock and Mill*, the river beneath the darkening sky, the tall trees, the peaked roof of the mill, the reflection in the water.

Paul and I didn't play together the whole weekend. We didn't make any plans, or race the bikes, or sit on the roof of the shed and talk as the sun set in the sky.

On Sunday night, when I was in bed, I lifted the corner of the British Naval Line. Without waiting for him to lift the Steamer, I said louder than usual, 'Do you want *The Lady Bold*?'

'What do you mean?' he answered.

'You can have it; I don't want it anymore.'

'Why don't you want it?'

'I just don't. You can have it.' I was glad for his voice through the crack, even if I had to give away *The Lady Bold* to hear it.

There was quiet for a while, then he said, 'You don't want to play with it anymore?'

'No. You can have it and you can keep it in your room.'

'What about the men?'

'The men too.'

'All of them?'

'Yes. All of them.'

'Are you sure?'

'Yes, I am sure,' I said. 'I am too old for them now.'

'Okay,' he said.

Then it was quiet. He wasn't going to say anything more. Now I wished I hadn't given him *The Lady Bold* when he wasn't even going to speak.

A long moment passed. I could smell the smoke from Uncle's cigarette under the door.

'Goodnight, Paul.'

'Night.'

I closed my eyes and remembered when we stood side by side at the top of Wallis, the way his hand in mine was part of the way I saw the world spread before us, as if it were his hand that gave it to me.

As I pedalled my bike to school the following Friday, I looked at the Grampian mountains on my right, at the green flats of Hughlon, at the wattle trees and stringybarks along the dirt road. Above it all, was the deep blue winter sky. This too was a landscape, I thought to myself, yet it was not like any of the landscapes in the book. The skies seemed brighter—wider. The trees held grey in the green of their leaves, and their trunks were ghostly white. Flowers formed in the shape of rounded brushes, and others were like the paws of a kangaroo. The birds were unlike any I had seen in the book. Which master had ever painted an emu? A cockatoo? Each new thought came as

I pushed down the pedals; this landscape is unique, down went the pedal, it can be painted, down went the pedal, if there were masters who painted Australian landscapes in the past—down went the pedal—could I be one in the future?

All week I had meant to tell Mrs St Clair about the book Uncle had given me. I wanted to show her some of the paintings. *Salisbury Cathedral from the Bishop's Ground* by Master Constable, *The Stone Breakers* by Master Courbet and *Shipping in a Storm* by Master Gudin. I wanted to share with Mrs St Clair the way Master Gudin painted the light shining through the storm clouds directly onto the ship as it plunged through the waves. Would the ship be saved, or would it be wrecked on the shore like Crusoe's? I wanted to talk to her about how different the masters were from each other in the way that they painted. The paintings I liked the most had no people. Or people that were so small they looked far away, as if they were not the most important part of the story.

Every day that week I had been meaning to show her. Today was Friday. Today would be the day.

Mrs St Clair stood at the front of the class. 'I am going to recite the first verse of a poem to you. It's called "It's like the Light", by Emily Dickinson. Allow yourselves to be inspired.'

The class was quiet as Mrs St Clair read:

It's like the Light –
A fashionless Delight –
It's like the Bee –
A dateless – Melody –

'When you are ready, class, you may begin.'

I put my brush to the paper and felt myself drawn into the landscape that I had seen from the road that morning. Since

I had been looking at *Letters from the Masters*, my work in Mrs St Clair's class felt more important, as if it had a place in a chain, the way each mountain had a place in the range. There were paintings that came before what I was doing, and there would be paintings that would come after.

'I feel as if I am there, Lawrence,' Mrs St Clair said, standing behind me. 'A fashionless delight indeed.'

I looked at my picture. Even though I did not have the landscape before me, it was there on the butcher's paper, Wallis in the light of my careless boyhood.

In the afternoon we sat at Mrs St Clair's feet while she read to us from Crusoe. *I could not forbear getting up to the top of a little mountain, and looking out to sea, in hopes of seeing a ship: then fancy that, at a vast distance, I spied a sail, please myself with the hopes of it, and, after looking steadily, till I was almost blind, lose it quite, and sit down and weep like a child, and thus increase my misery by my folly.*

After the reading Mrs St Clair asked the class questions. 'Pearl, what did Crusoe learn?'

'Hoping made Crusoe feel bad?' Pearl answered.

'If he did not hope, he would not have been so disappointed,' James added.

Mrs St Clair asked, 'Then would it have been better if he did not hope?'

'Wouldn't he have been sad all the time?' asked Peter.

'Yes, but the hope he did have wasn't real,' I said.

'It was folly,' Iris said. 'It said that at the end. Folly.'

We had so much to say we forgot to put up our hands, and yet we never interrupted each other.

'Thank you, Iris, but what if it had not been folly? What if he had spied a ship? Can I put that to you all?' said Mrs St Clair.

'Every time he was disappointed would have made him want to give up. That's no good. That would have made him tired,' said Ivy.

'I agree. It made him cry,' Robert said.

By listening together, we became one, yet we each understood Crusoe's struggle in our own way.

I never told Mrs St Clair about the book. It had weighed down my satchel all the way to school, and now it dug into the skin of my back as I pedalled home. Why didn't I show her the book? I noticed that Uncle never gave a book or anything else to Paul, and he did not tell Mother about it either.

15.

'WHERE IS HE?' I ASKED MOTHER when I came home from school that afternoon.

'Hello to you too, Lawrence,' she said, without looking up from her hoop. Mother was embroidering more since Uncle came. Three newly decorated miniature hoops had been pinned to the corridor wall, each with a blue bow. *Beverly Park,* in curly letters, a small farmhouse, and a bouquet of roses. 'Your uncle is milking the cow.'

I wandered down to Gert's shelter. Uncle was on the stool against the cow's side. I heard the milk hitting the sides of the pail, *squirt squirt, squirt squirt*, as Uncle's shoulders moved back and forth. 'Do you want a turn, Larry?' Uncle asked. How did he know I was there?

'She won't let me.'

'Of course she will.'

'She won't. Even Mother can't make her. She doesn't like boys.'

'What on earth doesn't she like about boys, I wonder.'

'Mother thinks some boys must have teased her in her old home and now she's wary.'

'We need to change that then, don't we?'

He turned around to me. His sleeves were rolled and I saw the hook on his arm curving upwards.

'Come on, come here.'

He crouched beside the stool. But I didn't want to go any closer to Gert.

'Come on,' said Uncle. 'I won't let her hurt you.'

'Are you sure?'

'Come on.'

I sat on the stool with Uncle beside me. The smell of his pomade mingled with the warm, grassy smell of Gert.

He put my hand around one of Gert's teats and kept his own hand on another. 'Here like this. Firm at the top and then the fingers all the way down, like a fan opening and closing. See?'

I watched the way he moved his hand.

'Take it easy, old girl, that's it, let the boy have a turn, come now, come now.' He stroked Gert's side. 'Go on, Larry, give it a try.'

I tried to make my fingers move like a fan, starting at the top of the cow's teat and going down, but no milk came. 'I can't.'

'Of course you can. Try again—firm at the top, then all the way down, finger by finger like the fan is closing.'

When he showed me, slowing down the movement so I could see, a thin stream of milk came from the teat down into the bucket. Gert shuffled and moaned.

'Easy does it, Gert, easy does it—it's only me and young Larry, old thing.' He nudged me. 'Go on, have another try.'

I did as Uncle said, holding the teat at the top and closing my fingers all the way to the bottom. A squirt of milk came down into the bucket. 'Yes! Uncle!'

'That's it, that's it. Again, just as you did, go on.'

I began at the top, my fingers closing around the teat all the way to the end.

'There, Gert, good girl, good old girl, let it down for Larry, come now, come now.'

I kept doing what he said until the milk came into the pail in one long straight stream. 'Look, Uncle!'

'There you go! There you go! Keep it up, Larry, keep it up!'

I moved my fingers the way he showed me while he talked to Gert and stroked her side. 'Come now, hush now, come, Gert, come, that's it now, that's it. Well done, Larry, well done, there you go, and Gert doesn't mind too much, do you, old dear?'

Suddenly, Uncle leaned in, took one of Gert's teats in his hand and squirted me. 'Got you! Ha!'

'Uncle!' I wiped my nose and lip, tasting warm milk on my tongue.

Gert stepped to the side and Uncle grabbed the pail just in time.

I pointed Gert's teat and squirted Uncle, milk hitting his chin.

'Ha! You got me! You got me!'

'Take that!' I laughed.

When the pail was full, Uncle and I walked up to the house. Before going inside, we turned, the bucket of milk between us, and looked to Wallis.

'Ah, Lawrence,' said Uncle.

The body of the mountain was grey and misty, and down beneath the rocks, the trees were deepest purple.

The next morning, as I walked past the bathroom, Uncle opened the door wearing only a towel around his middle. Another towel was draped over his shoulder. I felt embarrassed and wished I hadn't walked past just then. I looked away, and when I did so,

I noticed that one of Uncle's legs was smaller than the other, as though it belonged to Uncle when he was still a boy. The leg was turned inwards, and the skin was shiny and appeared taut as if it had been stretched. I looked up and into Uncle's eyes and he looked straight into mine. It was as though he didn't want his leg to be a secret anymore, as though he was tired of hiding it. 'Excuse me, Lawrence,' he said, and went to his room.

I went to school and did my drawing and helped Mother when I was home, and did not think of what I had seen when Uncle came out of the bathroom until I was in my bed that night. As I lay under the covers and waited for sleep, I pictured the skin, smoother on the shrunken leg, and how strong the other leg appeared by comparison. I had only ever seen Uncle in the suits that hung from him, loose, pulled in at the waistcoat and the cuffs, and then there he was with only a towel around his waist. I lifted the British Naval Line. 'Paul.'

I heard Paul lift the Steamer on his side. 'What?'

'I saw the leg,' I whispered.

'What?' he whispered back.

'Uncle's leg. The one he can't walk on properly. I saw it when he came out of the bathroom.'

'*Really?*'

'*Yes.*'

'What did it look like?'

'It was much smaller.'

'Smaller?'

'Yes. Like a boy's leg. But twisted.'

'Twisted?'

'Yes.'

'Did he know you saw it?'

'Yes. He was coming out of the bathroom. It was as if he wanted me to see it.'

'*Wanted* you to?'

'Yes.'

'God. *Why?* Was it horrible?'

'Horrible!' I whispered the word hard right up against the crack. 'It was like the ghoul from the Lombardy Mansion. Like the ghoul that caught the Lady Lavinia.'

'Did it have a face like the ghoul?'

'A mouth and a nose, but no eyes.'

'No eyes?'

'No. And it was hungry.'

'Did it have teeth?'

'Three rows. Like the teeth of a shark.'

'Did it come for you?'

'Yes, but I jumped out of the way.'

'Well done.'

'I told it where your room was though.'

'You bastard.'

'Bastard me.'

'Ha!' There was quiet for a while. Then he asked, 'Was it awful, Laurie?'

'Bloody awful.'

How good it was to be Paul's brother.

16.

MOTHER AND UNCLE WERE DRINKING Teacher's in front of the wood stove. 'Did you know there is a dance class on Saturday nights in Hamilton, Louise?' Uncle said. Paul and I looked up from our readers. 'I saw the poster in the butcher's window.'

'I did hear some of the wives talk about it.'

'But why don't you go?'

'It never crossed my mind.'

'You know I can manage.'

'Not every week like that, surely?'

'What do you mean? Why on earth not? I am here, aren't I?'

'Yes ... but ...'

'You would enjoy something like that, wouldn't you?'

'The wives do say it's great fun, but ...' Mother sipped from her glass.

'While I am here in the house, Lou, make use of me.'

'That sounds as if you are leaving us.'

'Not at all. But as you know I'll be in work again soon, and it's unlikely I'll have the hours I have now. Go on, Louise. At least give it a try. It will be good for you.'

'I suppose so. It's nice to be reminded of life outside of work and . . .'

'Outside of us,' said Paul.

Uncle spoke from his chair, without looking at Paul. 'Every mother needs a little time to herself, Paul. And we'll be sure to have our own fun. I think it's my turn to put together one of your aeroplanes.'

'I could give it a try, just once . . .' said Mother. 'And, Paul, you could try showing your uncle the way you put your models together.'

'Paul, I promise to do exactly as you tell me. Louise, you must go and dance and come back and show us your steps. Mustn't she, boys?'

'Yes, Uncle,' I said, but even as I said it, I wasn't sure. I wanted Mother to go out, but at the same time I wanted her to stay home.

'That's settled then,' said Uncle, taking a drink from his whisky.

Each night before I went to sleep, I pulled *Letters from the Masters* out from under my bed. Where will my eye travel first? I wondered. It was to the boat in Master Constable's *The Thames near Walton Bridge*, it was to the girl in Master Millet's *Woman Giving her Children a Meal* and it was to the flag in Master Delacroix's *Liberty Leading the People*. I would try and read the letters beside the paintings. *I have been living a hermit-like life, though always with my pencil in my hand*, Master Constable wrote to the Reverend John Fisher. *I see very clearly the halos of the dandelion* . . . Master Millet wrote to Alfred Sensier. *There has also been considerable perplexity as to whether the foremost aim of this method was to give employment to talent* . . . wrote Master Delacroix to the editor.

But the words were unfamiliar, and the writing difficult to read in my dim light. I was often woken by the book falling from my chest.

On Saturday afternoon, before her first dance class, I found Mother in the yard pegging the washing. I could hear Gert bellowing at the gate and I wanted to tell Mother that I could do the milking. Mother was standing at the clothesline, the basket of wet washing at her feet. Though it was cold she was not wearing her coat and I saw the outline of her legs where the dress was blown back by the wind. Mother swayed and hummed as she pegged one of Uncle's white shirts. I watched as she took hold of the shirt's arms, and held them behind her back. I turned away, suddenly embarrassed, and left her there, humming and swaying in the arms of the shirt-man.

The kitchen smelled of melting cheese and tuna fish; Uncle was making casserole while I was at the table working on the fourth ancient wonder—the Statue of Zeus. Mother came out of her bedroom. 'You know I could have taken care of dinner.'

'Louise, I can manage.'

'Reggie, are you sure?' Mother asked as she gathered up her gloves.

'Of course I am sure. I wish you would stop asking me.'

'Well, alright then. Alright.'

'Louise, it will be fun. Remember last time.'

'I do.' Mother patted down her hair. She wasn't wearing her scarf, and her dark green dress moved around her legs as if it were already dancing.

'You must have turned every head in Hamilton.'

'Oh, Reggie, really.' Mother blushed and picked up the keys to the Austin. 'Paul! Come out of your room and say goodbye to your mother.'

Paul's door opened. 'Goodbye, Mother.'

'Paul, Lawrence, you do need to have a bath this time, even if your uncle doesn't ask you to. Laurie, please!' Mother said, but she was smiling and would go dancing whether we took a bath or not.

Paul went back into his room after Mother left, while Uncle and I played chequers in the lounge.

'Always watch your back, Larry,' Uncle said, jumping two of my men.

'Darn!'

'No swearing, please.' Uncle smiled.

I pulled my vest over my head; it was cold outside, but Beverly was as warm as a summer's day. When it was just Mother, she burned the fire with the lever pressed flat, but Uncle opened it all the way.

'Paul, would you care to join us?' Uncle called to Paul.

There was no answer.

'Paul?'

'No!' Paul called through his closed door.

'Come out if you change your mind!'

Uncle jumped three more of my discs. 'Got you!' he said, pushing the discs from the board.

'No!'

'Didn't see that coming, did you?'

'Yes.'

'You did not. Liar!' He tickled my side. 'Come on, your turn.'

We played for a while more. Him jumping me, me jumping him, piling up the discs by the side of the board.

'Got you!' I said, taking the last man.

'You did indeed. Only one man, mind you. Not my three! Let me check the casserole.'

From the spare, the radio played music, the volume higher than it had ever been. Uncle drank from a new bottle of Teacher's, placing his glass down on the lace doily on the little round table beside the chair. A man sang, *Don't forget me, don't forget me, whatever seas you sail* . . .

'Ah, Mr Como!' said Uncle. He turned the music up even louder and took my hand. 'Come on!'

He pulled me to my feet, taking me into a turn, then swinging me back, doing the work for both of us. I could feel the body I could never see, warm and firm. He swung me around until I was dizzy, and when I almost fell, he caught me.

Paul came into the room. 'I'm hungry,' he said.

'What?' Uncle called out over the music.

'I'm hungry!' Paul stood in the middle of the lounge, hands on his hips.

Uncle said, 'Of course.' He turned down the music. 'Now you know why your mother enjoys dancing so much, right, Larry?' he said to me.

My head spun. 'Yes.'

'It isn't Larry,' said Paul. 'It's Laurie.'

'What's that, son?'

'It isn't Larry. We call him Laurie. Lawrence is Laurie.'

'Oh, I see. But I think Larry works well.' Uncle took a handkerchief from the pocket of his shirt. 'Very well—like the greatest actor of our time.' He wiped his forehead.

'Who is that?' I asked.

'Sir Laurence Olivier, of course.'

'Is he a master?'

'Of sorts, yes. Yes, he is. Not one of your master painters, another kind of master. One capable of extraordinary range and versatility. Yes, Lawrence, I think Larry suits you very well.'

Uncle had brought the whole world into Beverly, carrying with him countries and stories and other kinds of masters. Mother needed him and so did I. What was wrong with Paul?

Uncle, Paul and I sat at the table, set with Mother's good plates, and the tuna casserole in the centre. Uncle sipped from his Teacher's between mouthfuls of his dinner. Paul and I didn't speak; it felt as if it was up to Uncle and he didn't speak either. I wished Mother were home and that she could talk to Uncle. She would know the words to say. She could tell him her news and touch his arm. The quiet went on with only the sound of the forks scooping the casserole from the plates.

Then Paul asked, 'What were you doing before you came?'

'Didn't I already answer that?' Uncle said.

'No,' said Paul.

'Are you sure, Paul?'

'Yes.'

'I'd been travelling. Working.'

Uncle took a mouthful of his casserole and I saw the hook peeking from beneath his sleeve. Was it one side of an anchor? The root of a tree?

'I sold things, various things. I found I was good at that. I'm sure I told you all this. I like the business of people. I studied for a while. A course for business. And the arts course. But that was never my employment, only the lucky few . . . unless you could call appreciation a job, which it is, of course.' He dabbed at his mouth with his serviette. 'I craved change, perhaps that was my downfall. I don't want either of you boys to make the same mistakes. You both need to stay at something. Paul, your sport, the mechanics of things, how to put the pieces together. And Lawrence . . . Lawrence. Your art, your studies. I was always drawn to the new. Endeavours untried. The lure of the unexplored. But it is foolishness, in the end. All foolishness.' He clasped his glass between his hands. 'Louise and I didn't have the same opportunities that you boys have. Louise does a good job—and she has worked hard to raise you. She loves you, as you both know. She has come so far, since we were young . . .'

He was drifting. As though the Teacher's was a potion that took him back through time. It was always two short glasses, but when Mother was out, it seemed he kept going.

'It wasn't like that for us. Our mother was gone, and Father without any memory, shouting in his sleep; his battle went on long after the war was over—but you know that . . . the old stories . . . who cares for those stories now?' He put down his glass. '*Not I*, said the wolf. Not I. Eat up, boys, if it's there on your plate.'

'Did you go to war?' Paul asked.

Uncle paused. 'No,' he answered.

'Why not?'

'I told you about my leg, didn't I, Paul? The polio? Did I tell you?' Uncle put down his fork. 'Why don't you look? Then you can see why I didn't go to war. Why a number of grown men didn't go to war. Then you can learn how lucky you are that Salk and his team have worked so hard. Why I might be dancing in your lounge room tonight.'

He pulled up his trouser leg. You would never have known or guessed the leg inside it was twisted and shrunken. Every other part of him told a different story.

Paul's eyes narrowed as he looked at Uncle's leg.

'There,' said Uncle. 'That is why I did not go to war. Though, Paul, if I am going to be truthful, I may not have chosen to go anyway. It is too hard to say, since I did not have that choice.'

'Father went.' Paul looked up, his face set.

'He did. He believed in it.'

'And you didn't?'

'I did not. But nor was I content to know that my friends were being shot on the other side of the world for no good reason. I would have preferred to have been beside them. Trying at least. But as you now know, I could not.'

Uncle poured more Teacher's into his glass. Paul pushed his food around on his plate with his fork.

After we had helped Uncle with the dishes, Paul and I went to bed. I lay under my covers with the lights off, the dinner warm in my belly. The blinds were open, and I could see Wallis under a golden moon. I closed my eyes, and imagined Zeus, the fourth wonder, leaving his jewelled throne and crossing from mountain to mountain, from Wallis to Piccaninny to Abrupt to Signal Peak, all the way to Athens.

I heard someone open the door. Sensed someone in the room. Or was I dreaming? I gasped. Who was there?

Then Uncle whispered, 'Don't startle, Lawrence. It's only me.'

Why had Uncle come into my room? Had I done something wrong?

'Lawrence,' he whispered. He kneeled beside my bed, smelling of Teacher's and casserole and cigarette smoke.

I tried to sit up.

Uncle put his hand on my shoulder. 'No, don't stir, Lawrence.' He stroked my arm. 'Oh, sweet boy.' He leaned closer and kissed my cheek.

Mother said it was impossible that I would remember Father because I only met him twice. The first time, Mother said, he threw me so high in the air she was afraid I would fall. She said, 'Careful, Father!' Father caught me in his arms and said, 'I am teaching the boy to fly, Mother!' I thought of him now, with Uncle's kiss on my cheek.

Uncle reached under the blanket and put his hand on my thigh over my pyjamas. It was too heavy, too warm. I wanted him to take his hand away. He kissed my nose and chin and lips, and back to my cheek. I looked to the window; the night sky shone black and gold through the glass. Uncle said, 'Lawrence, it will all come to you in time.' He trailed his hand down the pants of my pyjamas. I wanted my uncle to leave. I wanted to whisper to Paul through the crack and wished he wasn't sleeping. I wished my mother was home and not learning to dance.

Uncle's face was too close to mine. Only Mother went so close, or Paul, when we wrestled. I couldn't speak. I thought, What could I have done wrong?

Uncle got in the bed, the springs creaking under his weight. He lay beside me and held me. He said, 'Lawrence, this is just for us.' He stroked my hair, then he placed his hand over my privates. There was only the fabric of my pyjamas between us.

Mother said to keep our hands to ourselves. We washed as she instructed, under our arms, behind our ears, soap on our bottoms and on our privates. She was always brisk and no fuss, and when we flicked water and wanted to play without our clothes after our bath, she said, *That's enough! Get dressed, please! Hands to yourselves!* She stood for no nonsense and said our privates were just that.

But this was my uncle, Mother's brother. There was nothing he didn't know and hadn't learned. He was very close, now, against me, his breath warm with tuna and Teacher's. He was moving, his breath on my ears, across my cheek, in my eyes and hair, hotter and hotter. I lay still. Heat came from Uncle's body. I could feel his fist knocking against my thigh. I didn't know what was happening. Wanted it to stop.

Uncle grunted, and all the air went out of him. I didn't move. After a while I heard the zip of his trousers.

'This is just between us,' he whispered. He sat up on the side of the bed. He touched my cheek. 'If we were to share it, it would destroy your mother.' He kissed me again, running his hand over my hair. 'Oh, Lawrence . . .' he said.

He got up and left the room. The smell of his pomade was on the sheet. I wished it were morning. What had I done?

I heard Mother's car pull up beside the house. I heard her in the kitchen talking to Uncle. 'Oh Reggie, it was terrific fun.'

'I can see the good it does you.'

I wished the night would end. I was always asleep when it was night and did all my living in the day. I hadn't known what the night held or how long it could be. That it could go on for so long it seemed it would never again be day.

17.

WHEN I CAME OUT OF my bedroom in the morning, Mother was in the kitchen making tea. I could still see the make-up she had been wearing the night before, outlining her blue eyes. There was a rose in her cheek as she placed a cup before Uncle. 'I can now do the foxtrot,' she said.

Uncle sat at the breakfast table, a smile on his face. 'I don't believe it.'

'Let me show you.' She held out her arms.

Whenever I saw Uncle around Beverly—climbing the ladder to do the gutters, or setting a trap for the rats, or fixing the bathroom tap—I thought that what happened in my bed the night of Mother's dance class must have been a dream. When I was beside him milking the cow, or showing him my drawing of the acacia branch, or telling him about Crusoe, then the dream belonged only to me, and had not happened. But later, when all the lights in the house were off, and I was lying in my bed, the night with Uncle returned to me. The way he came into my room, his kiss, the weight of his hand. The smell of tuna and Teacher's and cigarette smoke. Then I knew that what happened with Uncle had not been a dream and it did not belong only to me.

Before she left for work one morning Uncle asked Mother if he could drive her to work so he could use her car.

Mother said, 'What on earth do you want to buy that you need a car?'

Uncle dangled Mother's keys in the air. 'Never you mind, dear sister. Can I take your car, or can't I?'

'Of course you can. But don't be late picking me up.'

'Never,' said Uncle, slipping the keys into his pocket.

When we came home from school that afternoon, there was music playing from the lounge. *Toot, toot, Tootsie, goodbye! Toot, toot, Tootsie, don't cry! . . .*

I went into the lounge and saw Mother in Uncle's arms. 'That's not right! You spin here—' Mother pushed him in a circle '—and I go under here, like this . . .' She turned underneath his arms.

'You keep standing on my toes!'

'That's not my fault!'

'Whose fault is it, Lou?'

Uncle spun Mother very fast; she spun him back, knocking over the table that held the doilies. *Toot, toot, Tootsie, don't cry. Toot, toot, tootsie, goodbye!*

'Ahhh . . .' Mother laughed. 'No, Reggie!' She stamped her foot. 'You are not doing it right! You know you're not! You have to step . . . like this!' She tried to push him.

Uncle spun her; again too fast.

Mother giggled. 'Reggie!'

'What? I am trying! You are dancing like Maureen O'Halrohan!'

'Don't you dare!' Mother slapped his shoulder.

'Ouch! But you are! Heavy as a breeding sow!'

Mother shrieked and giggled. *Do it over again, watch for the mail: I'll never fail, If you don't get a letter, You'll know I'm in jail. Toot, toot, Tootsie, goodbye!*

'Mother?'

When they saw me, they stopped. 'Look!' said Mother, her face flushed with laughter. 'Look what he bought us. Not a penny to his name, and look!' She pointed to a gramophone player where a black record spun. *Toot, toot, Tootsie, goodbye! Toot, toot, Tootsie, goodbye!*

The following Saturday evening Mother prepared for her next dance class, spraying perfume on her wrists and fixing her hair. Paul put down the engine of his Messerschmitt. 'Mother, do you have to go?' he asked.

Uncle looked up from his newspaper. 'Of course she has to. What do you mean, Paul?'

'Do you have to go?' he asked.

'Paul . . . I . . .' Mother sounded uncertain.

'Do you have to?' he asked again.

I wasn't used to Paul asking Mother like that. He wasn't giving up.

'Can't you stay home?'

Mother looked to Uncle. 'Perhaps I shouldn't . . .'

'Louise, I am here, and it's one night in the week.'

'You are right—of course, you are right.'

'I am right, aren't I, boys?'

Uncle spoke to us from the big chair. 'You're going to allow your mother to go out, aren't you, to dance, to be with her friends?'

'Can I go, Lawrence?' Mother asked, smiling.

Uncle caught my eye.

'Yes, Mother,' I answered.

Paul didn't speak.

After Mother had left, Uncle made us dinner. He told Mother he was perfectly able; that men could cook as well as women and she shouldn't fuss. He stood at the bench chopping pumpkin and zucchini from Mrs Barry's garden. Steaks fried in the pan. I was working on my project at the kitchen table; the Hanging Gardens of Babylon.

'The most mysterious of all the wonders,' said Uncle.

'Why were they hanging?'

'I think they were built of terraces in order to look like mountains, so that Amytis felt less homesick. She came from the hills, you see. But they were easier to water that way too.' Uncle leaned over my chair and looked at my drawing. I had added my own vegetation; stringybarks, wattles and bottlebrush.

Paul was reading *Spooky Tales for the Brave*. It was hidden inside his mathematics pages. Mother would never allow him to bring a book like that home. Daniel Sheen had lent it to him and there were pictures of skeletons and a vampire.

Uncle stood at the stove and turned the steaks. Without looking at Paul, he said, 'Stories of vampires date back almost as far as those hanging gardens, did you know that, Paul?'

Paul snapped his mathematics book closed.

'Oh, don't stop reading your *Spooky Tales* because of me. As far as I am concerned, all reading for boys is good reading.'

He turned around, a cloth over his shoulder, holding two plates. 'Move everything from the table, gentlemen—dinner is served.'

Paul and I cleared the table.

'Mint and parsley sauce for the steaks,' he said, setting down a small jug. 'Care of Mrs Barry.'

As the three of us ate, my heart began to race. I looked down at the steak and the pumpkin and the zucchini as my heart pounded in my chest. I didn't want Uncle to hear it. What would he say? Uncle poured himself more Teacher's. My heart kept beating hard all the way through dinner. It was difficult to eat.

I was glad when Uncle cleared the plates. He said, 'I don't know about you boys, but I am really tired tonight. It's your mountain air, I suspect. How about our own reading time for the three of us? Does that sound acceptable?'

'Yes, Uncle,' I said.

'Yes,' said Paul.

I lay in my bed with the light off. Paul was asleep on the other side of the wall; I could hear him breathing. I wished, suddenly, that the crack would spread, splitting the wall until there was nothing between us at all. I pulled the blankets up to my chin as my heart started beating harder than it had at the dinner table.

He entered the room quietly, carrying with him the smell of steak and cigarette smoke. He came to the bed. I didn't know why he would come to my bed. Didn't he have enough of me during the day? Why did he want more?

The bed creaked when he sat down on it. He leaned over me. 'Oh, Larry,' he said, holding me against him. 'Lawrence . . .'

I wished he would leave.

Uncle touched my privates underneath my pyjamas, squeezing them and stroking them. I couldn't move. It felt as if he was touching a part of me that had never been touched or shared. The part that decided whether I lived or died.

He kissed me on the cheek, and then on my mouth, his hand on my backside feeling the skin. I wanted him to stop but knew it wasn't up to me. He began to move fast, pushing against me without making any sound, as if he was holding his breath.

I looked towards the window and thought of the mountain from the very top, the way I had seen it with Paul. All the other Grampian mountains linking and joined, rising and falling like waves. If Paul and I had stood at the top, our hands joined, and stepped from the cliff, would we have fallen or would we have flown?

I didn't know, anymore, if Paul was still asleep. If he had heard us, and told Mother it would destroy her. It would mean the end. Without him she could not endure.

In the morning Uncle was eating eggs when I came into the kitchen. Paul was at the table. Mother turned to me from the stove. 'There he is! Good morning, Lawrence.' Her eyes shone.

'Good morning, Mother.'

'I am making pancakes, Laurie. Your favourite.'

'Your mood is very good, my dear. Anyone would think you'd met a special someone at the classes. Louise . . . ?' Uncle looked at Mother over his cup of tea.

'Oh, don't be silly, Reggie.'

'Well?'

'Well, nothing.'

'It can't be long, surely.'

'Until what?' asked Paul.

'Oh, Reggie . . .' Mother placed a pancake in front of Uncle, then she brought him the syrup and the butter, moving around the kitchen as if she had only just stopped dancing.

That night I was lying in bed when I heard Paul whisper through the crack. 'Lawrence?'

I lifted the poster. 'What?'

'Do you think it's true?'

'What?'

'That Mother has met someone?'

'I don't know.'

'But she couldn't have, could she?' Paul asked. 'How many times does it take?'

'I don't know.' I whispered back. 'She's just dancing.'

'But Uncle said it himself.'

'No, he didn't,' I said, though I knew Paul was right, that Uncle had said it this morning.

'He did. You were there.'

'It wasn't what he meant.'

'But what if it's true, Laurie? What if she has met someone? What will happen?'

For the first time since Uncle came, Paul was asking me questions, needing answers, and I couldn't give them. I felt as if I were in a mist and could hardly see my brother at all. 'It's only dancing,' I said.

'But what if . . .'

'Goodnight, Paul.'

In my dream that night Paul called to me from the deck of *The Lady Bold*. I was in the water below, trying to swim through the waves. I knew that he wanted my attention, but I couldn't give it. The waves came one after the other.

18.

'I'LL TAKE PAUL TO CRICKET,' said Uncle the next morning. Paul and I were drying the dishes while Mother washed.

Mother said, 'Oh you don't have to do that, Reggie. Paul can ride his bicycle.'

'I would like to see the boy play.'

Mother placed a soapy platter into the rack. 'Oh, Reggie? Really?' She looked pleased.

'Really. It has been a while since I have seen a game.'

Paul flew his Messerschmitt over the chair. 'I can ride my bike.'

Uncle said, 'Nonsense. I'll take you. I'm sure you have work to catch up on, sister.'

'I do have work to do,' said Mother. 'And a pile of mending.'

Paul looked at Mother. 'Can't you come? I told Mr Tonks you'd be there. Other mothers will be there.'

Mother dried her hands on her apron. 'Mr Tonks will be very happy to meet your uncle, Paul.'

'I'll come, Paul,' I said. 'I'll watch the game.'

Paul looked at me angrily. 'I don't want you to watch the game.'

Mother's hands went to her hips. 'Paul! Apologise to your brother.'

'They have had you all to themselves for a long time, Louise. I suppose they have to grow up and be men one day,' said Uncle.

'I'll go to the game,' I said. 'Uncle doesn't have to go.'

Paul snapped, 'Why would you want to do that?'

Mother said, 'Paul! Lawrence wants to see you play. He is your brother.'

'I don't want him to see me play. Or Uncle. I'll ride my bike.'

Mother's mouth dropped open as Paul left the kitchen. 'I'm sorry, Reggie.'

'Louise, think nothing of it. The boy has never had a father and I am sure he doesn't want me impersonating one. Leave him be.'

I was glad that Paul was going to ride his bike and that Uncle wouldn't be taking him.

An hour later I found Paul at the front of the house, crouched over his bike. The back wheel was lying on the grass beside the chain.

'What's wrong with it?' I asked him.

'What does it look like?'

Just then, Uncle came out. 'What is it, Paul?'

Paul didn't answer.

'Need a hand?'

'I can manage,' Paul said.

Uncle went to him. 'Let me help. You'll be late for the match.'

'I can do it.'

'Are you sure?' Uncle crouched beside Paul. He turned the bike upside down. 'Pass me the chain.'

Paul passed him the chain.

'You wrap it round here . . .' Oil stained Uncle's hands as he clicked the chain into place. He was close to Paul, their shoulders touching. 'Now pass me the wheel . . .'

I stepped closer. 'Uncle . . . Paul can do it.'

Uncle pushed the back wheel into place. 'There, it's already done.'

Uncle stood the bike upright, rolling it back and forth across the grass. 'Good as new, Paul.'

Paul took the bike.

'I expect you to come home with even less rubber on those tyres. Ride like the wind, lad.'

Paul smiled and put his leg over the crossbar. 'Thank you, Uncle.'

'Give them hell!' Uncle called to him as Paul pedalled down the road.

Paul raised his fist high and kept riding.

Paul would be nine this year. I had started my birthday gift for him in woodwork—a box for his models. I was going to paint a fighter plane across the side and write his name—*Paul Loman*—in a flag from the cockpit.

I didn't want any of Uncle left over for Paul. If it happened to Paul, I wouldn't know what he was feeling or what it did or if he wanted it to stop. If it only happened to me, I could answer those questions for myself and that would be better than not knowing it for Paul.

'Can I show you a painting from the book, Uncle?'

'Of course,' said Uncle, following me inside.

That evening I started to feel sick. 'Go and lie down, Lawrence,' Mother said. 'I'll come and look in on you after dinner.'

'Yes, Mother.'

First I had to go to the outhouse. My stomach cramped as I sat over the bench. As soon as I pulled up my trousers I had to go again. I stayed there a long time. There was more and more. Each time I was finished I would have to go again. I don't know how long I was there; I began to feel very cold. When I came back into the house Mother said, 'You do look ill, Lawrence. Hop straight into bed.'

'Yes, Mother.'

I took Mrs St Clair's sketchbook and pencils from my satchel, and climbed into bed, pulling the covers up to my chin. I held the sketchbook and pencils under the blankets and thought of all the things Mrs St Clair had asked us to paint: flowers in a vase, the sky, the poem. I thought of Crusoe looking to the horizon for a ship. The book was almost finished and Mrs St Clair had set us questions. What lesson did Crusoe learn? How did he change? How do you think he would value that change? I thought of the ancient wonders—the Colossus and the Pyramid, the Hanging Gardens. And then I thought further back, to Mr Wade and the countries—Japan, where the religion was Shinto; Spain, where buildings were made by artists.

Mr Wade taught the class about those places, but Uncle had been there for himself. He knew about the architecture, the painting, the languages spoken. I held the sketchbook tighter and remembered the way Uncle entered my room. The way he put his hand on my privates, the way he moved, his breath, how hot he grew beside me.

Mother came into the room. 'Lawrence? Are you alright?'

'Mother, can you bring me the bucket?'

*

On Monday morning Mother woke me with a hand to my forehead. 'You still don't look right, Laurie. I will have to call the dairy.'

'Mother.' I sat up in the bed. 'I feel fine.'

Uncle came to the door.

'I'm alright,' I said.

'You were sick last night, Laurie. You aren't allowed to go to school until it's been twenty-four hours. Otherwise the whole class will go down.'

'Louise, I can take care of the boy.'

Mother turned to Uncle. 'Really, Reggie? You don't mind staying home? I'd ask Mrs Barry but she's due in at the hospital today.'

'Of course I'm sure. Don't think about it another minute.'

Paul came into my room wearing his school uniform. He said, 'Mother, Lawrence doesn't look sick.'

'I can't send him.'

'But he doesn't look—'

'Out of Laurie's room, Paul, I don't need you going down with it too.'

Paul stayed in the doorway.

'That's sorted then,' said Uncle. 'You go and do what you have to do to prepare for work and don't worry about a thing.'

'Thank you, Reggie. How did I ever manage without you?'

'You managed beautifully.'

Mother checked her watch. 'I'd better hurry.'

'I'll make you coffee.'

They left the room.

Paul was still there, standing in the doorway. 'You should come to school, Lawrence.'

'I can't.'

'Are you sure? You should come.'

'I can't.'

He looked all around the room, at the shelves and the bed and the poster and the window. He seemed worried. 'Do you want me to stay here?'

'How can you do that?'

'I could ride halfway then, after Mother's left, I could come back.'

'Why would you do that?'

'Do you want me to?'

'No,' I said.

Even though I said no, I did want him to. I wanted him to hide by the side of the road then I wanted him to come back, but I couldn't let him. Mother's wishes and Uncle's wishes were like a river that I wasn't big enough to stop.

'Okay, then,' he said. He looked at me one more time, then he left the room.

I pulled back the covers and went to the window. I saw Paul go out onto the driveway on his bike. I kept my eyes on him as he pedalled a short distance down the road. He stopped, his legs either side of the bike, turned and looked back to the house. *Come back, Paul.* After a long moment he put his feet on the pedals and kept going.

I went into the kitchen. It smelled of coffee. Uncle was sitting at the table reading the newspaper. 'Your mother has left, Lawrence. Is there anything I can get for you? How do you feel?'

'Alright.'

'Are you ready to eat?'

'No, thank you.'

'How lucky you are to have the day away from school.' He licked his thumb and turned the page of his newspaper.

'I like school.'

'But it's not your precious Friday art class.'

'No, but I like the other days too.'

'Of course you do. That's because you are clever.' Uncle put down the newspaper and went to the fridge. 'Larry, you look fine to me. You must have got it all out of your system.' I jerked away when he ruffled his hand through my hair. 'Larry, sometimes we think we know what is good for us, but it's not until we are much older that we understand.' He took the milk from the fridge.

I said, 'Uncle, I think I have to rest in my room.'

'Of course, of course, you go and do that. You rest and recover,' said Uncle, pouring milk into his coffee.

But instead of going to my room, I went all the way out the front door, down the side of the house, and around to the back yard. I could see Mrs Barry hanging up her washing next door. 'Mrs Barry!' I called to her and waved.

'Laurie! Hello there!'

'Hello, Mrs Barry.' I wanted to go through the gap in the fence and stay with Mrs Barry. I wanted to go inside with her and eat her meatloaf.

She came to the fence. 'Laurie, I am glad I saw you. Will you put some of Gert's manure over the fence for my turnips? I have to go in to the hospital, but when I come home I'll do the mulching.'

I went to the fence.

'Hey! Why aren't you in school? Are you alright? What are you doing still in your pyjamas?'

'I was sick yesterday.'

'Sick? What happened?'

'Sick in the stomach. Mother thinks it's catching so I had to stay home.'

'With your uncle?'

'Yes.'

Mrs Barry looked up to the house. 'It's a shame I have to go in to the hospital or you could stay with me. I can see you do look pale. Not at all yourself. Oh dear, Laurie. Where is he?'

'Inside.'

Mrs Barry frowned. 'Will he make you something to eat?'

'Yes.'

'How much longer is he staying? Has he told you?'

'I don't know. Until he finds work.'

'What sort of work is that?' She peered over my head again.

'I don't know. He ran a business. And he travels.'

'Yes, yes. I know about that. The travels.'

'Mother has been dancing.' I pulled at the crossvine that grew along the fence.

'Yes, yes, I know. Dancing.' Mrs Barry checked her watch. 'I need to go. Tell your mother if she needs any silverbeet I have more than I can use. I haven't seen her so much lately. Or you boys, for that matter.'

'Yes,' I said.

'I'd better be on my way . . . though I don't like to leave you when you're unwell. Forget the mulch. You had better go inside and get warm.' She looked up one more time towards the house. 'I suppose it's good for your mother.'

'Yes, it is.'

I grabbed again at the crossvine, and pulled, the leaves stinging my hand.

*

I walked slowly up to the house. When I reached the back door, I could hear the crackle of the radio coming from Uncle's room. I wished for Paul. I wished he and I were playing in the stream with *The Lady Bold*. I wished the water was pouring down from the top of the mountain and that the stream flowed all the way to the sea.

I did not go inside. Instead I walked slowly back outside, and down to the turnstile. There was the field where the orange trees were going to be planted. Where Father was going to spend all his time. Gert chewed her cud by the railing. I pulled up a handful of grass and stood at the fence with my hand outstretched. I was shivering with the cold. 'Gert. Come on, Gert.'

She stopped chewing and looked at me, swishing her tail over her rump.

'Come on, Gert, come on.'

She lowered her head and went on with her chewing.

I walked away from the fence and went into the shed. Cold came under the flannel of my pyjamas. The floor was freezing under my bare feet. I looked around at the rusted boiler, the old butter churn that Mother said was useless. The wooden walls, the damp loose rubble of its floor. There was nothing more to see. I left the shed and went back out to the yard. I noticed, in the bottom corner, the bunker door, against the short steep slope in the grass. I hadn't gone near there since I'd hidden from Paul before Uncle came. I walked down to the bunker and stood beside the door.

When I was in the bunker, the same ground that held Wallis—his roots, and the roots of all the trees, plants, grasses and flowers that grew around him—held me. I remembered the way being in the bunker had reminded me of the fur-lined rabbits' burrow. It had felt as if I would never be found.

I hooked my fingers around the handle to the bunker door and pulled, but the door didn't open. My arms were shaking. I tried again, pulling as hard as I could, but the door wouldn't budge. I stood there a moment longer.

I couldn't stop shivering; it seemed to be getting colder. I looked over the fence; Mrs Barry's car was gone now. I went through the door into the kitchen and all the ordinary things— apples in the bowl, white tablecloth, teapot, Mother's jar of pencils, bread in the bread bin—were in shadow.

I went into my room. There were all my own things: the Dick and Janes, the British Naval Line over the crack, the reading lamp, the shelf, my cupboard of clothes, and yet it was as if they had nothing to do with me, and I had never seen them before. I lay down on the bed.

There was a knock at the door. Uncle put his head around. 'May I come in?'

'Yes,' I said, sitting up.

Uncle hadn't been in my room before during the day. No man had. Only Mother and Paul. It was too small. Uncle's smell, his voice, his full-grown body took up too much space.

He said, 'Do you have something to read in here? Where is your precious book?'

I leaned down and pulled *Letters from the Masters* out from under the bed.

'Ah,' said Uncle, smiling. 'Your secret hiding place.'

He sat on the floor, his back against the side of the bed, and held out his hands. I gave him the book, and he flicked through the pages, stopping at one of the paintings. 'Right at the end of his life, that one. *Château Noir.*' He showed me a picture of a castle half hidden by blue and green trees. There was green in the blue and white sky too, as if the change from trees to sky was gradual, and one could easily become the other. You could see the strokes of the brush the master had made; he hadn't tried to hide them, as if he had intended it that way. Uncle read, 'From Cézanne to his friend, Emile Bernard . . . *As long as, inevitably, one proceeds from black to white, the former of these abstractions being a kind of point of rest for both eye and brain, we flounder about, we cannot achieve self-mastery, get possession of ourselves . . .*' He turned to me. 'Do you know what that means, Lawrence?'

'No.'

'I don't either, I was hoping you might be able to tell me.' He grinned. 'It's a lovely painting though, *Château Noir* . . . Do you know, Lawrence, I have seen this painting.'

'Really?' There was nothing Uncle hadn't seen and didn't know, and even though he didn't go to war, he would have gone if the choice was available to him. If the choice was not available to Father, he would be here instead of the Atlantic Star.

'Yes, really. And it was truly lovely.'

'Where did you see it?'

'In America. At the National Gallery.'

'You have been to America?'

'I have. And the galleries were sublime.'

'When did you go?'

'Years ago. Another lifetime.'

I felt myself pulled towards him like dust into Mother's hoover.

'Oh, Lawrence,' he said, closing the book and sliding it under the bed. He sat back and rolled up his sleeves. I saw the hook drawn into his arm.

He stood, touching his sleeve. He had seen me looking at the tattoo. 'More of youth's folly, I am afraid,' he said, pulling the blinds closed.

He came back to me, took my hand and kissed it, then he put it under the covers. 'You get some rest,' he said, then he left the room.

I lay back in the bed. When I closed my eyes, I saw the ink drawing on Uncle's arm, like a hook on the end of a line.

I needed to use the outhouse, but I didn't want to go. Wanted to stay in the bed. I don't know how much time was passing. My stomach cramped; I had no choice. I got out of bed. It was very cold as I left the room.

When I was passing the door of the spare, Uncle called out to me, 'Everything alright?' He was lying on his bed reading a magazine, the bottle of Teacher's open on the table beside him. He wore his suit pants with the crease, and his white shirt. 'Are you alright, Lawrence? Can I make you something to eat?'

I didn't answer him and kept going. I needed to use the outhouse very badly, the grass cold and damp as I walked down the path. I opened the outhouse door and pulled down my pyjama pants and sat over the bench. My heart was racing. I looked up at the strip of sky above the door and remembered the painting by Master Constable called *Cloud Study*. There was nothing in the painting but the clouds, grey with the gold light behind them. I heard birds singing and saw the carved leaves at the top of the door and the clouds passing in the strip of sky.

Then I smelled cigarette smoke. 'Lawrence, are you alright in there?'

I looked down and saw that I hadn't locked the door. 'Yes, I'm alright.'

'Are you sure?'

'Yes.'

I was still over the bench when Uncle put his head around the door. 'You've been out here a while, Larry. You'll catch your death. Come on up to the house.'

Only Mother and Paul had ever seen me in the toilet. My face burned.

Uncle went back outside and pulled the door closed. I felt myself shaking as I wiped my backside. When I pushed open the door, he was waiting for me against the fence, holding a cigarette. I had only ever seen him smoke at night after the day was done.

He said, 'For goodness sake, Larry, you'll freeze. Come on. I'll be in trouble with your mother if I let you catch cold on top of a poor stomach.'

He came to me and put an arm around my shoulder. I could feel the warmth of his body through the suit. I was cold in every part except where his arm was against me. As we walked up to the house, I felt, with each step, the unevenness of his legs.

I stood at the laundry sink and washed my hands.

Uncle waited. 'Come on, you need to get back under the covers.'

He followed me down the corridor and into my bedroom. I climbed into the bed and pulled the blankets over me. Uncle sat on the side of the bed and leaned down. I smelled Teacher's and cigarette smoke. He kissed my cheek, stroking his hand through my hair. I thought that he would stop at the first stroke, but he kept going, from my forehead, over my head, down to my neck, stroke after stroke, until his hand was like a rake over my skin. He said, 'Lawrence.'

I was falling downwards to where it was warm and dark, the way it had been for the baby rabbit in the fur-lined burrow. I felt myself dividing; there were two selves to choose from. One inside, one outside. Uncle reached under the blankets and slid his hand beneath the band of my pyjama pants. The divide closed at his touch. All of Uncle was grown, ahead of where I was. He knew things that grown-up people knew, he had grown-up people's thoughts, and strength. I was nothing. Knew nothing. My stomach rippled as he ran his fingers along the inner band of my pyjamas.

'Sorry for the cold,' he whispered.

He pulled down my pyjama pants. 'Lawrence, you mean a great deal to me and this is between us only. If we were to share this with your mother, it would be very dangerous, you do know that, don't you? We can't take that risk, do you understand?' He was so close to me, whispering the words. 'Do you understand, Lawrence? Tell me you do. You must tell me that you do. You must tell me that you understand it would destroy your mother, this thing that is between us.'

'Yes,' I said.

'Good, I want that to be clear,' he said. 'I want you to be as certain as I am. Can you tell me that you are?'

I didn't answer him.

'Lawrence? I need your answer. Can you give it to me?'

Yes, Uncle.'

'Good. Good boy.' Uncle touched my thighs, my privates and my backside. He climbed into the bed beside me, unzipped his trousers and pulled them down. Then he pressed his privates against my legs and backside.

I closed my eyes and imagined my father flying over the Atlantic Ocean in his Liberator. I saw the ocean beneath him, grey and stormy. I imagined the roar of his engine as he flew through the sky, blocking out all other sound. I saw the German U-boats on the water, not knowing that it was my father above them, not knowing that he was pulling back the trigger, that soon the bullets would rain down.

My face was in the pillow as I lay half underneath him. I could feel the heat that came from him, could hear his heavy breath. He was grown up; the feel and smell and heat of him was full of force and knowing. He was over the top of me now, like a clamp pushing my legs apart. My face was deep into the pillow; I could hardly breathe. I couldn't scream. Couldn't move or resist or fight him. Couldn't go against him with any part as he pushed against me with his privates.

I heard the roar of the German planes, louder and louder. When I looked down it seemed as if the ocean itself were on fire. Uncle's struggle became my struggle as he pushed into me; pain from my backside shooting along my spine. The fight was inside me, between all my parts, severing them, one from another. Flames leapt across the water. I wanted to press my hands to my ears but couldn't move my arms. I wanted it to stop but it kept going. The struggle kept going. Uncle pushing me forwards, then pulling me back, pushing me forwards, pulling me back. It would never stop. Then he gave one last push and grunted.

He lay over me. I was on fire underneath him, his sweat on my legs and back. The pain in my backside radiated outwards, like the crack in Mother's mirror.

He moved off me, lay beside me. 'Between us,' he said. 'Do you understand?'

I didn't answer him.

'Lawrence? Do you understand? Answer me, please.'

'Yes.'

He stood from the bed, pulling up his trousers. I heard him leave the room.

After he was gone I fell deeper and deeper, into the dark and quiet place underneath all life. One self thought I could be here forever; the other knew the time was almost over.

I woke when Uncle showed his head around the door. 'You need to get up and out of bed, Lawrence. Your mother will be home soon.'

I didn't move.

I don't know how much more time had passed when I heard him call from the other side of the door. 'Lawrence! Time to get up!'

My body was not my own. I was outside of the burning and the pain as I took a shirt and trousers from the cupboard and went slowly into the kitchen.

Uncle pulled out a chair and slid my seven wonders project across the table.

'Time for the Lighthouse of Alexandria,' he said.

19.

WHEN MOTHER CAME HOME, SHE asked, 'How are you, Lawrence? Feeling better?'

Uncle was at the breadboard slicing an orange. 'I think he is much better. No temperature for a start,' said Uncle, placing the orange quarters in front of me. 'How was work, Louise?'

'Same as usual, you know.'

'Same as usual? We can't have that.' He turned up the radio, taking her in his arms.

Mother made chicken soup. She watched while I lifted the spoon. 'He's quiet,' she said to Uncle. 'What do you think? Can he go back to school tomorrow?'

'Of course he can. Get some of your soup into him and he can face anything.'

Paul watched me too, never looking at Uncle.

My body ached and burned. I could hardly swallow.

*

That night I woke in my bed, cold snaking around my back. I heard them talking. I got out of bed and stood in the doorway.

'But why so soon, Reggie? I don't understand.'

'I'm sorry, Louise.'

'Is it something I have done?'

'No, no. It's nothing like that.'

'So why? Haven't you been happy here?'

'It's not that.'

'But you were going to look for work . . .'

'In Hamilton? At the dairy?'

'It was your dream too.'

'Was it?'

'Where will you go?'

'Sydney. I still have connections there.'

'But nothing certain.'

'What is ever certain?'

'Lots of things are certain. This family. Where you belong. What will I tell the boys? Lawrence?'

'You'll tell them that their uncle must work. Louise . . .'

'But you said it would be a new start.'

'There's no new start for me here.'

'And now you're going to leave me again.'

'Again?'

'Yes.'

'Don't see it that way.'

'You left me then and you're leaving me now.'

'There was nothing I could do.'

'Do you know what happened after you left?'

'I was sick . . .'

'Do you know what happened?'

'Louise, all that is in the past. So much time has gone by.'

'Time changes nothing!'

'Louise, for your own sake you must—'

'You don't know what happened!'

'I do. I—'

'You don't know—you left!'

'I do know, for God's sake!'

'Why did you come now at all?'

'I wanted to see you.'

'But why now? Not all the years before? You ran out of money, didn't you? Didn't you? That was all! No other reason!' Her voice was rising.

'You know that's not true.'

'It is true! What other reason? If all along you were going to leave?'

'To see you—you must know that . . .'

'I can't do it on my own!'

'But you have done it on your own for so long.'

'No! No! I don't want to, I don't want to! You can't leave!'

'Louise . . .'

'I can't do it! I can't do it! Don't leave me! Please, Reggie!'

'Louise . . .'

'Reggie, please, please . . .' She was begging him, crying. 'Please . . . please . . .'

'No, Louise. No.'

'That's it then? You're really leaving?'

'I am.'

I heard her walk away and the door of her bedroom close. It was because of what was between us. What else could it be? The cold came down over me like snow.

*

'Lawrence, Lawrence . . .' I woke to Mother at the side of my bed, her hand on my shoulder. 'I'm taking your uncle to the station,' she said. It was still dark outside.

I sat up in the bed. My back ached. 'Why?'

'He needs to leave.'

'But why?'

'I want you to take care of things until I'm home. Get you and Paul both to school.'

'But why?'

'Why what?' Mother snapped.

'Why is he leaving?'

'I don't know, Lawrence. Go back to sleep and give your brother breakfast when you both wake up. Make sure he does his laces and wears his coat.'

'Yes, Mother.'

'And don't be late for school.'

'Yes, Mother.'

She left the room.

My stomach cramped. Would Uncle tell Mother what was between us when they were in the car? My head pounded. I don't know how long I lay there. Or if I slept. I was very cold.

Paul came to my door. 'Where is Mother?'

'Taking Uncle to the station.'

'What for?'

I got out of the bed. The room was freezing. 'So he can catch the train.'

'Where to?'

'Sydney.'

'But why?'

'I don't know.'

'Has he gone?'

'Yes. We have to get ourselves to school.'

'Is he coming back?'

'No.'

'Good.'

'Get your uniform on. We can't be late.'

My back ached riding the bike to school.

'Hurry up!' Paul called to me.

I felt sick.

In class that day everything moved around me. I was sick and hot.

Mrs St Clair said, 'Lawrence? Are you alright?'

'Y . . . yes,' I said.

Uncle was gone because of me, because of the thing between us; Mother wanted him to stay and share her dream. It would destroy her. It would mean the end.

'I'm not sure,' said Mrs St Clair. 'I may need to speak with your mother.'

'P . . . p . . . please, no, Mrs St Clair.'

'Well, we shall see . . . perhaps you could stay home tomorrow.'

I didn't speak anymore. There were the windows and the rows of desks and the blackboard. I could see them from where I sat. This was the classroom, that was the teacher and they were the other children, I could see these things, but I was outside of them. Separate.

At the end of the day Paul was waiting for me at the racks. He said, 'Is he really not coming back?'

I got on my bike and started to push. I was shaking.

'Laurie? Laurie, is he really not coming back?' Paul pedalled beside me. 'Laurie?'

'What?' Every push down felt like the last. I didn't know if I could make it.

'Laurie!'

'What?'

'Is he never coming back?'

'No.'

'I'm glad.'

It was hard pedalling, Paul further and further ahead.

By the time I got to the house I was on foot, pushing the bike. I could hardly walk.

We found Mother sitting in one of the big chairs in the lounge. Her feet were pulled up underneath her. She looked small in the chair, like a girl. There were no sandwiches cut in quarters, no apples or glasses of milk on the table. The smell of Uncle's pomade was in the air. I thought, Is he here? Is he still here? I said, 'Mother?'

She didn't answer.

'Mother?' Paul said. 'Mother? Are you alright?'

She turned to us, her eyes red. The bird clock chimed four.

Mother picked up a crystal glass and threw it at the clock, knocking it from the mantle. 'Leave me alone! Go away from me!'

Paul followed me to the outhouse.

'Get lost,' I said.

He stood in the middle of the yard. I kept going, pulling open the outhouse door. There was the wooden bench, the bucket of sawdust, the strips of newspaper. I went inside, closing the door behind me, and pulled down my trousers. As I sat over the bench I felt sick—my heart began to race and sweat dripped down my back. I shut my eyes. Felt myself grow hot, and then cold. Squeezed my eyes shut tighter.

I was there in the house that was separate. Where Mother lived with Uncle. The Hartfields. I was in the bed. I heard them coming to the door. I knew the door would open any minute. I couldn't move my legs. I told my legs, Move! Move! Something was wrong, something I had done. I leaned forwards. My backside cramped.

I gripped the bench. I wanted to hold on, didn't want it to happen. If I could choose; if it were up to me. But I couldn't stop it. It was coming! *No! No, please, stop! Stop!*

I don't know when I got back to my room. Don't know how. There was vomit on my shoes, down the front of my school trousers. My bed wasn't mine anymore. Nothing was. I could smell the smoke of Uncle's cigarette, the pine of his hair pomade in my sheets. I felt his weight over me, my face in the pillow. I rolled to one side and another and then I cried.

Mother came into my room. She put her hand on my forehead. 'You are burning up, Lawrence! Lawrence, are you alright?'

My stomach clenched. I didn't want her hand against my skin. I couldn't cross the bridge.

'Oh, Lawrence, oh my dear. Oh dear.' She held me to her.

Her touch brought the horrors to the surface like drawing salve to a splinter. I wanted her to move back, to leave me, but I couldn't pull away, didn't have the strength.

'Paul! Paul! Where are you, Paul?' she cried out. 'Go and find Mrs Barry! Please, quickly, Paul—call Eileen!'

In my dream Uncle lifted his sleeve; the ship on his arm lay washed against the shore, the hull broken, sails torn. 'By the young Master Bonington,' he said.

I heard Mrs Barry say, 'The doctor is on the way, Louise.'

'Yes, yes,' said Mother, her voice afraid. 'Good.'

Paul was in and out of the room, his eyes wide.

Mother kept her hand to my forehead. I could barely stand it. 'Oh, my darling, Lawrence, please be still. My sweet boy, precious child . . .'

20.

MOTHER SENT US TO FIND mushrooms by the stream. 'Go on, you two, be back before dark,' she said, pressing the basket into my hands.

We pushed through the turnstile. Every step my eyes were on the mountain's peak, sharp and triangular, shredding the clouds. It was the first day Mother thought I was well enough to walk into the field. The first day back at school after weeks away. The first day I had to speak again, properly—to the teacher, the other children. Paul had heard me trying.

We came to the stream dripping over the moss, dampening the rocks. We crouched down, pulling at the mushrooms that grew there, making sure not to break the fine skins. I felt the soft brown flesh in my hands, saw Paul bent over the earth as I listened to the water trickling over the rocks, the breeze in the trees, and wished I did not have to leave. Did not have to return to school. Did not have to go anywhere.

Paul sat back on his haunches. 'What did Uncle do to you?'

I went still. My hands froze. 'Wh-wh-what d-d-do you mean?'

'What did he do to you?'

'Wh-what d-d-do you m-mean?'

'What did he do to you, Laurie?'

He looked into my face. I knew his eyes all the way back from the time when Mother brought him home from Stawell Hospital and let me give him the bottle. She said it was only me that could stop him crying.

My heart was hammering. 'Wh-wh . . .'

'You can tell me, Lawrence.'

'Wh-wh . . .'

'You can tell me. He's gone now.'

'F-f-f-f . . .'

'Laurie . . .'

'F-f-f-fuck off!' I stood, knocking over the basket, mushrooms spilling. 'F-f-f-fuck off!'

I walked away.

PART TWO

21.

I COULD NO LONGER HEAR so well what was being spoken—first by Mrs St Clair when I returned to fifth class, and then by Mrs June in sixth class, and then by all the teachers that followed. I was separate: from school and learning, from Mother and Paul, and from myself. My body grew tall, I had the parts of a man, but the parts did not speak to one another.

I was fifteen and sixteen and seventeen, and sat in class as the other boys did, but was not like other boys. I heard Mrs Barry say to Mother, *It reminds me of men back from the war.* But I kept going forward in the years, first form and second form and on to the final year. What else were they to do with me?

Paul grew too; not as tall, but broader, stronger. He continued to play sport, his arms and legs bound in muscle. He shaved every morning and wore men's scent under his arms. He was saving for a motorbike. He repaired Mother's Austin and then he sold the Austin and helped her buy a Ford. When his friends came to the house to collect him, to take him out, to his games, to parties, Paul said, 'This is Lawrence, my brother,' but he hardly looked at me.

Mrs Barry was one of the few people who did not ask from me what I could not give. I helped her work the vegetables in the garden and learned when it was time to plant pumpkin, zucchini and beans. I mulched Gert's pats with straw, and shovelled the mess over the fence. I helped Mrs Barry with everything that needed lifting and carrying and digging. She showed me her book of flora, teaching me the names of the plants that grew in the area—grevillea, banksia saxicola, golden heath. Mrs Barry and I found a new hat and shirt for the straw man and filled his body with fresh straw. He leaned over the garden, his lumpy arms outstretched, and we sat underneath him, drinking tea. Mrs Barry looked up at the straw man, then back at me. 'Relative of yours?' she said.

I did not paint anymore, although I continued to see opportunities where the search for something unseen might begin. I saw it in chimney smoke, in fallen branches, in spiders' webs. In nests, in rain and in rainbows. I saw it in the range of mountains, in the movement of clouds, in sunlight, in flowers on the branch, the beaks of birds. But *Letters from the Masters* stayed on the shelf beside my pochade box and my pencils, my sketchbook. At night I lay on my bed and looked to the black spine of *Letters from the Masters* on the shelf. I knew the paintings that were inside: Master Gericault's *Study of a Dapple Grey*, Master Courbet's *Burial at Ornans,* Master Manet's *Argenteuil*, Master Ingres' *Odalisque with Slave*. But I did not want to open the book. I kept my eyes on its spine as my stomach gripped and clenched.

Each day was marked by whether or not I would visit the outhouse. I lived a secret life of wanting to go, not going, and having to go. Every moment led to the same place. Every thought would be snagged on the one that came before, and all would be thoughts of the outhouse. My stomach cramped at nights.

I would wake up in the morning after it had been two or three or four days since I had been, sometimes five, sometimes six, and my backside would ache. I would come out of my room, my eyes cast down as if there was nowhere I was going, and nothing I intended to do. I would go through the kitchen door and feel Mother's eyes on my back. I would almost turn around, sit down at the table and eat my porridge. I would almost decide to wait. But it had already been a number of days; I had to go. So, I would leave the house, wishing Mother could not see me. Wishing Mother were blind.

Paul went down to the outhouse no trouble; he did not stop or wait or worry. He went at the same time every morning and was quick about it and made no fuss. He hummed a tune under his breath on his way down the path. I hated him. I wished he were blind too.

I would open the wooden door, hook the latch, and wait over the bench. I wished I could absent myself. Wished that I did not have a self. I hoped, *hoped*, that it would be for me as it was for Paul, quick and easy. My eyes on the strip of sky in the space between the door and the roof, the carved leaves, the framed sunflower, I would tense and wait, and then, when it began to come, wanted it to stop. *Please could it stop. Stop, please, stop.* Sweat would drip down my back and yet I would be cold. My legs would tremble but I could not move them. *Let it stop, let it stop, make it stop!*

If I tried, there was blood on the strips of newspaper, and if I did not try at all, nothing happened. I was caught between trying and not trying. Action and inaction. Forwards and retreat. I would stand, pull up my trousers, then need to go again. I would try again, and the same thing would happen. Sometimes it would be three or four times of thinking I would go, then not going, then trying again. Sometimes I would get as far as opening the outhouse door, stepping onto the path, before a pain took hold in my backside, like a fist, and I would have to go back inside. I could imagine Mother up at the house checking the bird clock, counting the minutes. I could imagine the look on her face, *What is wrong with Lawrence?*

I carried within me a conversation that did not end. *Must I go? Can I not go? Please, can I not go?*

The days were best when I did not go at all. I would say to myself, *Well, I went to the outhouse yesterday, today I do not have to go*, and even if I felt the inclination and wanted to go, I did my best to wait. But sometimes I could not wait. In the end, I could not control what my body needed. It was the body that chose.

I soon learned that the less I ate, the less I needed the outhouse. I left most of everything on my plate, I toyed with my food, pushing it this way and that with my fork, I did not eat the sandwiches Mother made, nor the biscuits she left on the dish, nor the slices of cheese, nor apples from the tree. I learned how little I needed, the difference it made. Mother said, *Lawrence, you are skin and bone, why won't you eat?* Paul rolled his eyes. *At least you can do that for her.*

Like the lines that marked the days in Mother's diary, reminding her when she needed to visit the bank, when she needed more flour from the Hamilton shops, extra feed for Gert, my days were marked by visits to the outhouse. My days, my months, my years.

And if I did not have it, my waiting to go, trying to go, being torn, being able, unable, what would have held my days together? What would have tied me to Beverly, to Hughlon, to the rest of the world?

22.

'PLEASE GO AND LOOK IN on Mrs Barry today, Lawrence,' Mother said as she left for work one morning. 'She has not been herself lately. Yesterday she barely came outdoors.'

'Y-y-y-y-yes, M-M-M-Mother.'

All that day I did not see Mrs Barry working her vegetable garden or hanging her washing. She did not take her tea onto the porch and smoke a cigarette. I did not see her at the front of her house tending her roses. In the afternoon I went to her door and knocked, listening for her steps.

'M-M-M-Mrs B-B-B-Barry?'

I heard nothing.

I opened her door and went inside. Mrs Barry's house was laid out just like ours, the same rooms, windows in the same position, bathroom and kitchen in the same place. But Mrs Barry's house was much less tidy; roses tied with ribbon hung from the curtain rails and doorknobs. Dying roses sat in jars on the tables and window ledges. There were tools and gardening gloves and empty plant pots on the kitchen table. I could smell the compost rotting in its bucket by the sink.

'M-M-M-M-Mrs B-B-B-Barry?'

I did not like to hear my voice inside the walls of the house. Did not want to hear the letters run over and over.

Mrs Barry raised her head from her pillow as I entered her bedroom. 'Lawrence.'

I did not want to go closer to her lying in her bed, the curtains drawn. Did not want to inhale the scent of her sweat, see her body loose in her nightdress, her grey hair spread across the pillow.

She lifted her hand. 'Lawrence. Please . . . come here.'

I sat on the chair beside the bed. 'I sh-sh-sh-sh c-c-c-call . . .'

'No, Lawrence, you mustn't call anyone.'

'Do-do-do you n-n-n-n-need any . . .'

'Nothing, nothing at all.'

She reached for my hand. Her fingers were too much pressure on my skin, too close, but I did not take my hand away. Could not. She wanted it there. Her need was the greater.

'Oh, dear boy. Your mother's pride and joy. Such a way about you . . .' She put my hand to her lips. 'Oh, Lawrence, dear boy, dear one.'

'Do-do-do-do is-is-is th-there s-s-s-s I-I-I-I . . . ?'

'Nothing, dear Lawrence. Stay. Just stay.'

I did not want her to look at me, to touch me, did not want to sit beside her.

'Lawrence, such a way . . .'

My stomach twisted.

I wanted only to pull away. But she kept my hand in hers and then she stopped speaking and looked into my eyes. There was nothing between my eyes and hers. She could see too much. The road inside. I fought the urge to cry.

'What a treasure you are,' she said.

I did not know why she wanted to be so close. Why would she not look away, leave me be?

'Dear little fellow . . .'

She kept looking into my eyes, her head resting on the pillow, her hair spread all about, like web. I could not look anywhere else. Tears came down my face. Dripped down my neck. Soon I no longer had a body and existed only in Mrs Barry's eyes. I did not need anything to be other than it was. There was no time. I had no pain and did not need or want for anything. I remembered the bunker, when I was under there with the earth all about, like a baby rabbit in its burrow. Held. I did not need or want to look away from Mrs Barry.

The room was dark when I heard Mother calling from the front, 'Lawrence? Are you in there? Mrs Barry?'

Mrs Barry's hand was cold in mine.

'I wonder who'll take over the place,' said Paul, after the funeral.

'She always vowed it would stay in the family.' Mother sniffed as she poured tea into our cups. 'I hope nobody comes. Nobody at all.'

I went down through the gap in the boards to Mrs Barry's vegetable garden. A few days ago, Mrs Barry had been planting celery and beetroot.

I sat on the ground beneath the straw man, eyes running black down his face. *Relative of yours?* I wished Mrs Barry was here. I looked up; the sun shone from behind the grey clouds, turning Wallis silver. 'Where did she go?' I asked him.

It was autumn; the air was cool. The leaves on the maple tree in Mrs Barry's yard were red and orange. Mrs Barry's gardening fork was still upright, stuck in the dirt where she had left it. I picked up the fork and turned the earth, then I put down the fork and used my hands. The earth was damp and dark as I cleared away the weeds, giving the celery and beetroot space in their rows. I don't know how long I was there, working the garden in the shadow of Wallis. *Yes, that's right, that's the way, Lawrence*, Mrs Barry whispered.

From then on Mother would bring home seeds in coloured packets, and I would scatter them, and press them in. I did not mind what grew. I would go down there, through the boards, and dig away. One winter Mother and Paul and I ate nothing but carrots, then the next there were no carrots at all and nothing but beetroots. Mother complained, *For goodness sake, Laurie, no more beetroot!*

The vegetables no longer sat in neat rows—the turnips grew among the spinach and the tomatoes among the carrots—but the garden kept providing vegetables. Potatoes and cauliflowers and rhubarb. Pumpkins left on the vine grew enormous, splitting at the sides. 'Did you grow these, straw man?' I asked him, leaning as though he might fall.

Every few months I would take hay from Gert's shelter and stuff the straw man, making sure his arms stuck out straight and his chest was full and round. I would straighten his hat, knot fresh twine about his ankles and tighten his belt. When I remembered, I would take the black marker and draw a new face, sometimes stern and judging, other times unsure.

23.

MOTHER HAD WRAPPED A TOWEL around my shoulders and was cutting my hair. 'Lawrence, I have asked Mr Brommell, and he is prepared to take you on at the dairy.' She dipped the comb in a bowl of water.

'M-M-M . . . I-I-I d-d-d . . .'

Mother waited as I tried to speak. *You are so like him.* Her good and curious boy. I both wanted to speak as others spoke and did not. Wanted the words kept close.

Mother snipped at the hair around my neck. 'They're looking for workers, Laurie. You're nineteen now. School is behind you, and you need to find employment.'

I wanted to stay home and do the chores. I wanted to work in the vegetable garden, in the shadow of the mountain. 'M-M-M n-n-n . . .' I looked down at Mother's bare feet. When had I last seen Mother's bare feet out of their work shoes, naked on the boards of the kitchen floor? I looked away.

'You must have work, Lawrence. Like everyone else. And it's a good time. Mr Brommell is expanding.'

'B-b-b-b . . . but . . . M . . . M . . .'

She came around to the front to cut the hair from my forehead, her body close to my face. I could smell her sweat, saw the damp circular patches beneath her sleeves as she lifted her arms. She tilted back my face with her hands and looked in my eyes. 'Please, Lawrence, can you try? I want to take you to see the dairy, and to meet Mr Brommell next week.'

I did not want to look at her face. Did not want to feel her fingers brush my ears, my cheeks. Lowered my eyes.

'Lawrence, can you do it? For me?'

Three days later we were in the car on the way to the dairy. The road was long and straight, and when I looked back, I could see the Grampians curving around Hughlon like an arm. 'Today is just a meeting with Mr Brommell, Laurie. It's just an introduction. Nothing to worry about,' said Mother, gripping the wheel.

I wished I did not have to go. I hoped I would not have to speak to anyone. I hoped no one asked me any questions. I sat beside Mother and watched the road, as we left Wallis further and further behind.

'Not much longer now,' said Mother.

In the distance I saw cattle grazing, the same deep black as Gert. Gert was old now, and when Mother and I took out the hay, Mother said, *What do I keep you for, Gert?*

'There it is,' said Mother.

I saw a collection of low brick buildings, three large silos and a tractor slashing the field. This was where Mother had been coming all these years—this was how she kept the wolf from the door.

'See the house?' Mother pointed to a double-storey house where smoke came from the chimney. 'That's where I have my office.'

We came to a gate where the sign read *Hamilton Modern Dairy, Est. 1946*. The car rattled as Mother drove over the grid. Some of the other workers waved at Mother as we climbed out of the car. I was aware that I was nineteen years old and was walking with my mother as though I was a boy much younger.

A man came towards us. 'Louise,' he said, taking off his hat. Mother said, 'Hello, Alan.'

'You must be Lawrence,' Alan said to me.

I looked away.

He said, 'Right, right, you're a big boy and should have no trouble.'

Mother took me into the main house. We went through the first door into an office. Mr Brommell was sitting behind a desk, but when he saw Mother he got to his feet. 'Louise, you're looking well.'

I could see how much Mr Brommell liked my mother, the way Alan had, as if he would do anything to please her, even if it was having me here. I saw Mother as they saw her, neat and tidy in her brown dress, except for her hair, trying to escape from underneath her spotted scarf.

'This place would never have run all these years without your mother—thank you for sharing her with us.' Mr Brommell put out his hand.

Mother nudged me, and though I did not want to, I shook Mr Brommell's hand.

'Let's go and see the milking parlour,' he said.

'Somehow I manage to avoid going down there,' said Mother, as we left the house with Mr Brommell.

'You prefer the bookwork, don't you, Louise?'

'Yes, I do. I did enough milking at home with my one cow. Ruined my poor hands.'

'Lots of my workers can't milk by hand at all anymore. But you're better suited to the books, I think, Louise.'

Mr Brommell turned to me as we walked over the muddy ground towards the low brick buildings I had seen from the road. 'She is clever, your mother. But I suppose you know that, don't you? How clever your mother is?'

'Oh, that's enough now, Mr Brommell,' Mother said. 'I am not so clever I didn't need a job from you.'

'True enough, Louise.' Mr Brommell smiled. 'Lawrence, have you ever been to a working dairy before?'

'N-n-n-n . . .'

'No, he has not, I'm afraid,' said Mother.

'Well, today we'll do the tour, although the only way to learn will be on the job.' We walked through the entrance to one of the smaller brick buildings. 'This is the workers' shed,' he said. 'Where you'll store your belongings, and where you'll come for tea break.' Inside the shed there was a large table, benches, chairs, rows of lockers and doors that led to bathrooms. 'Hygiene and cleanliness are our greatest priorities,' said Mr Brommell.

'Of course,' said Mother. 'Lawrence knows to always wash his hands.'

I wanted to shout at her. *Shut up!*

We followed Mr Brommell out of the workers' shed and into the biggest of the buildings.

'This is the milking parlour,' said Mr Brommell. 'It's called a herringbone—just like the fishbone, see?' He pointed to the way the stalls were laid out, each at an angle, in two long raised rows.

We walked down between the rows.

'This is the pit. The cows come in one end,' Mr Brommell said, 'and go out the other. You'll do a row at a time. The other men will show you. Don't look so worried, Louise.'

The milking parlour smelled of cattle and straw. Two men wearing white uniforms and white gumboots were hosing down the concrete, and three more were loading large cans of milk onto a truck. Mr Brommell showed us the cool rooms, the hayshed, equipment storage, and the parking bays for the milk trucks.

'You will need to be here by half past four in the morning to be ready for the first milk,' Mr Brommell said, as we were walking back up to Mother's car.

'I have arranged for Bill Granger to pick him up on his way past,' said Mother. 'Then he can take the bus home in the afternoon.'

'Not interested in learning to drive, son? My nephews are awful. Speeding the roads like a pair of hooligans.'

'No, he's not interested. It's Paul who can't stay away from the cars.'

'At least that's only one you have to worry about.'

'Yes,' said Mother. 'Yes, only one.'

I hated her. Only one.

I looked out to the cows in the fields, some grazing, others chewing their cud, the milk slowly increasing in their udders, as it had for Gert.

Mother stopped at her car. 'Thank you, Mr Brommell. Thank you for giving my Lawrence a go.' Tears welled in her eyes.

'That's no trouble, Louise.'

I would try; for Mother I would try.

24.

IT WAS PITCH-DARK WHEN MOTHER woke me, Monday morning one week later.

'Up you get, son. Porridge is on the stove. You'll need something warm in your stomach.'

It was as if she thought I was ten years old and could do nothing for myself.

'Bill Granger is never late,' she said as she bustled about the kitchen. 'You'll be waiting out the front. Alright, son? I would take you myself, but I don't start until nine.' She said the same things over and over.

'Y-Y-Y . . .'

Mother had learned not to wait for me to finish. 'You'll get used to the early mornings,' she said.

She checked the lunch she had made me for one more time, the bread and cheese, the oranges and the flask of tea. Then she packed it into my school satchel. 'Make sure to eat, Lawrence. You can't do a job like this with an empty stomach.'

She leaned against the chair, holding her side, rubbing at the pain that came and went.

'M-M-M-Mother?'

'I'm fine. You worry about yourself today, Laurie. Up you get to the road. Bill will be there right on time. You mustn't be late.'

It was not the way she spoke to Paul, even though he was younger by two years and still at school. She did not sound worried when she spoke to him. She was cross with him half the time. *Put your clothes in the laundry! Get off the telephone! Think less about the girls and more about your schoolwork!*

'Go on, out you go.' She put the satchel over my shoulder. 'And make sure not to miss the bus in the afternoon, Lawrence. Bill Granger won't be able to take you home, so you can't miss the bus. The driver is Frank Dern—he knows your stop.'

Mother had helped me with the timetable. The bus only came once in the afternoon and the walk from Hamilton Modern Dairy to the stop was twenty minutes.

Paul, who was standing at the open fridge and drinking straight from a bottle of milk, had said, *You should learn to drive, Lawrence.*

I hated him and wanted to hit him. I hated Mother, too, for showing me the timetable, carefully drawing a line underneath the last bus of the day.

'You better get out there. Bill Granger is never late, you don't want to keep him waiting,' she said.

'Th . . . th . . . tha . . .'

'Go on. Good luck, Lawrence.'

'Y-y-y.'

'Go on.'

Not once had she let me finish.

I left the house, the night air cold in my lungs. Cold under my coat, around my ears. Cold in my boots. These were the first days of winter, each one colder than the next. I looked to the outline of Wallis, standing at the front, brave enough to face the dangers, loved by his brothers—Abrupt and Piccaninny. 'Wallis . . .' I lifted my face to the last stars. In darkness the landscape rested, withdrew, concealed by the absence of light. How would it ever be possible to paint the night? It was only possible in contrast.

I remembered the painting by Master Caspar Friedrich, *The Giant Mountains*, in *Letters from the Masters*. The mountains were wreathed in mist, covered in snow. But the place my eye first travelled was the tree in the foreground. The black, leafless winter tree. It was the tree that told me most about the giant mountains of snow. It was the tree that gave the mountains their beauty. The leafless blackened tree and the bright white mountains were in relationship. I saw the painting as if the book was spread before me. *The Giant Mountains*, by Master Caspar Friedrich.

I looked down the road, dark as midnight. Mother had sent me too early. I blew steam into my cupped hands and stamped my numb feet. When I saw headlights, I drew breath. The truck pulled to the side and the door opened. I went to the truck and looked in. There was a man at the wheel much older than Mother.

'Lawrence,' Bill Granger said.

I climbed into the cabin beside him. I was glad Bill Granger did not speak to me as he drove back onto the road. I was grateful for that. I held tight to the satchel.

When Bill Granger drove over the grid, beneath the sign, *Hamilton Modern Dairy*, the cattle were waiting at the gate.

'Open her up, son,' Bill Granger said, stopping his truck.

'Wh-wh-wh . . . ?'

'Open the gate, son. Let them through.'

I climbed out of the truck. The air was full of the smell of cow as they stood in the herd, jostling and impatient. I unlatched the chain and opened the gate. The cows pushed past me, their bodies warm and familiar. Sisters to Gert.

Bill Granger parked by the fence. 'Come and put away your things, and we'll get you started.'

I followed him into the workers' shed.

'Stow your belongings in there.' He showed me an open locker.

I did not want to leave my satchel in the locker but could see I must do as the other men did. I saw them around the sheds, older than me, in white uniforms, white gumboots and white cloth caps over their heads.

Bill Granger took a folded uniform and a pair of gumboots from a cupboard beside the lockers. 'Change room through here.' He pointed to a doorway. 'From now on the uniform will be your responsibility and must be washed every day. You can pick up extras at the end of the week.'

I took the clothing and boots and went through. There were three men inside changing along the benches. They looked up at me and nodded. I looked away from the men, chose a cubicle and locked the door. I wished the men were not there, on the other side, as I took off my clothes.

When I came out, dressed in the uniform, *Hamilton Modern Dairy* sewn across the pocket, Bill Granger was waiting for me. After I had put my folded clothes into my locker, he said, 'This way.'

I followed him to the milking parlour. The large shed, with the stalls laid out like the backbone of a fish, was filling with cattle.

'Alan,' said Bill Granger, 'Louise's boy is here. Can you show the lad the ropes in the pit?'

'Right,' said Alan.

The cows came, one at a time, into the stalls.

'Over here, lad.'

I followed Alan into the walkway that ran between the two rows of stalls. Watched as he approached the cow in the first stall.

'Clean the udder first, lad, no dirt or flakes of skin. You see the flakes from the udder? A quick wash. See there.' He rubbed warm water with a sponge from a bucket over the udders of the cow. 'The idea is to get each cow done as fast as we can.' He looped a leather strap over her shoulders. 'Make sure the surcingle is hung forwards. The higher up towards her shoulders the better.' He took a steel pail from a row of hooks along the wall, with the four tubes attached, and went in under the cow. 'Keep the pail itself low and level. The vacuum inside the tubes will pull in the teat. Never force it or push. Just make sure the milk tubes are straight and open. They work the same as a thirsty calf, tug and pull. When the bucket is full, you unhook the pail, then take it to the cool room to be emptied into the cans.'

It was different to the way I had milked Gert at home; nestled against her side in the shelter, the heat from her belly full of Mrs Barry's spinach leaves against my cheek, the sound of the milk hitting the pail . . .

'As soon as a cow makes a mess we get in with the brush and hose,' said Alan.

As if she had heard us, the cow lifted her tail.

'There you go, son, good practice for you.'

Alan passed me the brush and shovel, and I got in and swept away the mess, using the hose to direct it into the guttering.

'When the cow is milked out, the surge needs to be removed, or it will lead to trouble. We don't want any dirt entering the pipes. Right, lad?'

I nodded.

Alan showed me how to remove the milking surge. 'All the pieces in warm water,' he said. 'The vacuum must be cleaned with a brush and checked for clogs or hair. Then hang your clean surge up here on the hooks to dry. These machines are better than the old lot,' said Alan. 'You will get it down to five minutes in no time.'

That morning I watched the other workers, remembering the steps. *Make sure the surcingle is hung forwards, unhook the pail, never force or push . . .*

I saw the way the cow went of its own accord out through the gates at the other end of the row as its udder was emptied. Three fresh lots entering the stalls until sixty had been milked. All around was the sound and smell of cattle—carrying with them the scent of grass and hay and fresh milk.

After the surges had been cleaned and returned to their hooks and the hoses flushed and the milk cans loaded into the trucks, a bell rang. We had been so busy at the work that I did not notice the sun had risen. All the workers left the parlour and walked towards the brick building where I had changed when I first arrived.

'Tea break,' said Alan.

I followed Alan. I hoped nobody would speak to me. I hoped I did not have to answer any questions or shake anyone's hand.

Inside the building the men made tea and pulled food from the fridges. I took my flask and my sandwich from my satchel. The men sat around tables and ate from tins of biscuits and spoke to each other, laughing and smoking and paying no attention to me as I left the shed.

I walked to a grassy hillock across from the milking parlour, sat facing east, the way I had come with Bill Granger that morning, and unscrewed the lid of my flask. I could see the cows grazing in the fields, the poddies chasing each other around the hay racks. All about me was green field and black cow. I drank from my flask. I had completed my first milk at Hamilton Modern Dairy. The tea tasted sweet and strong. I unwrapped the bread and cheese Mother had made for me. I did not think, for once, of how little I would eat. I did not think of the outhouse, or how soon it would be. I looked out at the fields of grass and further to the wheat, and the calves, and ate first one half of the sandwich and then the other, washing them down with the sweet warm tea. I felt the sandwich reach my stomach, anchoring me to the hillock on which I sat.

After the break the parlour had to be cleaned and hosed, the pumps and vacuums checked, and the hay replaced for the afternoon feed. I stayed close to Alan, watching, trying to help. He said, 'That's right, that's the way, well done.'

My shift was finished at two o'clock, when I returned to the changing cubicles and put on my clothes.

'Well done, lad,' said Alan. 'You won't take long to get the hang of it.'

'Th-th-th . . .'

'See you tomorrow, lad.' Alan had already learned not to wait for me to finish speaking.

As I walked towards the gate, I saw Mother's car parked by Bill Granger's truck; I knew Mother was in the house, in her office, doing the numbers, but she had told me not to wait for her. That when at work, we were not mother and son but ordinary workers, and she would see me when she returned home.

I walked out of Hamilton Modern Dairy, down the road towards the bus stop. I was glad to be on my own again, away from the other men, the buildings, the trucks coming and going, the concrete pit and pipes and hoses, the impatient cattle. I looked at the fields and the hay rolls and the white puffs of cloud in the cold blue sky. Fairy wrens flew in and out of the bottlebrush trees that lined the road, flicking their tails and bouncing between the branches. 'My first day,' I told the birds.

I waited at the shelter for the bus and looked out at the neighbouring farms. At the sheep and grass and gum trees. I could feel in my arms and legs the effort of the day, and the pleasure in rest. The bus soon came, as if it had known I was waiting. As if the bus itself carried the awareness that a man waited at a bus shelter to be brought home. And so it came. This was how the world worked.

When the doors opened, I saw the bus was empty. Mother had told me it would be this way; that it was a bus to pick up the workers from the orchards and bring them back into Hamilton.

I took a seat halfway down and turned to the window as the bus headed along the road, back to Hughlon. Soon I saw the long chain of the Southern Grampians. Then the mountains I knew best, Signal Peak, Piccaninny, Abrupt and, at the front, Wallis. 'Come!' he seemed to call.

I took long steps across the flat, my eyes on the vertical sides of the mountain. The last time I had climbed him I was with Paul. We had ridden our bikes across the field then laid the bikes aside when the trail became too steep. Paul was ahead of me, so I could see he did not fall behind. Our first time up the mountain. The day Uncle was to arrive. Paul did not want Uncle to come. How long since I had remembered? It was as if my working day at the dairy held me within itself, like a cup, allowing for my memory of the first climb, allowing me to climb now, and allowing for my thought of Uncle. *Paul did not want Uncle to come.* Heat rose to my face. My stomach clenched. I kept going.

The trail steepened, and my breath grew more rapid. I plucked a gum leaf from a branch, rubbing it between my fingers to smell the scent of eucalyptus. The earth was damp under my feet. I found a long stick and held it as a cane. I was the straw man! I had wrenched myself from the iron stake and was taking my first walk up the mountain, leaving a trail of straw in my wake. 'Good day to you.' I nodded to a pair of emus, lifting their long, nobbled legs. *The straw man speaks!*

I thought again of my day on the mountain with Paul from all the years before—the kangaroo bones on the plateau, the taste of apple, Paul's hand in mine. It was no longer a story, only fragments; our pirate battle on the summit, the wind about our heads, the wattle blossom caught in his hair. I kept walking, the stride of my legs—step after step, to the next and the next and the next—bringing back the past.

When I reached the summit, I was breathing hard, cold mountain air, though my body was warm. I walked to the edge of the rocks, where the valley of trees swept away to Abrupt. A single hawk circled the mountain. I sat at the edge, my arms around my knees, and watched the bird as it rode the wind, hovering, held.

I looked out in the direction of Hamilton, far below. I would go there, in Bill Granger's truck, and be in the world of the dairy, the world of men. I would do my work, then I would catch the bus home, and climb the mountain. This was where I would sit, right here, the wind about my head, and beneath the wind, beneath it all—silence.

25.

IT WAS NOT YET DAWN when I arrived at the dairy; the light of day began in the eyes of the cattle. I ran my hand over their backs as they pushed past me. Once I'd opened the gate they were on their way and nothing would stop them—but still I called to them in the darkness, my words flowing and complete. 'Hey, come on, come on, there now, through the gate now, that's right, there you go.' What was the difference, I wondered, between night and the coat of a dairy cow?

The last stars were fading in the sky as the animals settled in the herringbone, their hooves clipping on the concrete.

'Easy now, all easy,' I said to the cows as I cleaned the udder, hung the strap, attached the surge. Sliding my hand down their backs, the pressure coming on slowly until they could be sure of me and knew what was to come. *We are going down the valley, Going down the valley, Going tow'rd the setting of the sun; We are going down the valley, Going down the valley . . .* I sang under my breath, so they knew I meant no harm and would let down their milk.

Then, after the milking, the surge removed and the cows sent through to the hay laid out in the field, so they would be rested for the next milking. The cattle followed the same pathways they had made through the grass with their hooves every morning and evening, the tracks rutted, never straight as they followed first in a single line, then diverging like branches on a tree. There were sixty cows in total, none with a name, but a number tagged through the ear. I gave them my own names—Betts and Ears and Girl and Slow and Quickly Now and Queeny. I learned how each cow best milked, the lay of their udder, when they were due to calve, and which had a tendency to mastitis. I knew when they had given enough milk, and when they needed extra feed.

I was more with the cows and the milk than the men. A couple of times the other workers had asked questions—*Where do you live, son? How old are you? Who is your father?*—but they frowned or smirked as I tried to speak, and then they left me alone. Only Alan spoke to me; each day before I caught the bus for home, he gave me a nod and said, 'Well done, lad. That's the way.'

I sat in the same seat halfway down, looking through the window as the bus left the man-made things of the dairy behind—the buildings and silos and tractors and trucks and gleaming cans of milk. I learned the road, every postbox and pothole, every silo and waterway. Where the fir trees lined the paddocks, where the sheep grazed, where the trees lay fallen against the tussock grass. The layout of the farms, their names in iron letters over the gates—Bredlaw and Kennee and Linden Fields. I knew once I had passed the Trinity Lutheran Church it was not much further until I was home.

I leaned forwards in my seat when the Grampians came into view. For a time, it appeared as if the road was heading directly into the heart of Wallis. What was inside him? I wondered.

If you pulled him apart—his rocks and stringybarks and lilies and orchids and earth—so he lay scattered in pieces, would he grow again?

I was on my feet every hour from four o'clock in the morning, but there was not a single day I did not climb the mountain. In summer the sweat would drip down my face, my neck, and I would boil in my clothes as I walked to the music of blowflies. When I reached the summit, I would lie on the peak, my back against the warm rocks, waiting for the sun to set, washed in the pink light. When autumn came, the leaves on Mrs Barry's maple turned red and orange, and I could feel the cool air on either side of the long hot days. The sunsets then were pale yellow and purple and grey—dramatic events, to farewell the summer. Silent sky, sky as witness. Sky around the world. It was a wonder there was a man on earth who could tear his eyes from it more than an hour. In winter, the air was cold in my lungs, against my cheeks, as I walked towards the mountain, seeing the mists that clung to him, obscuring him. Wondering, was there ever a way a man could put his hands to the mist and see it there, in the cups of his palms? Mother said, 'You will catch your death, Lawrence,' but it was Mother who was growing slower, a hand to her side as she stood from her rocker. In spring came the rains and the flowers, parrot peas and lilies and kangaroo paw. Calves at the dairy, apples on the tree.

My days in a pattern like the scales of a pine cone: the milking of the cow, the rising of the sun, the climbing of the mountain. Years passed, two, three and four, until I had been working at Hamilton Modern Dairy for five years.

26.

ONE AFTERNOON MOTHER AND I were in the shelter, forking
the hay for Gert. Mother stuck the fork into the hay, and gasped,
dropping the pitchfork.

'M-M-Mother?'

She leaned against the fence, a hand to her chest.

'M-M-Mother?'

'Help me . . .' She struggled to breathe.

'Y-y-y-y . . .'

'Help me, Laurie . . .'

'Y-y-y-y . . .'

She leaned against me as we walked to the house. Past the
washing line hung with my whites, slowly up the back steps, onto
the porch and into the house. 'My room, please . . .'

I did not like to go into Mother's bedroom; the bed with its
patterned cover, the pillows, her empty shoes, her handkerchiefs
folded in squares. I did not want to breathe the air. Wanted to
look away. 'M-m-m . . . Are y-y-y-y-you . . . are you . . .'

'Let me rest. Finish the hay.'

'B-b-b-b . . .'

'Do the hay, Lawrence.'

After helping her to the bed I left the room and walked back down to the shelter to finish forking the hay. Was that what I ought to have done? I wasn't sure. What was wrong with Mother? Lately she had been tired. If she rested, would she then be the mother I knew? The mother who did not stop her chores until it was time for bed?

Mother did not get up to make the dinner. I looked in and she was sleeping. I closed her door, sat at the kitchen table and thought of all the meals Mother had prepared. How many times she had carried our full plates to the table. How many pies, how many chops, how much stew, cups of tea? I sat as the bird clock ticked from the lounge. I did not eat that night. I looked in one more time before going to bed and saw the rise and fall of her chest as she slept. Paul did not come home. He spent week-nights at the house of his girlfriend's parents, closer to his work.

The next morning, Mother did not get up to make porridge and pour tea into the flask. I put my head around her door. 'M-M-M-Mother?'

There was no answer.

'M-M-M . . . Mother?' I said again.

Mother spoke quietly without lifting her head from the pillow. 'I can't go to work anymore, Lawrence.'

'B-b-but w-w . . .'

'Bill Granger is never late. Go on, get ready. Be sure to make yourself some lunch.'

'Y-y-y-y . . .'

'Go on.'

I went into the kitchen and packed my own ham sandwiches and apples, made my own tea for the flask. It was not so hard to do. I returned to Mother's room. 'M-M-M . . . I-I-I . . .'

Mother's voice was strained. 'Bill Granger is never late.'

'Y-y-y-y-yes, M-M-M . . .'

'You need to be waiting.'

'B-b-b-b Mother . . . are . . . y-y-y . . .'

'Lawrence, go please.'

'Y-y-y . . .'

'Go on.'

I put my satchel over my shoulder and went onto the road. The only time Mother did not go to work was when I was a boy and was ill. I could not remember another time. She was never late. She did not like to miss a day or change things.

Mr Brommell came to me when I was hosing down the parlour after the milk. 'Your mother telephoned and said she wasn't well. Is she alright?'

'Y-y-y-y-yes.'

'Do you need me to send for the doctor?'

'N-n-n-n . . .'

'Please give her my best. I hope she recovers soon.'

'Y-y-y-y-yes.'

It was the first day Mother was not in the office doing the numbers. All that day I thought about her. Mr Brommell had asked me when I began at the dairy if I knew how clever my mother was. I had not given him an answer. When I showed Mother my reports from school, Mother said I was clever the way Uncle was clever. Not the way she was clever. But Mr Brommell was right: Mother was clever. She taught herself the books, mathematics, typing and inventory, and she looked after Paul and me at the same time. She was always there at the end of the day with tea biscuits and glasses of Gert's milk, and she kept the wolf from Beverly's door, all without Father. I hoped she was alright.

When I came home on the bus that afternoon, Mother was not in the kitchen. I went to her room and saw she was still lying in her bed. 'M-M-M-Mother?'

She turned around and pulled herself up against the pillow. Her hair was tangled around her face, all its shining golden colour faded. There were shadows under her eyes and her skin was pale. 'Was it alright?' she asked me.

'Y-y-y-y-y . . .'

'Good. Good.' She closed her eyes. Lines ran across her forehead, and from the corners of her mouth and eyes.

'M-M-M-M . . .'

She turned her head away from me.

'M-M-M-M, y-y-y-you . . .'

'Let me rest.'

She did not want to hear me try to speak.

I went into the kitchen and sat at the table. I remembered when it first became difficult to speak. All the years before.

I had been away from school a month after Uncle left. I had been quiet in those weeks. The doctor told Mother I was recovering, that was all, and I would soon be myself again. On my first day back, I remember icy winter clouds hung low in the sky as Paul and I pedalled down the road. Wallis was hidden in cloud; I kept my eyes on Paul's wheel turning ahead of mine.

When Mrs St Clair said, 'Welcome back,' I had nothing ready. When Mrs St Clair said, 'Lawrence, can you explain for the class what drove these explorers on? What discoveries had they made that gave them the determination?' I had no answer. I thought of all the words to choose. I asked myself, which word? I made my choice, but I did not want to let it go. 'M-m-m-m-m . . .'

Somebody laughed.

Mrs St Clair frowned. 'Lawrence?'

I tried again—'M-m-m-m-m'—but could not speak the word. *Men*. Or was it that I could, but did not wish to? Wanted words to remain within my own boundaries.

I don't think I spoke a single whole word that first day back. Roger Lenley chanted, *Lawrence got a stammer! Lawrence got a stammer!* Daniel Sheen joined him: *Lawrence got a stammer! Lawrence got a stammer! Not so smart now, Lawrence Loman, not so smart now! Lawrence got a stammer! Lawrence got a stammer!* More and more of the class. *Not so smart now, Laurie Loman, stammer stammer stammer, not so smart now, put your hand up now, Lawrence Loman!* I was trapped within a circle of boys.

Then Paul pushed through the circle, smaller than all of them, younger. He raised his fists. 'I'll tear your heads off! I'll tear your fucking heads off!' He came forwards, stepped close to Daniel, stepped close to Roger, to James, fists raised. He would have; he would have torn off their fucking heads with his own hands. The boys scattered, and left us.

But I remember pedalling home that afternoon, when the bus had passed and the road was quiet, Paul said, 'Lawrence, why are you talking that way?'

I pedalled faster, riding ahead. I could not answer; I did not want it to be with him too. *Let it happen with anyone but not with Paul; please, God, not with my brother.*

Words were the place my stammer ended, not where it began. There were breaks between things that had not been there before.

A thought would start on its course, but I could not follow it. Alone in my room, where I could sit against my wall, it was not as bad. The wall pushed me forwards, then took me back.

Mother soon learned how to speak in my place. She did not let me finish. Could not bear it. Is that what had made her so tired?

I did not leave the house that afternoon while Mother rested in her room. I did not walk to the mountain. Did not go outside at all. Remained sitting on the chair. The bird clock ticked three and four and five. The kitchen grew still; Mother's jars and vases and beaded doilies on the shelves, the chairs and table, the dresser and drawers and hoops on the wall, the cups and saucers swinging on their hooks, all came to rest. It began to rain.

Paul entered the kitchen wearing his mechanic's overalls, grease across his cheek, hair damp, pressed flat by his motorbike helmet. He had been at his new job nearly two years. He was part of a team at a mechanics. He saw me sitting at the table. He looked around the room, frowned and went into the lounge. He came back out and looked into the laundry. 'Where is she?' he asked.

'She i-i-i-is in th-th-th—'

'Where?' He walked through the back door and onto the porch. 'Mother?'

'Sh-sh-sh-sh . . .'

'Where?'

'Sh-sh-sh-sh . . .'

'For God's sake.' He went into her bedroom.

A minute later he came out and picked up the telephone. 'Ambulance, please. Beverly Park, Hughlon West Road . . . Yes, please . . . Hurry . . . I'm not sure . . . I can't tell . . . Yes.'

He put down the receiver. 'How long has she been like this, Lawrence?'

'I-I-I . . .'

'How long?'

'I-I-I . . .'

'Why didn't you call an ambulance?'

'I-I-I . . .'

'For Christ's sake, Lawrence!'

'N-N-N . . .'

The chair fell to the floor behind me as I lunged at him.

'What the hell?'

I slammed my fists into him; his body warm and hard under my hands. I wanted to hit him and kick him. Wanted to punch his face. Strangle him. I wanted him to fight. But he got me down and held my arm behind my back.

'Fuck, Lawrence,' he said.

I fought against him.

'Lawrence! The ambulance will be here soon.' He let me go, pushing me away, and went into Mother's room. I got up and sat on the kitchen chair, my heart pounding.

Paul directed the men to Mother's bedroom. He stood over the stretcher as they carried her out into the rain. It was Paul the men spoke to. *Warrnambool Hospital*, they told him. I wanted to cover her from the rain. Wanted to tell them, *Take care!* but could not speak the words. It was Paul who held Mother's hand as she lay in the back of the ambulance. I stood in the doorway of Beverly and watched as they drove down the road until they had disappeared.

I went inside. Droplets of water fell from my trousers and shirt collar. The bird clock ticked. I sat down at the kitchen table and looked up at the exposed beam that crossed the ceiling. There was a half-foot of space between the beam and the ceiling. I did not take my eyes from the beam, the grain, the circular notches, until my breathing grew steady, and I was no longer shaking. When I lay in my bed that night in the empty house—for Paul did not return—I pictured the beam, returning and returning to the beam until I slept.

I could see the shape of Mother's skull underneath her skin as she lay in the hospital bed. What was the difference between the bones and the life? She said, 'Lawrence, will you be alright?' Her breathing was laboured.

'M-M-Mother . . .'

She took my hand. 'Lawrence, I need to know you'll be alright.'

'M-M-Mother d-d-d-d . . .'

She was trying to cross the bridge. 'Lawrence, I . . .'

'M-M-M-M d-d-d-don't . . .'

'Lawrence, it's alright . . . I want you to be happy, to have what you want . . . Can you be happy?'

She deserved an answer, but I could not give one to her. There was something I wanted, before it was light, when I lay in my bed. But when I woke properly what I wanted was gone.

'Such a closed book,' she said. 'My son . . .' She reached out and touched my cheek.

I did not want her to touch my face. I wanted her to stay on her side.

She said, 'Lawrence, there's something I need to explain to you.' She struggled to sit.

'M-M-M-M no-no-no . . .'

'Lawrence, I need to tell you something. Please . . .' She could never let me finish a sentence. I had not spoken a single whole sentence to my mother since the day Uncle left.

'N-n-n-n-n . . .'

'Lawrence, please . . .' She put a hand to my arm. 'From the time your father was killed in the war there's been a pension,' she went on. 'I have saved it, for when I could no longer work. Or if you and Paul were to have a family, you might use it then . . .' Her voice was weak. 'I want you to have it, Lawrence. You will find the paperwork in my desk. It's all in your name. If anything happens, you will be able to manage. You can sell the land if you have to. I will tell your brother, if you need to sell the land . . . You will be alright. Do you understand, Lawrence?'

'Y-y-y . . .'

'Good.' She lay back against the pillow. All her life trying to keep the wolf from the door; she was still trying.

It had been two days since she had spoken. I was alone with her when she opened her eyes and looked at me. 'Reggie . . .' she said, reaching for my hand. 'Reggie . . .'

I wanted to pull away; I was not him.

'Reggie . . .' she said. 'Thank God . . . thank God . . .'

'N-N-N-N-N . . .' I could not speak the word, could not move past the letter, could not tell her that I was not him.

After Uncle left, when I was a boy of ten, Mother would sigh and speak to the air above the kitchen sink. *If only he hadn't left us, Lawrence.* Mother wrote letters to the address Uncle had given her. I saw her checking the letterbox at the front of the house in case he answered, lifting the little door, looking deep inside. Then standing straight, a hand to shield her eyes from the sun, staring down the road, day after day.

'Reggie.' She closed her eyes. Her hand in mine was the hand of a child.

27.

'YOU CAN STAY HERE, LAWRENCE. I know you'll want to.' Paul, still wearing the suit he wore to Mother's funeral, was packing his clothes into bags. A girl waited for him, in a car parked outside the house.

'Wh-wh-what ab-ab-ab-about y-y-y-y . . . ?'

'Bradley's offered me a job.'

'Wh-wh-wh . . .'

'The mechanics in Ararat. It's better than where I am now. A lot better. There's another bloke with a place, a spare room near work. You can stay here. I'll take Mother's car, but the rest is yours.'

He could not meet my eyes. He had defended my stammer all the way through school; it did not matter that he was younger, he would have killed for me. Paul pretended he never knew I could speak another way—had been free with my speech the way he or any other boy was free. But now he was leaving home and could not meet my eyes.

I followed him out to the gate. The girl waiting in the car drummed her fingers against the steering wheel.

'I'll come by in a week to pick up more of my things. I'll make sure you have what you need. You can call me, Lawrence, okay?'

He came to me and held me for one hard quick moment.

When I could no longer see their car on the road, I turned and looked at Beverly—her white boards and white paling fence, her red roof and green letterbox, her faded sign. *Beverly.* There she was without Paul or Mother inside, or Mrs Barry next door. I walked into the house, down the corridor and into the kitchen. I looked at Mother's side cupboard that held the wheat sheaf plates, her glasses, her ledger and half-finished hoops. I saw her rocker, her cardigan, her gumboots by the step. I heard the tick of the bird clock from the mantelpiece. The evidence of Mother was everywhere, though she herself was gone. The house was empty and would not fill again.

I had lived twenty-four years; there was not any part of Beverly or Wallis, and the fields around them, that I did not know. What more was there to see? I turned my attention to the beam above the kitchen. In places the stain appeared darker, but perhaps it was because of the way the light came through the window. The beam was wide, strong enough to support Beverly as it had for all the years. I went through the back door, down the path to the shed.

There was the rusted boiler, beside Mother's broken washer. The milking stool sat in the corner, beneath the steel pail hanging from its hook. The coil of rope was looped over a nail on the wall. I took the stool and the rope and left the shed. All doubt was gone. I did not think of Mother in the hospital, of Paul on his way to his new job, of Mrs Barry's empty house. Did not wonder what next. Thought only of the beam, the stool and the rope in my hands.

But as I passed the apple tree, a bird called through the branches. I turned and saw a crested pigeon, the bough beneath it heavy with apples. The feathers on the wings of the bird were lined in purple and gold, the point of its black crest jaunty atop its head. The pigeon called again, looking at me with its black eyes, ringed in orange. At that moment, it flew from its branch, disappearing in the direction of the field, drawing my gaze to Wallis. The body of the mountain was impossible to discern against the golden light that shone from behind him. He was the shape of a mountain only, as if he had not yet been filled with colour or texture. I did not turn away from the mountain, barely aware of the stool and the rope falling from my hands. There was something hidden inside Wallis, that was more than the vision of him, more than his body and his trees, more than the rocks and the earth that made him, something only I could reveal. Wallis was alone with the secret of himself. I wiped tears from my face. It was up to me.

Walking back into the house, I entered my room, and took the pochade box from the shelf. Ran my fingers over the label, *Artiste Propre*. I opened the lid. The coloured water paints sat in rows. Above, in their own compartment, were the three brushes and the dish for the sponges. In the slim drawer underneath were the thick sheets of drawing paper.

I took the paints into the kitchen. The squares of colour were dry and as hard as rock. I took a knife from the cupboard and cut out the hardened paints, crushing them into separate powders on a plate. I dipped one of the brushes in water and mixed and dabbed until the paint came alive.

I carried the pochade box, the plate and a jar of water down the path leading to the gap in Mrs Barry's fence on one side, and the outhouse on the other, and then on to the turnstile; my pathways around Beverly, grooves in the earth, where the grass no longer grew, like the tracks the cows made to the milking parlour.

I pushed my way through the turnstile into the field and then, where the grass was tussocky and soft, I sat, leaning my paper against the lid of the open box. Brush to the paper, it was not long before I was immersed in the sky over the mountain—an upwards sweep of grey and white cloud infused with light, over blue—then the summit of Wallis beneath. Brown and green and purple over green. It was Wallis as I had seen him, and it was more. It was the inside come to the outside.

I did not stop what I was doing until it began to grow dark. I slipped the paper into the box and began walking home. I breathed the air, moving slowly, passing through pockets of warmth and cold. The air about me, the fading light, the first star. Mother here, Mother gone. There was not a particle of life that did not change.

I reached Gert chewing her cud by the fence. She looked thin, her black coat draped over her bones. Was it the coat that gave her life? I stopped at the fence. 'Gert.' I held out my hand. She came to me, I looked into her eyes, milky and grey. I stroked Gert's neck. We lived lives in separate bodies, Gert in hers—licking from the salt block, dropping her manure, chewing her cud—and I in mine—riding with Bill Granger to the dairy, doing my work, coming home, walking and eating and using the outhouse—but at the same time our separateness was illusory; we made the same heat. 'Old Gert,' I said, running my hand over her face. 'Old cow.'

On the way back to the house I noticed how pink and bright were the cherry blossoms on the tree in Mrs Barry's yard. I went through the gap in the fence, snapped the end from a blossom-covered branch and took it with me into the kitchen. After setting the branch on the sill, I wiped crumbs from the bench with the rag, carried in a load of wood and lay kindling in the stove. Then I heated a cup of milk in the saucepan and cut an apple into quarters. I sat at the table to drink the warm milk and eat the apple. There were fewer thoughts between my actions, fewer questions. The apple tasted sweet, the milk creamy.

I walked to the window; the sky was now purple streaked with gold. Like the wings of the pigeon in the apple tree. There was nothing and nobody between me and the natural world. Mother was gone, Mrs Barry was gone, and Paul had moved away. I was alone, with nobody to observe me or think a thought about me or want something from me or be disappointed. All of Beverly's spaces—the house, the yard, the shed and woodpile and outhouse—were now private.

I took the watercolour painting of Wallis and the sky above from the pochade box and propped it up on the shelf, between Mother's salt and pepper shakers. It was like another window to the mountain.

I placed the cherry blossom beside the painting, went to my room and took *Letters from the Masters* down from the shelf. I switched on the reading lamp in the lounge, sat in Mother's rocker, and opened the book at a painting called *Sunset at Eragny* by Master Pissarro. I allowed my eyes to drift over the painting the same way the clouds drifted over its sky. I looked at the image this way, drifting, asking nothing, merely seeing. A row of poplar trees casting their shadows over a bright green field, beneath the setting sun. The sun was at the heart of the work, all of the painting misted in gold around the sun, translucent swirls of blue and pink, some horizontal, others at an angle, as if blown by the wind. I felt myself entering the field with Master Pissarro. I understood the living secret of the sunset at this place, Eragny.

There was a letter beside the painting, written in 1893, from Master Pissarro to his son Lucien. I read slowly—*Blessed are they who see beautiful things in humble places where other people see nothing. Everything is beautiful . . .*

I put down the book and looked around the house—at teacups in the lamplight, the bird clock on the mantelpiece, orange peel across the bench, at the roses and lilies in a vase left by the dairy for Mother. Her cardigan over the kitchen chair, unwashed potatoes, apples in a dish, the branch from the cherry blossom.

I took fresh paper and a lead pencil from the pochade box and sat back down in the rocker, placing my feet on the fender before the wood stove. I rested the paper on the box, my pencil making its steady grey marks across the paper. I drew the roses, the orange peel, the potatoes. These objects of the landscapes— these things, too, were roads. In stillness there was movement. As I drew, held within the soft light of the lamp, I spoke words from Master Pissarro's letter, '. . . *two willows, a little water, a bridge . . . everything is beautiful.*' The words were fully formed, bound within their consonants, one leading with ease to the next. '*Everything is beautiful.*'

Soon my stomach began to growl. I stood from the chair, setting aside my sketchbook. It was Mother who did the cooking; since she went to hospital, I barely remembered any of the ordinary things—what I did or if I slept or washed my hands and face.

I went to the cooling cabinet; a single pumpkin sat on the mesh that I could not recall bringing in from the vegetable garden. I carried the pumpkin to the kitchen bench and cut it in half, seeing that one half was rotten.

I lit the gas stove, as I had seen Mother do, cut the good side of the pumpkin into pieces, and placed them into the black pot. Then I poured in the water. Was this the way Mother prepared the soup? I waited for the water to boil, softening the pumpkin, then mashed it with a fork against the sides. Next I added salt and sugar, butter and cheese. Who cared if it was not the way Mother prepared the soup? I could do it as I chose. The same way I painted. Did not have to consult the cookery book, measure every ingredient. I cracked an egg into the pot.

Round and round with the wooden spoon over the stove. How soothing it was to see the orange liquid begin to bubble and thicken. I left it simmering and positioned the remaining half of the pumpkin on the table, setting it this way and that until I was satisfied. I opened my sketchbook again and drew, the vegetable's scattering of seeds, its softening flesh, the stringy hairs that grew from its damp centre, the vegetable's rot integral to its beauty.

When it seemed to me ready, I poured the soup from the black pot into my bowl.

There it was before me, its scent sweet and earthy. I did not play with the soup, turning it this way and that with the spoon, seeing how little I could take.

I swallowed every mouthful, sweet pumpkin dripping down my chin.

After I had eaten, I went to the bathroom and turned on the taps over the bath. I had not taken a bath since I was a boy. Without removing my clothing, I turned off the light and lowered myself into the water. Steam rose around me. I slid down the bath so the water came over my ears and eyes. I was Ophelia by Master Millais, my clothing floating around me like weeds in a stream.

28.

PAUL CAME TO THE HOUSE a few days later. I opened the front
door when I heard his motorbike. He pulled off his helmet and
stood before me, in his leather jacket, his motorbike parked
on the grass. He was of the world. Could travel across it on a
motorbike. I hated him.

'I-I-I n-n-n-n . . .'

He said, 'What?'

'I n-n-need . . .'

'What do you need?'

'I n-n-n-n-need . . . p-p-p-paint.'

'Paint?'

'I will give you m-m-m-m-money. C-c-c-can you you you . . . ?'

He frowned. 'What do you mean? What sort of paint?'

'P-p-p-paint.'

'Are you going to paint the house?'

'Oi-oi-oi-oil oil p-p-p-paints, oil paints. Can-can-can-canvases.
P-p-p-paper.' I was older. I came first, knew everything in class,
it was me who led the way up the mountain. The harder it was
to speak the more I hated him.

He sighed, looking away from me.

'P-P-P-Paul . . .'

'Where, for God's sake, do I get those things?'

'I-I-I-I . . . I don't don't . . .'

'Forget it. Do you know exactly what you need?'

'I-I-I-I I don't don't . . .' I shrugged. I was helpless. Did not know where to begin.

'Look . . . Don't worry about it. I'll find them. I'll find something.'

'Th-th-th . . . thank you. Th-th-th-thank you, Paul.'

Our eyes met. When we were boys, he could only catch me if I slowed down enough to let him. The questions he asked. The answers I could give.

'Are you going to let me inside? I have to see what else you're going to need. You can't eat bloody paint.'

'Y-y-y-y-yes.' He followed me down the corridor.

My days found a new pattern after Mother died. I woke when it was dark and readied myself for work; preparing my flask, sandwiches, apples from the tree. Then out to the road to wait for Bill Granger. My shift began with opening the gate for the cows and ended with hosing away their dung from the pit. Then home on the bus, when I would look through the window, knowing the mountain was coming, that I would see him at the head of the chain, any moment, then seeing him, still there, the road heading into him, as if it would end in him, as if there were no other place to go, nothing beyond him. Arriving home, making sure I had fresh paper in my pochade box, clean brushes, water, and out through the turnstile.

Was it my eye telling my hand? Did my hand know without being told? Master Friedrich wrote, *The artist's feeling is his law.* Was it feeling that made a painting? Or was it some other inclination? I stayed on the same branches over and over with the black and the green, strokes becoming smaller. Who cared what made the painting? Only that it was made. Only to do it and do it and do it. The leaves formed under my brush until they made a canopy, sheltering me as I worked.

I did not count the hours that passed; my body grew tired but other parts of me had never been more alive and did not need or want to stop. Master Cézanne wrote that the fingers wanted to paint until something was formed. I did not want to stop until there was enough on the paper to carry me through to the following day.

But when the light began to fade—as light must always fade—I stopped what I was doing, pushed the paper into the shelves of the pochade box, and began the journey home. I would find some treasure to carry with me as I went—a stone, feathers, a branch, flowers. Back to Beverly to make something for my dinner—bread and sausage, cheese and bully beef or sardines and beans from Paul's boxes. Mrs Barry's vegetables: tomato, carrots, silverbeet. I ate the dinner without cooking, or with cooking. I ate standing on the porch looking at the sunset. I ate leaning against the kitchen wall looking through the window. I ate in the rocker, rocking as I ate, my mind left behind in the fields, on the mountain, my mind in the painting, beneath the canopy, my mind in the book, the letters. I ate with one hand holding the paintbrush, I ate bread stained with the day's paint and drank from a glass marked by a fingerprint of cadmium yellow.

Every night I read a different letter. Master Delacroix wrote to Pierret, *I have seen here a play on Faust. The most diabolical thing imaginable.* Master Otto Runge wrote to Goethe, *It is a great relief to me to see the fulfilment of my dearest wish.* Master Turner wrote to Trimmer, *I lament that all hope of the pleasure of seeing you, or getting to Heston, must for the present probably vanish.* I copied the words on paper with a pencil, travelling the letters, each one its own miniature sketch. A sentence, like a painting, was a road. *I adore you, words who are sensitive to our sufferings, words . . . with the scent of vibrant silks . . .* wrote Master Ensor. *Adore . . . sufferings . . . silks. Letters from the Masters* gave me words to describe painting, words with which to understand, words to name. Every letter in the book was written to me. I was not alone. I remembered Crusoe and his story. Words made sentences and sentences made stories and stories made Crusoe; he had stayed with me as if he were my brother and I had known him all my life.

Every night I lay on Mother's bed and opened the book at Master Constable's letter to the Reverend John Fisher. *My skies have not been neglected, though they have often failed in execution.* I whispered the words, '*not been neglected . . . often failed . . .*' I ran my fingers over the painting that was beside the letter. It was Dedham Mill, again and again. I watched the master's brush begin to paint, the tiny strokes of the disembodied brush like a lullaby, *sh sh sh sh* as the Stour, the Dedham Mill, the dark trees and the evening sky appeared before me. By the time the brush was deep into the branches I was asleep.

I painted twenty-eight watercolours of the mountain, which I pinned above the stove, over the taps, and the shelves, above the sink. As I stirred the porridge in the morning I could look to the paintings and see where they needed more attention, and where they might have benefitted from less. Each painting was a window. I wished Mother had done the same with my parrot peas. 'The parrot peas,' I said. 'The parrot peas.' Ha!

Since Mother was gone, I went to the outhouse at whatever time I chose. *Now I will go, now I will not go. I need to go but I will resist, I will wait and go later.* I did not have to wait until Mother was out of the house. I no longer had to feel her eyes on my back as I left the kitchen and walked down the path. I did not have to worry if Mrs Barry saw me from her yard. Fewer of my thoughts led to the outhouse, and I feared it less. Other things concerned me. Where did the light fall? What colours did I seek? What was my purpose?

Because I was not so concerned about my visits to the outhouse, I ate more of the dinners I made; more of the bully beef, the soup, the sardines and baked beans, more of the pumpkin and cheese, potatoes and butter and rhubarb and tea biscuits. Since Mother died, my belly was full and there was new strength in my body.

'Lawrence!' Two weeks later Paul called for me from the front of the house. 'Lawrence!'

When I came out the front, Paul was unstrapping a large box from the back of his motorbike. 'I don't know if this is what you want, but it's a start. Not the most expensive, but not the cheapest either.'

'Wh-wh-wh-wh . . .'

'I bought them in Melbourne.'

I could hardly believe it. 'Y-y-y . . . ?'

'Yes, all the way into the city. I made a day of it.'

I took the box from him. He had brought them to me. He had been to Melbourne. I loved him and hated him. Wanted to embrace him and to punch him.

'How's it going out here? You alright on your own?'

The box felt heavy.

'Lawrence?'

'Y-y-y-y . . . yes.' I wanted to be with the box. Did not want to speak with him.

'Good seeing you too, Laurie.' Paul pulled his helmet over his head. 'I'll come by in a few days with groceries.'

'Y . . . yes y-y-y . . .' I said over my shoulder.

I heard the roar of his motorbike as he drove away and did not mind that he had left and could ride as fast as that, and travel where he wanted. Buy paints in the city.

I carried the box into the house, placed it on the kitchen table, tore away the tape, and opened it. The paints were called *24 Stanmore's Oils* and came in a long white and silver tin. I opened the lid and picked up three tubes—Parisian blue, rose madder, viridian. My mouth watered. I counted five small canvases, five sketchbooks and a dozen drawing pencils. I unrolled a fabric pouch and found eight paintbrushes of different thicknesses. Paul!

I ran my hands over the canvases and the empty pages of the sketchbooks, and the pencils and the set of *24 Stanmore's Oils*. I remembered the day of my tenth birthday, when Mother gave me *The Lady Bold*. Paul and I as we left the house, heading for the stream, our imaginary ocean where the soldiers and pirates fought to the death. Now, here, with the paints in my hands, I thought, This is better. Better!

At the bottom of the box was a catalogue, like the catalogues Mother kept for clothing and sheets and household items. It read *Parker's Art Supplies, Melbourne.* I placed the catalogue carefully in Mother's desk and left the house. I found three long narrow pieces of wood, almost as tall as myself, at the side where Mother used to park the Austin. I intersected them at the top, using fence wire, then nailed another shorter plank midway, to make a shelf. 'There,' I said. 'There,' as the hammer went down.

After setting the makeshift easel in the middle of the kitchen, I rearranged the pochade box so that it could hold twelve of the oils and the palette, and three of the brushes from the roll. I placed fresh paper and one of the smaller canvases into the compartment beneath the lid. I took a leather belt from my cupboard and tacked each end to the pochade box so that it made a strap. The metal cup could be tied by the handle to the strap.

That evening I lit the fire in the wood stove, sat in Mother's rocker and studied the catalogue from Parker's. There were different kinds of paints listed: Horrings Water Palette, Genoa Oils, Thirty-six Colours Comprehensive, 12 Acrylic Starter Set. There was a multitude of drawing pencils: ebony Fabers, Derwents, Blendwels. There were crayons: Milton Bradley's broad lines, Ludwig soft pastels, Talens coloured. I turned the page and saw canvases of all sizes, 24 x 30 inches, 36 x 48 inches, 18 x 24 inches, then sketchbooks with paper of different kinds: Edgeley's, Normandy's, Artists Own. There was thick Dover's drawing paper, Edgeley's set paper, and Drawers Professional. There were pastels and inks and charcoals, as well as cleaning products. There were palettes, brushes and sponges. I rocked Mother's chair back and forth, back and forth, and the fire warmed my feet. Now there was a reason; a reason for a wage. I milked the cow and the milk went to the city and I was paid. The money went to Parker's, and the paint came back to me and that was how the world turned. 'Ha ha! Milk to paint, milk to paint, ha ha! What is the difference?' I spoke to my feet resting against the guard. 'What is the difference?'

I lay in bed that night and could not sleep. Although I had been on the earth for twenty-four years, it was as if my life was only beginning now. This was the first day the bird clock had ticked. I switched on the lamp, picked up *Letters from the Masters*, and turned to a painting by Master Millet. A field in spring, a rainbow arching over rain-filled clouds. I ran my fingers over the trees in the foreground, heavy with fruit, the path of dirt, the sky of blue and grey. Beside the painting was a letter by Master Millet to the historian Alfred Sensier. *I see far more in the countryside than charm, I see infinite splendours*. I switched off the lamp, closed my eyes and was there, beneath the rainbow in the field of infinite splendours.

The next afternoon, after I came home from the dairy, I walked out to the field with my pochade box over my shoulder and my easel under my arm. When I was halfway to the mountain, I dug the legs of the easel into the ground, then I rested my canvas across its shelf. I had intended to paint Wallis but found myself instead drawn upwards. The first layer of sky held dense white cloud after that palest blue.

Master Constable wrote in his letter to the Reverend John Fisher, *It will be difficult to name a class of landscape in which the sky is not the key note . . . The sky is the source of light in nature, and governs everything . . .* I had believed Wallis to be the central feature of so many of my paintings, but perhaps it was a trick of the eye. Master Constable said the sky was the governing feature, though the sky must appear incidental. I looked at the mountain, then above. It was the sky that showed me the nature of Wallis. It was the sky that gave me the mountain. 'Ha!' Here I was, twenty-four years old, and learning something new. Ha! I put my brush to the canvas. The sky was endless, and this work, this painting that I did unobserved, that so preoccupied me, this too had no end.

The oils Paul brought me allowed me the freedom of exploration; I could work on a single painting for days, travelling deeper, making changes, staying longer in the smallest of places. I was as a man who had been hungry all his life and was only now taking his dinner. There was nothing missing from my plate, nothing. I was eating, I was eating! I barely noticed cold or stammer or other workers able to sit and speak and drink tea together. These were of no concern to me. Painting was a play between my eyes and my hands, two parts that spoke to each other when other parts could not. I would think of painting as the cattle entered the herringbone, as I strapped the surcingle over their shoulders, as I listened to the pump of the surge, as I cleaned the pipes and swept the sullied water into the pit. I would see the painting and listen to it, for what it wanted from me, all the way home on the bus. And in the doing of these things—this work at the dairy, all the while thinking of my painting—the painting was unfolding, revealing itself to me whether I stood at the canvas or not. During my break I would inhabit a landscape of paint—burnt umber, gold ochre, brown oxide and red; the brush was ever at work, moving across the canvas, knowing where it was needed, my eyes open or closed.

Riding with Bill Granger in the truck, changing into my whites, milking and cleaning and sweeping and singing softly to the cows in their stalls. Tea and ham sandwiches on the hillock for my break—how satisfying it was to know what came next, and then to have it come next, as I guessed it would, knew it would, and there it was, without diversion or disappointment. Men were the same as cattle! As the cow made her way to the herringbone, the trail formed by a thousand times a thousand hooves upon the grass, so a man made his way to Hamilton Modern Dairy, did his work there, and headed home on the bus to his paints.

The bus ride was a drawn-out anticipation of the work that would begin as soon as I was home, a work that called upon a part that belonged to nobody but me. I inhabited two worlds: the man-made world of Hamilton Modern Dairy, and another world of sky, of landscape, of nature in translation. I could put my hands to my face any time of any day and smell a mix of dairy cow and oil paint.

29.

I MADE A LIST, BREAKING the words into single syllables. *Raw si-enn-a. Blue co-balt. Mag-en-ta.* I took my time choosing the colours, imagining how they might combine, the colour between colour. I stayed up late into the night putting the list together, preparing myself to speak it, practising the words, *Rankins mineral turpentine, two sable rounds, one sable fan, one filbert and two bristle flats.*

Picking up the catalogue, I dialled the number.

A woman answered. 'Parker's Art Supplies, Moira Parker speaking.'

'I-I-I. M-m-m . . .' I could not move past the first letter. 'I-I-I . . . I w-w-w-wou-wou . . .'

'Excuse me?' the woman said. 'Can I help you?'

'I w-w-w-w . . .'

'Yes?'

'I-I-I-I . . .' I could not speak. Could not make the words. There was a silence. I lowered the receiver.

'Please, can I help you? Hello? Can I help you?'

223

It was not possible. I turned my head to the window and saw Wallis overlooking Beverly, overlooking me inside Beverly's walls, using the telephone. All the ways he wanted to be seen with the paint I was trying to order.

'Are you there? Is anybody there? Hello?'

I raised the telephone. 'An or-der. I w-w-w-w-want to to to p-p-p-place an o-o-o-orr.'

'Oh yes. Good. Good. Thought I'd lost you then. I can help you with that. For pick up or delivery?'

'D-d-d-del . . .'

'Delivery. Good. Do you know what you want?'

'Y-y-y-y . . .'

'Good. That makes it easier. Do you want to tell me now?'

'Yes. Y-y-y . . .'

'I have a better idea. Could you give me your name, please?'

'L-L-L-Lawrence. My my my name is L-L-L-Lawrence. L-L-L-Loman. Lawrence Loman.'

'Well, Mr Loman, do you think you could send me a list of the products you wish to purchase? And an address? Then we can have them delivered and you can pay cash on delivery, if that suits.'

'Y-y-y-yes . . .'

'Good.' She was brisk and made me think of Mother. Knowing how to get the job done and not waste a minute. 'Will this be a regular order, or is this just a once-off?'

'R-r-r-reg . . .'

'Regular. Good. Perhaps the best idea, then, is if you send us a list, address it to me, Moira Parker, and I will make sure that everything is put together and packed right for postal. Alright? How does that sound, Mr Loman?'

'G-g-g-g-g-good. Very good.'

'Wonderful. I will be anticipating your list. You are in Victoria?'

'Y-y . . . yes.'

'Good. Shouldn't be too long then. Let me give you our postal address—though I take it you have the catalogue?'

'Y-y-y . . .'

'It doesn't matter. I will give it to you again regardless. Remember, cash on delivery or it will be returned. Are you ready with a pen?'

'Y-y-yes.'

'Here we go then. Parker's Art Supplies, Attention Moira Parker—that's me—Moira Parker, 7 Tribble Lane, Melbourne 3000. Got all that?'

'Y-y-yes.'

'Good, Mr Loman. I look forward to receiving your list.'

'Th-th-th-thank you.'

'Goodbye, sir, and have a nice day.'

I wrote a new list for Moira Parker, as tidy as I could. *Scarlet, crimson, cobalt, aquamarine. Fabriano 36 sheets, Canson 36 sheets, Tiziano 36 sheets.* Master Ensor wrote, *I love to draw beautiful words, like trumpets of light.* The written word held more of the light than the spoken. My own trumpets of light ran straight across, all made of letters, each one sitting on an invisible seat, the *g* with its long tail, the *i* and the *j* with their dots. The *t* and the *l* and the *f* standing tall, like miniature umbrellas for the word beneath. What a joy it was to make a word, each one with its own shape, to communicate its meaning. It was a list not only for me, it was for another. *Moira Parker*. Moira Parker was Master Fuseli's Charis, listening while Thetis attempted to explain.

After I had completed the list, I folded it in two and placed it in an envelope from Mother's desk. I wrote the address for *Parker's Art Supplies* on the face of the envelope, *7 Tribble Lane, Melbourne 3000, To the Attention of Moira Parker*, then pressed a stamp of Queen Elizabeth onto its top right corner.

The next morning, I set off for the postbox at the end of Hughlon West Road. I did not think I would see anybody from the town of Hughlon. I might see trucks on their way to the orchard or the sheep farm. But fewer on a Sunday. I might not see anyone at all. The road was my own. Spring's wildflowers lined the road. Parrot peas and lilies and pink fuchsia. Wallis and the family of mountains behind him was to my right. I could turn to him and hear his silence as I might hear it from the summit. I could imagine that pathway. My legs took up a swing of their own, each stride moving my thoughts forwards into new paintings and the list in its envelope, on its way to Moira Parker. At the same time as having thoughts I observed the landscape, hay in fresh-cut rolls, the tracks of the tractors through the wheat, the crisscross of fences, the passing clouds, the kestrels and the parrots, the green of the grass in spring, each blade its own shade, each and every living thing its own colour, its own nature. I sang, *'Reach for the sky, reach for the sky, hands up high, hands up high, we are climbing sunshine mountain, you and I, you and I!'*

There at last, where the road forked one way to Hughlon Consolidated and one way to Hamilton Modern Dairy, was the red postbox waiting for my letter to Moira Parker. I read the words that I had printed on the envelope. *Parker's Art Supplies, To the Attention of Moira Parker*. I touched the words, briefly, then placed the envelope into the box.

30.

SHERBOURNE CANVASES OF ALL SIZES leaned against the walls of the corridor, the lounge, the laundry and the bedrooms. Even the sides of the bathtub. Every room was covered in different aspects of the landscape. The natural world up close, and from afar. The landscape in rain, hail and sunshine. Sky where the cloud was like a wide dark lid, a layer over the fields. Sky where cloud was pulled apart like white wool. Sky with cloud in plumes like smoke. Cloud lit with gold.

When Paul came, he frowned, and said, *For God's sake*. He could never stay long. He brought food—oats, bread, cheese, ham and beef strips, taking money from Mother's account to pay for it. I wanted to see him, had waited for him, listening for the sound of his engine on the road, and then as soon as he was there, I wanted him to leave. Did not want him to hear me speak or see the way I lived. But then weeks would pass, and I would again listen for the sound of his engine on the road.

Once he came to the house smelling of flowers.

'Wh-wh-wh-what is that s-s-smell?'

'What smell?'

'F-f-f-f-flowers, flowers, r-ro-ro-roses. H-h-h-h-honey.'
I sniffed him.

He blushed. 'It's Ruth.'

'Wh-wh-wh-wh-who . . . ?'

'The girl I am going to marry.'

I hated him.

I ordered supplies from Moira Parker every few months. After I sent the order, the questions would begin: *When will the postal van arrive with my paints? When?* I found myself looking at the mud and the ground and the grass and wondering could I make my own viridian? My own umber? My own crimson from Mrs Barry's camellia flowers? Could I still paint if the postal van never came? I would have to ask Paul, but I did not want to ask Paul. Did not want to ask him ever again.

Every day I hoped I might arrive home from Hamilton Modern Dairy and see the postal van coming down the road, even though I knew full well that the van did not come until four o'clock. And even after four o'clock, at the same time as hoping, I did not believe that it was possible. That I, Lawrence Loman, might cause such an event, like the delivery of a box from Parker's Art Supplies. It was not possible, and yet I hoped that it was. Every truck I heard pass along the road, I would go to the front door to see if it was the postal van. And it was not the postal van. If there had not been a delivery in some time, I chose not to climb the mountain, not to leave the house, and to wait instead. Day after day after day. Then, on one of my days of waiting, when I thought I could bear it no longer, I would hear the sound of the postal van and then I would go out the front to see the postal van parked on the grass.

I had caused the box to arrive. I had sent the list. I had not needed Paul. I was sure the box would not arrive, and it had arrived. My name was written on the boxes—*To Lawrence Loman*. I was he. Paul had withdrawn the money for me in preparation and I had had it ready since making the order. *Parker's Art Supplies, To the Attention of Moira Parker*. Charis to my Thetis. I would give the driver the envelope and take the boxes inside. I would look at the boxes and understand a chain of happenings that included me. My first telephone call to Parker's, a man of twenty-four years, my list in the mail, Moira Parker's reading of the list, her packing of the boxes, their journey from Melbourne to Hughlon, and finally their arrival at my door. The transformation then of paint into image. I had earned the money milking the cows at Hamilton Modern Dairy. The milk was delivered to the townspeople and the hospitals and the schools the way the arts supplies were delivered to me.

31.

THE COWS WERE IN THEIR stalls and I was at the top of the row, when I saw a small boy enter the pit. He walked slowly past the cows until he came to me.

'Does it hurt?' he asked.

'Wh-wh-what?'

'The thing—the thing that does the milking, on the cow, does it hurt?'

'Th-th-th-thing? The s-s-s-surge?'

'Yes.'

'I-I-I d-d-d-don't th-th . . . N-n-n-no.'

He crouched nearer to the cow's udder. 'It looks as if it should hurt, though, doesn't it?'

The boy wore a brown jumper patterned with black diamonds, and gumboots that appeared too large. His hair stuck up in knots at the back of his head as though it was not long since he had left his bed.

'Colin! Colin!' I heard a man calling. It was Mr Roy Pease, the crop manager. I turned and saw him silhouetted in the light at the end of the pit. 'Colin, what did I tell you? You are not to come down here. Stay out of the way of the animals!'

'Better go,' the boy said to me, and walked quickly to Mr Pease. Mr Pease ushered him out and the boy was gone. I wondered if Mr Pease was the boy's father. But why would he have the boy here with him? There had never been a boy or a child here before.

I returned to my work, releasing the cow from the surge. At tea break I took my flask to the hillock and sat facing in the direction of Wallis. I poured tea from my flask and unwrapped my bread and cheese as the sunshine warmed my back.

I could see the cows that would soon calve in the nearby field, bulging with the new life. Soon there would be poddies. The cows were black-and-whites, like Gert. It was contrast that showed colour. It was not black on its own, it was black against white; it was not blue on its own, it was blue against white and green and black.

I sipped my tea, ate my apple and stretched my legs in the grass. I wondered how to paint the grass so the field could be revealed, along with the individual blades themselves. For there was no field, there were only the blades of individual grass that made it.

I looked around for the boy.

That afternoon I came home and walked through the house, expecting Mother. My solitude came to me afresh every day since she died. I poured myself water from the tap and looked through the window over the sink. 'Where did you go, Mother?'

I left the house with my easel under my arm, and the pochade box strapped over my shoulder. Perhaps the answer to the question, Where did Mother go? was contained within the act of painting.

Perhaps that was why I did it so often since she died. Every time the landscape asked to be painted—the mountain, the fields, the valleys—it was trying to reveal to me something about its living self, but it was also an attempt to answer the broader question, Where did Mother go? And not only Mother, but also Mrs Barry, Father over the Atlantic, and everybody else who once lived. To paint the living was to express its temporary nature, its fleeting beauty. Where had it come from and where did it go? Master Pissarro's sunsets, Master Friedrich's mountains, Master Turner's skies, as much as they were about the subject, were about the world beyond the subject. Where Mother was.

I looked about me as I pushed through the stile, at the fields and the range of mountains and the bright grey winter sky. The world without Mother was enormous. As if it had expanded in her absence. I was more aware than I had ever been of change in the natural world, and of beauty. Any decision I made about which aspect I liked best was challenged by the one that followed. It was the beginning of winter, cold and subdued. A time when nature concealed its colours, a time for introspection, for seeing unassuming detail. This was the time that was the richest. Though I would think the same no doubt when the first buds of spring showed their colours!

I set up the canvas in the field, and as I painted the range behind Wallis, rolling across the sky in a series of sharp peaks, up and down like a sea of hard stone and rock, I felt myself emptied into the landscape and filled by it, and it was not until I was walking home that I thought again of the boy in the milking parlour.

It was as I was returning to the sheds after the tea break the following day that I saw him. He was trailing his hand along the fence that ran the length of the calving field. I never saw boys anywhere. Paul and I were once boys. Everyone then was a boy. Boys poured from the gates of Hughlon Consolidated, boys at Paul's cricket matches, boys filling the school bus. I was among them, and I was just the same. But that was long ago. A lifetime. I walked slowly, watching him, as he stopped to swing back along the fence, looking up, his head tilted to the sky, his hair dark and untidy. Today he wore a green jumper.

I was close enough now to hear that he was singing. '*Oranges and lemons say the bells of St Clement's, You owe me five farthings say the bells of St Martin's . . .*' Trailing his hand up and down the fence, then swinging back, holding the rail with both hands and looking to the sky. '*When will you pay me, say the bells at Old Bailey, When I grow rich say the bells at Shoreditch.*'

I did not want to look away; the dairy buildings behind the boy, the blue sky above, the calves in the poddy field, the boy singing at the fence. How would it be to render such a scene in paint, a scene that included a boy?

He swung around and saw me. 'Hello.'

I nodded. I did not want to speak. Did not want my voice in the same picture as the boy.

He let go of the fence and came towards me. 'Have you finished the milking?'

He was so much smaller than me, smaller than anyone I had seen for a long time.

'Y-y-y-yes. Yes.'

'So what are you going to do now?'

His face was open, his eyes blue. It was as if he had looked at the sky so long, swinging from the fence, his face upturned, that the sky had gone inside his eyes.

Across the way I saw the other men heading back to work. I began to walk towards the parlour. Mr Brommell did not stand lateness.

The boy came with me. 'I am here because my mother is away and it's holidays from school. She had to go because her own mother is ill. I have to come with my father to work because of that. Otherwise I would be seeing my friends at home.'

I did not speak.

'Dad won't let me near the cows. I would like to give them a pat when the suckers are on and tell them it will soon be over. But Dad thinks I might get kicked. He wants me to stay in the house. Do you think I would get kicked?'

I wanted, suddenly, to smile. 'I-I-I d-d-d-don't think th-th-th-they w-w-w-would would m-m-mind.'

The boy did not seem to notice how long it took for me to answer. He waited.

'I think I could be their friend. Do you think I could be their friend?'

'Y-y-y-yes,' I said. 'Yes.'

We were at the entrance to the parlour; I raised my hand to him before going inside.

All the way home on the bus I thought about the things the boy said. He was on holidays from school, he would like to go nearer to the cows, could he be their friend? As I walked to the base of Wallis, as I did my painting of the first trees, as I picked fuchsias and black-eyed Susans and returned to Beverly, placing flowers in the jar, eating sardines and beans from their cans, wiping the bench and rinsing the cup, I imagined answering his questions. *The cows won't kick you, no, boy; here, come closer and see where the surge goes and come and touch her, she won't kick, there is nothing to fear.*

When I went outside to gather kindling, I spied a small bird's nest fallen to the ground.

I brought the nest inside and placed it on the table. I lit the wood stove, then I sat in Mother's rocker and read Master Ingres' letter to his friend, M. Varcollier. *I so much enjoy giving free rein to my pen on subjects of which I know you are as fond as I am that it brings tears to my eyes, and makes me tremble with a happiness I cannot describe.*

'*A happiness I cannot describe,*' I said into the quiet of the kitchen.

I looked to the nest on the table.

I opened my sketchbook and sharpened my drawing pencil. My pencil made its strokes, *sh sh sh* across the paper, in time with the crickets and the frogs, and the tick of the bird clock. I had never made a drawing for anybody. It was the subject itself I did the drawing for, and then, when it was done, it was time for the next subject. But this time the boy, Colin, was part of the drawing. The image shaped itself around my efforts to share something with him. It was a different way to work, and the tenderness I felt for the subject I felt also for the object, which was the boy, Colin.

When I looked at what I had done I saw and experienced for myself the care with which the mother bird had made the nest. How vital was the nest, for without it there was no home for the life that was to come. And because I had made the drawing with the boy in mind, in a sense, for him, the drawing, was an act of communication. *A happiness I cannot describe.*

I pinned the drawing to the wall over the rocker.

That night in Mother's bed I dreamed of colour. I could not discern any single shape or character. The colours moved apart and around me. Each colour had a voice not made by a body. In the dream the language made sense. I too was colour only. But when I woke in the morning there was no sense. Only feeling. Warm and pleased.

After preparing my lunch and my flask of tea, just as I was about to put the nest into my satchel, I looked up and saw last night's drawing pinned to the wall. I unpinned it and folded it carefully around the nest. Then I pushed the parcel into the satchel.

I had never sought out another person at the dairy before. Had never waited for anybody. I knew my position. Sometimes Peter Boer and Jock might pay me attention. *H-h-h-h-how are you today, L-L-L-L-Lawrence? You o-o-o-okay?* But mostly they left me alone; Mr Brommell liked his workers to get on, and any reports of trouble he took steps.

Mr Roy Pease, the boy's father, worked Mr Brommell's wheat crops and did not come into the parlour. So why was I looking down the row of stalls for the boy when it was not likely he would appear? The boy knew he was not to enter the herringbone—his father had warned him only the day before. And yet, all the while the cows were in the stalls, flicking their tails and letting down their milk, I looked for him. I found myself impatient for the tea break, which I never had been before, in case I might see him. Time was slow to pass. I was separate to the cows, did not feel grateful for the milk they gave, the warmth from their coats, their gentle eyes. Instead I was cross with them when they shuffled sideways or kicked at the surge. As if they were responsible for the boy's absence. The cows!

Finally, the bell rang for tea break. I took my satchel from the locker and walked to the hillock. I hardly tasted my tea or my bread. I kept searching for the boy but saw only the usual things: the cows now relieved and grazing; the men smoking outside the sheds; the milk trucks parked outside the parlour. Everything in its place. Why was I waiting for him? Colin was a boy, here at the dairy because his mother was away. It made no sense to wait for him. But I found myself continuing to look for him regardless, as though the looking for him came from a part of myself that did not ask the question why and did not give up.

At the end of the break I threw the remains of my tea at my feet and watched as the droplets seeped into the grass. He was not coming. I was not going to see him again.

But as I got to my feet, there he was, walking around the side of the sheds. He waved at me. Today he wore the brown jumper with the row of black diamonds. I had wanted to see him so much; now to see him was pleasing beyond my understanding. I felt again within me the dream of colour.

I walked towards him, seeing too the scene that held him: the dairy sheds, Master Corot's grazing cattle, the clean blue sky.

'I almost didn't come today,' he said. 'I nearly went with my aunt instead. But I'm glad I came. I saw the truck that waits to take the milk. All the cans they have to lift. What if there was a crash? What if the milk spilled on the road?'

I kept my satchel over my shoulder. When I was at home it was easy to imagine myself giving the nest to the boy, but here, now, it was not as I had pictured. I did not want anyone to see me give the boy the nest. I wished for privacy with him. But how was that to happen? Where could we go?

'How was the milking this morning? Did the cows try and kick anyone?' The boy asked me as if he had seen the milking too many times to count and was sorry to have missed it this time.

'No no no no tr-tr-trouble. N-n-n-n-no kick-kick-kicking.'

When I spoke the boy's blue eyes were calm; no shadow crossed them as a shadow crossed Paul's eyes and Mother's eyes and the eyes of the other workers at Hamilton Modern Dairy and every teacher and child at Hughlon Consolidated. In the boy's eyes there was space and time. I could not imagine reaching their end. Like the eyes of Master della Francesca's Child, they were patient. 'Th-th-the c-c-c-cows g-g-g-g-gave no no no no trouble.'

'Only milk.'

'O-o-o-only milk.' Ha!

Just before we were in full view of the sheds, when I could see no other workers, I stopped and took my satchel from my shoulder. I unbuckled the satchel and pulled out the parcel, a little crushed, and held it out to the boy.

'What is it?'

'O-o-o-open it.'

He opened the paper and saw the nest. 'Where did you find it?'

'At at at my my h-h-house. At my house. In the g-g-g-grass.'

'Your house?'

'Y-y-y-yes. Yes.' Nobody stopped us or saw us. 'L-l-l-l-look.' I showed him the drawing of the nest on the crumpled paper.

'Oh . . . it's a drawing. A drawing of the nest.'

I nodded.

'Did you do it?'

'Y-y-yes.'

'It looks real.'

'Y-y-yes.'

He looked closely at the nest itself. 'I hope the mother made another and there were no smashed eggs.'

'No no no s-s-smashed e-e-eggs.'

He held the nest up, turning it around so he could see underneath. 'It would have done a very good job.'

'Y-y-y-y-yes.'

Each time I spoke, he waited. Then I heard the hoses turned on and the scrape of the shovels on the cement as the men returned to work.

The boy came with me as I walked to the sheds. Peter Boer was at the gate and looked across at me and then at the boy.

Colin said, 'Thank you for the nest. And for the drawing. When I find some eggs in need of a home, I will put them in the nest. Then I will put the nest in a tree and perhaps the mother will come back and sit on the eggs.'

'Y-y-y-yes.'

'I will still have the drawing to remind me.'

'Y-y-es.'

Colin ran off in his too large gumboots, as if he was on his way right then, at that very moment, to find eggs. I watched him, so much smaller than everybody else, his knotted hair, his narrow legs.

That day, when I saw Peter Boer speaking with Jock and Mr Pease, and the three turning to look at me, I was above them, like Master Runge's angels.

When I came home that afternoon I wanted very much to paint. But I had no clean canvases and did not wish to work into one of my old paintings. Nor did I have any clean drawing paper. I had made an order with Moira Parker and was waiting on the delivery.

I took up a pile of old newspapers that had been left under the sink. I went outside with the remains of my watercolour paints and faced Wallis on the porch. But he was not the driving subject.

I laid the newspaper out across the boards and began to paint. Soon the boy's eyes appeared before me over the words. *A new prime minister* . . . His dark and knotted hair. *Fuel prices continue to rise* . . . His chin, his cheeks. *Last Sydney tram* . . . I had to imagine for myself the distance between the ear and the curve of the neck, the brow and the nose, the eye and the forehead. *Queen is flying home today* . . . *HMAS* Vengeance *returned* . . .

I painted twelve sheets of newspaper. Each painting the boy emerged more clearly. Each painting simpler, with fewer lines, less paint. I hardly needed him there to show him. At sunset, I took the paintings inside and pinned them to the walls. I stood back and saw Colin's face beside drawings of leaves and drawings of rhubarb and drawings of Gert's hooves. I did not object to using newspaper; it was contrast and contradiction that created meaning.

But by the time night fell, watercolour on newspaper was not enough. I looked through the various canvases that leaned against the walls, some half-finished and discarded. I chose a smaller canvas, 18 x 24 inches, where I had painted a path that led into the trees, just before the track that led up the mountain.

I was not accustomed to using the oils indoors at night. I finished my painting with daylight, then, if I was so inclined, drew with my pencils. But tonight, with the fire lit in the stove, the smell of oil paint thick in the house, I painted the boy on the path. He was unobserved. Like other subjects there was something inside him that could not be seen with the naked eye. Only I could see it. Because it was seen *through* me. In that moment of painting the boy, I understood that I was a filter—it was landscape as seen through me. Still life as seen through me. I understood, then, that I was in every painting, and I was here too, with the boy.

It was the light that struck me. It came from the sky but also emanated from him, the subject and central focus of the painting. He shone with light. He wore no shirt. I had not intended that the boy wear no shirt. I had seen him in his woollen jumpers— brown and green. He now appeared in his long trousers, his upper body dressed only by the light.

Tomorrow was Sunday. I would not see Colin until Monday. But I had the painting and could work into it as long as I needed. White into the sky, darker green on the first tree. The field in which the boy stood was a rich flax, in contrast to his dark hair.

The boy was oblivious to me. He was alone in the image, and that was the strength of the picture; his solitude, in the light.

32.

ON MONDAY MORNING, SITTING IN Bill Granger's truck,
I thought, it will not be long now.

'They say the sun is meant to shine today,' Bill Granger said.

'Y-y-y-yes.'

'So they say.'

Bill Granger had taken me to work in his truck all these years
because Louise had asked him to; he had rarely spoken to me.
But this morning he had done so.

'Yes, s-s-s-sun.'

I looked for the boy as soon as I was out of the truck. I looked
for him on my way to the parlour, I looked for him as I was
cleaning the udders of the cows, I looked for him as I attached
the surge, knowing at the same time that he was not there, that
I would not see him for many hours.

When it was time for the morning break, I took my flask and
my sandwich and went to the hillock. I drank the tea to soften
the bread, and watched the sky, the high curving grey clouds,

the white clouds drifting beneath, and thought, It will not be long now. But I did not see Colin in the morning break. Nor did I see him when I returned to the sheds.

My chest tightened. I had been certain I would see him. I had imagined it with every brushstroke from Saturday afternoon to Monday morning. I thought, since I did not see him in the morning break, I would see him at the lunch break. But what if I did not see him at the lunch break? What if I did not see him at all?

I looked for him every minute, whether I knew he would be there or not. He did not come at the lunch break, and he was not there in the afternoon. I did not want to clean and stack the tanks, did not want to put out the hay, did not want to brush out the surges. Did not care for Alan's words when he told me I had done well.

As I walked to the bus, Peter Boer called out, 'Waiting for your f-f-f-f-friend?'

Jock laughed and Peter Boer spat on the ground.

In the bus on the way home I did not look through the window for the mountains or think of climbing Wallis or wonder what I might paint next. I thought of the boy. The longer I did not see him the more I wanted to see him, and the more I wanted to see him, the greater my doubt that I would. There was no separation between pain and the boy. The stammer lodged in my thoughts. I hoped I would see him, was sure I would. What had made me sure? It was because I had wanted it, and that was all. The boy did not think of me. Why would he? The longing to see him was replaced with a shame, greater than the pain of his absence.

When I arrived home, I did not know what to do. I did not want to climb the mountain, did not want to paint. I turned away from the image of the boy on the canvas, went into the kitchen and raised my eyes to the beam. How long had it been since I had looked to it? There it was. Its familiar grain, its notches, its uneven stain. I decided I would leave the house; the beam would still be there when I returned. I walked down to the bottom of the yard and through the fence to Mrs Barry's garden. I took the gardening fork that was stuck in the dirt and began to turn over the rows of earth and cut the dead leaves away from the cabbages that grew. I pulled up three potatoes and two carrots.

I went inside with the potatoes and the carrots. I lit the wood stove and as I crouched before its open door, the flames catching, I did not think of either the boy or the beam. I stood at the bench and cut the carrots and the potatoes and made myself soup with ham and carrot and potato. I stirred the soup, not looking away from the potatoes and the carrots that not long before had been growing in Mrs Barry's vegetable garden. I poured the soup into my bowl, making sure none spilled, keeping my attention with the bowl and the rising steam. I did not think or look beyond the soup.

As I lay in my bed I turned to the window and saw the stars in the night sky. The stars glittered. If I did not identify them as stars or sky, told myself no story about them, saw them without knowledge, without history or thought—the pain in my chest eased, and the question, *Will I see him again?* was silenced.

As soon as I arrived at the dairy the next morning, I began to search for him. I looked over the backs of cows, between stalls, and along the pit. I looked towards Mr Brommell's house, and out at the crops of wheat beyond the dairy, all the while my chest in a vice. Why could I not give up? I thought of the beam, its solid width above the kitchen, put there all the years before by Mrs Barry's father. The boy and the beam. Back and forth.

'Lawrence!' Colin called to me on my way to the bus stop at the end of my working day.

Peter Boer and Jock and Mr Roy Pease watched as the boy came to me.

'I found eggs.'

I did not care that the men watched me; I hardly saw them. They did not matter to me. It was the boy! I was seeing the boy! He was here! Real!

'One was smashed, and one was not. I put them both in the nest.' His face was bright and open. 'I found them on the ground. They had no mother.'

Every second of waiting for him had been worth it.

'I don't know if they will hatch. Do you think they will hatch?'

'I-I-I . . . I-I-I don't know.'

Even with the bus on its way, and Peter Boer and Jock and the boy's father close by, he was patient.

'I am keeping the nest inside, and I have put a blanket over the eggs. I stuck the drawing to the wall above the nest. Like a mirror.'

I could feel the stare of the other workers. 'I-I-I have to to to g-g-g-go.'

'Will you be here tomorrow?'

I nodded.

'There is something I want to show you. I'll see you tomorrow.'

*

246

I could not feel the ground beneath my feet as I walked along the road to the bus. Barely noticed the roll of thunder, the cold. Today I had seen Colin. When I did not see him on Monday, I had been certain I would never see him again. And today I had seen him.

As soon as I was home, I dropped my satchel on the table, not stopping for my pochade box, not considering which brush, which paint. I walked down through the yard, not stopping to say a word to the straw man, to pick a snail from a cabbage, to lean against the turnstile. The boy had said, *There is something I want to show you. I will see you tomorrow.* Tomorrow! As I strode through the field I was showered in rain, rain on my head, down my cheeks, under my collar. I was on my way to the mountain, as all about me grew the splendours of spring; tinsel lilies, grevillea, pink heath and, there ahead, Master Millet's rainbow.

That evening I sat in the rocker before the woodstove and read from *Letters from the Masters*. My painting of the boy leaned against the guard by my feet. The painting was not yet complete; the trees, the grass, the path itself—all needed work. I intended to take my time. As I sat, gently rocking, I drifted from the flames behind the glass, to the book—*Barque of Dante, View of a Rocky Coast by Moonlight*—to the boy in my painting. The light and its source.

After my dinner, I lay in the bath in darkness, my clothes floating around me. Colin had thought about me as he searched for eggs and a blanket to cover them, he thought about me as he chose the right place for the nest on his shelf, as he placed my drawing above the nest, he thought about me just as I was thinking about him now.

I stepped out of the bath and peeled off my clothes, leaving them in a wet pile at my feet. I stood naked, dripping bath water. I had learned not to look down at my body. If I did not look down, I had no body. But now, in the darkness of the small bathroom, I placed my hands against my chest, felt the muscle, the bones, the damp hair. Colin had searched for the eggs because I had given him the nest. He had put my drawing on his wall. I had caused these things to happen. To the boy, I was real, as he was real to me. I lowered my hands, to my privates.

I did not ask for them, did not ask for any part of my body. For what purpose were they put there? I shivered. Was it this way for others? Or was it only my own privates that carried a warning?

I took the towel from the rail and dried myself, then I went to the bedroom. I got into the bed, without dressing, pulling the covers over myself. I could feel all the parts of my body where the sheet touched. I was still damp. My skin tingled. I could still feel my privates without touching them.

I rolled to my side. I was almost twenty-five years old. I was not like Paul. Paul and Ruth. Paul working at his garage, repairing cars. Paul in the world away from Beverly, and from me. He had always been with girls and liked girls. He had told Mother. He had said, *I like her, Mother, I like her, she is pretty. I think I will take her out, Mother, what do you think? Do you like her?*

What did I like? I had no knowledge of what I liked. In the early morning, before I was properly awake, I felt a sweetness and a longing. But it was gone before I could name it, as if it were afraid.

The weight of the blankets, the sheet against my skin, my body growing warmer. I recalled the touch of our fingers as I passed Colin the nest within its drawing. I remembered it, over and over—him smiling first, or smiling after, the touch lasting a single second and then five seconds, him holding out his hands for the nest, me holding out mine. The story would begin at the beginning; his face, curious as I opened the satchel, the nest itself, the loosening weave, his eyes, the touch of our hands. Then it would draw to a close, only to begin again. At the same time as saying I could not have it, I allowed myself to take it. Again and again, all that night.

33

'THIS IS WHAT I WANTED to show you. See the troll?' Colin held a long ragged piece of bark.

It was my morning break and I was sitting with the boy on the hillock.

'Hidden in the wood. See?' He pointed. 'See? That's the nose. There.'

'Y-y-y-yes!' I did see the troll, its fierce mouth and eyes indented in the bark.

'And there is the chin, see?'

As he traced the line of the troll's chin our fingers touched.

'If you see it, that means it's real and that it could come to life. Did you know that?'

'N-n-n-no.'

'Your house, where you live, do you get scared there?'

'N-n-n-no.'

'But you live alone, don't you? My father said you did.'

'Y-y-yes.'

'But you don't get scared?'

'N-n-no.'

'Even if it came to life?'

'Wh-wh-what?'

'The troll. If the troll came to life. Would you be scared?' He raised the bark-troll, swinging it from side to side. *'Beware, beware, for I live in the forest, beware, beware for I live by the sea, beware, beware for I live in the mountain, beware, beware, for it's you that I see! Ooooooohhhh,'* he sang, his eyes wide. *'Ooooohhhh.* You take it.' He passed me the troll. 'I would get scared.'

Mr Roy Pease came from around the side of the shed. 'Colin!' he shouted. 'Up to the house!'

'I better go,' he said. 'I hope you don't get scared.' Then he was away, running back to his father, his legs ungainly, like the poddies', too long for his body.

I carried the troll with me to my locker, pushing it into my satchel. The boy sees things as I do, I thought. The hidden life.

Peter Boer and Jock stared at me. Peter Boer said, 'What did you put in your bag?'

'N-n-n-n-n-n . . .'

'What did he give you?'

'N-n-n-n-n-n . . .'

They came close. Jock said, 'You're a bloody weirdo.'

'N-n-n-n-n . . .'

Peter Boer said, 'I'm watching you. You aren't right in the h-h-h-head, L-L-L-L-Lawrence.'

'Al-al-al . . .'

'You're a freak. You only got the job because Brommell was after your old lady.'

'Right then, back to work,' Alan called from the door.

They left me alone. But I hardly cared about them. The boy

had given me a gift. I was Master Vidosky's prince receiving the crown in Malbork Castle.

When I arrived home that afternoon, I lifted the bark troll carefully from my satchel, running my fingers over his rough surface. Pieces of him had broken away and lay at the bottom of the leather. *'Beware, beware, for I live in the forest, beware, beware, for I live by the sea!'*

I placed the troll on the shelf, then I set up my easel in the lounge and began to work into the painting of the boy. It was the light from him, and from the sky, that explained the painting. The boy was on his way to the trees where he would no longer be seen; his light was fleeting.

Soon I found myself looking at things inside the house as if they might be a gift for the boy—the skeleton of a frog? The feather from a parrot? How old is he? I wondered. He must be ten. He is ten, I decided. What gift? Stone with a streak of crystal?

I sat in the rocker and ate my dinner of bully beef and cabbage in front of the wood stove, the image of the boy again at my feet, resting on the guard. Could I give him flowers dried the way Mrs Barry dried the roses? Could I draw him a bird? What about a painting? Leaving my plate on the floor, I looked through one of the stacks. I found a recent painting on a smaller canvas. It was the view from Wallis, just before a storm. I was pleased with the painting on the day I had completed it; the perspective was accurate, the great curving valley of trees that led to Abrupt, the turbulence in the sky overhead. I had been soaked on my return to Beverly, the canvas safely tucked under my coat. I smiled at the memory, placing the painting on the kitchen table.

*

'You did this?'

'Y-y-y-yes.'

We were sitting on the hillock, at my break.

He turned my picture in his hands. 'Is this what you like to do? Paint?'

'Y-y-y-yes.' I wanted to share it, tell him, as if it were a confession. 'Yes, I do.'

'Oh. It's really good.'

He pointed to a corner of the sky in the painting, a square of blue surrounded by grey and darker grey clouds. 'A storm is coming,' he said.

'Yes.' I pointed to the light on the other side of the canvas. 'Th-th-th-then it changes.'

There was life in that part of the sky that wanted to make itself known. It was the transition. The tension between light and dark, calm and storm.

'It's all weathers,' he said, 'in one sky.' I could feel his weight come and go against my side as he spoke.

'Yes. Yes.'

'Do you always know what you want to paint?'

'I-I-I . . . I don't know, don't know. Sometimes not until I am painting.'

'Oh. Yes. That's the same as me when I write a story at school—I never know what will happen. That's what I like about it.' He traced his finger around the frame of storm cloud in my picture. 'Where were you when you painted it?'

'I-I-I was up up on the m-m-m-mountain. On the the the to-to-top.'

'Which one?'

'M-M-M-M . . .' I tried again. 'M-M-M-M . . .' I did not think I could do it. What if I could never say the word? Never reach him? 'M-M-M . . .'

I could not do it.

I glanced at the boy. He was in no hurry. He was looking at my picture. Tilting the canvas one way, and then another.

I took a breath, noticed the cows grazing, the calves growing taller in the field next door, the smoke from the Brommells' chimney. I released the breath. 'It was Mount Wallis,' I said. 'I painted it from the top of Mount Wallis.'

'Do you live near there?'

'Yes,' I said.

He put his hand on my knee and turned his body to look back to the shed. At that moment Mr Roy Pease and Peter Boer and Jock came out of the milking parlour. Mr Roy Pease shouted, 'Come here now, boy!'

'I have to go,' the boy said, getting to his feet. He still held my painting in his hands.

I had not thought about where he might keep the painting once I had given it to him. I had not planned where he might hide it. For then I realised that I did want him to hide it; that I wanted him to keep it between us.

'I keep checking the eggs, but nothing has hatched.'

I watched him leave. I could see Peter Boer and Jock staring at me, caps low over their eyes as the boy walked towards them, carrying the canvas.

At home that evening, I wondered where the boy had put my painting. I hoped that it was in his own bedroom, for his eyes only. Perhaps he had put it with the drawing of the nest, perhaps they were together, the two pictures, the sky and the nest, somewhere hidden. I did not want Mr Roy Pease to see it, or a brother or a sister if he had one. The painting was just for him. When I next saw him, I would speak to him about it, *Colin, this is between us. Tell me you understand, I need to know you understand . . .*

What a comfort it was to open the gate for the herd the next morning. 'All easy,' I called. 'All easy.' I knew the hours would soon pass and Mr Roy Pease would bring his son to see me. What else does a man need but cows waiting at the gate, and a boy on his way?

At morning break, he came and sat down beside me on the hillock. 'Look,' he said, taking a paper from his pocket. He spread his drawing across our knees. 'It's called *Battle of the Vikings.*'

I looked at the drawing he had made; soldiers with horned helmets manned the deck of a boat on a stormy sea. Rafts carrying men dressed in cloaks were crossing the sea towards the boat. It made me think of Paul and our games. Were all boys the same everywhere?

I would ask him, in a moment, where he had put my painting. I would not interrupt his story, I would wait, and then I would ask him. *Where did you put my painting, Colin? Did anybody else see the painting?* I would tell him, *This is between us.*

'That's the sign of the clan,' he said, pointing to the red circle he had drawn on the sail. 'Those men are the Anglo-Saxons.'

Our heads were almost touching as we looked over the drawing.

'See the rafts coming across? They're the Franks. That's the enemy.'

Colin's hair fell over his face. His lips were the same colour as the inside of a strawberry.

'Oi!' Mr Roy Pease shouted down to us.

Neither of us moved as Mr Roy Pease marched across the grass. 'I told you to stay in the house!'

Colin called, 'But I don't want to stay in the house!'

Peter Boer and Jock watched from the fence.

Mr Roy Pease grabbed Colin's arm. 'Get up to the house now!'

'But . . . why do I . . . ?'

'Get up to the house!' He pushed Colin.

Colin started to cry. I heard a sound, like rushing water between my ears.

'But . . .'

'Go!'

Colin stumbled, crying, running across the grass towards the Brommell house.

Mr Roy Pease pushed me to the ground when I tried to stand, then he kicked me in the stomach. 'Dirty creep!'

I saw Peter Boer and Jock coming towards us. Mr Roy Pease kicked me again, in the stomach, the face. I put my hands over my eyes. Peter Boer picked me up by the collar and hit my nose and chin. When I fell, Jock kicked me in the backside.

Mr Roy Pease stood over me. 'I'll tell Brommell myself, don't worry about that.'

When I opened my eyes, his lines were blurred.

'Stay away from my son. Do you hear me?' He kicked me again in the backside. Then he walked away.

Peter Boer kicked me in my privates. 'I would have left you dead.'

Jock kicked me in the back. And again in my face. 'Better off dead.'

*

I could hardly see. I don't know how I stood, how I walked. I had to get home. There was pain down my back and in my stomach and privates. I had to keep going.

Soon I heard the horn of the bus. It pulled in, though we were not at the stop. The doors opened. It was Mr Dern. He looked at my blood-stained uniform then away as I reached for the railing, pulling myself up the steps. I was the only passenger.

Mr Dern closed the doors and the bus drove back out onto the road. Some time later—I don't know how long, had I slept?—I heard him call, 'Your stop.'

The doors opened. I almost fell down the steps.

There was Wallis, glowing and dark across the field. Did he see me? Did he care? I kept going. One foot in front of the other. Beverly was not much further, her red roof, her letterbox, her faded sign . . . at last I was home. I pushed open the door. There was the wood stove, the rocker, the cups and plates and pots and pans, my paintings and drawings. There was the troll in the bark.

I went to Mother's room and lay on the bed. Each blow I had been dealt opened a passageway for the pain. The pain rose above me; soon I could not see through it, like the mists that covered Wallis in winter. I closed my eyes. In my dream Colin hovered in the branches, above the people, his arms wide, like an angel in *The Birth of Venus*.

I did not know how much time passed. I did not know if it was night or day. I stayed in the bed. I was cold, shivering. I knew the door would soon open, and that he would come into the room, that I would rise towards him.

34.

I WOKE TO THE SOUND of the telephone. The room was in darkness. It was only ever Paul who rang on the telephone. I put my feet onto the floor. I was shaking. I looked down and saw that I was still wearing my uniform, *Hamilton Modern Dairy* written across the bloody pocket of my shirt. I saw my white gumboots, spattered with dried blood, on the floor by the bed. My throat burned. How long had I been in bed? I looked into the mirror over Mother's dresser and saw my face black and bruised. My left eye was swollen closed.

I went out of the room, moving slowly. I did not want my thoughts. Mr Roy Pease shouting at Colin, *Get up to the house now!* Colin crying. Peter Boer hitting me.

I made it to the kitchen sink and the telephone stopped ringing. Each thought was as much pain as a boot to the side. *Stay away from my son.* Peter Boer standing over me. *I would have left you for dead.* I took a glass and placed it under the tap, turned on the water. *But I don't want to stay in the house!* The boy's cry.

As the glass filled, I looked to the beam over the kitchen. I kept my eyes on the beam as I drank. I sat in Mother's rocker, holding the empty glass, my eyes on the beam. The telephone rang again and again. I was both hot and cold and was reminded of another time I was both hot and cold, many years before. I kept my eyes on the beam and thought of Mother's milking stool. The way Mother would tuck the stool in close to Gert's side as she worked. I thought of the rope coiled on its nail in the shed. I do not know how long I was there, rocking in Mother's chair, night becoming day, day becoming night, picturing the way the rope would swing over the beam. I do not know what time it was when I stood from the rocker.

I opened the back door and stepped down from the porch. There was Wallis in the clouds. What was he? He did nothing. Changed nothing. Could not see me. If he was pulled apart, and lay in pieces on the ground, he would not grow again. I went on my way to the shed, the grass icy beneath my bare feet. Then something caught my eye in the bottom corner of the yard—the door to the bunker in the sloping ground. I stopped in my tracks. I had not noticed or thought about the bunker for many years. Passing the shed, I crossed to the bunker door. Hooking my fingers through the iron handle, I took a breath, then pulled. The door did not open. I pulled again. The door stayed tight. One more time, I thought.

The bunker was filled with dirt, almost up to the frame that held the door. Room only for one boy of nine years old to hide, if the door was closed over him. I scooped up a handful of the dirt. I remembered the feeling of Wallis above the earth as I lay underneath. I remembered Paul calling from the other side. I stood and walked back to the house.

Once inside I did not look to the beam; I thought of the space on the other side of the bunker door. I filled the kettle and set it on the stove to boil. I shook tea-leaves from the jar into the tin pot. I put three spoons of sugar in my cup. As I poured the boiling water from the kettle into the pot, I thought of the rabbit warren that Paul and I had found in the field. The way the deepest burrow was lined with fur pulled from the mother's body. When I was in the bunker it had reminded me of the rabbit's burrow. Fur-lined, close and dark. The earth all about me.

I walked out onto the porch with my tea—steam from my breath mingling with steam from the cup. The tea was sweet and warming.

I returned to the shed. I took the shovel from against the wall without looking to the stool or the coil of rope, and crossed to the bunker. I began to dig out the dirt from behind the door. I was aware of the pain in my body, but it was separate to me, as though there was a twin outside of me and the pain belonged to him. I kept digging, striking the shovel into the hard-packed dirt. I pitied the twin but could do nothing to help him. I repeated the same action, striking the shovel into the hard-packed dirt, tossing the dirt into the grass beside the door. The dirt had been there since Paul and I were boys and did not want to shift. But I kept going, all thoughts contained within the action while the twin standing beside the door ached and burned. Striking the shovel into the earth, gathering the hard-packed dirt, and throwing it into the grass beside the slope. I would not go to Hamilton Modern Dairy again—in went the shovel. I would not see the cows again—in went the shovel. It would be Peter Boer who opened the gate—in went the shovel. In went the shovel, I will not see you again, Colin.

I was weak. My throat was on fire. I dropped the spade beside the pile of dirt and walked up to the house. After drinking from the tap, I took two apples from the bowl and sat on the porch in the canopy swing. I sliced the apples into pieces and looked at Wallis as I rocked the canopy swing. He was purple. The sky around him white and silver and grey. I watched night fall around me, remaining in the canopy swing until it seemed the air was made of ice. I was enveloped in so much cold I grew warm within it. Then hot. I went inside and climbed into Mother's bed, pulling the covers over me. I saw Wallis through the window, tall in his purple coat, lavender hat atop his head, like the pigeon's crest.

I did not know what time of day it was when I was woken again by the telephone. The ground tipped and swayed as I left the bedroom. I went into the kitchen and picked up the receiver. 'Y-y-y-yes . . . ?' Each time I spoke to Paul the same humiliation.

'Lawrence? Lawrence? Are you alright?'

'Y . . . Y . . . Y . . .'

'Why didn't you answer before? What happened? You know I was about to get on the bike and come over. What happened at the dairy?'

'N . . . n . . . n . . .' I was tired of it. The days of trying to speak were coming to an end.

'When are you going back?' He never once waited for me to finish.

'N . . . n . . . n . . .'

'Lawrence, I have spoken with Brommell—he is expecting you to return to work. What happened?'

'I . . . I . . . I . . .'

'You have to go back, Lawrence.'

'N . . . n . . . n . . .'

'You need the job.'

'I . . . I . . . I . . .'

'What the hell happened?'

'N . . . n . . . n . . .'

'Alan said there was a fight. Did somebody hurt you?'

'N . . . n . . . n . . . no.'

'I know some of those guys are trouble. Peter Boer. And his mate. I can speak to them . . .'

'No . . . no . . .'

All the years in the schoolyard, Paul to my defence, fists held high. The long ride home on the bicycles that first day. *Why do you talk like that, Lawrence?* I hated him.

'Lawrence?'

'N-n-n-n-n . . . N-n-n . . . No! No!'

'Alright! Settle down . . . settle down . . . I'll come around on Friday. We can talk about it then. Brommell says you can take the week.' He hung up the telephone.

I looked through the window; it was growing dark, but I did not light the wood stove. Was barely aware of the cold, or of my hunger. Still wearing my muddy uniform, I returned to Mother's bed. The boy had cried. He did not want to go to the house. I felt a weight against my chest. How many days since I had seen him?

I turned my face to the wall and pictured the growing pile of dirt beside the slope that held the bunker door. I thought of the shovel striking the earth, tossing the dirt into the grass, the space on the other side of the door growing deeper.

*

When I next opened my eyes, there was sunlight through Mother's window. My left eye stung. When I moved there was pain that spread from my privates, throughout my back, to my neck, shoulders and jaw. Pain began in the privates, as if that was their function, to disperse it to the rest.

I thought of Colin's face and was gripped with pain. I pulled myself up and put my feet to the ground. My heart pounded. I got up out of Mother's bed, left the bedroom and went through to the back door. I looked down to the bunker. I could see the pile of dirt on the grass beside the slope. I took a deep breath. Wallis was dark at his base, grey cloud swirling about his head. My heart slowed as I breathed in the air so cold it burned.

I went inside, and took the jar of oats from the cupboard. I poured some into the pot and added water, stirring the pot over the stove. When the porridge was ready, I stood on the porch in my bare feet and ate as the pigeons and warblers called to each other across the yard.

At first, I did not think I could do it, the muscles in my back were so tight and torn. But I soon warmed up, and after a time, I could not feel anything but the shovel breaking the earth, gathering the dirt, tipping the dirt into the grass. Whenever I looked up, there was Wallis, the sky moving about him. I was suspended between the mountain and the growing pile of dirt as the sweat dripped from my forehead.

When I no longer had the strength to dig, I stepped out of the sloped tunnel, and saw that it was much deeper, and was made of a steel floor and steel sheet walls on four sides. Tomorrow I would continue. *Knock knock*.

*

I lost count of how many days I worked at the bunker. My body continued to dig in my dreams. The striking of the earth, the tossing of the dirt, the deepening space. One morning I went down to the bunker, opened the door and saw it with fresh eyes; it must have been two foot by three foot, was made of two walls, a roof, a floor that sloped into the earth, all built from corrugated iron. The bunker was deep enough now that fire could pass over the ground above, protecting whoever was inside. I stepped down the sloped metal floor. Underneath the sheeting on one side the bunker went deeper, into the earth itself. I turned to Wallis, solid and grey over Beverly. 'Wallis,' I said, then closed the bunker door behind me.

I pulled the bunker door closed over my head.

There was no light. I made my way down the slope, crawling into the deeper space under the wall on one side. I pulled off my uniform and felt the cool earth pressing against my skin. I shut my eyes, breathed deeply.

I came to rest the way I did when I was a boy and Paul was on the other side of the door. When I was held by the earth, with only the mountain who knew. Safe as the rabbit. I listened to my own breath until I could not hear it at all. Until I had no body, and was outside of my thoughts, living without living.

35.

PAUL WAS IN MY KITCHEN. 'You have to, Lawrence,' he said.

'N-n-n-n . . .'

'I've spoken to Mr Brommell. He's had a talk with the men.'

'N-n-n . . .'

'Lawrence. These things happen.'

'N-n-n-n . . . No, Paul. No.'

'Just like that? What are you going to do about money?'

'M-M-M-Mother l-l-l-left me m-m-m . . .'

'You're just going to use that? You're twenty-five years old, Lawrence. You're not a cripple. You can work. Brommell was happy with the job you did. More than happy.'

'I-I-I-I . . .'

'What?'

'I d-d-d . . .'

'What?'

'I don't don't don't . . .'

'What?'

'I am not go-go-go-going back. S-s-s-s-sell s-s-s-s-some of the l-l-l-land. Sell it. Sell it. I-I-I-I am not g-g-g . . .'

'Sell the land?'

'To-to-to-to the or-or-or-orchard.'

'Hell, Lawrence. No. No. I don't want us to do that.'

He looked out the window. Walked to the back door, opened it.

'I need to look at Mother's accounts. Maybe there's enough . . .'

'She s-s-said . . .'

'I know, she said there was enough. I know. Let me see. I'll have to go the bank. Hell, Lawrence.'

I selected a clean canvas and prepared my pochade box, adding aureolin, coral, deepest violet to my palette. I placed the last of the apples, the tea biscuits and a flask of tea into my satchel. Dressed in my low hat and my belted trousers, my undershirt, my shirt, my woollen coat, I walked out of Beverly with my pochade box and satchel over my shoulder, my easel under my arm. I walked with my old clothes against my skin, the air warming within them. I went past the straw man, leaning closer to the ground, no face left but black stain. If the straw man was stirring porridge at the stove in the house, and I was standing by the garden with my arms splayed, what would be the difference? I smiled. The air was fresh in my lungs as I pushed through the turnstile, its creak like a song.

I soon reached the stream. The sound of running water in harmony with all sound from the mountain, birds, breeze, leaves. I cupped my hand, callused, paint-stained—in the stream, the water tasting of moss and earth. The sun cast dappled shadows along the path, disappearing behind trees, then reappearing. I breathed the scent of eucalyptus as I opened the easel, readied the canvas.

The brushstrokes described the flat of the field before me, as I painted into its hidden life, green on violet, green on coral, green on aquamarine, every stroke different to the one that had come before. Above the field, greater than the field, the day's key note. Aureolin on blue and white. It was the sky that told the painting's story, the sky that revealed change. I looked about me at the red-and-green parrots, the gold and green in the throat of the dove, at the wild winter flowers in bloom—the purple fan and the yellow guinea. This was the world for me; there was Wallis above and the bunker below, and here was I, between them with my tray of colours.

PART THREE

1994

36.

IT WAS SUNSET. I WAS ON the back porch in Mother's canopy swing, looking over the day's work. I imagined the clouds on the canvas extending beyond its border, obscuring my hands as I drifted over the work. Seeing, without thinking or purpose, empty, finally, of the need to paint. Butterfly sang through the open window—*Io sono la fanciulla più lieta del Giappone*. I sang with her, *The happiest girl in Japan*, and drank from my bottle of beer.

A truck came down the road. Sometimes they went past on their way to the orchards. My attention remained with the painting; the moment before the clouds spilled their rain. I heard the truck stop next door. I lifted my eyes from the canvas. Trucks did not stop at Mrs Barry's house.

I heard a second vehicle pull up next door, followed by voices and the doors of the truck and the car opening and closing. A man said, 'You just let us know where you want the furniture. We'll leave the boxes in the kitchen.'

'Thanks,' a woman answered.

A girl said, 'No way. Come off it, Mum.'

A dog barked. There had never been a dog at Beverly. Gert would not have liked it, nor would the birds.

I got to my feet, went through the back door and stood at the side window where I could best see into Mrs Barry's yard. Two men were carrying a table into the house. A black dog bounded around their feet. It must be a mistake—these people had taken a wrong turn. Perhaps they thought this was the orchard. And as soon as they discovered their mistake they would leave in their truck and I could sit again in the canopy swing and drink from my bottle of beer.

The girl sat down on a coffee table on the grass. I wondered how old she was. I did not know how old girls were. She wore shorts full of tears and a t-shirt that showed her navel. It said: *Wake me when it's over.*

I watched as the two men unloaded all of the furniture and boxes from the back of the truck. The black dog ran about, sniffing at the trees and fences. My stomach clenched.

A boy came out of the house—a boy of probably ten years—his eyes on the pages of a book. He did not look up from the pages as he walked towards the truck. I watched as the boy tripped over a box sitting on the grass. He stopped and looked up, and for a moment I thought he had seen me through the window.

He was a narrow boy, his hair dark. His hair was like Colin's hair. I did not think of Colin. It had been many years not thinking of Colin. For one moment I thought, It *is* Colin. It is Colin. What a foolish thought. It could not be Colin. Colin would be a man now. But the same hair. Knotted and dark. The same narrow, long-legged body.

The dog barked.

'Kids! Help me in here, will you? I can't do this shit on my own!' the mother called from Mrs Barry's back porch.

What did the woman mean? What did she want the children to help her do? Why was she carrying things inside the house?

My thoughts crossed. It is not happening, it is not happening as I fear it is happening. Yet it *is* happening, it *is* happening.

I forced myself from the window.

As soon as I left the window I wanted to return.

I went to the telephone, following the numbers on the piece of paper Paul had pinned to the wall.

'Paul Paul P-P-P . . .'

'Lawrence? Is everything alright?'

'P-P-P . . .'

'Yes?'

'Th-th-th . . . There are . . . There are . . .'

'What is it?'

'Th-th-th-th-there there there . . .'

'Lawrence, what it is?'

'There there there . . .' Each word an obstacle. 'There are there are there are p-p . . .'

'What?'

Why could he never wait for me?

'P-p-p-p-people . . .'

'People? Where?'

'N-n-n-next door come into-to-to Mrs B-B-B-Barry's.'

'Into the Barrys'?'

'Y-y-y-y-yes, yes . . . P-p-p-please c-c-c-c-come come come.'

'I will, Lawrence.'

'C-c-c-c-come n-n-n-n . . .'

'I will come tomorrow.'

'N-n-n-n . . .'

'I can't come now. I have work to do. I won't be able to come until tomorrow.'

'B-b-b-b . . . but . . .'

'I can't come sooner, Lawrence. I'll be there tomorrow.'

I put down the telephone. He was coming; not until tomorrow, but he was coming. And then he would tell the people next door they had to leave. That they had arrived at the wrong house. That there was somewhere else they belonged. I went to the window. I could see them moving down there. Their voices travelled. Laughter, shouting.

I could not settle, could not sit, or paint, or read. I walked up and down the kitchen. Pine cones on the shelf, carrots and onions in the bowl, sketches pinned to the walls: feathers, potatoes sprouting, cups and plates and spoons. There was the ham bone on the bench, the remains of the bread and the paintbrushes and the cloudy water and the jars and rags. Everything in its place. I walked into Mother's room, out, down the corridor, into the lounge. Looked through my windows—the back, the window over the sink, the window in my old room. Wallis appeared dusty and veiled through the glass. I returned to the side window. How much longer until they left?

When evening fell, I did not want to draw. I drew every evening, even with my wrist aching from the day's painting. My feet up on the fender, fire lit or unlit, sketchbook on my knee. Days of the leaf, the apple core, the possum bone. But not today.

I went to the fridge, took out a bottle of beer and drank standing at the sink. My head swam. Paul began to leave bottles of beer in my boxes of supplies years ago. I soon learned to drink only at the end of the day, when there was nothing left to put onto the canvas. Learned to measure out the way beer allowed me to detach from the work so that I did not ask of the painting,

What now? Beer, too, was in service of painting. But not like this. Not at the sink, the whole bottle. The downfall of Master Hals, Master van Gogh.

How I hated to miss the sunset. Every evening the sky in new colours, new formations. But I would have to wait until they were gone. I walked from room to room, window to window. Lights turned on in Mrs Barry's. When Mrs Barry had been living next door, I did not recall ever seeing so many lights. I could sense the presence of the family even when I could not hear them or see them.

I did not want to look at *Letters from the Masters*. Did not want to read Master Ensor's trumpets of light, tracing my fingers over the syllables. Did not want to try my current favourites on the tongue—*festive, virgin, pertinacity*—to speak them into the quiet of my kitchen, windows open, allowing the words to flow out into the landscape that I would paint the following day. Did not wish to stand in my kitchen with the wood stove alight, seeing the flames through the glass, heating my socks over the iron, drying my boots so I could crack away the mud, ready for tomorrow's walk.

I went to Mother's room and closed the blinds. I wondered if the family could see me through their windows, closing the blinds in mine. Then not only would I be aware of them, but they would be aware of me. I felt sick. I did not know what to do with my questions.

I went to Mother's bed and lay facing the wall, listening to the tick of the bird clock from the lounge. My stomach ached. What if I needed to use the outhouse? What then? Would they see me? I thought of the family; the mother calling for help, the girl calling back, the relentless bark of the dog, the boy as he came from the house, his eyes on the pages of his book. What was in the world of those pages? I remembered Mrs St Clair reading to us in the fifth class, *Man is a short-sighted creature*. I remembered Crusoe's island, his solitude, the clarity of his thinking. That was the world Defoe's pages gave us in the fifth class; each day, Crusoe looking across to the ocean that encircled him, for a boat that might rescue him from his *Island of Despair*. Wave after wave washed up against the shore until at last I slept.

37.

THE NEXT MORNING, BEFORE I was properly awake, I thought, Soon I will leave the bedroom, place the kettle on the stove and stand on the porch while I wait for it to boil. Then it returned to me. There were people next door. I left the bed and went into the kitchen. I stood at the side window and pulled back the blinds. There was no sign of any life at Mrs Barry's. Had it been a dream? Had the family realised its mistake and left? The truck carrying the furniture was gone. But what about the other car?

A light turned on in the kitchen next door.

I could not leave the house. I would have to wait for Paul. Perhaps he would tell me when the people next door would leave. Perhaps he would explain the mistake. I crossed from one side of the room to the other.

The stammer was in my thoughts. If I tried to speak—*salon, composition, Prix de Rome*—the words would jam at the first letters. I looked at the bird clock. Seven o'clock. What time would Paul be here? He could not come until after he finished his work. It could be four o'clock. It could be five o'clock. Even later. He could not say.

It was cold in the house. I opened the iron door of the wood stove but did not ready the fire. I crossed to the side window, the front window and back to the wood stove. Again opened the iron door but could not seem to set the kindling, strike the match. Went to the front door but did not open it, only stood there. I did not know what to do. I walked to the back door, put my hand on the handle.

The dog barked from Mrs Barry's yard. I looked again at the bird clock. One quarter of an hour had passed. I looked away from the clock, noted the time, then turned to the clock to see the time again. Over and over. I did not know how the hours were to pass. I heard voices, the mother shouting to the girl, the girl to the mother, the dog barking. But nothing from the boy. His was the quiet voice, the concentrated voice, oblivious to the world outside his pages. A narrow, dark-haired boy. Were all boys this way?

I went to the tap over the sink and filled a glass of water. Soon they would be gone. Paul would come and explain. He would say, *They leave today, Lawrence, it has been a mistake.* I drank the water, left the glass in the sink, checked the bird clock, looked through the windows, lifted the wood stove door, returned to the sink, drank again. The air inside the house grew thick.

For the first time, trapped inside, I noticed the canvases around Beverly's walls. Paintings leaned against each other in every part of the house, smaller paintings hidden behind larger ones, many standing, others in uneven piles. There was no part of Beverly free of my work. The corridor one-third its natural size! I did not know until then how many pictures I had painted. When a painting was complete, it remained here, belonging to my understanding of the landscape in the minutes and hours and days in which I had painted it. And then I would begin afresh, on a new canvas.

I ran my fingers over the surface of a painting of the morning sky. It was the light at dawn, translucent, tentative. The canvas, like every canvas in the room, seemed to me to be a living thing, not merely an object, plain and ordinary, but a soul contained within an object. *Paint into me, Lawrence, there, where I need light.* Today, trapped in my house, I saw my paintings as if they were a family, springing from the same source. My children, here, against the walls of Beverly. *How my whole life, even in its best moments, falls short of this sweetness . . .* Master Rodin wrote to Emile. I touched the layers of paint on a picture of Mount Abrupt, painted from Wallis. The valley that led to him dense with trees. I picked up the canvas. Who had painted this? Had the straw man pulled himself from the garden, stolen my pochade box from the kitchen and set himself up on the mountain?

An image of Gert caught my attention. The cow was standing in the field to the right of the turnstile; it was dusk, and the sky was pink and grey and palest yellow, a gentle descent into night. Gert's head was turned towards me. I sat on my haunches in the corridor running my fingers over the thick black of her coat.

One evening, many years ago, I found Gert behind the shelter, lying on her side. She bellowed, straining to lift her head. I crouched beside her. She moaned, her eyes rolling. Her belly was bloated, though her bones protruded in her hips and hindquarters. Her legs stuck out stiff and straight. She moaned again as she tried to raise her head. I sat down beside her. Her head dropped into the grass. Gert had been at Beverly since I was a boy. All the years she was in the field, in the shelter, at the trough. Her breath came hard in and out of her nostrils when I took her head in my lap. The sky turned purple. Soon she stopped breathing.

I held her head in my lap, and rocked forwards, then back, forwards, then back. *Old cow, old girl, old friend to Beverly and to me.* I stayed long after she had passed, my hands on her neck, stroking the length of her coat. *Old girl, sweet cow, dear friend.* There was no difference between Gert's coat and the night, shades of black upon black.

Looking at the painting now I was reminded afresh. 'Gert . . .' I wished I could look through the window and see her standing at the fence by the shelter once more. Must all things pass? Was there no other way? Perhaps that was why I painted— because there was no other way.

I put away the picture and continued to look through the canvases, selecting those which needed attention and placing them over the windows, darkening the house. I left only the side window uncovered, the one that gave me a view into the Barry's yard. I had created the paintings, and the paintings repaid my efforts by shielding me from the world outside. I was grateful. I thought I had not lived with a family since Mother died and Paul left, but I was wrong; I had been living with one since I began to paint.

As night fell, I switched on the electric light so I could continue to look into the work. I no longer felt a prisoner. I had climbed the mountain countless times; I did not need to do so again. Master Constable wrote that it was the scenes he saw on the Stour before he was ten years old that made him a painter. I too had seen all I needed to see. Even if the sky disappeared—if I should open the door in the morning, look up and see only darkness—I could keep painting it and every sky would be new.

'Lawrence!' Paul called from the front door. For a moment I wondered why Paul was here. But then I remembered. I put down the canvas and went to the front door. Paul was already in the corridor, carrying two boxes. He didn't usually come inside—he gave me my boxes at the door, or outside the house. But today he came into the kitchen. He placed the boxes on the table. I noticed a smear of grease across his cheek. We were both marked—Paul with his car grease, me with my paint.

'Christ,' said Paul, as he looked around.

My landscapes covered the house: the field, the red roof of Beverly, the grey slate of Mrs Barry's, the peak of Wallis as seen from the porch, Wallis at sunset, Wallis in summer, the sky from Wallis, the valley that led to him—all there for Paul to see. He shook his head, eyebrows raised. I wanted to turn the faces of my paintings to the walls. Wanted to push Paul out. Punch him.

He turned to me. 'I've been next door, Laurie,' he said. 'They have moved in. They are here to stay.'

Had I heard him correctly? Here to stay? Sweat covered my body. 'No no no n-n-n-n th-th-th-they c-c-can't c-c-c-c . . .'

'Calm down, Lawrence.'

'B-b-b-but . . . h-h-h-how . . .'

'There isn't anything we can do about it. They own the land. It's her family. Mrs Barry's.' Paul walked to the back door and opened it. 'Christ, how long since you've opened a window in here?'

'N-n-no no no no . . .'

'Lawrence, take it easy.'

'No no no no n-n-n . . .'

He faced me. 'They're here to stay. You're going to have to get used to it.'

I saw the contempt and impatience for me in his eyes. Two houses close by, one mine, the other empty. That was the picture in which I lived. Now a family had arrived next door.

'They seem alright, Lawrence. You still have all the space you need. You leave them alone, and I'm sure they'll leave you alone.'

'Th-th-th-th-th-they are here to to to to to . . . ?'

'Yes, yes, here to stay.'

'N-n-n-n-no no . . .'

'I don't understand what you're trying to say.'

I knew it had nothing to do with Paul, that Paul could not stop it, yet I blamed him. 'Y-y-y-you . . .' My thoughts were disconnected, incomplete. 'Y-y-y-y-y-y . . .'

'You can't have it all your way out here forever. They seem okay. The property is big enough.'

'N-n-n-n-n-no! No! No! No!'

I paced from one end of the kitchen to another. Even as I was resisting, I knew there was nothing that could be done. I picked up a plate sitting on the kitchen table and threw it at Paul's feet.

'What the hell? Lawrence!'

The plate shattered.

I hated him.

'I have to get home.' He put his hand on one of the boxes. 'There should be enough for a while. There is soap there too. Use it.'

I wanted to punch his head.

At the door, he stopped. 'There's nothing I can do about it, Lawrence.'

He said the words as if he was saying something small,

insignificant. *The tap cannot be fixed. There is a tile needs replacing. You must clean the gutters.*

'I'll come by again next week. You should tidy the place up, Laurie—I had no idea.'

And then he was gone.

I pulled a beer from one of the boxes and drank. Fuck him. I put the needle on *Butterfly. Gran perla di sensale!* sang Pinkerton. I closed the back door. I did not remove the canvases from the windows. I could hear the mother screaming at the girl and the girl screeching back. The lives of other people. Every sound cut too deep. Years of living here alone, now this? It was impossible. The emptiness of Mrs Barry's house was necessary to Beverly, Beverly could only be inhabited if the Barry house was not. *Ah! quei ciottoli mi hanno sfiaccato!* sang Sharpless. But the music did not speak to me. Was, for the first time, foreign. I finished the bottle of beer, took another and sat in Mother's rocker.

Master Vidosky, the last master in the book, wrote to his friend Vladimir in 1905: *Last night I attended the premiere of* Madame Butterfly. *Never have I been so moved, transported to the cliff where the poor girl waited. Each musical phrase a gift. How I long to paint as the Italian composes! I listen to the opera on my gramophone endlessly.*

I had wondered, what was a musical phrase? Who was Madame Butterfly and why did she wait? Master Vidosky painted the sea in the moonlight, he painted boats and lighthouses. Why did he want to paint as the Italian composes?

I looked at the record player Uncle had given Mother, sitting in the same corner where he had placed it all the years before.

I wondered if that was Master Vidosky's gramophone. Could it play the opera as Master Vidosky had once heard it? That evening, I sat at the kitchen table and wrote my list for Paul.

mineral turpentine
tea biscuits
tea-leaves
beer bottles
beef strips
nails
cheese
seeds for cauliflower
a gardening fork
Madame Butterfly

When Paul arrived the next day, I gave him the list. 'Laurie?' He looked up at me. 'What's this?'

'What?'

'This.' He pointed. '*Madame Butterfly*.'

'It's m-m-m-m . . .'

'It's what?'

Why could he not wait? Not even once? 'M-m-m-music.'

He frowned. 'You want this?'

I growled at him. It was only ever food supplies from Grady's. Seeds. Once the paint and canvases, before I purchased them for myself. Sometimes hardware. But he was there anyway—he had told me that; he was at the hardware store, it was no trouble. It was the only time I had asked. I hated to ask. But who was Madame Butterfly? I needed to know. What did it mean, each musical phrase a gift?

'How will you play it, this music?'

'On the r-r-r-record . . . on . . . the the r-r-r-rec-rec-rec . . .'

'Lawrence, that thing is ancient. I played records on it when I was a kid. You can't use it.'

I growled at him again. It was only ever ham bone and cheese and butter and nails.

'Alright, alright. Let me see. Let me sort something out. It could take a while.' He left the house grumbling.

The next time he came he pulled a slim square package in a brown paper bag from one of the boxes.

'Wh-wh-what . . . ?'

'Yes, Lawrence, it is. You can thank me later.' He gave me the package.

I pulled the record from the paper. On the cover there was a picture of a black-haired girl in a bright orange gown looking out to sea from the edge of a cliff.

'Do you know how the record player works, Lawrence?'

'M-m-m I th-th-th . . .' I could not remember, did not play records.

'Here . . . let's see . . .' He sighed loudly and came down the corridor. 'Can you tidy up the place? Imagine what Mother would say . . .'

I wanted to smack him, my hand across his mouth.

He went to the record player on the shelf, took down the player and placed it on the coffee table, then he plugged the cord into the wall. 'Still gets power, that's a start. Take out one of the records and give it to me, Lawrence.'

I looked at the record cover; there were the lyrics in Italian in a booklet inside the cover with an English translation. I took the first of the three records from the cardboard and passed it to Paul.

'Okay, you put the record on the player like so . . . You lift the needle. Did you ever do this, Laurie?' He lifted the arm on the side of the player and brought it down on the record. A crackle came from the player. 'Sweetest sound in the world,' said Paul.

As the music played I was aware of my mouth falling open.

I did not want Paul to see me listening. I did not want him to hear it. 'Th . . . th . . . th . . . thank you, thank you, Paul, thank you. Thank you . . .'

'Okay, okay, I'm going. *Madame Butterfly* is all yours.' He smiled at me. 'Glad you like it. Anything else you need?'

'N-n-n-no no! No!'

'Alright, alright . . . I'm going.'

Once he had left the house, I returned to the player, put the needle back onto the record and sat in Mother's rocker. The music was made of a number of instruments and voices combining, one indiscernible from another, the way paint combines on the canvas. I leaned back against the rocker as the music flooded over me. *Butterfly* held my private self, turned it slowly about the room. Master Vidosky had been right; each musical phrase was a gift, and I received them with gratitude. I was transported, as Master Vidosky had been, to the cliff with Cio Cio San. I too waited for Pinkerton, believed he would return to me. I too took my father's knife. At the end of the last record there were tears on my face.

After a time, I learned every word in English and in Italian. Language too was a road to travel. *Amore, addio, addio! Piccolo amor!* When the player broke, I wrote *new player* on my list for Paul. Paul said, *Christ, Laurie,* and brought me one.

I pushed myself back and forth in the rocker, my feet on the guard. *Butterfly* could not reach me now. The family next door came between me and the happiest girl in Japan. I longed for the bunker . . . My thoughts turned to the boy drifting from the house with his eyes on the pages of the book. I rocked back and forth. What world did the pages hold for the boy? What did he see there? What did he do? *For sudden joys, like griefs, confound at first.* As the fifth class listened to Mrs St Clair we walked the island with Crusoe, we too felt the anguish at the loss of his ship, trembled alongside him at the sight of footprints in the sand. Was it the same story the boy read in his book?

38.

I DO NOT KNOW HOW many hours I lay awake in Mother's bed that night; I was restless, uncomfortable. I crossed to the window and drew back the blinds. 'Wallis . . .' I touched the glass. I did not leave Mother's room at night. I knew the position of the dresser and the chair, the cupboard and the shelf, the tick of the bird clock from the lounge. Every night I lay in the bed until daylight appeared between the slats. But this night the walls of the room pressed in on me, the air too close. I left the bed, went into the kitchen and switched on the lamp. Beverly seemed smaller, crowded with paintings—field on field, mountain after mountain, sunset and sunrise. The floor was thick with my drawings: the heart of the orchid, over and over; wattle flowers on the branch, the same branch from every angle; the sprouting onion, the onion in half, the onion skin. I was suffocating.

Through the side window, a single light shone over Mrs Barry's porch.

I pulled on my coat and black woollen hat and pushed open the back door. I stepped down into the yard, not looking to the house as I followed the path, past the bunker and the outhouse, past the straw man and the vegetable garden, to the turnstile.

Once through the stile, beyond the sight of Mrs Barry's house, I could breathe more easily, inhaling lungfuls of the cool clean air. As I followed the path through the field, I looked up at a sky awash with stars. I was accustomed to closing my doors when night fell, now here I was, walking into the night. I could see the black bulk of Wallis ahead; he had his own shade of darkness, as did the sky, the fields, the trees, the sheep, even me. My own darkness! I kept going, alive between my thoughts, experiencing space in this cleansed and rested world. I could have walked the path with my eyes closed; knew every step. Listened as I walked. Branches snapping, the song of frogs, of crickets, wind in the trees, my own footsteps, the breath as it came and left my body—these sounds became new, amplified. The music of the night. All these years it had played outside my door and only now could I hear it. Perhaps it was not as bad as I had first thought that a family had come to live next door. They had given me the night!

I placed my hand on the trunk of a peeling stringybark, his body papery and rough, then crossed to another and another along the path, touching their trunks and branches, their skin alive under my hands. Warmth spread from my centre, out through my clothes.

The trail steepened, my breath coming faster; every inhalation an invitation, every exhalation a release. All the years of breathing, from the minute I was born, and only now did I appreciate the opportunity an exhalation afforded me. Just as Crusoe learned that he could choose the bright or the dark, so could I.

When I came to the first rocky outcrop, I lay on my back against the rocks. The moon was a narrow crescent, the rest of his circular self in shadow. I put my arms over my head, palms open to the stars, to the gleaming black blanket of sky. I felt the night take away the years, years of manhood, years of isolation, years of painting, years of thought, years from my body, releasing me from them until I was young again. Moon! Stars! Mountain! Who are you and who am I beneath you? *"Whence are we?"*

I chose my largest canvas and set it up on the easel in the middle of the lounge. I selected the oils—ivory black and lamp black, iridescent white, Prussian blue. I prepared rag and brushes and turpentine. I chose the third record and placed the needle where Butterfly denounces her god. There was no one else who could do what I could do. My body stiff and slow, my hand aching, ready. I closed my eyes and was there again, my face to the sky.

All that day I was contained within my painting. The field beneath the stars. Night drew me into night like a road, a road into the living and invisible self of the field, the aspect that contained the answer to the question, Where did Mother go? Where did Mrs Barry go? Father? Gert? I was barely aware of the arguments between mother and daughter next door, the protests of the boy, the dog.

At some time in the afternoon my stomach began to cramp. I stamped my feet and held my breath. I would wait. I turned hot then cold then hot again. I sat in the rocker and refused. Soon the urge receded. I sat and waited and was glad when the urge did not return. I went back to my work seeing the night reveal itself in my living room. Hour after hour. I did not step away from the easel until my stomach growled.

When had I last eaten? I dug around in the boxes Paul had left on the kitchen table: bread, cheese, cured sausage. I longed for potatoes and carrots and celery from the garden next door. I made ham and pea soup, cutting the ham, having no peas, adding water. Crumbling biscuits into the pot. Sprinkling salt. It would do for the week. I sat cold in the rocker and ate the soup without peas, my eyes on the painting. *Greater depth*, it said. *Why in your painting must the night end?* Halfway through my soup I stood, brush in hand, tripping over the bowl, spilling soup as I returned to the canvas.

It was dark outside when I left the house and walked the path to the outhouse. After closing the wooden door behind me, I looked to the decoration of carved leaves against the ribbon of night sky. It was not Lawrence unbuckling his belt, not Lawrence over the bench, the pain like a knife.

Every night that followed, I pulled on my winter coat, my black woollen hat, and walked across the field to the first outcrop on the mountain. There, I lay on my back on the rocks and looked to the sky. Each night the waxing moon glowed brighter, bathing me in its light. And as I was drawn upwards, I was made young again, as if the years of my manhood had never been lived. I was as young as the boy who lay asleep in Mrs Barry's house, the light of the moon across his cheek.

When I returned to Beverly, just before dawn, I drank a bottle of beer standing at the sink, then fell into the bed drenched in cool and quiet night.

I rose in the morning and made my pot of tea, but I did not stand on the porch with my cup, resting my eyes on the landscape, as I was accustomed to doing. Instead, I returned to my work, hand aching from the efforts of the day before. The night sky rested against the easel in the middle of Beverly's lounge. Juices rushed in my mouth—the anticipation of tea and painting. Ha! Tea and painting—the two were good friends! What did it matter, that my knuckles were swollen, my wrist aching, pursued by *the devil arthritis*. The brush and the paint drew me back into the night. Black paint covered my hands. I hardly heard them next door—the ring of the telephone, the girl and her music. Other girls her age in the yard. I was at the work of discovery, learning the texture, the density and the light, of night. Sometimes I slept, and would wake with my mouth dry from dreams—black into black, deeper and deeper, the stars, the field, the brush. I could not see and did not want to see daylight. I did not tend the vegetable garden, did not listen to *Butterfly*, did not sit on the back porch in the canopy swing as the sun set over the mountain.

After two weeks, the moon was full, its light obscuring the stars. I was weary, my hand in the mornings tight as a claw. Once it had loosened, I could not work for long before it would stiffen and cramp again.

I was trapped in the scent of myself. The bedsheets, the used cups, the uneaten dinner on the stove, the cabbage rotting on the sill. My socks and trousers, my woollen hat. I longed to go out into the day. Wanted sunshine on my face. I wondered what might be growing, what surprise; I wished for the dirt in my hands as I pulled away the creeping thistle and the dandelion. Craved the orange of carrot, the red of tomato.

The painting of the night leaned against the wood stove, swirling with stars, the field in shining blackness. I wanted to be with it, but if I looked at it a minute longer, I would be sick. I wanted suddenly to be away from the image of the night, and it too wanted to be away from me. I turned the canvas around so it faced the wall. But I did not feel pleased to see it shamed and turned it back. I walked the length of the kitchen, wall to wall, wall to wall.

There was a knock at the door. Sharp and quick. *Knock knock knock*. I crossed to Mother's rocker and sat. Who could it be? *Knock knock knock*.

'Hello, there, hello!' It was the girl from Mrs Barry's calling at the door. 'Hello!'

I kept rocking.

'Hello in there!'

'We know you're in there.' They were laughing at me, like Peter Boer. Like Jock. Like the other children at Hughlon Consolidated. *Not so smart now, Lawrence.*

'Shhhh . . .'

'Hey there! We're your new neighbours come to say hello.'

I could not go to the door. Could only rock in Mother's chair.

'Hello! Are you in there?'

It was the girl—I could tell—not the mother. But there was another voice, too; I guessed it must be the boy. Why had they come? What did they want? Paul said they would leave me alone, and now they were at my door. I kept rocking.

The knocking stopped. I stayed in the chair. Back and forth back and forth. There was only the door between the family and me. Not enough! Back and forth, back and forth. How much time was passing? Rocking distorted time. Back and forth, back and forth. Were my eyes open or closed? I needed to use the outhouse very badly. My stomach ached. I had to go. I opened the back door and, without looking to Mrs Barry's house, walked the path down through the yard.

I kept my eyes on Mother's framed card of the sunflowers, only the smallest hint of gold remaining as I pulled down my trousers. My stomach cramped. *Knock knock knock.* Who was there, knocking on the door of the outhouse? Someone was there! *Knock knock knock.* It was not real. I was imagining the sound. I grew hot. *Knock knock knock.* It was as if the act of imagining the sound had made it real. Now it was real! Who was at the door? *Knock knock knock. Knock knock knock.* I could not move forwards, could not retreat. My stomach gripped and cramped. *Knock knock knock.* I leaned forwards. I wanted to, knew the pleasure, wanted it. Wanted it!

I threw in the sawdust shavings from the bucket. I could not forgive myself. Shame like a blade.

I pulled open the door, taking a breath of the cold clear air. The last of spring. It was not possible for me to return to the house. Not possible. I kept my eyes low and walked down the path, past the bunker door towards the turnstile.

39.

AS I WAS GOING PAST the break in Mrs Barry's fence, I saw the boy beside the vegetable garden. He was digging at the dirt with his bare hands, working away with the same deep absorption as when reading his book. He looked up and saw me.

'You're home,' he said, sounding surprised.

I could not speak.

'We knocked a while ago but you didn't answer.'

I did not respond.

He looked down at the hole that he was digging. 'I'm making a pond.' He pointed at Beverly.

'You live there by yourself, don't you?'

I nodded, slowly.

'Now we live here too.' His voice was soft and clear. The voice of a boy. 'Didn't you hear us at your door?'

I said nothing.

'Next time we'll knock louder.' He returned to his work. 'Tanya didn't want to come, she wanted to stay in the city. But I did.'

The boy looked to be ten years old, as I had first thought when I had seen him through my window.

'What's so good about the city? Things are expensive.' The skin of his arm was flecked with dirt. 'There won't be as much trouble for Tanya out here. That's what Mum is hoping.'

'David! David!' the mother called from the house.

'That's me,' the boy said. He stood, brushing dirt from his trousers, wiping mud across his cheek. 'What's your name?' he asked.

It had never been more important. This moment. My own name. 'L . . . L . . . L . . .' But it was not possible. 'L . . . L . . . L . . .' I could not.

Then the boy smiled at me.

I took a breath. 'L . . . L . . . Lawrence,' I said.

'David!' his mother called again from the house.

'Better go,' said David. 'See you, Lawrence.'

Lawrence. I watched as he ran up to the house. His long and narrow legs, his shirt, hanging over his trousers.

It was as if I had only just arrived on the earth. There was Wallis before me, but I could hardly recognise him. Did not know the trees at his base, nor the sky towards which they grew. I began to walk towards the mountain, sunshine moving through me as though I were transparent. I was, for once, without thought.

I accepted all things as I walked. Accepted my boots that pressed into the toes with each step, and my pants that hung too loose, the shirt that scratched with the movement of my arms. Accepted the stiffness in my joints as I pushed and swung my way up, the bones growing closer over the years. I forgave them, forgave every part of my body, the body of a man as old as me.

Soon I came to the stream, now barely a trickle. I accepted the tiny grains of creek bed that entered the cup of my hand before I drank. Accepted the hard ground under my knees. Accepted the moment that was here, accepted it as it passed, accepted the one to follow.

When I reached the summit, I did not ask how it might be painted—it was enough to see the world lit with gold, the trees covering the mountain like a ragged coat, the mountain itself as the river was to Master Cézanne. Ever unfolding.

I do not know how long I was on the mountain that day. Resting against him. Inhaling him. Seeing his birds and his stream and stones. Raising my hand to his emus and wallabies, his blue-tongued lizard. Viewing the world from his summit; the valley and the fields and the roads beyond. The red roof of Beverly, the grey slate of Mrs Barry's. I had been starved of light. I was as Master Corot when he discovered the oak trees at Bas-Bréau. Master van Gogh and his poppies. Master Friedrich and his forests of pine.

I came down slowly as the sun began to set. I stopped when I reached the turnstile, and looked at the sky; grey and gold resisting the darkness. The place between day and night. How I longed for my brushes and paint! Too late! I continued on my way. When I passed the outhouse, I did not wonder, What will happen when I need to go there? When I passed the bunker, I did not ask, How much longer? When I looked to Mrs Barry's house, I did not think, What if they see me? I thought, instead, of the boy's face. Of the way he had asked me my name. When had I last shared my name?

Once inside the house, I took the first record from its paper sleeve. '*Dei crucci la trama smaglia il sorriso . . .*' I sang with Suzuki. *A smile breaks through a web of trouble.*

I readied the fire, tearing used pages from my sketchbook—nests, bulbs and banksia men—and crumpling them into balls.

Said to myself—myself who never tossed a page, never let go of any object—said to myself, What do I care? and tossed my drawings into the stove. I laid the kindling, piled the wood, then struck the match. I sat and watched the flames catch, arrested by their movement, their sound and warmth. The fire held me as beer held me, as painting held me, as *Butterfly* held me.

My stomach gurgled, empty. I closed the iron door and went to the kitchen—finding cheese and corned beef, pressing them between slices of bread. I opened a bottle of beer and sat with the sandwich and the bottle by the stove. Feet on the guard, warmed by the fire, I ate my dinner. Beer and bread—was there ever a better friendship? Back and forth, back and forth.

When my plate was empty, I took *Letters from the Masters* from the shelf. This night I did not look at the shorelines and hills and skies. Not the mills and haystacks and bodies of water. I turned instead to the paintings of people. I touched the skin, the cheeks, the hair, the legs and arms of Leonidas at Thermompylae, the men and women in *The Feast of Achelous*, *Christ as He Entered Brussels*. Human bodies as mysterious as the sky. Roads that did not end. Later, I lay on Mother's bed, and though sleep did not come, I did not object. I lay in all my clothes as the heat from the stove entered the room, wrapping itself around the cold, insisting, *Now, change*.

As I filled the kettle the next morning, I thought about the way the boy's face opened to me. I pictured him making his pond, his mud-flecked arms. I looked down at Mother's tin pot in my hands—the same pot I had been using since she died, taken from the same place on the shelf—surrounded by drawings and used teaspoons and the sugar bag, the saucer with its stain, the dried wedge of lemon, the dusty wing of a moth—still lifes in every object. The boy's smile was a doorway to endless possibilities. I spooned in the leaves and poured the water. The teapot that steeped the leaves, the pale pink lines of the chipped cup, the lemons, shrinking and withering, the wood in the basket, the feathers—the way these objects sat beside each other, their relationship accidental and yet meaningful, intended, contradictory. 'Ha! Inside too is a landscape.'

I opened the back door to the early morning sun. Summer was almost here. I prepared Indian yellow, cadmium yellow and titanium white on my palette. I pulled two kitchen chairs into the doorway, sitting on one and resting a canvas on the other. I drank from the tea, the cup warming my hands, the steam rising, then I placed the cup on the floor beside my chair. I took up my brush, not minding the pain in my hand, as if it were a friend to me. Welcome, pain, paint with me, take tea with me. Steam rose from my cup, dust floated in the light.

I poured myself tea after tea from the pot, replacing my cup on the floor, leaving ring upon ring drying on Mother's wooden boards. I painted into the sun, layers of yellow into yellow. Immersion in light. Sun across my knees, sun in the sky, sun on my canvas. Could I not keep going, contained forever within this one emerging world of light? Must I inhabit another?

It seemed I must; after some hours, I could barely move my right hand, my stomach was empty, sour with hunger. Everything changes. Even passion. I needed air. Needed to be away from the scent of paint. I stood from my chair, rubbing my back, and placed the painting of the sun beside the painting of the night. I looked at them leaning against the wall. Night beside day, sun beside moon, one turning to the next. My head throbbed; I could no longer look at the paintings, and they no longer wanted to be seen. Demanded to be left alone, to grow, as Mrs Barry's radishes grew before they were ready for the soup pot.

I pushed my fingers through the holes at the end of my pockets and walked the path past the outhouse and the bunker, past the gap in the fence between Mrs Barry's and Beverly, keeping my eyes on the trail. I did not look to where I had seen him the day before. Did not search for things I might show him, the lizards, the blue treasures collected by the bower bird, the faces of trolls.

I sat on the rocks by the stream, close to the base of Wallis, and pulled off my boots and then my socks, stiff with wearing. I wriggled my toes. Hello, old toes. I pushed my feet into the stones under the shallow water. Look at those old feet with the marks from the socks pressed into the skin, so pleased to be out of their boots. Look at them. I lifted my feet from the water and noticed the dark hairs on each toe, the nails yellowing, like rind, uneven and discoloured. My feet, old friends that had carried me to the peak of the mountain, how many years? I watched the water move over my feet, blurring and softening their lines, creatures transformed by light and water. I turned my hands palms up, then over again. More old friends come to join us by the stream: one stiff, the knuckles swollen, worse every winter. I saw the swipes of paint across the palms; Indian and cadmium yellow. It occurred to me I had never seen my hands without paint. 'Ha!' Was that the way they were made? Covered in paint from the day I was born? What a shock for poor Mother. Ha!

My body came from the sleeves of my clothes, the cuffs and the hems, the collar, but that was all I knew of it, or had known. I inhabited my body from the inside only—it was the means to paint and did not hold my interest. But today I felt the sun on my face and saw my feet transformed in water, my paint-covered hands, and thought perhaps my body was more.

I lay down on my back against the damp clumps of mountain grass, my feet in the icy stream, and felt the earth against me, arms and legs and head supported. The earth beneath gave me a sense of my arms and legs and head. Did the earth know I was there? Did the Château Noir know that Master Cézanne stood before him? Did the clouds know that Master Constable had stood beneath them? Did the Rocky Bay know that Master Turner was on the shore with his brush?

I listened to the trickling stream. It was my body that had given me this moment, the sound and the sense of the mountain beneath me; my body that inhaled the mountain air, my body that exhaled. It was my body that lived. Perhaps then I *was* my body. Perhaps all the subjects within the portraits of the masters—the Women Plucking Geese, the Hunter in the Dunes, the Riders on the Beach—were their bodies. Was that what a person was?

As I walked back to Beverly, rested and cooled, I pushed my hands deeper into my pockets. There were holes in the pockets of all my clothes. If I did not have to carry my satchel or my pochade box and easel, my hands found a home in my pockets. My shoulders rose and stooped, my legs took their strides long and fast, my head down, and that was how we walked, all the parts of my body and me. It was the earth that had told me I had parts and was made of them and was inseparable from them. Was it thought that made the body, or did body make the thought?

Today my thoughts asked, *Will I see him? Will he be there? Making his pond? Scooping out the dirt, his dark hair knotted, so I could see the way he must have lain to cause the tangles?*

But when I walked past the fence, he was not there. I saw the beginnings of the pond, the untidy borders of the vegetable garden, the rocks and ferns, the straw man leaning, all a frame for the boy who was missing.

I forced myself to keep walking. I did not want to. Wanted to wait by the pond—the pond that would be—but did not. What was this feeling inside me? This longing? This anticipation? When did I last know it? I was as rusted as the boiler in the shed. Stiff with time.

40.

'HURRY UP, TANYA, YOU DON'T want to be late for your first day of school!'

'Get off my back, Mum.'

'You can't wear that to school.'

I listened to them arguing next door as I drank my tea.

'Why not?'

'Just take off the skirt, and put on your uniform.'

'Mum!'

'David, let the dog out and get a move on!'

The girl again. 'No way, Mum. It's not you who has to start at a new school. Why should it be up to you?'

'Tanya, give me a break. Hurry up!'

I saw David through the window, throwing the ball for the dog, and the dog leaping into the air to catch it. He was wearing his school uniform. The dog brought the ball back to the boy, dropping it at his feet. The boy picked it up and threw it again. 'There you go, girl! There you go, Mol!'

'David, time to go!'

I watched as David kneeled before the dog and put his arms around her. He leaned forwards and pressed his head against the animal's side. The dog sat, panting, in the boy's embrace. The boy whispered something close to the dog's ear, then he patted the dog's head and stood.

'David, hurry!' his mother called.

But the boy was in no hurry. He took his time as he made his way up to the house. Drifting.

'David!' the mother called again. 'Get a move on!'

I heard the opening and closing of car doors, then the car as it drove out onto the road. When it had been gone a few moments, I heard it backfire, once, and continue driving. The boy and his sister were going to school as Paul and I had once gone to school. I wondered, would the mother return? Or was she like our own mother, working in Hamilton? I waited for the sound of her car and when, after an hour, I did not hear it, I was sure she would not return until day's end. I was alone with Beverly.

At first, I did not know what to do; I could use the outhouse, go to the bunker, walk into the field. But which? I removed my canvases from the windows and opened the back door. I understood that my solitude was temporary and wished for the way it had been before the family arrived, yet at the same time felt glad that it was not. Wanted the boy once more in the yard with his arms around the dog.

But how pleasurable it was to walk the boundaries of Beverly unobserved. To breathe the air, to witness my surroundings, to speak words. 'Reformation! Labyrinth! Propensity!' Today it was Master von Menzel. 'Materialism! Attitude! Brilliant!'

I crossed to the shed, collected the secateurs and cut away the blackberry bushes that threatened to choke the stile. I allowed my thoughts to wander. They pulled this way and that, like the branches at which I cut—the painting of the sun, when was it time to make an order from Moira Parker, the boy throwing the ball. The force of his young arm. His smile. The dark blue of his school uniform against his skin. His seriousness. His young voice. It was as if a person damaged his voice every day that he grew older until he was a man with a voice as rough and uneven as gravel!

The green branches fell around my feet as I worked. My hands stung, torn by thorns. I plucked the fat black berries from the bush, put them in my mouth and kept cutting. My mouth filled with the sweet juice. 'Everything is bursting into life.' I spoke Master Corot's words without stammer, as I raked the branches. The turnstile, free at last from the thorny blackberry, swung with ease. '*E poi la nave appare. E poi la nave Bianca!*' I sang.

On my way back to the house I looked through the gap in the fence; beetroot stalks and rhubarb grew in the centre, tomato plants competed with carrots. The straw man grinned at me. I wished I could go and crouch by the garden, place my hands in the dirt, turn the earth, clear the weeds. I sighed and went on my way towards the house.

Once inside, I filled the kettle and placed it on the stove. I checked the clock. Time had never meant anything to me, and now with what frequency did I look to the birds over the mantle? As if I were waiting. I sipped my tea and added sugar and added more sugar, and then more, and again checked the clock. How much longer until I heard the school bus coming down the road?

'David, you bloody vacancy! Don't leave your shit outside my room!'

I crossed to the side window.

They were home.

The boy came into the yard and threw the ball for the dog. It was as if the whole long day was a simply a distraction for the boy from throwing the ball for his dog! I saw the flash of black as the dog leaped. Sometimes the boy was where I could see him from the window, then he would move too far down the yard and I could only hear his voice.

'Mol! Mol! Drop. Mol, *drop*!'

'No way . . . it's a freak zone. You have no idea. Oh God . . . I cannot get my head around it. No. Fucking miles. Yeah . . . no way . . .'

At first, I thought the girl was talking to herself, then I realised she had pulled the telephone out to the porch.

'It's the bloody middle of nowhere. I know . . . oh, it looks good—too long but, you know . . . you could cut the hem . . . That's what I did! I'm not kidding . . . You should come . . . yeah . . . we'll tell her I'm at yours, then we'll tell yours you're at mine . . . no . . . he's cute . . . he's really cute.'

The mother returned later, just before nightfall. The fighting began soon after. 'Don't speak to me that way, Tanya! When are you going to learn?'

'Don't hold your breath.'

'You're an idiot if you don't see what an opportunity this is.'

'You are kidding me. An opportunity? Really?'

'You just got yourself expelled, in case you've forgotten.'

'Suspended.'

'There's no difference. How much longer was it going to last there?'

I thought of the boy as I had first seen him, his eyes on the pages of his book, inhabiting his own world.

*

Every morning I heard the family coming in and out of the house as they prepared for school, then driving away in the car. Each day the boy and the girl returned on the school bus, their mother returning some hours later in the car. When I knew the pattern, and could anticipate it, I felt Beverly further returned to me. I could go wherever I wanted, use the outhouse, the bunker, walk up the mountain, drink tea on the porch in the canopy swing, or beer under the apple tree. Eating apples, tossing the cores at Gert's empty shelter, as I waited for him to return. I was distracted from painting. Roamed Beverly, aimless and enjoying my aimlessness. A painting demanded much. I had not known until now, how much. A painting asked me to walk down its road knowing there was no end, an act of surrender.

My attention was elsewhere.

41.

IT WAS SATURDAY. I HEARD THE mother call from the front of the house, 'Tanya, I don't want you leaving the place, okay? I'll be home by three.' Then a single car door opening and closing. She was going to work, leaving the boy and his sister alone. Our own mother went to Hamilton Modern Dairy every Saturday and left Paul and I at home. The whole day we did as we wished—climbed and hid, fought and raced, wrestled and ate Mrs Barry's meatloaf, all the while waiting for Mother.

I wondered what I should do . . . Ought I to leave the house and climb the mountain? It was warm and sunny. I could paint the blue sky interspersed with cumulus from the summit. But, no, no, I did not want to climb the mountain. No, I did not. I tried working into my painting of the sun but could not find my way. I was restless.

The sister played music from her bedroom, the window wide open. A man sang to the cherry blossom in Mrs Barry's yard. *What you talking about on the street? Don't know what it is to feel the heat? Going to treat you like you're my own, my own sweet treat. Because you're mine, because you're mine.* The man sounded angry. As if he were declaring war on the landscape, the world of Beverly and Wallis. But I did not object. This morning I did not object. *Going to treat you like you're my own, my own sweet treat. Because you're mine, because you're mine.*

I decided to walk down the path to the pond. There must be a reason I would walk down the path to the pond, but what could it be? I wondered what that reason might be all the way to the gap in the fence.

He was crouched over his pond, his back to me. A plastic bucket lay on its side next to him. The pond was wider now. I watched as he worked, scooping the dirt with his hands. How committed he was to his task.

I could have stood there all day, watching him.

He turned to pick up his bucket and saw me. 'Oh, it's you.' He opened his arms wide. 'Look. Even bigger.' His eyes were as deep as the Sea of Galilee. He returned to his digging. 'I can put in rocks, and weeds, and Mum said she would buy fish from Hamilton.' He scooped out more of the dirt. 'Where we lived in the city you couldn't have a pond. Tanya thinks it's the worst coming here. I mean, school is pretty bad. I hate being new. But the fish will be good. I wonder if you can buy them in Hamilton?' Then he was quiet and there was only the sound of his hands scraping at the wet ground.

Was he waiting for me to speak? I did not want to disappoint him. As I disappointed Paul. Mother, Mrs St Clair, Mr Brommell. I continued to watch him. If the boy had a shovel, he could dig out more of the dirt. It would not hurt the skin of his hands, as it must. The boy kept scraping. I walked away from him and back up to the house. I was sure I had left the shovel leaning against the front porch for some task or another? As I went through the house I wondered if there was something else I could give him. I looked around the kitchen. What would a boy do with a teacup, dried leaves, a cicada's shell? I went into Paul's old room. A small glass jar sat on the shelf. I picked it up; three marbles clattered around its base.

I collected the shovel from the front and went back down through the yard with the jar. But I could not see him! Was the fishpond already so deep he might be hidden inside? But no. He was not inside his pond. Of course he was not. I had taken too long. He was not there. He had returned to the people inside his home. Had not been able to wait. I remembered Colin as he ran towards the Brommells' house. Then there was only the empty place the boy left behind. The boy of ten, what happened to him, where did he go?

I left the shovel and the glass jar in the pond and returned to Beverly.

I walked up and down the kitchen. I moved into the lounge and did it there. Pacing past canvases and brushes, sardine cans and beer bottles, empty tubes of paint, used rags, sketchbooks filled with drawings. I kept going up and down. Pacing from the lounge to the bedroom, the bedroom to the laundry, the laundry to the spare. The medal in its place on the shelf, its ribbon arms dusty and faded, surrounded by newspaper, empty soup cans, pencil stubs. How did they come to be in here? I returned to the lounge and picked up *Letters from the Masters. Illuminating, patronage, Rome. Consolation, primary, phenomena. Zealous, beneficial.* What did any of those words mean? Even the paintings were closed to me. I tossed the book to the floor and pushed Mother's rocker back and forth. I had taken too long for the boy. He could not wait. When would I see him again? I did not know. Did not know. I left the rocker and crossed to the kitchen chair. I had wanted to give him a gift.

I thought I had time. Was sure I had the time. I was mistaken.
I left the kitchen chair and sat in the rocker. Back and forth,
back and forth.

When night at last fell and the lights next door were out but
for the one over the porch—how I longed to smash it with a
stone—I walked to the bottom corner of the yard. I had to go
down there—even at the risk of being seen. The bunker was
a stroke in the painting of my days. How old was I now? Was
I forty years? Fifty years? Sixty? I searched for Wallis in the
starless night and could not see him. It was as if the mountain
had disappeared. I pulled the bunker door closed behind me.

42

THE NEXT TIME I WENT down to the gap in the fence I saw the shovel lying across the widening pond and the jar filled with stones wedged between rocks. I looked up and nodded at the straw man as a sweetness spread throughout my body. 'The boy found a use for the shovel, straw man, and for my gift.' I picked up the shovel, stepped into the pond and worked at the sides. When the pond was smooth and even, I stood the shovel upright in the ground. It seemed it was the shovel did the talking between the boy and me. The next time he came here he would see the shovel upright in the dirt and he would know it was me who put it there, just as I knew now it was him who had left it lying flat.

Early the next morning, I took the steel milking pail from its hook in the shed and headed for the turnstile. I carried the pail by its handle, recalling other times when I had carried it for Mother, taking the extra to Mrs Barry's for the patients with no hope. I crossed the field towards Wallis. I did not bring the pochade box, or any canvas, or paper and pencils. As I walked,

I had the sense of where spring had been, could feel him, behind me, the growth that would soon die. All was in flux; all was change. 'For what?' I asked the morning. 'To where? Ha!'

Wallis became damper and cooler the higher I walked, the pail swinging by my side. In and out, in and out, one breath leading to the next, like my steps up the trail. I was aware of myself as a part of the landscape, just as the spiky grass trees and the bundled guineas were a part of the landscape. I did not question the value of the grass or the guineas, so why should I question my own?

I came to a place close to the base of Wallis where the stream made the ground marshy, and puddled, where the ferns and the balga and the purple moss flowers gave shade and kept the earth moist.

I sat by the muddy ground and watched.

I had seen frogs on many of my walks, hidden behind rocks, blinking beneath ferns and leaves, camouflaged. I had listened to their song from the back porch all my life—a natural music to my tasks, my pleasures. This morning I sat still and quiet, looking into the leaves, into the rocks, the water. I bent forwards, my fingers oversized and clumsy as I lifted the plants, pushing aside the wet stones.

I saw one, his skin indistinguishable from the brown and curling stems of the ferns, his small eyes blinking, tiny bulbs. I moved slowly, my old hands and wrists like gnarled branches over the stream. Slowly, slowly, I came down over him. 'Got you.' I held him between my hands, lifting him to my face. The frog and me eye to eye. I smiled. 'Hello, boy, *blink blink*.' I placed my sticky gift into the pail. His throat bulged in and out. I watched him hop to the side, the steel wall too steep for him to climb. 'Not for long, little man.'

I returned to my task, sitting in the quiet of the damp and shaded pocket, until I saw another. I leaned in, hands over the puddle. Slowly now . . . 'Got you.'

I put the second into the pail with the first.

I kept my eyes on the rocks and the leaves and the puddles, the water barely flowing, and did not move. Time could do what it wanted. It could pass, or it could stand still. The third frog was on his way, no matter what time did.

Did anybody know that a man waited by a puddle, at the base of a mountain, to catch a frog? Who knew? Mother? Father? Mrs Barry? I was unsure of how long I sat. My body ached, and my backside grew damp and cold. A storm might rage around me, fiercer than Master Rembrandt's, and I would not move. I was as the mountain.

At last I saw him, not yet fully grown, his legs half tail. Down I came over him. 'I am absolute lord and lawgiver.' I spoke the words into the glade, or was it Crusoe himself helping me catch the frogs? I looked at the creature in my cupped hands, noting the markings down his back, the way the darker brown sat beside the lighter, the balance in his stripes, his bright round eyes. I had painted the landscape all these years, but I had forgotten the frogs! I looked at his legs newly forming, readying the animal for a life of jumping, of swimming and climbing. I saw what he would become, his unlived possibilities. 'Little man . . . Clever fellow,' I whispered to him. Smaller than the other two, he was the real gift. The boy could watch him as he grew. I placed the frog in the pail, then I broke ferns at the stem and added them to the water, along with rocks and sticks. I got to my feet—how my knees ached!—and carried the pail as carefully as I could back along the trail.

*

I kept the three inside for the day, checking them every little while. 'It will not be long,' I told them, pushing away the weeds as they tried to make their way up the sides.

Before the boy would be home from school that day I went under the house. There, among discarded planks and bricks and sleepers I found a large piece of black plastic. I pulled out the plastic, spread it in the sun and swept it with the porch broom, scrubbing at the mould and mud caught in the cracks. 'Yes, yes, that's it, that's it, that's the way.'

My work was interrupted by a magpie calling to me from the porch railing. The bird looked at me, head to the side. *What are you doing, Lawrence?*

I shooed the bird away with the broom. 'Go and talk to the straw man!'

The plastic lay clean and smooth across the porch. 'There, now. There.' I rolled the sheet under my arm. Then suddenly the thought came to me: What if he is not there? What if he does not come again? The plastic was rolled and ready, the frogs waited in the pail. What would I do?

I would go anyway. Why not? Why shouldn't I go?

I made my way down the yard, carrying the roll of plastic and the pail, to the break in the fence. I looked into Mrs Barry's yard. The boy was there, sitting in his empty pond, but he was not alone. I had not expected the girl would be there too, one leg over the other on the grass, yellow thongs on her feet, the dog beside her. She held a cigarette between red fingernails.

I raised the pail towards the boy. The dog lifted his head.

'What's in the bucket?' the girl asked, blowing out smoke. Her shirt was orange, her shorts were torn, her long hair pulled high. She stood out in the landscape like rubbish.

I set the pail down close to the boy.

The girl leaned forwards and looked into the pail. 'I can't see anything,' she said, reaching in and moving one of the rocks. 'Eeeek!' she shrieked.

'What is it?' asked the boy, coming closer. 'Oh, look! Frogs. Two. No, three!'

I unrolled the plastic sheet.

'Going to wrap one of us up in that?' the girl asked.

'Shut up, Tanya . . .' David said.

'That's how you get rid of a body—didn't you know, Dave? You wrap it in plastic.' The girl ashed her cigarette into the pond. 'Then you dump it.'

I did not think the girl would be there. When I was imagining this moment, she was not there. It was only the boy. Thoughts and longings are one way, then the world happens in its own way. Yet the moment would not have happened at all if I had not seen it, would it? Who else made the picture?

I said to the boy, 'Y-y-y . . . you n-n-n . . . to to to m-m . . .'

'He wants you to get out of the pond, David,' the girl said. 'Isn't that what you want, mister?'

I nodded.

'Oh.' The boy climbed out of the pond.

I got down on my hands and knees and tucked the thick black plastic into the corners of the pond. I pushed it under rocks and dug it into the ground at the top and pulled it taut. The boy watched, sometimes looking into the pail. I was aware of my body, awkward and oversized as I worked. It seemed a body changed its size depending on who was placed beside it! The girl smoked and slapped at the mosquitoes biting at her thighs. The pond was now lined with the black plastic.

'What about the water?' the girl said.

'Th-th-the h-h-h-hose . . .'

'Where's that?'

'T-t-t-t-tank.'

The dog sniffed at the pail. 'Sick 'em, Rex,' said Tanya.

David pushed the dog away. 'Leave them alone, Mol.'

I stood to get the hose. Why was she here? Her garish colours, her torn clothes, legs a feast for the mosquitoes. It was between me and the boy. I uncoiled the hose and turned the tap. I felt her eyes on me as I dragged the hose through the gap. I could imagine her thoughts. Her questions. *Who is he? Why can't he talk? What's wrong with him?* I wanted, then, to stop, return to Beverly, at the same time as I wanted to keep going towards them. To go forwards, to retreat.

What part chose?

I directed the hose at the pond. 'I can hold it, if you like,' said the boy, as he got to his feet. Every part of him was put together in the right way. Everybody else, including myself, put together in the wrong way—feet too big, backs curved, heads oversized, hands too small, the lines without symmetry. But not him. He was perfect.

I passed him the hose, the water slamming against the plastic.

Tanya said, 'How come you've been hiding?'

'He hasn't been hiding,' said David.

'Well, we haven't seen him much, have we? And the other week when we came around he didn't answer the door.'

'You don't always answer the door, Tanya,' the boy said.

'Not if I know it's you that's knocking.' Tanya picked up a stone and threw it into the pond.

'Hey,' said the boy, frowning.

Tanya took a long pull from her cigarette. She narrowed her eyes, examining me through the smoke. She had the same features as her brother, the same dark hair and grey eyes, the same colour on the cheeks, the same long limbs, but in the boy they were gentle and inviting; in the girl they were sharp, cold, impenetrable. Opposing interpretations of the same beauty.

She stood. 'God, this place is disgusting. Frogs and bloody mud and bloody weirdos.' She flicked her cigarette into the grass and stepped on it. I watched her bottom as she walked away, hungry enough to eat its own shorts.

'Don't worry about her,' said the boy. 'She's always like that.' He snorted.

It was as if we shared a secret. I heard it in the snort from his boyish nose. Ha! And then I did not object that the sister had been there because she had pushed us closer. Perhaps whoever had put her there knew that it would!

The water was almost at the top of the pond. 'Shall I run up and turn it off?' he asked me.

I nodded. Watched as he ran to the tap, his legs long and ungainly, as Colin's had been. His back, his loose long shorts that needed a belt to hold them closer to his waist. His bare calves.

The water stopped from the hose and he came back down. 'Can the frogs go in now?'

I nodded. Passed him the pail. Watched as he reached in and lifted out a frog.

The boy held the creature in the palm of his hand, his fingers curled around it like a small cave. He brought it to his face. 'You are about to go to your new home,' he said. 'I hope you like it.' He lowered the frog onto a rock in the pond. 'There you go, frog,' he said. 'I will go back for your friends, while you get to know the place.'

He reached again into the pail. His long arms, his fingernails each with a miniature crescent of mud, his bare knees, bruised.

He lifted another frog from the pail and placed him onto the side of the pond. The frog hopped under a clump of weeds.

'I'll need more of those,' he said. 'Those weeds. Next time could I go with you?' he asked, lifting the last frog from the pail.

'Y-y-yes,' I said.

'I am going to make the sides higher so they can't escape.' His shirt lifted as he scraped at the dirt, exposing the pale skin of his back.

'David! David!' his sister called from the house.

David sat on his haunches. 'There wasn't even a yard in our old place,' he said. 'And now we have all this.' He swept his arm wide, indicating the mountain, the fields and forest, the sky, as if it all belonged to him.

'David! Get up here!' It was his sister.

'Got to go. Thank you for the frogs, Lawrence. And for the pond.' He smiled at me. *Lawrence*.

It did belong to him; it all belonged to him.

I watched him leave.

43.

I WALKED BACK INTO BEVERLY'S yard, noticing how long the grass had grown. How covered the yard was in sticks and branches and leaves that had fallen from the trees. There was paper and rubbish on the grass too, that must have come from inside Beverly. I lived like a man on a path of stones across water, one foot yet to land. I did things between stones I could not recall. When did I leave such a mess? I went to Gert's shelter and rolled the iron drum lying on its side up into the middle of the yard. Next I gathered the fallen branches and leaves and rubbish and placed them in the drum. I found old newspaper and crumpled the sheets, tossing them in with the rest. Then I struck the match, waited for the smoke to rise.

I took the rusted push mower from the shed and pushed it up and down, cutting the thick grass in long criss-crossing tracks until the sweat dripped down my back. After I was finished the yard appeared enormous, reminding me of the years when Mother was alive. Paul would kick the football all the way to the back fence before running to retrieve it. I had forgotten the space was so big.

I returned to the house; how cluttered and untidy it had become! Why did I not see it before? I picked up a drawing from the floor, of Gert at the turnstile, tracing with my fingers the cow's face, the circular stile. The drawing was years old. The line of the horizon was poorly placed; I could not tell if I was above or below Gert. How far my drawing had come! I crumpled the picture of Gert and stuffed it into the wood basket.

I gathered the drawings that lined the floors of every room. Drawings of nests made of twig and bark and string, until the drawings of nests became drawings of vegetables; twisted carrots, pumpkins in half, cauliflower stalks. The bathroom floor was covered with drawings of apples from Mother's tree—the apple freshly picked, the apple rotten, the apple core. Mother's bedroom was abandoned feathers, butterfly wings, the skeletons of possums. When did they line the floors in this way, my muddy boot prints across the lead? I gathered them into my arms, the mistakes of my past, and took them out to the fire.

Next I took all the rubbish boxes and packets and anything I knew would burn down to the drum. I placed all the empty tubes of paint and tin cans, and bottles of turpentine into used boxes from Parker's Art Supplies and carried them to the front of the house. Paul could take them away with him when he next brought supplies. He had offered to do so often enough.

Dust rose up around me as I swept the floors, singing with the girls of *Butterfly*, '*Gioia a te sia, dolce amica, ma pria di varcar.*' I could now see the grooves and knots in the oak boards, their texture and warmth. I rubbed at the windows with a rag—how green was the yard through the glass, how bright the apple tree. I washed every dish, cleared the window ledges and cornices of dust, the corpses of flies, spider webs. I took canvases from the house and placed them on the porch where they could feel the sun on their faces.

As I was there on the porch, I heard the sound of the postal van. For the first time I had not been waiting, wondering when it would come.

When had I last sent an order? Was it before the family had moved in next door, or since? Today, for the first time, I had not waited. I had not anticipated its coming, had not noticed that I would soon need paint or paper or pencils. Had not been waiting or wondering when would it come and thinking perhaps it will not come, will not come at all, and then what would I do? This time, for the first time, the boxes had simply arrived.

I went out the front, and saw the postman pulling out my boxes from the back of his van. Paul had organised the payment, as he had done for some time now, and I signed his book. I brought the boxes inside and placed them on the kitchen table. It occurred to me then, if the boxes arrived without my thinking that they would not, perhaps it was not my waiting and my doubting that made the postal van come. The postal van came because I had sent an order to Moira Parker, she had read the order and boxed the supplies, then the postal van had brought them to me. That was why they arrived. Not because I had suffered for them. My next thought was one I had not had before—*I do not need to suffer so.* My thoughts led easily one to the next, without stammer. What had given me this new life, this space between thoughts? *I do not need to suffer so!*

I did not immediately open the boxes as I was accustomed to doing. No. I was content to have them sit on the empty table, on the freshly swept oak floors, in the light that poured through the windows.

44.

'HEY, THERE!' IT WAS THE mother, calling over the fence. 'Hey!'

I was on the porch, on my way inside the house, when she stepped through the gap.

I turned around.

'Hi,' she said.

Short dark hair, longer on one side, a line of silver hoops down her ears, black lines underneath her eyes. Tears in the knees of her jeans.

'Hey there,' she said as she came up the yard towards me. 'I'm Rachel. Rach.' She held a mug in her hand stained with drips of coffee. 'It's Lawrence, isn't it?'

I nodded.

'Sorry it's taken me so long. But you know, just trying to get settled . . .'

I could tell there were words she wanted me to say. That she was waiting for them.

She looked at me over her cup. 'Crazy, isn't it, both of us out here in the middle of nowhere, and we haven't officially met? So—hello.'

323

Again, she was waiting.

'I hope the kids don't piss you off . . . They told me about the frogs. That was nice. That would have been good for Dave.' She looked around, worried, hoping, hoping it was nice, hoping it was good. She said, 'You've been here a long time, haven't you?' She was looking up to Beverly when she asked—at the yard, and the outhouse. My back porch. Like she was searching for something. She said, 'I hope they don't piss you off.' A hard smile, there and gone. 'They piss me off.'

'I get back from work late—just the first thing I could find. At the hospital in Hamilton. I'm an aide out there. Anyway, it's good to know you're here . . . Your brother came around. Paul.' She brightened at this. 'He seems alright. Seems really nice. Said he'd fix my car if I needed it. Good to have family, right?'

She was asking directly now.

'Y-y-y-yes.'

Shadows crossed her eyes. There was silence before she spoke again, looking over to Mrs Barry's house.

'Good when this place came through. Last of the old brothers kicked the bucket, and it fell to us. Like magic, hey, when that happens?' She ran her hand over the shorter side of her hair. 'Just in the nick of time. Tanya chucked out of school, debts up to my eyeballs.' It was as if she were talking to herself. 'We're not allowed to sell it. That's the deal. We have to stay. That's the only thing. Bloody ridiculous, if you ask me.'

The dog barked, bounding through the fence into Beverly's yard, past the woman, to me. The animal had no sense of where she ended and I began. Sniffed at my trousers. Jumped up on me, paws against my thighs.

The woman grabbed the dog by the collar, coffee spilling from her cup. 'Come on, Mol. Sorry about that. She's got a terrible bark, I know. Great guard dog, I suppose. Not that we need one. Paul said you were always here. So that's good. Nice to know.'

She drained her cup over the dirt, still holding on to the dog. 'He told me you looked after the vegetable garden at the bottom of our yard. Listen, you can keep it going, if you like. I mean, if you don't mind us taking what you grow. Sharing it, I mean. I'm shit at gardening and I can't see Tanya taking it up any time soon.' She rolled her eyes. 'So just . . . yeah, garden it, or whatever. And I'll just take what you don't need. Maybe I can give you my number at work, and if there's any trouble—I mean, you know, anything with the kids while I'm not there—you can call that number.'

She pulled on the last ring in her ear then shook her head. 'Bloody hell,' she said. She checked her watch. 'I got to go. Nice to meet you, anyway. If the kids give you the shits, let me know.'

She looked at me one more time, then she was gone, dragging the dog behind her.

I turned and went inside. I sat in Mother's rocker. Rachel was the mother of the boy. Rach. I had a mother who took care of my brother and me. And next door, where Rachel and David and Tanya now lived, Mrs Barry had lived, and she had watched over us when our mother was at work. I rocked the chair. Mothers could not always keep their sons safe.

After I met Rachel, I counted five days that passed without speaking to the boy. Was it because of the mother that I did not see him? I had walked down to the gap in the fence, I had looked in at the pond, but he was not there. The dog had come into my yard many times, wandering about, sniffing every fence post and paling. I did not want the dog sniffing the borders and doing her business. Did not want the sudden way the dog moved and jumped and barked. The dog was an intrusion. I could do nothing about her and saw her often. The only times I saw the boy was in the mornings before he left for school, when I watched him through the side window, throwing the ball for the animal. Why did he play with the dog so many hours? Throwing the ball over and over?

Why must you be with the dog, David?

The next Saturday morning, I decided to work the vegetable garden. The mother had told me to do so and I had eaten few vegetables since the family arrived. Was I choosing a time when the mother, Rach, would not be at home? I asked myself. But it was not until now that I had the inclination! It was only now, this Saturday morning. I was not sure whether David or his sister were at home; I had not heard them. It was quiet next door. Rachel had said I was welcome to it, she said to keep it going, to work it and share it. I looked through my side window and could not see the boy or his sister or the dog in the yard.

I pulled on my boots, took the iron pot, and went down to the gap in the fence. The day would soon be warm, the land was drying as the summer grew longer.

The plastic sheet had retained the water in the boy's pond. I picked up a stick and stirred the weeds. The third frog swam from one side to the other, his legs almost formed. I looked up; the straw man was pointing at me. 'What?' I frowned at him, turning my attention to the vegetables, running my hand through new tomatoes on their stems, the stalks of carrots. I pulled away the snails that had been eating the bean leaves. I could see the holes left by the aphids. Dandelions and creepers grew between the rows. I turned the earth with the gardening fork; what a pleasure it was, the tearing sound of the tiny roots of weeds, leaving space in the soil. I uncovered one last potato, small and sprouting, as I cleared the beds, removing pests, feeling the leaves in my hands, the sun on my shoulders. My thoughts turned to the soup that I would prepare; the way it would bubble on the stove, with the ham bone and the salt, carrots and beans rising to the surface, tomatoes lending richness. I imagined the boy coming down to the bottom of the garden to check the frogs, to speak of the fish that his mother was going to buy. I said to him, without stammer, 'Have some soup.'

I soon grew warm and wanted to pull off my jacket, though I did not. I wished I had Gert's manure to feed the garden. I would ask Paul, and he would bring a load. He would bring fresh seeds too, if I asked him, and I could plant corn, and the corn would bubble, yellow and bright, beside the carrots. Soup too was a picture. A balance of colours.

'Hey there, what are you doing?'

I looked up.

The boy was coming towards me. His hands were hidden in his sleeves so that I saw only the tips of his fingers. His shorts showed his pale knees. He came slowly down, to where I was, under the straw man, with my iron pot.

'What are you doing?'

'V-v-v-v . . .' I wished the word was there and came for me the way it came for others. I wished it and at the same time wanted the word to remain with me. Yearned for outward expression, needed privacy—my longings too, in contradiction. What was not?

The boy sat down on the grass.

I tried again. 'V-v-v . . . I-I-I . . .'

It did not feel as if the boy were waiting for me. He was not in a hurry. He had never been in a hurry. He looked at me, or he did not. His eyes on other things—the yard, the field, the sky.

'Vegetables,' I said.

'Oh.' He leaned over and took a bean from my pot. He tore the outer shell and the row of beans inside spilled onto the grass. 'What do you do with these?'

'S-s-s-soup.'

'Really?'

'Y-y-y-yes.'

'These too?' He picked up one of the carrots.

'Y-y-y-yes.'

'It's dirty.'

'Y-y-y-yes.'

'It looks like it comes from under the ground.'

'Yes. Yes. It does.'

'I hope you wash it first.'

'Y-y-yes.' I wanted to smile. 'I-i-i-it's a r-r-r-root. It is the root o-o-o-of the p-p-p-plant.'

I remembered all that I had taught Paul, the questions I could answer, and if there was one that I could not I could learn the answer. I could ask Mr Wade, or Mrs St Clair. I could go to the library and find the answer in a book. *What is the capital of China? What is the world's largest river? Name the seventh ancient wonder.*

I sat back beside the boy, leaning on my hands as we faced Wallis. Summer showed his every corrugation; the mountain had shed the fears of the colder months and was ready to be seen.

'Have you been up there?' the boy asked.

'Y-y-yes. Yes.'

'What's it like?'

'G-g-g . . . It is . . . it is . . . good. Good.'

'It must be dangerous. So high.' He twisted blades of grass in his fingers, pulling them.

I shrugged. 'N-n-n-no. N-n-not d-d-d-dangerous.'

'I would like to go there.'

'To to to the top?'

'Yes.'

'It's a l-l-l-long way. A long climb.'

'How long?'

'T-t-t-two hours. Or th-th-th-three hours. Or m-m-m-more.'

'That's not long. I did school camp once and we did a day walk.'

To take him to the summit, as I had been with Paul so many years ago? The two of us climbing Wallis . . . it was something I might imagine from Mother's rocker. It was something I might imagine as I climbed alone. It was not something that could happen. And yet many things had happened as I wanted them. Paints from Moira Parker. *Madame Butterfly* on the player. The boy here beside me. 'W-w-w-would you like to?'

'Yes. Could we?' he asked.

I didn't know. Was it possible?

'I'd really like to.'

'We c-c-could . . . we could . . . we could . . . go on a S-S-S-Saturday. Saturday.'

'When Mum is at work?'

'Yes.'

'Does Tanya have to come?'

'D-d-d-do you want her to?'

'No.'

'Alright. Alright. Alright. N-n-n-no.'

'I hope we get to the top.'

'We n-n-n-need to go early.'

'I get up early. I get up before Tanya. She sleeps in. She'd sleep in until lunchtime if I didn't wake her.'

'Al-al-alright. B-b-b-but you will need to t-t-tell her, tell her.'

'I can leave a note.'

'A n-n-note?'

'That's what she does to me. Leaves notes. *Home later. Don't tell Mum.* I can leave a note too.'

'Very early. W-w-w-we need to l-l-l-leave early, before the h-h-h-heat.'

We looked at Wallis.

'It's a long way,' he said.

'Y-y-y-yes.'

We sat among the vegetables, alongside the beans and tomatoes and carrots, and for a while we did not speak. Wallis inspired silence. He was Homer in *The Apotheosis* on the highest step. I wanted to place my hand upon the boy's head.

He stood. 'Next Saturday then?'

'Y-y-y-yes.'

'All the way to the top?'

'Y-y-yes.'

'I won't tell anyone.'

'N-no.'

'Early.'

'Yes. I will be here, at this spot. Early.'

'So will I.'

45.

THE EVENING BEFORE WE HAD planned to walk I looked once again through the kitchen window at the sky. Every day since we had made our plan, I had looked at the sky and asked myself, What if it rains? Will we not go? What if there is a storm? I reminded myself that at this time of year it would probably be warm. But each time I looked at the sky I wondered the same thing, What if it rains? What if we cannot go? It did not matter how many times I told myself that it was probably going to be fair weather, still I found myself asking the question, What if it rains? Will we not go?

And now it was the last day of waiting and the afternoon sky looked clear and had been clear, for every minute of the past week.

When had I last walked in the company of another? I wondered as I added carrots to my soup. Paul, all those years ago. How many? Forty? Was it more? Not long after my tenth birthday. The day Uncle arrived. Mother had left us while she went into town to collect him from the station, and Paul and I had climbed the mountain. How enormous the world seemed from the summit, Paul's hand in mine. I remembered the sense that although my adventures would be alone, it was the feeling of Paul's hand in mine that would enable them. But Paul and I did not go there together again.

And tomorrow the boy and I were going up the mountain. I stirred the soup in the pot, looking about me at the shelves that held the teacups and saucers and bowls, at the pine cones and stones and drying leaves amid them. There was relationship between that which was fresh from nature and that which had travelled further. The cone and the cup, the bowl and the leaf. There was relationship where you could not first see it.

I took the scissors from the drawer, went to my front porch where the gum tree flowered pink and white. I cut away an armful of the blossoms, then returned to the kitchen and placed them in Mother's vase. Had I known the way the pink of the blossom would sit against the green of the vase? Or was true beauty accidental? Or perhaps beauty was everywhere, depending only on the eye that sees it.

I stood in the kitchen with the warmth of the sun across my face and my thoughts of beauty. I wanted to take off my coat. I only took off my coat to sleep, or when I had my bath, keeping on my other clothes. Clothing, too, needed a wash! I remembered Mother scrubbing at my clothing over the washer board when I was a boy. Standing at the line in her work dress and rubber boots, pegging socks and sheets with the same hands that had milked Gert and done the numbers.

Mother's hands.

The veins that ran from her wrists to the crooks of her arms.

Her worry for us. Mother's worry left us free to roam. She carried it for Paul and me in the veins that ran from her wrists to the crooks of her elbows. Clever Mother. Mother no longer here. Mother a memory.

I looked around the house; the past had entered Beverly and I was at peace with it, and at peace with what was to come. Soup on the stove, sun across my cheek, the pink and white blossoms in the vase. '*Non più bella e d'assai fanciulla io vidi mai di questa Butterfly!*' I sang, as I pulled off my coat. The kitchen smelled of soup and blossom, eucalyptus. Scent, too, was in relationship. Scent, too, was a road to a place that was not for the reaching.

I sat in the rocker and looked through *Letters from the Masters*. Unbound pages slipped to the floor. As I reminded myself to take care, to order glue from Moira Parker, or string, a portrait of a man on one of the pages caught my eye. I ran my fingers over his face, his brown coat with its high collar. He turned to me as if I had interrupted him. *What is it that you want?* he seemed to ask. Beside the portrait was a note: *Runge painted this self-portrait in the year of his death.* I had never been interested before in self-portraiture. My interest was in the world without the image of myself. Miraculous. Faultless. But Master Runge had my attention. The way the light fell across his forehead, the look in his eyes. He was not angry. But nor did he show warmth. His eyes challenged me. Asked of me: *What do you have to say for yourself?* In that same year he did the painting, Runge died. But in the time he painted the portrait he did not know he would die. He was alive, with only thoughts that pertained to his life, real and vital to him, as if it would not end. 'And yet he died.' A man lived with effort and intention, he suffered, he knew he would die, and yet he painted. I shook my head. Why was it so difficult to understand?

I read Master Runge's letter to Goethe. *A firm belief that there is a definite spiritual connection between the elements may finally bring the painter a consolation and cheerfulness to which he cannot attain by any other means . . .* 'Consolation, cheerfulness, spiritual.' I spoke the words aloud while looking at the portrait. 'Elements, definite, attain.' Words that became mine in the speaking, complex in shape, layered, precise.

I stood from the rocker, went into Mother's room, which was in shadow, to the drawers where she had kept her pearls and her perfume and her gloves. I dragged the drawers out through the door—they were heavy and knocked awkwardly against the frame on either side—and into the kitchen. The last of the day's light showed the mirror. I had caught my own reflection in the windowpane often enough but only ever in part. I never looked long, did not like the surprise. The last time I had looked squarely into the mirror my face had been bruised and blackened. How many years since then? I turned on the kitchen lamp and angled the mirror so it would cast my reflection in adequate light.

I failed to recognise the man I saw in the glass. Was it me? How old was I? I did not want to be this man I did not know, covered in hair, lined, eyes dark and inscrutable under heavy brows. I wanted to turn away. But Masters Runge and Friedrich and Rossetti did not turn away. Their self-portraits were not designed to flatter or beautify; they were merely another object to paint, an object living and accessible. Master Runge had something he wanted to show the world, through the filter of his hand and eye, the filter of his experience, his desire, and he used his face to do so. The face was a landscape, separate to the artist. A road into the question. I existed ageless within my ageing body, looking out through its eyes, as Master Runge had looked through his.

I set a clean canvas up on the dresser's marble top, leaning it against the small cupboards on one side. I took up my palette.

Readied the jar of water, the rags and brushes. I looked again at the face I saw reflected in the mirror; not as if it were my own, but as I looked at the mountain, or the apple, or the leaf. I worked first into the hair, unruly, dark, running this way and that. Burnt umber and brown ochre, copper and ivory black. From the hair down to the forehead, its small scar—from what I did not know, could not recall—working into the indentation, the way it crossed the natural lines. Painting into the ears that showed themselves from beneath the hair. The beard, grey and dark, the cragged cheeks, the uneven skin. I saw the deep lines across the forehead, and the deep lines from the eyes, more down either side of the chin. I saw the last of the sun across this face of lines and made no judgement, only looked, without effort, for what would show itself in the strokes of the brush. On my way, on my way, at last, down over the dark brows, into the eyes.

It was only when night fell that I stood back, switched on the lamp to better see what I had done. I gasped. Was this me? Was I creator or subject? I saw within my own painted eyes the closest I had ever been to answering, Where did the road within every painting lead? The closest I had been to knowing where Mrs Barry had gone, Mother, old Gert, all things that must die, as the frogs in David's pond must die, as the doves must die, the vegetables in the garden and, one day, myself. I was filled with tenderness for all who would die, who lived without knowing why, and for the man who had appeared on the canvas. How much did we choose? Gert could not choose, Mrs Barry could not choose, and I could not choose.

I placed the portrait beside the mirror on Mother's drawers and stirred the soup at the stove. '*Ah! dolce notte! quante stelle!*' I sang as I stretched the fingers of my aching hand. Standing at the window, I saw Butterfly's night of stars. For once I did not object to the light in the windows from the house next door. I wondered what the boy was doing in there. Was he thinking of our walk?

Only David and I knew about the plan to climb the mountain. David's mother would be at her work at the hospital. David would leave a note for his sister. Tanya did not wake until late—lunchtime, the boy had told me—and then she would see the note, not until then. I wanted the night to pass so the morning would come and the secret I shared with the boy could unfold before us. I wanted it more than I had wanted supplies from Parker's, more than I wanted to paint Wallis, more than I had wanted to give Colin the nest. I wanted the night to pass, and for the next day to begin. Begin! Begin, new day! Yet still I relished knowing that the night was not gone, that the night was still here, because all that was to come was still on its way. And the morning *would* come; there was nothing anybody could do to stop it, and when it came, there I would be, at the pond, waiting.

I went to Mother's bed and switched off the light. Did not want the morning to arrive, and wanted it to, very much. I lay hour after hour, between night and day, wanting and not wanting, desire and destination.

46.

I WAS WOKEN BY A sharp pain in my backside. I sat up in the bed, seeing light through the slats of the blind. My stomach clenched. It was not as at other times when I could wait. I was hot and cold, trembling. I walked down to the outhouse, not looking up from the track, pulling the wooden door closed behind me, hooking the latch. I kept my eyes on the carved top of the door as I pulled down my trousers. I kept my eyes there, on the strip of sky, my focus outwards, away from myself.

My knees were weak when I stood, shaking. I pulled up my trousers and opened the door. There was Wallis, rays of gold over his north face, the sky promising blue. Palest blue mountain. The jewel of the Grampians. I held the door until I stopped shaking. It was the first morning on earth. The first tick of the bird clock.

I went about the kitchen making tea and packing the satchel. Apples and beef strips, oranges and cheese, bread, tea biscuits enough for two. I hummed as I tied the enamel cup to the strap, the cup that the boy and I would soon share. *'Tutto estatico d'amor,*

337

ride il ciel!' I cut wedges of cheese and wrapped Mrs Barry's tomatoes in a cloth, placing them in the side pouch reserved for the turpentine. I packed a knife and a slab of butter. Then I put the satchel over my shoulder and looked around Beverly, at the player, Mother's rocker. The wood stove. The soup bowl. The pink and white blossoms in the vase. *Goodbye, goodbye.*

I pulled on my woollen hat, went out through Beverly's back door and down to the pond. I had not expected that the boy would be there. Not yet. I knew that I would wait for him, wanted to wait for him, relished the anticipation. I looked up at the straw man, his face leaking, more scarred it seemed with every passing day, and wanted, suddenly, to shake his hand. *Today we are going up the mountain, the boy and I.* Then there would be another who knew my secret. I smiled. A smile for the straw man. Master Rodin wrote to Verhaeren: . . . *my whole life, even in its best moments, falls short of this sweetness.*

I checked Mrs Barry's house and saw that the driveway was empty. The mother had left for the day. The back door was closed, and the blinds were drawn across the windows. *What if he does not come?* I thought suddenly. Why had I not considered this possibility? That the boy would not come. Why would the boy want to climb the mountain with me, a man of fifty or more? I could not think of the answer. There was no answer. Or was there? Perhaps there was an answer to the question, and it was this: there was no reason he would want to. What did I have to offer the boy? A jar of stones? Three frogs? A shovel? I would not wait a minute longer—I would go inside and paint. Forget the mountain. I looked at the sky. It was a good day for climbing—that was true enough. If the boy did not come, perhaps I could go on my own. Perhaps the boy was a dream, and if he was a dream, then I could carry the dream of him on

my back. Share my lunch with the dream. Speak to it. Summer
was in the air, cool before the heat—yes, a good day for climbing.
It would be just as pleasant with the dream of the boy as with
the real. My satchel was ready with apples and oranges, tomatoes
and cheese, bread and the beef strips that Paul thought I liked.
The enamel cup tied to the strap. I would go regardless.

Perhaps I could rock while I waited a little longer for the
boy. Just a little longer. I could rock against the fence. I did
the first motion forwards, then the first motion back, and then
decided I would not rock. I stood in one place and wondered,
What was it that threatened when I wanted to rock? What did
the motion contain?

Then I saw him.

I raised my hand to David as he walked towards me. As I had
thought of him, wished for him, dreamed of him. There he was.
Was he born of the pictures in my mind?

'I didn't know if you would remember,' he said.

'Y-y-y-yes,' I said. 'Yes.'

He wore a hooded jacket, long belted trousers, and his school
shoes. He had no bag or satchel of his own.

I am older, I thought. It is up to me. The recognition of this
moved me. It was just as when Paul and I were boys.

As we walked past the straw man, the boy stopped and
pointed. 'Did you make him?' he asked me.

'I d-d-did.'

The boy stood beneath the tall figure made of old straw,
unwanted clothing. 'Don't wake my sister,' he said to the straw
man, a sparkle in his eyes.

Ha! The boy and the straw man were friends! Who would
have known?

The turnstile creaked its song once for me and once for David as we pushed our way through. We did not speak, our bodies taking their time to wake to the motion of our walking, our ears growing accustomed to the sound of one another's footsteps, to the song of the warbler and the dove and the kookaburra's laughter. Sheep grazed, in the distance; a tractor was parked in the field, ready to slash the hay. I could see the orchard's bluestone farmhouse, and the buildings that surrounded it. Horses fed at the hay nets by the stables. The day itself, whether painted or not, was a work of art. I wondered, Who made it so? For whose delight was the day?

I stayed behind him on the track as we approached the forest of stringybarks; slowing down my pace, my eyes on his legs as he walked the shaded path through the trees—I wanted him to find his own way, to show me that he could. Soon we came to the trail that led steeply up the mountain. With Wallis there was no warning. It was the same with every mountain in the range—they sprang from the land almost vertical.

'Are y-y-y-you you you you ready to start s-s-s-start the climb?'

'Ready as I'll ever be!' the boy called back.

I felt myself smile, unfamiliar, almost painful. I let it come across my old face and did not will it immediately away. *Ready as I'll ever be!* Young sailor. Pirate.

I heard the boy singing a tune under his breath as he walked. The tune came and went, sung only for himself, carrying him further to a place inside himself. I too had places within me. In this way we were the same. Painting took me to those places; and *Butterfly* and beer. Walking up the mountain.

The bush came close around us as we climbed; acacia and parrot peas and redgums. Black cockatoos with yellow tails squawked in the banksias, pulling at the pods. The scent of eucalyptus filled the air.

'I don't know about the school,' the boy said.

'Wh-wh-wh-what?'

'I said I don't know about the school.'

'Wh-wh-wh d-d-d-do you mean?' I asked him.

'School is hard work.'

'Th-th-th-that is g-g-good, isn't it?'

'Not really. I don't mean it in a good way. I mean . . .'

'What w-w-would you rather do?'

'I don't know. Read.'

'Wh-wh-what d-d-d-do you read?'

'Adventures mainly. I like escapes. I like space. I like castles. I like gangs who escape. Adventures with boats.'

'What do you like about boats?' Speaking with the boy was different to speaking with anybody else. He was in no hurry.

'Cabins. The mast. The rigging.'

'Ha. Cabins. Yes, rigging, yes. Up to the top.' I recalled *The Raft of the Medusa* by Master Gericault, *The Storm* by Master Gudin, and Master Friedrich's *Seascape by Moonlight*. I was with the boy and his story, and at the same time it gave me memories and pictures and stories of my own. Was this conversation? For one to offer, the other to receive? Words leading to other words, words to pictures?

'I like battles,' he said.

'Y-y-yes. Battles. Adventure.'

'I like battles where you really don't know who will win. It could be either side. I like the battle to keep going and going and you just don't know who will win. I like it when there are two sides and you know which side you want to win, but it just

341

doesn't look like it and you keep hoping, even if it looks like your side won't win, you can't help it, you keep hoping.'

'You like that?'

'Yes. I hate it, but I like it.'

'What do you mean?' I asked him.

'I hate worrying and hoping, but I can't help it. I keep thinking the good guys have to win, they have to, even if it looks like they won't. It's a bad feeling and it's a good feeling.'

'At the same time.'

'Yes. Yes, at the same time.'

I wondered if all boys were this way. Enthusiastic, sharing passions, loyalties, and finding it all a pleasure. I am sure I was once this way. David was restoring my boyhood to me. This walk, the air warm and clear, both empty and rich—the contradiction. Our feet led our talk, pushing the ideas forwards and upwards, contained by the broad body of Wallis. I was not alone. I knew it then in conversation with the boy. *I have been alone, and I am no longer alone.*

He went on with his talk. 'And then, when the good guys do win, I feel glad. Even when I finish the book, I still think about the way they won. How close it came. I will go over that moment the most. Like, if I am in my bed and the lights are off, there will be that battle again that looked like the good guys would lose. I go back to the start, even when I know what will happen. Like with every pirate killed, even the captain, except for one, the youngest one who you think couldn't do anything, couldn't make any difference, what difference could he make? Then he does a trick—some kind of trick that nobody thought of—he turns the sails around or he steers the ship into rocks when the soldiers are sleeping, or he does something—*something*—and he wins. That's what I like. I don't think about anything else.'

It was better than listening to *Butterfly*, or the call of birds, or the song of the frogs, or any other listening I could recall. I saw every picture as he spoke; the battle and the ocean and the trick of the youngest pirate. I inhaled the crisp air and listened to the talk of the boy, his ideas and words leading easily to the next, and me here on the mountain with him, a man, knowing the way, guiding us to our destination and yet allowing him to take the lead.

David stopped and bent down to look at something at his feet.

'What is it?' I asked him.

'Look.' He pointed at a centipede beside the path, curled around its sac, its colours glowing in bright rings. Huron purple, lime green, canary yellow. 'What's it doing?'

'Laying eggs, I think.'

'Oh. Will it stay to look after them?' He squatted and looked closer.

'Yes. I think it will. For a short time, at least.'

'Oh. I like its colours. The red legs.'

'I do too.'

He stood. 'You could put those colours in your paintings, couldn't you?'

'I could. I could.' I did not stammer. Here with this one person, this one boy in all the world.

'Next time you should. A caterpillar with red legs.' He looked up at me, eyes shining. 'These colours, they belong in a painting.'

He was right; the colours of the centipede would go very well in my painting. The boy was thinking of me when he spoke, of what might bring me pleasure, satisfaction. Of what was meaningful to me. How long since I had known what that might feel like? To be considered in this way. We kept walking. The sky above was free of cloud. In all of the paintings by the masters

I could not recall a sky so clear and blue. Every painting in the book was from the continent of Europe, first introduced to me by Mr Wade in the fourth class. France. Germany. The Netherlands. Today's sky was particular to *this* place. This country must have its own masters, I thought, to paint its own infinite splendours. Who were the masters of this country? I wondered. I thought then of all my paintings leaning against Beverly's walls. The sky at every time of day and night. If I did not paint the skies of Hughlon, they would not be recorded, known. Their uniqueness never captured. It had been up to me. All the years . . . How I enjoyed my thoughts as the boy and I walked! Considering the European continent and our own continent, the sky and its particularities. Each step sent one thought forwards to the next, with the appropriate time and space between—no single thought repeating, catching me within it. Perhaps the day's key note was freedom, or was it connection? I felt comfortably within my own boundaries, at the same time as connected with another. I could enjoy my questions about the nature of a sky and where it belonged and who had painted it, but I remained at the same time aware of the presence of the boy, and curious about that which held his attention.

I watched him as he found his way ahead of me, David in his blue belted trousers, his dark hair, twigs catching in his clothes, light around him. It was as if he belonged here, and not to that other world below the mountain. Perhaps neither of us belonged to the world below the mountain at all, and would never be returned to it, because it did not suit us, was not ours, we—the boy and I—would forever be compelled by the worlds we carried within us. Separate to each other, at the same time close, in relationship like the objects in a still life—the cone and the cup, the bowl and the leaf. Here, together on the mountain,

He turned around to me. 'We must be getting higher,' he said, swishing his stick through the air.

I do not need to live another day, I thought. This can be my last.

I nodded at the path up ahead. 'We can rest soon—a little further.'

I heard his breathing grow heavier as we continued to walk. I wished that I could carry him on my back—I knew I would not offer—but still I wished it, the way we wish for things every day, the way we fall asleep dreaming and wishing for the things we want that cannot happen. Life it seemed, was a platform for dreams of the things that we could not have.

Soon the path opened out, and we were at the first ridge. There was a trickle of water over the rocks dampening the ground.

'Let's take a rest,' I said.

David stood at the edge of the plateau and took off his jacket. 'It's getting hotter,' he said.

'Yes.'

'What mountain is that across there?' He pointed at the sheer sides of Mount Abrupt.

'Abrupt. Mount Abrupt.'

'I wonder if there is a boy and a man standing on Mount Abrupt looking at us right now, asking what mountain is that?'

I smiled. 'I wonder.' I untied the enamel cup from its strap.

He turned around to me. 'Is it much further?'

I set the cup underneath the trickle of water before returning to the boy. 'Not much further.' I took the bag from my shoulder and brought out an apple, using the knife to cut it into pieces in the palm of my hand. I leaned against the rock, feeling the sun warm across my back.

The boy sat beside me.

'You are lucky you can do whatever you want,' he said, taking a slice of apple from my open hand.

I laughed. *You can do whatever you want.* He crunched noisily on the hard fruit. Ha!

'My sister is a bitch.'

'That's not the right way to talk,' I said. Each word was contained within its first and last letters. We were away from the past, and future, in a time and place where I could speak. Wanted to.

'It's the truth. My sister is a bitch. She lies.'

'She is still your sister.'

'Who cares?'

'You will care one day. You care now. Don't use language like that.'

'Hmph.' He sounded angry. Suddenly, unexpectedly, I wanted to laugh again. What a delight it was to want to laugh, and then to choose not to. I had not known it was possible. Now I did know it. Whatever it cost me, I wanted to know it always.

'Why are you alone here?' David asked.

'What do you mean?'

'Where is your family?'

'I have a brother.'

'No, I mean . . .'

'You mean a wife. Children.' I stood to fetch the cup of water.

'Yes.'

'Not everyone does that.'

'Mostly they do. I don't know anyone that doesn't.'

'It's not for everyone.'

I brought the cup to him and watched as he drank, seeing the way he wiped his mouth before passing the cup to me. There was a pressure in my chest . . . I could not imagine that these things—drinking and wiping and passing the cup—had ever been done before in the same way.

'Why not?'

'I . . . don't know. I am interested in other things.'

'What things?'

I wanted to tell him that I was interested in him. But it was enough just to be with him, responding to his curiosity. Watching him. Absorbing him. For in every minute, every second we had together, I was aware of the minutes and the seconds that we would not have. I felt them as acutely as these now. I had to prepare for them. The time when he would be elsewhere. Was it possible to ache for what would disappear at the same time as loving what was here now? I did not know. I did not know anything. Nothing had prepared me. The book of letters could not prepare me. Painting could not prepare me. Wallis could not prepare me. There was nothing else I knew.

'The other kids think I'm a freak. They don't want to be my friend.'

'Oh.'

'I don't have many friends yet.'

'Oh.'

'I mean, you're my friend. And that's good. Yeah, it's good. You're old, but you still do things.'

Ha!

He stood and tossed a stone over the plateau's edge. 'Do we keep going?'

'Yes,' I said. 'We keep going.' It was a matter of not thinking of the words. *Keep going.* Not the *k* and the *g* and the *n*, not the shape and sound of the words, but the idea of movement. And that I wanted to agree with him. That was my intention—to communicate with him that I wanted to *keep going*. The boy was the key. My need to agree, to encourage him. It was a day of illuminations. I wanted the day to *keep going*.

I packed the satchel and retied the cup. Picked David's jacket up from the grass and passed it to him.

'Thank you,' he answered, tying the jacket about his waist, the sleeves like a pair of arms.

The sun was warmer now. We kept climbing the trail, the mountain leading us, giving us work to do, yes, but invitingly, wanting our footfalls against his wide and solitary body. Up and up and up, the mountain listening to the boy's song as I heard it, seeing his back as I saw it, jacket around his waist, arms swinging, seeing his neck, his size and youth, all the ways he had yet to grow, seeing these things as I saw them, seeing him change his pace, slow and fast then stopping, then slow again, then a run. I could never tell and nor could the mountain.

We came to the place where the path flattened before the last cluster of stringybarks. The boy ran up ahead. Then he turned to me. The trees were behind him, the sun was not yet high in the sky. 'Pretty close now, I reckon!' he called to me.

This is how I will paint you, I thought. For I knew that I would paint the boy, in that moment as he turned to me, the trees thickening behind him, the summer light falling across his face and torso. His stillness, his vulnerability, the light over him, from the sun, but at the same time emanating from him. I knew I would paint him, as I had once painted another boy.

David turned and began to walk again, and I followed along the path into the trees. He snapped a small branch from a banksia. 'Lenny Pilkins said, "Your sister's a slut."'

'What?'

'Lenny Pilkins said that. He says whatever he wants because his father is a policeman. He said, "Your sister's a slut."'

'What did you say?'

'I didn't say anything.'

'He was wrong to say it.'

'I don't know if he was wrong to say it. When I told Tanya, she said, "So what?"'

'Oh. Oh.'

'That's why we moved here. Because of Tanya.'

'Wasn't it because the house came to you?'

'Yes, that too. We needed the money. My dad didn't make enough. I mean—any.'

'Where is he now?'

'He's back in the city.' David whipped at a tree with his branch. 'Mum doesn't want to live with him anymore. She reckons he's useless.'

'Oh. Oh . . . Useless.' I wondered what that meant. To be useless or useful.

'She said he just gives her more work to do. That she should have known, that his own mother warned her he was useless.'

'Oh. Oh I see.'

What was it that made a man useful? Was my own father useful? He had been there only to put my brother and me in Mother's stomach. Did that make him useful or useless? He was useful in the war, wasn't he? But then he was killed in his plane. Was his death useful or useless?

The boy said, 'I don't think he's useless. He just can't do a job. He just can't. He doesn't like them.'

'What?'

'Jobs.'

'Oh.'

I thought of my own employment at the dairy. I did like that job. It was my last job. I no longer had a job. Perhaps I was as useless as the boy's father.

He was quiet again as the path took us through the stringy-barks, the summer orchids bursting pink against the trunks. My eyes moved from the pink and yellow fuchsia to the purple lily to the white heath that grew around the base of the eucalypts, then back to the boy. Why was it so difficult to look away? His tousled hair. The way he swung his small branch, looking everywhere, the insects as interesting to him as the clouds. It occurred to me that the boy contained a time within him that had passed. A time that I had longed for since it was lost to me. He held that time within him, the boy up ahead on the path, singing his tune. Carelessly, without effort. It was a time natural to him. I looked at David and felt keenly the loss of that time, at the same time as feeling it returned to me. By him. How strange and contradictory were relationships? Sadness and delight. Loss and gain. Solitude and togetherness, all walked hand in hand.

My thoughts were interrupted by the path as it grew steeper, made of large rocks and loose stones. It would be harder for the boy. 'Let me go in front, David,' I said.

He stood back as I passed. His face was damp with sweat, his cheeks hot and pink. When the rocks were too high, I held out my hand to him. That was how we did it, higher and higher. First, he would try himself, and I let him try—more than once I let him—and then, when it was clear the distance was too great, I held out my hand.

At last we reached the summit.

We stood on the flat rocks. There was Abrupt at the front to the east, then behind him Piccaninny and, further, Signal

Peak and between them the sweeping tree-filled valleys. Below the range in the wide flat world, the patchwork of fields, sheep and horses grazing, the bluestone orchard. Over the years new farmhouses had been built, with their accompanying outbuildings—sheds and silos. And there were more roads, and more traffic moving along them. But many things had not changed: the road that led to Hamilton Modern Dairy, its distant fir trees, the Trinity Lutheran Church. And there, Beverly Park and Mrs Barry's house.

I was aware of the silence. Silence between ourselves. Silence within ourselves. Silence on the mountain. I felt the boy and I drawn beyond our limitations, as if the silence had the power to do so. For a moment, I could have turned to the boy beside me and seen it was my brother, Paul. It was again that day, Paul not wanting Uncle's arrival, and I beside him looking forward to it.

He stood closer to the edge. 'I can see all the way to the town,' he said.

'And further.'

'And further, yes.'

It was as if all space within me had been cluttered with that which I did not need—fearful thoughts, thoughts of anger and dread, as well as the small irritations of every day, the tedium of living, my needs—dinner, the outhouse, more paint—was now emptying from me. The view, the breeze, the sunlight, the mountain and all that it showed us moved through this new inner space. I experienced the boy's presence in every part of myself. A sweetness that did not exclude my privates, as if they too belonged, held purpose.

'Look,' I said. Above us flew a pair of hawks.

The boy turned his face to the sky.

'There,' I said.

He followed the path of the hawks with his finger as they circled. 'You don't see them in the city,' he said.

I smiled. My smile readier, warmer every time. 'No, I expect you don't.'

We sat against the rocks and I took the rest of the food from the satchel—bread and beef strips, cheese and butter. I could feel the heat of the sun loosening me like beer. '*Vanno e vengono a prova, a norma che vi giova, nello stesso locale alternar nuovi aspetti ai consueti.*'

'What are you singing?' he asked me.

'What?' I cut the cheese into thick slices and buttered the bread.

'You were singing.'

'Was I?'

'Yes. What was it? The song.'

Every moment in his company told me I was heard. 'It is Goro.' I passed him bread and cheese and beef.

'Who's that?'

'Goro. He is a man in *Madame Butterfly.*'

'What's that?'

He took a bite of the sandwich, the bread and cheese distorting the shape of his words. It made me want to smile. Why did he have this effect, the smallest things, his eating of the bread and speaking and the crumbs flying as he spoke?

'It's an opera. A story of Butterfly.'

'What did Butterfly do?'

'She blindfolded her child. The child she had with Pinkerton. She covered the child's eyes. Then she . . .'

'What?'

I swallowed the knot in my throat. 'She took her own life.'

'Oh. How did she do that?'

'With her father's knife.'

'Oh. That's sad.' *Sad.* Yes, it was sad. 'Why do you sing songs from something so sad?'

'It is beautiful. *Madame Butterfly* is beautiful. There is beauty in sadness.' I was not aware that I knew this until I spoke it. Yet the masters knew it. There was sadness in Master Rethel's *Dance of Death*, in Master Munch's self-portrait, in Master Rossetti's *Beata Beatrix*. I did not know if it was the masters who had taught me, or *Butterfly*, or speaking to the boy. Perhaps these things could not be separated.

'Oh,' the boy responded. 'You know a lot.'

His attention moved to a lizard as it darted out from beneath a rock.

I knew nothing.

We were on the way home now. The boy was once more in front, but this time it was a scramble, with Wallis himself tipping us down. How satisfying it was to find the right place for the foot with all the momentum of the mountain's weight behind us.

'Take care,' I called to the boy. 'Take care as you go!'

I wanted to run with him, the way Paul and I had run the day we climbed down the mountain, so we would be back in time for Mother. But the boy had not climbed before; I had to watch over him. Was this the nature of responsibility?

The walk across the field was more difficult for David. He was slower. I longed again to carry him. But I could see the boy was making his own choices. Had things he wanted for himself, things he wanted to learn. I wanted to give him that. Wanted those discoveries for him. Was this how my father might have felt? Was this what it was to be a father?

Halfway across the field he stopped. 'I am glad we came to Hughlon,' he said. 'I wouldn't have climbed the mountain if we hadn't.'

'Yes.' It was as if a hand was pressed against my chest.

As we approached the turnstile, I felt the cares of our return. The boy had his family. He had to go to school. But still, I reminded myself, he was next door. I could see him in his yard through my window. I could find him by the pond, with the frogs.

When we pushed through the stile and entered Beverly's yard, I heard voices, laughter, girls.

'Tanya must have friends here,' said David.

Tanya was by the pond with two other girls. All of them with coloured nails and hair knotted and t-shirts torn with words: *Slam it Girl Wake me Move It.* All of them puffing cigarettes. Tanya glanced at her watch. 'Starting to get worried,' she said. 'What have you guys been doing?'

'We climbed the mountain,' said David. 'Didn't you read the note?'

It was the two of us, then, against the sister and her friends.

'I read it, but I didn't believe it.' She pointed to Wallis. 'Up there?'

'All the way,' said David.

'All the way? Really?' Tanya looked at the other girls, eyebrows raised.

The girls grinned.

'Who are you?' David asked them.

'Megan,' one said.

'I'm Jennifer,' said the other.

'Mum didn't say you could have friends over, Tanya.'

'She didn't say you could go up the mountain with Mr Weird either.'

Megan and Jennifer gasped, then giggled.

'Shut up, Tanya.'

I turned to leave.

'Goodbye, Lawrence,' said the boy. 'Thanks for today.'

The boy had spoken my name. Had thanked me. His day with me had made his move to Hughlon worth it. I did not feel my feet as I walked up to Beverly. Was this how it was for the hawk making circles in the sky?

47.

I PLAYED *BUTTERFLY*, SOMETIMES IN sequence, when Pinkerton first arrives, and other times out of sequence, beginning at his desertion, or Butterfly's death. I did the same with my memories of the day as I sat in Mother's rocker; waiting for David by the vegetable garden, fearing he would not come, then seeing him as he raised his hand to me. Or beginning at the descent of Wallis, where we spoke very little, accustomed to each other's presence and enjoying the pace. Then I would return to the path up the mountain, the boy ahead of me, his narrow legs, the way he swung at the branches and hummed, like me, existing in myriad worlds. I rocked back and forth in the rocker as we looked over the cliff edge that showed us the valley and fields and roads from above. I tasted again the sweet apple, the tough bread and salted beef, saw again his mouth as he ate, as he drank, wiping water from his lips. The delight in his face when he discovered the centipede.

Mother's dresser sat in the light of the kitchen, its mirror reflecting the dishes and the hanging pots and the dirty plates.

Yet from another angle the same cracked mirror reflected the rich and mellowing light through the windows, the green fields, the green yard and the apple tree, the red breast of the flame robin as he hopped along the fence. I lifted the self-portrait, held it to the light and looked into the eyes. What do you want? I asked the man.

I do not know when I went to Mother's bed and turned off the lamp. I did not want to sleep. Did not need to. I had not eaten since we returned from the mountain, nor did I want to. The day played itself over and over; Wallis in the summer sun, the boy's smile, the orchids bursting into flower. Sweetness spread throughout my body. I closed my eyes. In darkness I could absent myself. The sweetness and the longing were not mine. The night enclosed me as I drew in the cool air, fresh from the mountain, through Mother's open window. Long slow breaths, keeping my body still as the longing and sweetness increased. It was the desire to be joined. Foot to leg, leg to thigh, thigh to hip, hip to privates, privates to back and shoulders, head and thoughts. How long had it been since I was whole?

I imagined his face as he asked his questions, told me of the school, spoke to me about his family. His books. I imagined him against my back as I carried him up the mountain, his hands over my shoulders, his breath against my ear.

I held one hand to my chest as I felt with the other the skin beneath the waistband of my trousers. The sweetness pooled under the waistband, where my hand lay. A sensation seeking more of itself. I touched my privates to direct the stream of urine, that was all. They did not belong to me. But to whom did they belong, if not to me? I was trembling, the sweetness increasing as I placed my hand against my privates.

I closed my eyes tighter. I did not live. Could not. The sweetness was separate to me. My breathing grew heavier. Sweetness building like a wave.

But what was that? There was someone in the room! Someone coming towards me! I reached for the light—where was the light? The switch? I heard the lamp hit the floor. I wanted to cry out. Wanted to scream. But the scream was caught, turned inwards. Where was the light? Where had it gone? The wall was there. I put my back to him, facing the wall.

He took up all the space; there was nothing left over for me.

A panel of heat spread across my back, along my arms, down my legs and into my privates. I was covered in sweat. I got up from the bed. Did not look through the side window to Mrs Barry's yard. Did not step into my boots or pull on my hat. I kept my eyes on the path as I walked to the bunker.

There was the boy, and then there were my thoughts about the boy. One was a seed, the other a tree, full grown, its branches hung with lights. There was the real and living David, both ordinary and incandescent, as Master Raphael's child, and then there was the world the boy gave me—a set of hopes and dreams, pictures and conversations we might have, roads we might travel.

I began my painting; sap green, phthalo green, and Payne's grey on my palette. The boy appeared on the path as I had seen him, ahead of me, before the trees thickened. I was reminded of another painting, from long ago, another boy before the trees. And just like that painting, there was the light emanating from the boy's naked torso, but also from the sky above. There were the trees into which he would soon disappear, the light and the trees as essential to the painting as the boy himself.

They framed him, gave him context; the picture was a dialogue between setting and subject. Master Constable was right; the painting was more than its central figure—it was the subject's relationship to the landscape in which he was placed, and the light that revealed him. These aspects of the painting spoke to each other—the boy's solitude, the light that emanated from him and from the sky—hard to tell the difference—the path through the high pale grass, the trees ahead—in conversation with each other like the parts of a body, all the work of my knotted and lumpen hand. This painting of the boy the product—the pain in my hand its foundation. How could something so ugly create such beauty?

When I needed rest, I placed the painting of the boy beside my self-portrait on Mother's dresser. I put the needle on *Butterfly*, took a bottle of beer from the fridge and sat in the canopy swing looking to the mountain. I swung the seat as I drank. My hand was tight as a clamp. I tried to open my swollen fingers, and smiled. If the pain wanted a place, why not my hand? Let it come. *Come, you devil arthritis, make your home in me.* I sipped my beer. The music took me to the cliff where Butterfly waited, looking out to sea, and then it took me further. What in this world was there left to paint?

48.

I WOULD SEE HER SOMETIMES. The mother. She would wave at me, smiling, uncertain, hoping that it was good that I was there, hoping it was lucky we had each other in the middle of nowhere. I watched her go out to her car wearing her nurse's aide uniform, coffee cup in hand. I saw her drag her hand through her hair, shorter on one side, touch the rings that lined her ears, looking back to Mrs Barry's house one last time. She carried her children in her body—the mother—driving down the road to keep the wolf from the door.

It was a Saturday, and she was not yet home from the hospital. I was working in the vegetable garden, surrounded by enormous zucchinis, bursting at the sides, spilling their white flesh. David lay on his front by the pond. The straw man leaned over us, one arm to the sky. Music played from Tanya's bedroom, *Oh girl, you look so good, you look so good like you know you should, for me.*

'We don't see Dad anymore,' David said, dipping his hand into the water.

'Did you . . . did you . . . before?'

'Yes. Not that much after he moved out. Only sometimes. When he needed money.'

'Oh.'

David lifted his hand from the water; green weeds hung from his fingers. 'He is a pretty good father. I mean . . . he's pretty good. He takes an interest. And he does turn up to things. Mum says he doesn't, but he does. Now he doesn't come over at all. We're too far away.'

'Oh.'

'But I like it here. I like it here more than in the city.' He rolled onto his back. 'A lot more room!' he shouted. Suddenly. Very loud. *Ha!*

I heard a door slam. Tanya was coming down the yard towards us carrying cups, a bottle of beer. Biscuits. 'Hey!' she called to us. She placed the two cups side by side on the grass. 'What are you two losers up to?'

David said, 'You're the loser.'

'Yeah, right.' The cups wobbled on the grass as Tanya poured in the beer. 'Mum just rang. They asked her to do a double shift. She won't be home for ages.' She opened the packet of biscuits. 'Tim Tam for you, van Gogh?'

Master van Gogh! Weaver at the Loom!

'Don't look so surprised. Don't you think I know anything?'

I took a chocolate biscuit from the row. So did she. The frogs croaked to each other across the water. The girl sat on the grass, her dress riding up, revealing the dimpled skin of her thighs. The same as the women in Master Ingres's *The Golden Age*.

'Like what you see?' she said to me.

David said, 'In other hemispheres it's light. It's only dark here, in this one.'

'Do you find what he says interesting?' Tanya asked me, sipping from her cup.

'Shut up, Tanya,' David said.

361

'I don't.' She took another long drink.

'So?' said David.

Tanya pointed at the straw man. 'He needs a new face.'

I looked at the leaking eyes and mouth. The stain of his scars.

'Yes.' I drank the beer from the cup and ate the biscuit. Beer and biscuit. New friends. We sat, the three of us, belonging, not belonging, the straw man as witness. A tooth began to ache at the back of my mouth.

The next day I was in the vegetable garden, picking leaves of silverbeet. I hoped that time in the garden would distract me from my aching tooth. David pulled up the cuffs of his trousers and put his feet into the pond. The dog sniffed at the sides.

'I don't think we'll ever get the fish,' the boy said.

'You have the frogs.'

'Yeah. But it's not the same.'

'Why won't you get the fish?'

I wished I could have added them to my list for Paul.

butter

nails

beef strips

fish for the boy's pond

'I don't know. I keep asking. It just hasn't happened. It's Mum's hours. Someone has to make the money.'

'Oh. Oh.'

I gathered the leaves of the silverbeet in my arms. When I got to my feet the boy did the same. When I stepped through the fence, the boy followed, the dog at his heels. I had not asked the boy to come with me—and yet here he was. Life could surprise a man, even one as old as me.

'What are you going to do with those?' The boy pointed to the leaves.

'Boil them.'

'That's it? Just boil them?'

'With ham.'

'More soup?'

'More soup.'

'Sounds disgusting.'

He was following me to the house.

'Is your mother not home?' I asked him.

'No,' he said. 'Extra shifts.'

He stepped up behind me onto Beverly's back porch.

'It sure is hot,' he said.

The dog's pink tongue dripped as he panted at the boy's feet.

'Would you like . . . would you like a drink?' It was as if I had a second body behind the first that made its own choices, decided things, did things I did not understand. A twin attached that I could not cut away. It was this twin who offered the boy water. This twin who wanted the boy to wait for him.

'Yes.'

I went into the house. When I looked back through the open door the boy was there, sitting on the edge of the porch, his head against the beam, one hand on the dog's back. He is sad, I thought. The boy is sad.

I put the silverbeet on the bench, filled a cup with water, then went back outside. David turned around and held out his hands.

When he had drunk the water, he placed the cup on the boards beside him. 'It's Christmas soon,' he said.

'Oh. Yes.'

'What do you do at Christmas?'

I recalled Christmases from when I was a boy. Gifts under the tree. Mother hanging stockings from the mantelpiece. Christmas pudding with Mrs Barry. I did not recall any Christmases later. What happened to them? 'I . . . I don't know.'

'When school finishes, we're going to the city. To see Dad. And our cousins. We're going for just over a week.'

'Oh.'

He stood. 'Thanks for the drink, Lawrence. Come on, Mol.'

The dog followed the boy out of my yard.

The boy was going away. My tooth throbbed. When was Christmas? I knew the days and the months by the way the landscape changed. I knew the month by the colour of the grass in the fields, by the nature of the skies, by the temperature and whether the stream held water, whether the orchids were in bloom. When was Christmas?

Two days later I heard more noise than usual coming from Mrs Barry's house. The mother's shouting and calling, arguments between the sister and the mother. The dog whining. The opening and closing of car doors.

'Get a move on, kids! I want to be in Melbourne for lunch.'

'I don't want Mol on my lap!' Tanya shouted. 'She drools.'

'Can you get David's gear into the car?'

I did not hear the boy, but I knew he was there, his eyes on the pages of his book.

The dog barked and I heard the rumble of the car's engine. I went to my front door and watched the car disappear down the road, stunned by the quiet left behind. The family was gone.

The boy was gone. I looked at the sky; there was not a single cloud, only an endless expanse of blue. I could sense the heat of the day ahead. If I wanted to go outside it would be best to go now. Today I could do whatever I pleased, unobserved. Wasn't that what I wanted?

I went back inside the house. 'No, it is not,' I said to the cup and saucer on the sill. 'No, it is not.' I did not want to go outside. I had not climbed the mountain since I had done so with the boy. Had not wanted to. Did not want to use the outhouse. Did not want to go to the bunker. Did not know what I wanted. My toothache was worse. Worse every day. 'Damned tooth! Damned pain! Useless!' I paced the room, my hand to my jaw.

49.

I LOOKED AT THE TWO paintings; the self-portrait and the boy—
one on the dresser and one on the easel. Pressing white and raw
umber from the tubes onto the palette, I worked into the boy's
arms. I was only with the boy's arms, distracted at last from the
ache in my mouth, distracted from his absence. The boy's arms
were contained within the leaves on the branches behind him.
The central point was his torso, his head and the light around
him. But his arms were as necessary to the balance of the piece
as was the light.

I do not know how much time passed. There was no time.
I was only with the boy's arms. And when I could no longer see
them with clarity, and was weary of looking, instead of sitting on
the porch or walking to the field, I ignored the pain in my fingers,
my wrist, my jaw and turned my attention to the self-portrait.
Working into the eyes of the man in the picture, glancing into
the mirror when I needed, glancing at the boy on his canvas
beside me. I wanted to remove from the eyes of the man their
endpoint, and create in paint space, light, feeling. Most of all,
life. But life eternal. Transcendent life.

I painted until the brush fell from my fingers onto the marble top of the dresser, smudging its surface with Venetian red. When I tried to pick up the brush, I could not open my fingers. I boiled water and poured it over a towel, then wrapped my hand in the hot wet towel. I went to the back porch, sat in the canopy swing nursing my hand, and looked at Wallis, at the drying world about him: the field at his base, paler each day, the sky its startling blue, the burning sun. Sweat dripped from under my arms. I thought of the way the boy leaned against the post, missing his father. I wished that the family were home: Tanya and her smoking and screeching; the mother shouting at her daughter; the dog and its ridiculous relentless bark. I thought, I have been alone here for a long time. I did not play *Butterfly*. Did not move from the canopy swing. My tooth continued to ache, and then to pulse, as if my heart was caught in my damned tooth. When the urge came to use the outhouse, I resisted. Night fell. My hand was no better, I grew hot. I would not go to the outhouse.

It was not until the first stars appeared that I stood from the canopy swing and went inside. I picked up *Letters from the Masters* from the seat of the rocker and sat in its place, opening the book at a painting by Master Whistler. *Old Battersea Bridge: Nocturne—Blue and Gold*. Master Whistler wrote, *As music is the poetry of sound, so is painting the poetry of sight*. I kept my eyes on the gold that fell from the sky in the painting, the gold in the windows of the buildings that lined the shore, the gold in the water. I would turn to another page, hardly see what was there, and return to the bridge, over and over.

I was in my bed, facing the wall, and he was behind me. He said, 'Turn around,' but I did not want to turn from the wall.

He said it again. 'Turn around.' He placed his hands on my back. I turned and looked into his eyes. My trousers were wet. I shook with heat and cold. When I raised my head, the blood rushed in my ears. I thought, tomorrow I will pull it out. Tomorrow.

50.

I LOOKED AT PAUL'S CALENDAR and counted the days. Which day was Christmas? The twenty-fifth of December. I only needed to count seven days from that day. He would return January the first. He had said he was going for a week. *Just over.* I did not know what I would do until then. What did I ever do before he came?

I could not concentrate on any one thing. Could not complete any task. Could not work the vegetable patch for more than a few minutes, could not walk past the turnstile, could not drink more than a sip of tea, could not eat more than a bite of apple. My tooth was too tender. I could not even paint; my fingers curled painfully towards my palm. How much more time? There was a constant throbbing pain in my mouth. I could not settle. The chair? Not the chair. The bed? Not the bed. The canopy swing? Not the canopy swing. *Butterfly* meant nothing to me, was noise only. My thoughts rattled one to the next, between the waves of pain coming from my jaw. What to do? The garden? No, not the garden. And not the painting, the book, the dinner or the drawing. Nothing. The stammer was throughout.

I was certain that he would not return. I looked at the
Battersea Bridge many times, but then would close the book,
and wonder, what now? The house was hot. Too hot. I could not
separate my thoughts. I wondered, What if he does not return?
I was waiting for his return at the same time as believing it would
not come. Just as I had waited for Colin. Just like the moment
in the outhouse between the beginning and the end. It was not
possible to go forwards, not possible to retreat. I waited for his
return the way I waited for the postal van. I thought, He will
not return. I will not see him again. But at the same time as
thinking I would not see him, I listened for the car and asked
myself, How much longer? Even through the pain in my tooth
I asked it. How much longer? My thoughts made a mockery
of me. I asked myself, What if I do not see him? There was no
answer that I could endure. I took ice from the freezer, wrapped
it in a rag and pressed it to my cheek. I could not eat, could not
draw. There was no place to give me comfort.

Paul came into the house. I was propped up in Mother's bed,
neither asleep nor properly awake. Hot. Why this damned heat?
'Why didn't you answer the door?' Paul said.
'I-I-I d-d-d wh-wh-wh . . .' My tooth pounded.
'What's wrong?'
'N-n-n-n . . .' I got out of the bed and went into the kitchen,
every step like a hammer to my jaw. I had not heard Paul at the
door. Had not been ready.
Paul followed me to the kitchen. 'Lawrence, is there something
wrong?'
'It's I-I-I i-it's . . .' I put my hand to my mouth.
'Have you got a toothache?'

'Mmmm . . .'

'You'll need to see a dentist.'

'N-n-n-n . . .'

'Lawrence, it's probably infected. I'll make an appointment.'

'N-n-n-n . . .'

'It's happening, Lawrence.'

I could not fight him; I would have to do as he said.

Paul looked around the house. His eyes over my canvases, brushes and jars of water, milky with paint, paper on the floor, the walls, beer bottles, dishes at the sink, dishes on the chairs. Who was he to look at my house?

'I'll see if I can get you in tomorrow. Pick up the bloody phone when I call, okay?'

He walked to the front door.

'Clean yourself up, Lawrence. You need to shave.'

'Wh-wh-wh . . . ?'

He said, 'How are the new neighbours?'

I shrugged. Speaking harder with him than with anybody. I hated him. Hated that he brought supplies.

'So, it's going okay?'

Fuck you. *Going okay, going okay.* 'Y-y-y-yes, okay. Okay.'

'Right then. I have to get home. Been a long week.'

There was still the grease across his face, grease on his clothes. I wished suddenly to reach out and wipe it from his cheek. Touch his face, the shadows beneath his eyes. He had three children. Three mouths to feed. He had the wife to feed. Me to feed.

'See you next time, Laurie.'

The only one to call me Laurie. 'Y-y-y-yes.'

I wanted him to leave, but as soon as he did, I wanted him to return. Wanted to be close to him, hear his laughter, then wanted him gone forever.

*

That night I dreamed that I bit the rabbit trap Mrs Barry's father set in the field. When I woke my mouth was open and dry, my head aching.

In the morning, Paul called from the front door.

I came to the door, every step sending fresh waves of pain across my jaw.

Paul looked me up and down. 'Jesus, Lawrence . . . I can't take you into town like that.' He checked his watch. 'You need to change . . .'

I looked down at my clothes. The trousers were covered in mud, the hem of the shirt stiff with dried paint.

'And you need to shave. How long has it been?'

Paul's face was smooth. He shaved every day. I did not know when I had last shaved.

'Come on. We still have time. Go clean yourself up.'

'Wh-wh-wh . . .'

'You need to shave, Lawrence.'

'Wh-wh-wh . . .'

'A shave. Go in the bathroom and give yourself a shave.'

'I-I-I . . .'

'For Christ's sake,' he said, pulling out a kitchen chair. 'Sit down.'

'Wh-wh-wh . . . ?'

'Come on.' He pulled the chair out further.

I sat on the chair. When was the last time I'd fought him? How many years? It was before Mother passed. Before the ambulance arrived at the house. I knocked him to the ground and hit him.

Paul went to the kitchen drawer and returned with the scissors. Then he took a bowl from the cupboard and went into the bathroom. I heard the tap running. He came back out with the bowl full of warm soapy water and a towel over his shoulder. A razor blade floated in the bowl. When he put the towel across my chest, his hand touched my neck.

I flinched. 'N-n-n . . .' I put my hand on my jaw. Painful to touch. My head was worse. 'N-n-n . . . C-c-c-c . . .'

'Relax, Lawrence.' Paul stood before me at the table, his strong body in his mechanic's uniform, grease on his forearms; I could not fight him.

I sighed.

'Laurie, we have to. You look like a bloody bushranger.'

He sat on the chair opposite me and began cutting off my beard. It fell in dark brown and grey tufts to the floor. Hair on my knees. Hair around Paul's boots. When he soaped my face, I pulled away from him.

'Take it easy, Laurie . . .'

He stood before me with the razor. Nobody had come so close in a long time. He held my chin with one hand and drew the razor down my cheek with the other. I smelled soap from the dish. I thought, Why do you come? I remembered Paul as he was when we were boys riding our bicycles home from school, his wheel against mine, mine against his. I remembered him in the apple tree, throwing apples.

He drew the razor down my chin. He was too close; I did not want to look into his eyes. Did not want to. All the years were there; our whispered conversations through the wall, our attempts to eat Mrs Barry's meatloaf, our games, our laughter.

He kept shaving, under my nose, down my neck. Washing away the suds and the hair. I listened to the sound of his hand in the dish of water, the scrape of the razor down my face, his breath.

He picked up the towel and dried my face. 'Done,' he said. 'You look ten years younger. Handsome devil.'

'H-h-h-how o-o-old . . . ?'

'You're fifty-one, Lawrence. Fifty-one, okay? Can you go and change your clothes?'

Who was he to know how old I was? It had always been me who had known. The seven ancient wonders. Why did the mother rabbit pull the fur from her body? What did Crusoe learn by leaving his home? It had always been me and not Paul who knew. Who was he? Why did he still come?

'Go and change your clothes. You must have something cleaner.'

'F-f-f-f . . .'

'Get a move on.'

'F-f-f-f . . .'

'Lawrence . . . you . . .'

'F-f-f-fuck you!'

'Lawrence!'

'F-f-f-f . . .'

'Alright, alright.' Paul frowned. 'Forget it. Let's go.'

I followed him out to the car.

I remembered the road, the Trinity Lutheran Church, the sheep farms, the fir trees and the pines through the window of the bus. The drive in Bill Granger's truck before the sun was up. The cows would be waiting for me to open the gate—*all easy, that's the way, all easy.*

Today there were few cars on the road, and I thought, I can do this, I can visit the dentist with my brother.

But when we came into town, I did not recognise anything. Not the roads or the streets or the buildings. So many people and cars and shops, all in a hurry, impatient. The women dressed in garish colours, wearing shoes that tapped loudly along the pavement. Men climbing out of trucks. Speaking with each other. All moving quickly, sure of their direction. I was one thing, and they were another.

Paul saw it, glancing at me and away, keeping the distance between us as we walked crossed the road. Ashamed we were brothers. Born to the same mother, all those years before, growing up in the same house . . .

Paul took me into a white brick building.

My tooth pounded in my head.

Paul spoke to the woman at the desk. 'This is my brother, Lawrence Loman. I told you we were coming.'

I kept my eyes low.

She said, 'Through the door to your left, please.'

'Go on, Lawrence,' said Paul.

I did not want to go into the room. Wanted to leave the building. Return home.

'Lawrence.' Paul nodded towards the entrance of the room. 'Go on.'

I swallowed hard. We bombed Pawville, destroying its school, its church, its roads. We dug for buried money at the Marbles. Helped Mrs Barry make the straw man. We walked the mountain, me behind him making sure he did not fall, seeing his patched trousers, the wattle blossom caught in his hair . . .

Paul put his hand on my back. 'Go on, Lawrence.'

I hated him.

I went into the room and saw a long flat red chair. The light in the room was very bright. A nurse wearing a white dress said, 'Can you get on the chair, please.'

I clambered into the long chair. Where to put my arms, my legs. Why so easy for others?

'Just lie back if you could, Mr Loman.'

I lay back. The light in the room came from a large lamp overhead. I did not know such a light existed, so white it was almost blue.

The nurse wore a badge that said *Hamilton Smiles Dentistry*. I was shaking and wanted to use the outhouse.

A man in a white coat entered the room. 'I am Dr Peters. Can you open your mouth for me, Mr Loman?'

I did not want to. Wanted to leave the room and return to Beverly. Pull out my tooth with the pliers.

'If you could open your mouth wide,' the dentist said.

I could see the look on the face of the nurse when I opened my mouth. She wanted to turn away. As if I were not human. As if I had spent so much time with Wallis, I had become a part of him that had only just broken away, leaving a trail of dirt in my wake.

The minutes grew long as the dentist pushed the needle into my gum. I was hot and cold, shaking. 'Arrggh . . . arrghh.'

'What is it?' the nurse asked.

'Are you alright, Mr Loman?'

'Arrggh . . . arrghh.'

'We have to wait for the anaesthetic, Mr Loman.'

We waited. As I had always waited, caught between advance and retreat, the beginning and the end, sweat under my clothes.

'Are you ready, Mr Loman?' the nurse asked.

I could not answer as the dentist clamped the iron tool over the tooth. I heard the sound of the tooth breaking from me like rock shattering.

'Arrghh . . . argghh!'

'You can sit forwards now, Mr Loman.'

I wanted to cry.

'Please sit forwards and spit into the sink now, Mr Loman,' the nurse said, her hand on my shoulder.

I did not want her touch. Wanted her to step away, leave me be. Why could I never choose?

Blood circled the white sink. My backside cramped.

The dentist padded my gum with cotton wool. Tears came from my eyes, dripping down the sides of my face, into my ears.

I walked out of the room, my hand on my cheek. Paul was waiting for me. His eyes met mine. When we were boys, I was the one who showed him, *There is the spider's web, the rabbit's burrow, yes, we can climb higher, come on, Paul, this way.*

'Jesus,' Paul said.

I wanted to hit him.

On our way back to the car, he told me he needed to stop at the supermarket for supplies.

'N-n-n-n-n-n . . . !'

'But it'll mean an extra trip . . . we're so close. Lawrence, you can stay in the car. We have to get you some painkillers . . .'

'N-n-n-n-n-n-no no no . . .'

'Settle down . . .'

'N-n-n-n-n . . .' Why was he always telling me to settle down? I wanted to put my hands around his throat.

'Please . . .'

'T-t-t-t-take take take . . .' The swollen mouth and gum made it even harder to speak. I could feel the eyes of people on the street.

'Alright . . . alright! Alright. I'm taking you home. Let's just get across the road.'

I held my hand over my mouth and closed my eyes. As Paul drove, I pictured Wallis, and me, the missing piece, returning. Held. My face was numb, swollen. It did not belong to me.

'We're here,' Paul said.

I opened my eyes. There was Beverly, her red roof, her white fence, her door with its square of frosted glass. I got out of the car.

'But you won't have anything for the pain . . .' Paul said.

I shut the car door.

'That's my pleasure, no problem at all, Lawrence,' Paul said behind me.

Beverly, for the pain, only Beverly.

I barely heard him drive away.

I did not look at Wallis as I walked down past the vegetable garden, past the straw man to the bunker. I opened the door, crawled into the tunnel, and pulled off my clothes. I went down into the furthest space, under the wall. I lay there, the earth all about me, pulling my limbs in close, arms around my knees. I breathed in, and slowly out, contained within the silence.

I was in Mother's chair before the stove, unaware of whether I was rocking or not rocking. I ran my tongue over the space in my mouth where my tooth had been, sore to touch. I could not go into the town again. Could not be in the world; if I did not know it before, I knew it now. All of my teeth could rot. Damn my teeth. Damn life. Damn living. It was not possible to leave one thought and go cleanly to the next. The book lay open on the floor. The beam was there, behind me, running the length of the kitchen, but I did not look to it. I was still waiting. Could not give up.

Another night was on the way when I heard the sound of a car engine next door.

51.

THE POSTER OF THE RED Funnel Steamer in Paul's room was long gone; the crack in the boards between the rooms plain to see. I looked around at the space that was Paul's before he left Beverly. Building his model planes, practising his reader with Mother, catch-up mathematics at the kitchen table . . . I stepped over canvases and paint and empty bottles and sat on Paul's boyhood bed. Paul had left, he was at his business, his garage, and would go home to a place I had never seen, to a family I did not know. I looked around at his blue and green and red ribbons, pinned to the walls. Rewards for his sports. I could see him now standing before his stumps at the Stawell Oval, holding his bat, his face set, ready. I picked up one of his model Liberators from the window ledge. *Take that, Kraut!*

He had brought his wife to Beverly Park once. Ruth. I had been living here on my own for some years. I do not know how many, I was still young, I remember that. He came to bring me supplies. She got out of the car behind him. She was pregnant. Paul had not told me she was coming. He had not told me she was pregnant. That he would be a father. She put her hand to the lower part of her back as she walked towards me, smiling. Like Mother, she wore a scarf. I could see her hair underneath the scarf, a long brown ponytail, hanging over the front of her shoulder. She was coming towards me, where I stood at the front of the house, waiting for my boxes. I was not prepared. She was smiling. So much smaller than me, than Paul, even with her swollen belly.

I felt my mouth drop open. I was tall, so far from the ground, my long untidy legs in stained trousers, torn at the knee, torn at the pocket from the pressure of my fists. The ground was so far from me. As she came towards me—a woman, not Mother or Mrs Barry, with a child inside her—I made a sound. Groaned.

She stopped.

Paul said, 'Lawrence, this is my wife, Ruth.'

He had not told me. Had not warned me. I turned to him. 'No!'

Paul's face dropped. 'Lawrence!'

'N-n-n-n-no!'

'It's okay,' said Ruth, 'I can wait in the car.' She sounded worried now.

'No!' I shouted. I was older. Who was he to have a wife with a scarf over her hair, the skirt with the same flowers, her stomach round, her smile, her hand extended. 'No!' I shouted. 'No! No!' It was happening, my actions, my force and my shout, without me choosing, but if it was not me choosing the words, their volume and force, who was it?

'I'm sorry, Ruth, I should've told him. I'm sorry.'

'No!' I shouted. 'N-n-n-n-no!'

'It's alright, really,' she said, before turning back to the car. 'Next time.'

But there was no next time. I would not have a *next time*.

I ran my fingers over the crack in the wall. It was not merely because of the way I had behaved towards his wife that I did not see her again, or his children. He could have tried. Paul. He could have put up with my indignation. It was because he did not want to see me through his wife's eyes. His children's eyes. I was the past and they were his future—he could not bear the collision.

I sighed. I was not in Paul's room to think of my brother. I got onto my hands and knees—my back stiff, old back, old knees—and peered under the bed. Mother used the space for storage, blankets and pillows, bags of clothing. I groped in the darkness until I felt the edges of a large box. I pulled out the box and opened it.

There she was. The gift Mother had given me on my tenth birthday. *The Lady Bold* and the box of men. *Happy Birthday, Lawrence.* Ten candles on the cake, never-ending lights in the glass. Paul and I in the stream, our rafts of bark. I lifted out the boat; her sails torn and ragged, her body scratched, rigging snapped, the name *The Lady Bold* now faded. I touched the letters. There was a missing 'B'. *The Lady Old.* I laughed. *The Lady Old! The Lady Old.* 'Ha!' You and me both, boat. 'Ha ha!' I ran my fingers up the broken ladder and down the stern, blowing dust from the deck. The pirates and soldiers were in their wooden box, fewer now than when Mother had given me the gift when I was a boy turning ten. Yesterday.

I carried *The Lady Old* and her men into the kitchen. *The Lady Old.* 'Ha!' I stood at the sink and scrubbed away the dirt lodged in the grooves of the deck. 'Har har, me farties . . .' The soldiers spilled their blood that day, their arms lopped off at the joint!

I went to Mother's kitchen drawers, and found string and glue, needle and thread, matches and small nails.

How enormous and callused and clumsy my fingers were, holding the white thread! How difficult it was to see the tiny knots! It took me a long time to thread the cotton through Mother's needle, holding it as far from my eyes as I could. 'Did it!' I declared when the cotton, wet from my tongue, was at last through the hole.

I repaired the tears in the sails, rocking in Mother's chair. Was I not just like Louise with her hoops? We are not so different, Mother, you and I. I used the string to repair the rigging. It was a different colour to the original but could pass for rope with a little ochre. By cutting matchsticks with Mother's sewing scissors, then gluing them into the gaps, I could repair the hull. Using two small nails, I replaced the broken pieces of the steering wheel, gluing matches in-between for the spokes. I worked until the rigging on the boat was taut, her crow's nest with its circular railing in place, the two sets of oars ready at her sides.

Leaving the boat on the bench, I chose the colours from the Battersea Bridge from the pochade box—ultramarine blue and gold. I found my finest brush then prepared the turpentine and the rag. For seven days there had been nothing I had wanted to do, then the family returned and here I was, blue and gold on the palette, brush in hand. Was there no end to life's surprises?

I painted a thick stripe of blue around her body, then I painted over the words *The Lady Bold* in gold. Barely noticing the sounds of their homecoming—laughter, telephones and music, the barking of the dog. Cars in the drive.

I left *The Lady Bold* to dry on the bench under the window. Then I opened the little wooden box. Paul was not at the mechanics shop with the other workers, not with his children, not with his wife. He was here, lying in the box alongside the wooden men. Taking turns as pirate and soldier and coming out only now that I had opened the lid. *What did he do to you?* he asked me.

'Fuck off, Paul.'

I tipped out the wooden men, picking up each in turn and painting the red coats afresh in vermillion. I fashioned new arms and legs from more matchsticks and cut one of Mother's lace doilies into tiny strips to make new headscarves. Then I set the men along the edge of the table to dry. 'Har har . . .' Redcoats and pirates prepared for battle. *The Lady Bold* sat ready on the bench, looking as good as she did the day Mother gave her to me for my birthday—better for her scars.

But there was something missing.

I went to Mother's clock and ran my fingers over the birds—it had been a long time since they had drunk from the dish. The day Mother had thrown the glass at the mantelpiece. After Uncle left. I snapped one of the birds from the clock. 'You will have a new place today, little fellow.' All the ticks he had heard, all the years. And yet there was still change. Still time.

I glued the bird to the bow of *The Lady Bold*.

'There now. Tick, tick.'

After I heard the mother leave the house the next morning, I went out to the canopy swing with my tea. It would be another hot day. I did not know how long I would have to wait. From over the fence I heard the slap of the ball as it hit the dog's jaw. *If you want me the way that I want you, give me your sugar, give me your sugar.* Tanya's music played loudly through her window.

Soon I heard the voice of another girl—the friend of Tanya. They were laughing together. I did not leave my place beneath the canopy. I looked at Wallis. How long had he been there, in his place in the chain? Was there ever a world without him? I doubted Wallis had ever asked himself, *How much longer?*

At last David put his head between the boards. My chest tightened.

'Hello, Lawrence!' he called up to me and waved.

I waved back.

The boy came through the boards into my yard. Never in a hurry, never in a straight path, always curves to his direction. I wondered, as he drifted towards me, Has the boy come from my painting? Stepped from my canvas? Was that where he was born?

'Hi,' he said.

The dog was at his feet. I had seen it all unfolding this way, but I had not seen the dog, and yet here was the dog, beside the boy. Why was it only ever *almost*? I stood from the canopy swing, waiting as the boy came to my back steps.

'What did you do for Christmas?' he asked me.

I did not want or need to speak, only to listen to him, and could have listened all of my days.

'Did you stay here?'

'Yes . . . yes. Here . . . here.'

The boy stood on the grass looking up at me, and I stood on the porch looking down. This moment, like all moments, was moving forwards to the next. I could not stop it, as much as I wanted to. For as much as I longed for what came next, when I would give the boy his gift, I wished it did not have to happen at all.

'It's pretty hot, isn't it?' David wiped his hand across his face.

'Yes. Yes, hot.'

I thought, I should look elsewhere, at something else, and could not. Did not. All the ways in which he was right, his perfect lines, more perfect each time I saw him. Master Roqueleman wrote to his teacher that perfection was death. And yet the boy was perfect and was not death. Any idea or thought I had held its contradiction. Life was a riddle. Who made it so?

David said, 'I saw my father.'

'Oh. Yes.'

'Yeah. It was good. He's a good father. Mum doesn't think so. But he is good. He's just broke. But there's a lot he can do. He just isn't sure.' He kicked softly at the bottom step and looked up at me. 'Did you get any presents?'

'No, no. B-b-b-but . . .'

The boy waited.

'B-b-b . . .' I could not move past the first letter.

And yet I too was once a child of ten, my hand free of pain, no lines on my face, my voice pure, my speech flowing. I took a deep breath. 'But I have something for you.'

'You do?'

'Yes. Yes.'

'What is it?'

'A gift.'

'Where is it?'

'It's . . . it's inside.'

'Inside?'

'Yes.' Then I thought, Yes, it is inside, when I could just as easily have brought it outside. Then, unbidden, came the question: Why did I leave the gift for the boy inside? I did not want to answer.

'Inside the house?'

'Yes.'

'Oh.' He looked at Beverly's door. 'I didn't think you would have a present for me.'

'I do.'

'But I don't have anything for you.'

'No. No.'

He chewed at his lip, turned and looked back down towards the gap in the fence. I knew, then, that he had been warned.

'I have it ready.'

'Now?'

'Yes.'

'Okay.' He stepped up onto my porch.

I opened the door for him, and he came inside. The dog tried to follow, but I closed the door in front of her, shutting her out. She whined in objection on the other side, and then was quiet.

The boy was inside my house. The distance between him and my longing was closing. I felt myself standing at the meeting place of dream and real, thought and real, painting and real.

David looked around, at the objects along the shelves—the pine cones and pumpkins and feathers and stones, at the canvases all about, at the chairs and tables and every surface covered in tubes of paint, empty or full, the sketchbooks, and pencils. I saw then how much there was for the boy to see. I saw Beverly with fresh eyes, that she was the place for me to live and work, as Master Liebermann's room was to him, and Master Sickert's room was to him, and Master Courbet's room was to him. These places were described in *Letters from the Masters* as *studios*. This, then, was my studio. It was the boy that showed me as he had shown me everything else that mattered.

David walked slowly about the room, running his hand over my shelves, looking at the walls covered in drawings. He did not try to direct the course of his wandering and his observations.

He allowed life to take him. As if he knew there might be other, more interesting ways to experience his surroundings. Paul and Mother and Mrs Barry and anyone I had ever known from the years before, when I did know people, Mr Brommell and Alan and Bill Granger, even the postal delivery truck driver, even Moira Parker when she took my order on the telephone, all in a hurry, all with purpose and direction, except for the boy.

He had not yet seen the boat.

'Your house is a mess,' he said.

I wanted to laugh.

'You're lucky—you don't have anybody to make you clean it up.'

'I did clean it up.'

'I'd hate to see it when it's messy.'

Ha!

'My mother never leaves me alone. If I could live like you, I would. I would never tidy a single thing.'

'No.'

'No way. And I would still know where everything was.'

'Yes, I am sure.'

'Because all the mess would be mine.'

'Yes.'

'I bet you know where everything is.'

'Yes. No. Not everything.'

'You'd know every picture.'

'Yes. Look.' I pointed to *The Lady Bold*, gleaming on the wooden seas of my kitchen table.

He turned to me, eyebrows raised.

I nodded.

He stepped towards the boat, then looked back at me. Again, I nodded.

He went to the boat, ran his hands down the rigging, touched the boat starboard, then port. Touched the oars that came from the side, and then the matchstick steering wheel. He raised *The Lady Bold* up, the boat wider than his chest, and turned it in the air. 'It's for me . . . to keep?' He asked as if he was not accustomed to a world that could deliver to him what he most wanted.

'Yes. The box too.'

'The box?'

'Yes. Open it.'

He took the wooden box and opened the lid, taking out a pirate, running his fingers over the scarf that bound his head, his wooden body. 'A pirate . . .'

'Yes, yes.'

'And soldiers.'

'The enemy.'

'Are you sure?'

'Yes.'

'Is it from the olden days?'

Ha! 'Yes, yes. The olden days. Yes.' Then I had the thought, I was from the olden days! Just like every master in the book. And everything else I loved. All from the olden days.

'Was this yours? I mean, when you were a kid?'

'Yes.'

'What age were you when you got this?'

'Older than you, I . . . I think, yes, older.'

'How old?'

'I was ten. It was my birthday. My tenth birthday.' A hard pain rose in my throat. My eyes prickled.

'I am ten,' he said.

'Yes, yes.' The age of all boys.

He placed a soldier in the crow's nest. 'Man the decks! Enemy craft approaching!'

I wanted to touch his cheek. He stood so close, it would take so little . . . and yet I did not. Could not. I did not want to see my hand—worn and lined, marked with dirt and paint—so close to the face of the young boy. But I longed to feel his skin. Wanted to tell him something in the touch that I could not tell him another way. My gratitude. My affection. Wanted to tell him these things, wanted to very much.

'I can play with the boat in the pond.'

'Yes.'

I reminded myself that if he were here now, he would always be here. I would always have him in this way. I could play the memory over and over, the way I did to *Butterfly*. I could take them over and over, the copied moments, always longing to be here, in this one. The original.

'I'll need to add more water. Make it deeper. Make it so if a man fell overboard he really would drown.' He turned a pirate in his hands.

'Yes.'

'Is it really for me? I mean . . . are you sure?'

'Yes. Yes.'

'I've never had a present as good as this.'

'Yes.'

'Thank you, Lawrence.'

He opened the kitchen door, *The Lady Bold* in his arms, and was gone.

I sat at the kitchen table in the heat of the afternoon as Beverly grew still around me. All was in its place—furniture, objects on the shelves, the walls and ceiling, floors and stumps, and even me, the man in the room, sitting at the table. I closed my eyes and turned my gaze inwards. Saw emptiness and fullness side by side. Soon I would cut the bread, slice the apple, drink from the bottle of beer.

The next time I looked to the window, night had fallen.

52.

IN THE DAYS THAT FOLLOWED, my thoughts burrowed down into a warren where each narrow passage opened into a nest lined with fur. I was there with the boy in different ways. We spoke, he took my hand, smiled at me. He was behind me, his hands on my back. He was before me as I reached for him and touched his cheek. I did it over and over, the boy patient, unafraid. I needed only my thoughts of him. Did not need to paint. Did not need food in my belly. Could not feel the ache in my hand and in my wrist, did not mind being inside Beverly in the heat, did not object to the mother or the sister or the dog. I was held by my thoughts of the boy, one after another, as they flowed into each other without distinction. We were together in the yard, we were together in the bunker, we were together on the mountain. When he grew weary, I carried him on my back, his arms over my shoulders. We leaned against the warm rocks at the first plateau, legs spread before us, eating bread and cheese. We sucked the juice from wedges of orange. The boy placed the bright peel against his teeth the way Paul did when we were boys, his mouth grinning orange. How I laughed. Nothing could take me from him. We climbed Master Derain's mountains in Collioure, rested in Master Böcklin's fields, crossed Master Bonington's bridge in Paris. We walked the shores of Plymouth Bay and Stoney Bay and sailed the boat in St Dominique. We were *The Lady Bold*'s only crew. Steering her matchstick wheel, climbing her ladders of string, manning the oil-painted deck. Frogs croaked their greeting as we sailed the seas of heat and cold. He came into my waking thoughts when he had barely left my dreams. The songs of *Butterfly* lifted me from Beverly, drew me into the stars. It became difficult to find my way back. My chest ached. I was hollow. Yet if I was away from the thoughts of him, the pain of their return was brutal and painful. I could not eat even if I wanted to.

I stood on the porch. The mother, Rach, was on the bottom step, coffee cup in her hands. She raised her cup to me. 'Hi, Lawrence.'

The stammer began in my thoughts. How I wished I could turn away, pretend she was not there.

'I just wanted to say thank you—thank you for the great present. The boat. It was . . . it was pretty special.'

I could hear how much she wanted it to be great, special.

'He's been playing with it. Yeah. He really likes it. It's just, Lawrence . . . I want him to make friends. I mean, when school goes back, I want him to make some friends his own age, you know? Maybe it would be better if he didn't . . . if he didn't, you know, come over here. It's good he's taken his head out of his book, but it's just . . .'

'Mum!' the girl, Tanya, called.

Rachel checked her watch. 'Late again. God.' She looked at me, her cup raised to her mouth, like a visor, 'Don't take this the wrong way, it's just that, it was a good present, but . . . maybe just no more . . . just, let him find his feet here. You know?'

She lowered the cup. She was looking at me, waiting.

I stood there, and did not speak, did not, though I knew the words she wanted.

I was woken that night by my privates. Sweetness and desire, beginning there, radiating outwards along my arms and legs, up to my chest, and neck, my face, my lips. Nerves tingling. I kept my eyes closed; I was the feeling only, without self. Without identity. But then, as I opened my eyes, I became aware that it was me, the man, Lawrence, here in the bed. Lawrence, in whose skin I had lived all my life, through whose eyes I had always seen. I was uncertain—felt the promise of a sweetness offered, but were they my privates or the privates of another? I sensed the presence of another yet knew I was alone. If I tried to speak, even to the boy with whom I could always speak, I would not be able to shape a single word. I could not move the covers, though I was hot. Wanted the covers over me as if they might protect me—but from what?

Thoughts of the boy, the mountain, the walk, our time together, were suddenly terrible. I could not find a place for them. How had they occurred? Did I make them happen? The thoughts caught, one behind the other, like the letters I tried to speak. I was too small to contain the horrors that were planted in me, the tree grown too big, severing the parts so that one could not speak to another, not the feet to the legs, the legs to the back, the back to the privates to the head. My stomach clenched and twisted with shame.

I followed the path to the outhouse, keeping my eyes on the grassless track. All the years I had walked it, all the years Mother and Paul had walked it, all of us taking the same path to the outhouse. Yet I did not look upon Mother and Paul with judgement, carrying their strips of newspaper, fresh sawdust in the bucket. I envied their calm. The tune on their breath. Why was it so different for me?

I pulled open the door and went inside, took down my trousers. I was shaking. 'Ah ... ah ...' Who was it moaning? There were tears in my throat, my eyes. Why must it happen over and over? Why not just once?

When I woke in the morning there was nothing but the boy. I saw my hands before me making the tea, pouring the oatmeal into the pot, taking up the wooden spoon. But they were disembodied, like the hands of Master Bouguereau. Only David was real. I put the needle on the record at any time of the day now, no longer waiting for the sun to set. *Amiche, io son venuta, al richiamo d'amor.* When the record came to its end, the needle returning to rest, the music continued to play. So it was with the thoughts of the boy. Not layered with *yes* or *no*, *I will* or *I will not*. Not layered with the past, or with the future. He appeared before me as eternal as Master Eeckhout's celestial beings. I saw David in every room, through every window. I saw him in the sky, the mountain, in the branches of the apple tree. I spoke to him, each word fully formed and leading to the next. There was nothing unspoken, nothing we did not share. When the moon shone through the slats in the blinds, I wanted to be awake in its light, to see him again and again lifting the frogs with such care.

I stayed within the house. I was exhausted. I was on fire within Beverly's walls. I was dying of a thirst that could not be quenched. The boy was throughout. It was what I wanted—this desire—and yet I wanted it gone, finished. I wanted it and was tormented by it.

I painted. As if by painting I could take myself to the point, free myself. But painting fell short. Even painting, even Puccini fell short. Even beer. I was a home I had been forbidden to return to. When would it end?

I crossed the yard, not looking left or right. I pulled open the bunker door, took off my clothes. Took a breath, waited, released the breath. I did it again. I did it again. And again. I waited for my second self, but there was no divide. My thoughts continued. My desire did not cease.

53.

BEFORE DAVID CAME TO LIVE at the house next door, I knew what to do when the day began, when to make my tea, when to sit on the porch in the canopy swing, when to paint, drink my bottle of beer. I hardly had to think. Now, every decision was made of a thousand questions. *Should I? Would I? What if, what if? Yes, if that, then this; if this, then that*, on and on, until finally I left the house. I was not on my way to see if the boy was there, by the pond, no—I was on my way to the mountain. I did not have my pochade box, my easel or my drawing book. Did not have a cup for water, though the day was hot, but that was where I was going. I walked down the yard in the same clothes as I always wore—woollen hat, trousers, boots, coat. I kept my fists deep in my pockets—grateful for the familiar ache of my right hand. Something I could recognise. There was nothing else I could recognise. I was damp with sweat. Why was I wearing such clothes? Why had I always worn them?

I would not stop at the fence to see if he was there. I would not look into Mrs Barry's yard to see if he was throwing the ball for the dog. I would go on my way, to the mountain.

I heard voices through the gap in the boards.

'Your men have only just seen the ship.' .

'From the shore.'

'Yes. And they bomb it.'

'Yah! Yah! Go, Tom, go!'

I heard laughter, splashing water. David was with another boy. They were playing with *The Lady Bold*, in the pond.

'Got you! Man overboard!'

'Shark bait!'

'Har harrr!'

They were boys, as Paul and I were once boys, playing in the stream.

I looked up and saw the straw man on the other side of the fence, pointing to the sky. 'We are no longer boys,' I whispered. 'You and I.' I could not join the two friends playing in the pond next door, fighting their battles.

I turned to Wallis, his peak bright and sharp in the sky. I was myself again, my own familiar self, Lawrence Loman, leaving the boy behind.

As I climbed the mountain, the world in its summer glory rushed to meet me; blue-headed lorikeets and blue-winged wrens and rosellas flew in and out of the papery branches of the stringybarks. Heath and white gum and spider lilies bloomed between the trees. I heard the buzz of the flower wasps and the dragonflies and blowflies and the crickets, a music made of the wings of insects. The snap of dry balga. Warm mountain air in the leaves. Wallis had always been here—either looking over me, or beneath my feet as I climbed his pathways. I felt the sweat in my socks, down my back, under my hat as I took my long steps up the mountain, my bold steps, my long legs; did any man have legs as long as mine? There was nothing more that I needed. I had one thought after another with enough space to join them, and enough to keep them separate. There was no stammer in any part. I would not see the boy again, did not want to. I wondered, When was I last free?

As I reached the summit, a wind blew the branches of trees and the leaves, and blew cumulus across the sky. It blew around my head, and against my body. I turned in circles, my arms stretched as wide as the straw man. All of life was changing, and I was changing. I thought of all the paintings to come, and my desire to paint them. There was no end. 'So glad to be alive, even in this pestiferous world!' The wind carried Master Ingres' words out over the cliff to join the circling hawks: *So glad to be alive! So glad to be alive!*

Yet even as these fresh and spacious thoughts came to me, I knew that I would return, that I would see him again. Even in my relief, in my bliss, I knew. Perhaps it was the knowledge of my return that allowed the thoughts at all. Or was it seeing him again that had given me bliss?

54.

I WAS SITTING IN MOTHER'S rocker, feet against the guard, when there was a sharp knock at the door. I did not want to open the door and hoped the knocking would stop. But it did not stop. I began to rock in the chair and did not go to the door. But the knocking went on.

I left the chair and walked down the corridor. The house was hot; my face sweating. I wished there was nobody knocking, wished they would go away.

I opened the door. It was Tanya and another girl—the girl that I had met with David. What was her name? The dog was with them, tongue hanging from its mouth.

Tanya said, 'Can we come in? You remember Megan?'

'N-n-n-n . . .'

'Not for long, Lawrence, we locked ourselves out of the house. Mum and David will be home soon.'

Tanya walked past me down the corridor. The dog followed.

'God, it's hot in here. Come on, Megan,' she called to her friend. 'Don't you have a fan, Lawrence?'

Megan looked at me. I stood back from the door and she came inside. I had no choice but to follow her into my house.

Tanya was in the lounge, leaning against the couch, the dog at her legs. 'Thanks, Lawrence. I thought I left out a spare key. But anyway, you're here, so nothing to worry about, right?' She looked around the room. 'Do you realise this is the first time I've actually come into your house? David's been here but not me.' She crossed to a painting of Beverly from the mountain top that leaned against the wall. 'So, this is what you do in here all day . . .' she said, standing the painting upright.

'N-n-n . . .'

'What do you think, Megan? What do you think of these?'

Megan shrugged.

The dog walked around the room sniffing at furniture, tubes of paint, shoes.

Tanya turned to the dishes and the rubbish and the still lifes that had once again gathered on my shelves. How did they get there, the cockatoo's feather, the mushroom, the drying leaves?

'What a mess, Lawrence.' She crossed to the side window. 'You get a good view into our yard from here, don't you?'

I did not answer.

'You do. You can see almost all the way to our back verandah.' She turned around. 'It's pretty much the same as ours inside. Except ours is tidier.' She sat down on Mother's rocker. 'Mind if I smoke?'

I shook my head.

'Do you want one, Lawrence?' She pulled a packet of cigarettes from her bag.

'N-n-n-n . . .'

'Megan?'

Megan came further into the room. 'Sure.'

'You really don't want one?' Tanya tapped two cigarettes out of the packet.

'N-n-n-n . . .'

'Suit yourself.'

She set me a pace. It was like being in the classroom again at Hughlon Consolidated.

Tanya put the two cigarettes into her mouth, then she pulled a pink lighter from her pocket and sucked back on the cigarettes. 'Here you go, Megs,' she said, passing the other girl a lit cigarette. As she leaned forwards her dress rose up, showing her legs all the way to her underwear. She sat back down on Mother's rocker. 'Sit down, Megan.'

Megan looked around. 'Where?'

I saw her notice my boots on the floor, my worn socks, empty skins, stained in the toe and the heel.

'On the couch.'

Megan pulled a face.

'Don't be rude to our host,' Tanya said. 'Go on. Sit down.'

Megan pushed away clothes, papers, tin cans, a fork and rags crusted with dried paint.

'You seriously don't mind if we smoke, do you, Lawrence?' Tanya flicked the pink lighter, rocking back and forth in the chair.

She made me think of Peter Boer and Jock at the dairy, all the years before. My visit to the dentist. The nurse in the white uniform, looking over my open mouth. 'N-n-n . . .'

'Just what I thought.' She rocked in the chair, flicking her lighter. *Flick flick. Flick flick.* When she stood, the empty chair kept up its rocking behind her. She crossed back to the side window. 'That was a pretty good present you gave David. I mean, it was old-fashioned, but it was cool. Did you see it, Megan? Did I show you David's boat?'

'No,' Megan said.

'It was cool. From the olden days. David tried to take it into Stawell pool but the lifeguard said no go. Unhygenic. Plastic only. Shame.' She turned to me. 'How come David gets the present? Why don't I get a present?' She leaned back against the wall. 'What's wrong with me?'

I swallowed. 'I-I-I . . . n-n-n . . . I-I-I . . .'

'It's okay, Lawrence, I'm only teasing you. Nothing I need here. That's unless you want to do a painting of me . . .' She stepped away from the wall and walked around the room, looking at my pictures. 'Most paintings of girls, they're in the nude, aren't they? Isn't that right? Like, the paintings in the museums, I mean the really famous ones, the girls are in the nude, right?'

I shrugged. The smoke from the cigarettes filled the room. The stammer was in all parts.

'Isn't that right, Lawrence? About the girls in those paintings?'

I could not hear what was being spoken. What was being asked. Could not understand. The smoke from the cigarettes was coming between her questions and my answers. 'I-I-I . . .'

'Megan, it's true, right? I mean, did your school ever take you on an excursion to the art gallery? My school in the city did. You might not get to do that out here. Too far away. But we went and the girls in the paintings never wore clothes. And they were all fat. Fat girls everywhere lying on beds. Did you ever get to see that, Megan?'

Megan shook her head.

'Well, it's gross. You're not missing anything. You may as well stay out here in Nowhere Central. Girls are fat here too.' She sighed.

Everything stopped. Megan on the couch, Tanya leaning

against the bench, and me standing at the entrance. Still life in Beverly's lounge. Who was choosing this?

Then Tanya went to the record player. 'Fuck, it gets hot out here. And there's no beach. That sucks.' She leaned over the player. 'I mean, it was hot in the city, but at least you could get to the beach.' Her legs were long like David's but were the legs of a girl. New to me. The way she leaned . . .

'Can I play your music?'

'N-n-n-n . . .'

'Oh, come on, I love music—don't you, Megan? Plus, it's a record player. That's cool. Old school.'

She put the needle on *Butterfly*. I heard the crackle before Pinkerton sang, *E soffitto . . . e pareti . . .*

'You go to the discos out here, don't you, Megan? The blue light?'

'Yeah, sometimes.' Megan blew out smoke.

'Oh, this is great.' She began to sing at the top of her voice, her hands outstretched as if she was putting on a show. 'Ahhhhh! Ahhh!'

Megan giggled.

'T-t-t-t-turn it turn it turn . . .'

'Turn it turn it . . .' Tanya copied. 'What are you trying to say, Lawrence?' She turned up the music.

I tried to speak. 'T-t-t-t . . .'

'What? I can't hear you!'

I tried again. 'T-t-t n-n-n-no no . . .'

'Oh, relax. It's great. Great music.' She turned it louder. *Qui, o la . . . secondo*, sang Goro.

Tanya butted her cigarette out in a cup at the sink, then she pulled Megan from the couch. 'Aaaaaaaaahhhhhh! Ahhhhhh-hhhh!' she pretended to sing as she swung Megan around the room, dancing. The dog barked. They laughed, and sang, and danced, all girls' arms and legs and short dresses across my floor.

'No n-n-n-no . . .' I came towards them, wanting them to stop. *Capisco! Capisco! Un altro*, sang Pinkerton.

'Oohhh, get away from us!' Tanya shrieked and giggled.

The girls fell to the floor, crashing into the player, knocking it to the ground. The needle scratched against the record and the player was silent. Tanya and Megan went quiet. I stood, my heart pounding, chest heaving.

Tanya got up from the floor, straightening her skirt. 'Sorry, Lawrence. I hope we didn't break it.' She picked up the player. The arm of the needle came free in her hand. 'Oops.'

'Sorry,' Megan said.

'I suppose we should go,' said Tanya, putting the player on the table. She checked her watch. 'I think they must be home by now.' She took another look around the room, then she crossed to my painting of the boy where it rested against Mother's dresser. 'Is this David?'

'I . . . I . . . I . . . n . . . n . . . n . . .'

'Is this my brother?'

'N . . . n . . . n . . . I-I-I . . .' All of me stammering, in thought and in speech.

'It's him, isn't it?' She looked at the painting, then back at me, eyes narrowing. 'Shall I take it and give it to him? Or maybe I should give it to Mum. Would you mind that, Lawrence? If I gave it to Mum?'

'N-n-n-n-n . . .'

'I think the words you're looking for might be, *Please don't*.'

Megan said, 'Let's go, Tanya. I think your mum could be home. I think I heard the car.'

Tanya put the painting back against the dresser. 'You like my stupid brother, don't you, Lawrence?'

'I-I-I-I . . .'

'The word you are looking for is *Yes*.'

'I-I-I-I . . .'

'*Yes*, Lawrence. That's the word. Not that hard. Y-E-S. *Yes*. Come on, Megan, let's get out of here. I hate this place.' She walked towards the door. 'It's a fucking dump.' She opened the door and the girls were gone.

I looked around the room. It was altered. The same objects, but no longer any relationship. Not the chair to the floor, the window to the wall, the saucer to the cup. Only discordance. I picked up the painting of the boy and slid down the wall. I was pushed forwards by the wall and held.

55.

DAY FOLLOWED DAY OF BOILING heat. The fields that surrounded Wallis were the colour of pale straw. The land crackled, brittle and thirsty. I sat beneath the canopy of the swing and waited for the heat to pass, my hand aching in my lap. I did not want to work on anything new, was interested in two paintings only: the boy and the self-portrait. But I did not want to develop them further, only to look at them. To look and look again. At the two paintings, side by side.

The first stroke of colour like a doorway, the road on the other side, into the hidden life, calling, *Show me.* Travelling the road as long as my hand and daylight and hunger would allow, travelling until there was nothing left, then returning, painful at first, like silence following sound. Being home again, in the canopy swing on the porch, the sun setting, casting the summer sky in pink, drifting over the scene on the canvas, as if it had been painted by a man I did not know, had never known. The pain of separation, overnight, before the return, and returning and returning until the painting sickened, and begged, *No more.*

*

Paul was at the front of the house with supplies. 'Dry out here, Lawrence. It's a bad summer. You should clear out the gutters. Rake the leaves.' He said the same things every year. 'It's a hell of a season. The orchards are all irrigating. You've got nothing out here. You've only got the hose.'

'N-n-n—I don't don't n-n-n . . .' The stammer worse with him than with anyone.

'How are the neighbours?'

'O-o-o-okay.'

'I told you it would be okay.'

'Y-y-y-y-yes.'

'I brought you beer. Meat. What's wrong with your hand?'

'N-n-n-nothing wr-wr-wr-wrong.'

'The way you were holding it.'

'N-n-n-n-nothing.'

'Is there something wrong?'

'N-n-n-n . . .'

'You want to show me?'

'No no.'

'Okay. Okay, fine.' He put the boxes on the front step. He had paid. It was my money, but he took care of it, as he took care of everything. I hated him. 'So they leave you alone next door?'

'Yeah. Yes.'

'You look thin. Thinner. You need to eat.'

'I-I-I eat I eat.'

'Eat more.'

'I-I-I . . . I eat eat eat . . .'

'Okay, you said.'

I picked up the boxes.

He took my arm. 'Are you alright, Laurie?'
What did he do to you?
I pulled away from him, picked up the boxes and left him there.

Night had fallen and the long hot day was at last left behind.
I was inside Beverly, looking into the trees that lay ahead of the
boy on my canvas; tomorrow I would begin again, when it might
be cooler. I touched the trees on the canvas; wanted to work into
their branches. There was a knock at the back door. Before the
family came, there was never a knock at my door, and now, how
many? I leaned the canvas against the wall and opened the door.
The boy stood on the threshold, holding *The Lady Bold* in his
arms. 'It's broken,' he said.

Behind the boy, through the open door, was the night. The
vast black sky, the stars like silver dust, the dark mountains.
I stood in the doorway, drawn to the night behind the boy.
Wanted, suddenly, to tell him, *It is yours, everything, Beverly,
the house, the shed, the fences and bunker, the acres for the orange
trees, all of it, yours.* Then to walk past him and into the night,
never to return.

The boy held out the boat. 'It's got a hole in the deck, see,
and the water gets in. The rigging snapped, too. Do you think
you can fix it?'

Without waiting for an answer, he came into my kitchen.

I closed the door behind him. Closed the door on the night.
I was not going anywhere.

'Do you think it can be fixed?'

I took the boat from him, seeing the damage to the deck.

'Can you do it?'

'Yes.' I put the boat on the table.

'Will it take long?'

'Not long, no.'

'Tanya has a friend at the house. Jared. Mum wouldn't like it, but she's working the late shift for double the rate. Jared and Tanya are on the couch.'

'Oh.'

'I don't know when Mum'll be home. She called and said she was going to try and get one of the other aides to cover for her. Then Jared showed up. Tanya met him at the pool. Mum said Tanya could have a friend over, but she didn't know it was going to be Jared.'

He stopped talking and looked around Beverly, as he had done the first time he came inside. He moved slowly, drifting, trailing his hand over stones, brushes, feathers, paint. I thought, He did not need to come. He wanted to come. He does not want to be at home. It did not matter then that his sister had been inside Beverly with her friend, that they played my record and broke the player, and it did not matter that they smoked the cigarettes, and that the sister saw my painting of David. None of it mattered because the boy was here, and wanted to be here. It was his choice. The girls altered the house and now the boy was altering it again.

David stopped at a painting of night that leaned against the back of the couch. He picked up the canvas.

'Night,' I said.

'But there's light.' He pointed to the corner of the canvas, at the sun shining through.

'Yes.'

'Not much night to go, is there?'

'No, not much.'

As we looked together the painting seemed to deepen, darken, at the same time as the corner that showed the light grew brighter. The combined act of our looking changed the way we saw the image. I did not need another moment of my life—this could be the last. And yet, as soon as I had the thought, *This could be the last*, another moment, like the light in the painting, was on its way. My hand touched the boy's fingers on the canvas.

He turned to me. 'Have you got anything to eat?'

'I do.'

'What?'

'Biscuits. Cheese.'

'Can I have some?'

'Yes.'

'And something to drink?'

'Yes.'

I took biscuits down from the cupboard and the cheese from the fridge. 'Do you like tea?' I asked him.

'If it's got enough sugar. And milk.'

'Condensed milk?'

'Good, yes, and sugar.'

I boiled the kettle and found the sugar. 'You put in the sugar,' I said. I brought down two cups, placing one in front of him on the coffee table.

He moved clothes and paints and paper from the couch, sat down and spooned sugar into his empty cup. We waited for the kettle to boil. He did not speak. I did not speak. The lamp in the corner lit only the circle around itself. Much of the room was in shadow; the paintings themselves, shadows. It was another moment on the way to the next, and I was both in it and outside of it. Yet was it not the same for all moments? One part engaged, another observing. Two selves.

The kettle on the gas ring shot steam into the air. I stood, went to the kettle and poured the boiling water into the pot. I cut the cheese into thick slices and put them on a plate with the biscuits. I waited as the leaves steeped in the hot water, not needing to hurry. The next moments were coming, no matter what, nothing could stop them. I placed Mother's cosy over the pot, picked up the plate of biscuits and cheese, and returned to him on the couch, putting the plate on the coffee table.

I sat beside him. He took one of the biscuits from the plate, holding it in his hands. I poured tea into both cups, then I tipped the tin of sweet milk over his and we watched as it left the can in a long sticky string. The boy stirred his cup then he placed the spoon on the table and dipped the biscuit into the tea. I looked only at the boy, at the way he sat in his blue shorts, his knees, small bruises down the front of his legs, his t-shirt, his narrow arms—the arms that had dug the pond and held the frogs and turned the pages of his book. I watched him eat, dipping the biscuit into the tea, eating the tea-filled part of the biscuit, dipping again. Crumbs spilled down the front of his shirt. I wanted to smile. There was nothing in him that needed to be other than it was.

'Your house is the same as ours on the inside. I mean, they are different, but the shape is the same. At first you don't think so, because of the different things inside, but they're the same.' David got to his feet and walked into the corridor. 'The living room. The kitchen. The big bedroom at the front.' He looked around the house. 'The two at the back.' He went to the room at the end. The room I had when I was a boy. 'In my house, this is my room.'

There were biscuit crumbs on the table, and across the couch where he had been sitting. A puddle of tea surrounded his cup.

I looked from the boy to the evidence of the boy, the spilled crumbs and sugar and tea. The ring left behind by the tin of sweet milk. I wanted to be here in this moment, but I also wanted to hold the moment for the future, when I would look at the evidence of the boy's presence and tell myself, *He was here*. There would never be enough of what I wanted. I could hardly be in this moment because of what I wanted in the next.

I stood and joined David in the entrance to the room of my boyhood. When Paul had slept on the other side of the wall. There was my single bed, crowded with canvases and rubbish and boxes. I stood just behind him in the doorway. Longed to put my fingers on his neck, his ears, move down him and touch his back. It was the only thing I wanted: to touch him. Not exclusive of the person that he was, not exclusive of the things he said, the things he liked, that mattered to him, but inclusive. The boy inside his body, was what I wanted. His hidden self.

I went closer.

He said, 'Is that your room?'

'It was. When I was a child.'

'How did I know that?' he said. 'And this is where I sleep now. Only in my own house.'

'Yes.' My voice sounded deep and scratched and intrusive, and I wished that I had a different voice, a voice as smooth as Butterfly's. I did not take my eyes from the back of his head. The knots in his hair. My throat was dry. His head, his neck and shoulders, his whole boy's self, full of possibilities for learning, for growing up and forwards and finding out what this life—*his* life—was for.

I reached out and touched his hair. It was as though I had been missing my privates, until now. As if they did not belong, were misshapen and wrong, and must be hidden, the way Uncle's leg was hidden inside his suit. Now my privates did belong, and had a place, and I wanted them there. Flooding with sweetness and sensation. A feeling that was more than painting, more than walking, more than seeing the world from the mountain top. I wanted to kiss the back of his neck, where it disappeared under the collar of his shirt. Wanted to pull the shirt away and kiss where the skin curved into his shoulder. Wanted to hold him against me.

'Why isn't it your room anymore?' he asked.

I was transported to a time long ago. A time in this bedroom when I was safe, enveloped in the moments before sleep.

'You could have any room in the house, why not this one?'

A time when my brother slept in the room on the other side of the wall, his long sleeping breaths my lullaby. I would travel the body of the mountain, drifting slowly upwards.

'Why don't you sleep in here?'

I touched his head, his hair, placed my hand on his shoulder. Stepped closer. 'David . . .'

Glass shattered.

'Pervert!' the boy's sister screamed. The head of the shovel broke the window.

Someone was banging at the back door, shouting. The door swung open. A man came into the room.

'David! David!' the mother was screaming. She came towards me, hit me in the chest. 'Get away from him! Don't touch him!'

I fell back.

David cried, 'No! Mum, no!'

The man kicked me in the stomach.

'Don't, Jared!' David tried to push him away.

Tanya screamed, 'Freak!'

I crawled to the wall, hands over my face as the blows came down over me, against my back, into my stomach, my face. Is this how it must always end?

'How could you make us come here?' the girl screamed. 'How could you?'

'David, are you alright? Did he hurt you?' The mother took the boy in her arms.

I reached the wall.

I do not know how long I was there. Rocking breaks time into motion. Any time can pass. It is entering time and leaving time. Was I rocking or being rocked? I no longer heard sound, could not feel anything outside of rocking, the wall pushing me forwards, taking me back.

56.

SOON THE HOUSE WAS EMPTY, quiet. I did not stop rocking. I was sitting in water. Did not look into the faces of the men as they came into the room. Saw their bodies in pieces; the dark blue of uniformed legs, backs, chests as they lifted me away from the wall.

'N-n-n-n-n . . . !'

I fell from the arms of the men like kindling. Like the straw man.

'You're coming with us . . .'

'N-n-n-n-n-n!'

'Settle down . . .'

'N-n-n-n—' I could not move past the letter. 'N-n-n-n . . .' Could not say, *No*. Could not say, *Don't, please don't*. Could not say, *Stop*.

One of the men said, 'You're under arrest.' The other locked handcuffs around my wrists.

They took me outside, where the heat from the road collided with the cold beneath my skin. I did not want the light of day in my eyes, closed them against it, but the light peeled back my skin like bark. I was pushed into the police car, then they drove me away from Beverly. From Wallis.

I felt the years. I do not know when they passed. What happened in them? My body against the seat, my hands in the cuffs, my feet on the floor of the car—to whom did they belong? My head, neck, ears—to whom did they belong? I was inside that flesh, but I was not that flesh. I was as Master Runge, looking out from the inside, the flesh a cage.

I do not know how long I was in the car. I never knew how long I was anywhere. I kept rocking by thinking of rocking, pushed forwards by the seat, held by the seat. An abyss opened between thoughts. Like trying to cross to Mother. I held onto the raft of the *Medusa* as the storm raged, the raft rising to the crest of one wave—the apex of change, of fright, of loss—and falling back, before the next.

'Settle down,' one of the men in the front seat of the car said.

But I had not spoken. Had not moved. Had I?

The horizon could not save the men from drowning.

A policewoman led me to the cell. I found a wall and pressed myself against it. The cell was brightly lit. I was unshielded, exposed. Did not have my pochade box or book of *Letters from the Masters*. Did not have Wallis or Beverly or the bunker. Time was passing. It did not matter that the birds no longer drank from the dish.

I was in my bed, lulled by the slow breaths of Paul on the other side of the wall, on my way to sleep. Mother was in Hamilton, at the dinner dance. Wallis that day had been shrouded in mist. I was drifting. Soon it would be painting again with Mrs St Clair. Everything I saw had two lives— one real, one in paint. Uncle understood. Uncle with the seam that ran the length of his trousers, his shoes with the stripe, his uneven walk, the hook drawn into his arm. Uncle hidden inside his suit. Uncle with the case that told another story. Which story did I choose?

That night he had made us casserole, told Mother to enjoy herself. We had seen her pink cheeks, her red lips and golden hair, free at last from its scarf—the beauty she would soon share with Hamilton. If it were not for him, for Uncle, Mother would not have endured. I was almost asleep when the door opened.

I heard him walk to the bed, made slow by his leg, too late for Salk and his team. The smell of pomade, of casserole and cigarette smoke and Teacher's. He brought the world into my bedroom. I was not big enough. He came to the bed, kissed me. I turned my head as his shirt sleeve rose, and saw what was drawn into the skin, where the hook led.

I sat on a chair at a table. An empty chair was on the other side. Paul came into the room with a policeman. He said, 'Laurie . . .' His face was white with new lines across his forehead. There were shadows beneath his eyes. He sat at the table and the policeman stayed behind me. 'Lawrence, what happened?'

'Y-y-y-y . . .'

'What?'

'You you you . . .'

'Lawrence? What is it?' He never gave me the chance to speak the words.

'You you you you . . .'

'Lawrence?'

'You know know know!'

'Who?'

'You know know know know!'

'What do you mean? What are you talking about?'

I was on him, my fists against him. I was his older brother; there was nothing of me he did not love. How many times had we wrestled and punched and hit each other, our strength saved for each other, given to each other like gifts? I could feel him under the skin of my hands as if I was once more ten years old. I pushed against him and wanted him to fight me.

'Lawrence . . . stop . . . stop . . .'

Wanted him to resist, wanted to feel him pushing back. *Fight me!*

'Lawrence, you need to calm down . . .'

'N-n-n-n-n-no no no!' I tried to hit him, to punch his face.

'Lawrence . . . Lawrence!'

'N-n-n-n-n-n-n . . .' I wanted to kill him. Wanted to tear his legs off, cut his head from his neck, put out his eyes . . .

'Lawrence! Lawrence, stop!'

Fight me, fight me. Wanted to rip out his stinking hair. Wanted to take the axe from the woodpile, cut off his monster leg, his privates. Put him in pieces, a knife in his eyes, sever his thoughts from his body, the man from the boy. Who was he, my uncle, inside his body, who was he? Who was he?

The policeman put his arms around my back. 'Settle down!'

My heart pounded faster and faster with the words trapped inside. I struggled against the man. 'No no no stop! Stop! Stop! Help me! Help me!'

'Settle down, now!'

'Lawrence! Lawrence!'

I was heaving, panting. 'No no stop stop! No no! No no no help help me!'

'It's okay, it's okay,' Paul said. 'I've got him. Take it easy, Lawrence, take it easy.'

'Stop stop stop! No no no!'

'It's okay, everything's okay.' He put his arms around me; he was my brother, Paul. He waited in the entrance to my room, told me to come with him to school, told me to come with him on the bike, he said we did not have to go to school, we could climb the mountain, he did not want me to stay in the house.

'Lawrence, I . . . I . . .' This time it was his letters jamming and trapped. 'Lawrence, no . . . it's not . . . no, it isn't . . .' His eyes turned red. He looked across at me and the years of our vanished boyhood were there in the room between us. 'Laurie . . .' He let his tears fall and he grabbed my shirt. He cried, his crying not flowing outwards in song like Butterfly at the cliff, but trapped, hurting him. 'Laurie, Laurie.'

'Time's up.' The policeman led me back to the cell.

Time changed nothing. Time compacted. Yesterday is today, yesterday is now. Forty years and yesterday, what was the difference? Uncle came to me in the cell. It was impossible to hide. He saw it all and knew it all and could choose. It was the years he had lived, the places he had travelled, the things that he had learned. Uncle over me, his weight, his sweat and heat. I lifted my face from the pillow, turned my head and saw *The Lady Bold* drawn onto the skin of his arm. I stood on the bow as the deck burst into flames.

*

The light of early morning over Wallis—lavender and palest yellow. Translucent yellow, light infused. Clouds rose from my pochade box, *Artiste Propre*, drifting up to the sky. I stood on the rocks behind *Two Men by the Sea*. I was both inside and outside the painting. The sun spread before the soldiers, no part of the sky it did not fill. Divine light.

Coming through the clouds, my father in his Liberator, room behind him for one more. 'How high shall we fly, my boy?'

In the morning, the policeman unlocked the door of my cell. 'Charges have been dropped.'

Paul was behind him. I could not look at him. I followed the man out of the cell.

There was the world outside the cell that I could not be part of, so much of it, so full of information, so busy. I could not absorb it. Had no space. Paul was beside me as we walked out to his car. Heat rose in waves from the road, and from the buildings, and from the people in the streets. I held my hands pressed under the pits of my arms. Damp, shaking. Paul opened the door to his car. I got into it and he drove the car away from the police station. Away from the city. I leaned into the seat and rocked, forwards and back, my eyes closed.

Paul said, 'The boy told Rachel you never did anything. Never touched him. She has agreed that if . . . if you move away, Lawrence, they're prepared to forget it.'

I could hardly hear him. What was it he was saying? We were in the heat of the car on the drive away from the city, heading home. That was enough. I did not want to listen. Did not want anyone near me.

'We're going to have to find somewhere else for you. We'll have to sell. There has to be somewhere else . . . somewhere you'll be comfortable . . . We have to think about it, Lawrence. You won't be able to stay here.'

I could not understand his words; they made no sense to me. I thought only of Beverly. Her place in the wide flat field.

'Apparently the kid has disappeared. Run away. Rachel thinks he's gone back to the city to find his father.' His words were sound only; I did not care for them.

It was almost night when Paul stopped the car outside Beverly. She was as she had always been. I opened the car door.

'Lawrence! We need to talk . . . okay? I'll call you to talk about things . . . about what we have to do!'

I got out of the car, stumbling towards the house.

'I'll call you tomorrow, Lawrence. Pick up the telephone, okay?' He drove away.

As I came closer, Beverly was not as I had remembered. She was bricks and tile, plaster and boards only. She was stumps and glass only. She was form without meaning. Without life.

I opened the front door, walked down the corridor into the lounge. There was the smashed glass of my side window. There was *The Lady Bold* broken on the floor. There was the back door swinging from its hinges. Beverly had been invaded. I picked up *Letters from the Masters* from the seat of Mother's rocker, flicked through the pages. What did those letters and pictures mean? *Hoarfrost*, *Le Déjeuner sur L'Herbe*, *The Abbey in the Oakwood*—what were they to me? Nothing—they meant nothing. I let the book drop to the floor. The pochade box sat on the kitchen table. I ran my fingers over the wood, opened the trays, saw the tubes of paint, the brushes, the dishes for the sponge. Pushed the box to the edge of the table, let it fall.

There were my paintings; paintings of night, of field, sky and star and cliff and leaf and stream and branch and sun and mountain, leaning against the walls and the furniture and sitting in piles on the floor. There were the self-portrait and the painting of the boy on Mother's dresser, beside the broken mirror. I picked up the self-portrait, running my fingers over its surface. It was nothing but paint. Nothing but art supplies. All of the paintings were nothing. They were not living. Had never lived. I let the portrait fall from my hands and looked into the mirror. My eyes like shards of glass.

I saw my mother's face.

She had never crossed the bridge to save me—it did not matter the reports I brought home from school, did not matter how clever I was, the talent I showed. Each day she waited for a letter from him that never came. It was not me she wanted to meet on the other side.

I went through the back door, onto the porch. Night was falling over Wallis. I saw him as he was. A mountain made of rock and earth. If he was pulled apart, spread into pieces across the field, he would not grow again. Wallis did not live. He saw nothing. Every tree, and blade of grass, every flower and bird and stone, the field for the oranges, the tracks through the grass to the bunker, the outhouse, the vegetable garden, the straw man, the turnstile. They did not live.

I went into Beverly, lay on Mother's bed. I was alone. I had been alone since I was a boy of ten.

57.

WHEN I WOKE, COVERED IN sweat, I did not know where I was, and did not care. I turned and slept again. The bird clock no longer ticked from the lounge. Who knew how much time was passing? I heard knocking. Was it a dream? Who was at my door? The knocking continued.

I got up slowly, my body stiff and slow. My hand was cramped, fingers curled. I could not move them. The knocking went on. I had never been so hot.

I went down the corridor.

It was the girl, the dog at her feet. She waved a hand in front of her nose. 'You stink.'

I felt the sweat drip from my forehead. Was that why the girl had knocked on my door, to tell me that I stank?

'We can't find David,' she said. 'Don't worry, you're off the hook, he was missing before you came home. We're leaving now to get him back from Dad.' She looked over my shoulder, at the house behind me. She shook her head. 'Anyway, Mum didn't want me coming over. But I'm not scared of you.' I heard the horn of the mother's car from the road. 'I'll be glad to get out of here. Enjoy your last days in this dump, Lawrence.'

I watched from my doorway as she got into the mother's car at the front of the house. The dog leaned, panting, through one of the windows. I did not see the mother's face where she sat behind the wheel. When the girl closed the car door, she lifted her pink lighter and flicked it through the open window. I watched until the car was gone.

I went down the corridor into the house. I sat in Mother's rocker. I felt as if I was caught inside the wood stove it was so hot. The telephone rang. I stood and went through the back door onto the porch. A hot wind swirled around the house, blowing dust and grit into my eyes. It was hotter than I could remember. But I did not object, did not object to the wind and the storm of dust and the heat. Did not need it to be otherwise. My throat was dry, but I had no desire for water.

I sat in the canopy swing listening to the creak of the bars as it moved. Time passed. It did not matter what happened, time passed. 'To where?' I asked the wind. 'For what?' I slept again, on the porch, under the canopy.

I woke to the sound of the roaring wind. The telephone was still ringing inside. I smelled smoke. I squinted into the sun; there was smoke over Wallis, smoke across the range. The wind was deafening. The telephone rang and rang. Above Wallis, there was no longer cloud, no longer sky, only smoke. I did not move. The smoke billowed from the mountain as if it began inside him, passing through his skin of trees and rocks and earth to fill the sky. I got to my feet. Stepped down from the porch. There was the straw man, pointing to the fire. I coughed and pressed my hand to my eyes. Smoke burned my throat as I stumbled, half blinded, towards the bunker. Fire had come again.

Was that someone coming through the darkness? I went down through the yard, through the smoke. It was him. The boy.

'What are you doing here?' I shouted above the wind.

I could not hear his answer.

'David, what are you doing here?'

'Hiding!' His face was streaked with dirt and sweat.

'What?'

'Hiding!'

'Why?'

'From Mum. From Tanya. It was Mum who called the police. That's why they came!'

I looked past the boy at the fire moving down into the trees at the base of the mountain. It was almost impossible to see through, a storm of heat and smoke and dust. 'I was on the way to the top. That's where I was going! But it was too hot!'

I grabbed his hand and pulled him towards me.

'Let me go!'

I hauled him towards the bunker.

'No! Get away from me!'

When I dragged open the bunker door, he got away from me, running for the turnstile.

I ran after him, catching him by the arm.

'No! Let me go!'

'No!'

'Let me go!'

'Get inside!' I pulled him back towards the bunker.

'No! Leave me alone!' he cried.

'Get inside,' I shouted, pushing him ahead of me into the entrance of the bunker. 'Get inside!'

'No! No! Leave me alone! Don't touch me!'

'David . . .' I took him by his shoulders. He was shaking, crying. 'You have to go in there, David.'

'No!'

'You have to.'

'No. I don't want to.'

'You must. The fire is coming.' I pushed him through the door.

'What about you?'

'Go on—go in there.'

'But . . .'

'Go!'

He slipped down the tunnel. 'What about you?'

I looked at him, where he crouched in the entrance. He was only a boy, only ten years old. There was nothing he had done wrong. Nothing he could do wrong. I was a man of fifty years or more—yet I loved him. I picked up the door. 'You must stay there. Stay inside.'

I looked at him, one more moment, until the next.

Then I shut the door over him, closing him in.

Turning to the mountain, I could see the fire passing through the trees, crossing the field. It would soon reach the yard.

I went quickly into the house, picked up the telephone and called Paul's number.

'Paul?'

'Lawrence! Lawrence! I've been trying to call you! There's a fire! Are you okay?'

'The boy . . .'

'You have to get out, Lawrence! There's a truck leaving from the orchard. I've told them to—'

'The boy is in the bunker. He will be safe in the bunker.'

'What? What boy?'

'David.'

'In the bunker?'

'Yes.'

'What are you—?'

'Paul?'

'Yes?'

'The boy is in the bunker. Do you understand? You must come for him, he will be safe in there, but you must come.'

'What the hell?'

'Do you understand?'

'Yes, yes, Lawrence, I understand! He is in the bunker. David.'

'Good. Yes.'

There was a moment of silence between us.

'Lawrence?'

He was my brother. He had always come with supplies. Had not refused me anything. Had not left me. He had tried. 'I love you, Paul.' I put down the telephone and went back out onto the porch.

I looked to the sun burning behind the smoke. Sun of Pissarro, Friedrich, Munch, burning in the skies of Courbet, Millet, Constable. Wallis and the rest of the Grampian mountains behind him, the trees at his base and the field in which he grew, were on fire. I crossed the yard, past the straw man—*Good bye, straw man*—pushed through the turnstile and into the field. Crusoe called to me from the flames. *And what am I and all the other creatures, wild and tame, humane and brutal? Whence are we?* Butterfly waited on the summit. *Amiche, io son venuta al richiamo d'amor!* Friends, I come to the call of love!

My stride was long, my body powerful, all parts in communion. One self, contained within the parts, the other extending beyond them. I was on my way; today I would learn, where did the road lead?

Epilogue

THIS WAS HOW CLOSE THE fires had come. Moira Parker looked out over the blackened ranges. *Please don't let him have died.* She had prayed on the drive from Melbourne. She had told her new partner, Andersen, that she needed to check up on someone who may have been in trouble in the fires. He had said, Okay, he valued what she knew about managing the business, trusted her decisions. He had spent all his time running galleries, talking to artists—this was his side venture. Moira knew her fair share about painting; it was a successful partnership.

Many of the houses in the township of Hughlon had burned, but not all. She pulled up at Beverly Park—the house was completely untouched. Moira Parker was relieved. How many deliveries had she addressed to Beverly Park over the years? She climbed out of her car and walked to the front door of the house. Lawrence was alright. Thank God.

A woman was collecting mail from the letterbox at the front of the house next door. There was a boy with her, a black dog at his heels.

The woman called out to Moira Parker, 'There's nobody there.'

'What?'

'The man who lived there—he isn't there anymore.'

'What? Where is he?'

'They think he was caught in the fire.' The woman nodded in the direction of the mountains. 'It came right up to the house, then the wind changed in the nick of time. We were lucky.'

'Oh no, that's terrible. About Lawrence, I mean.'

So, Mr Loman had not been spared. How terrible. She'd had a feeling something had happened . . . That was why she was here, wasn't it?

'Are you . . . family?' the woman asked.

Moira Parker hesitated. She was not family. But she needed to get into the house. 'Yes—yes, family.'

'I think the place is open. I mean, if you need to go inside. I think it's a mess in there. His brother is on the way to deal with it.'

'Oh . . . yes. Yes, I would like to go inside. Poor Lawrence . . .'

'Yeah. Poor Lawrence.'

'I'll go in and take a look around.'

'Sure,' the woman said, ushering her son and the dog into her own house. 'Get a move on, Dave.'

The boy looked at her for a moment, then went inside.

Moira Parker opened the front door to Beverly Park. Oil paint—she knew that smell—and rubbish. Turpentine. Smoke.

When her eyes adjusted to the darkness, she found herself looking around at paintings. Paintings on the walls, down the corridor, paintings against every surface. Mostly landscape, though she was struck by a portrait of a man, which instinct told her was a self-portrait of the artist, and another painting of a boy standing on a path, on his way into a cluster of trees. She stood and looked at the work for a long time. Her body flushed. She could not seem to move. Finally, she fumbled for her phone. 'Mr Andersen, you need to get out here . . . as soon as you can, please. I have found something . . . a body of work . . . something astonishing. Please come. Now.'

Moira Parker dropped her phone and wept.

Acknowledgements

The author would like to acknowledge the Gunditjmara, and
the Eastern Maar peoples—the Traditional Custodians of the
land in which this novel is set.

The author also wishes to acknowledge:

'It's like the Light' by Emily Dickinson (first published in 1896)
Robinson Crusoe by Daniel Defoe (first published in 1719)
Madama Butterfly, an opera by Giacomo Puccini (1904), based on
   the short story 'Madame Butterfly' by John Luther Long (1898)
'Toot, Toot, Tootsie (Goo' Bye!)', song lyrics by Gus Kahn, Ernie
   Erdman, Danny Russo (written in 1922)

And the following artists:

Arnold Böcklin
Richard Parkes Bonington
William-Adolphe Bouguereau
Jan Brueghel the Elder
Paul Cézanne
John Constable
Jean-Baptiste-Camille Corot
Raffaello Sanzio da Urbino

Jacques-Louis David
Eugène Delacroix
Piero della Francesca
André Derain
James Ensor
Caspar David Friedrich
Henry Fuseli
Francisco Goya
Antione-Jean Gros
Théodore Gudin
Jean-Auguste-Dominique Ingres
Max Liebermann
John Martin
John Everett Millais
Jean-François Millet
Edvard Munch
Camille Pissarro
Alfred Rethel
Auguste Rodin
Dante Gabriel Rossetti
Peter Paul Rubens
Philipp Otto Runge
Walter Sickert
J.M.W. Turner
Gerbrand van den Eeckhout
Vincent van Gogh
Rembrandt van Rijn
Adolph Friedrich Erdmann von Menzel
James Abbott McNeill Whistler